PRAI~~SE FOR~~
THE OTHER SIDE OF GOOD

"Bravo to E. A. Coe for managing such a fast-paced, complicated plot with lots of characters and still making me care about every one of them! I loved the way he handled Theo's character to keep me guessing about whether he was a 'good guy' or a 'bad guy.' It's a tribute to the author's deft handling of human complexity that this character is quite a bit of both.

"I came away from this book feeling not only entertained by an exciting, nail-biting story but also better informed about the terrible problem of human trafficking. Since reading it, I've done a little research, and it's a far bigger problem everywhere than I had realized.

"If the author has a sequel or series in mind, I'll be first in line, because I really want to see what might happen next."

—**Elizabeth Cottrell**, Author of *Heartspoken*

"E. A. Coe's new book, *The Other Side Of Good*, is a police thriller narrated in a straightforward style reminiscent of *Dragnet*, but replete with characters far more complex than Sergeant Joe Friday. Commander Denton Jones is an introspective detective. He assumes nothing but is open to everything.

"The unfolding mystery keeps you reading as the intrigue builds. How does an honest cop cope with an uneasy friendship with his childhood best friend, who is the kingpin in the most powerful drug cartel in Cincinnati? What is more, the complexities of the kingpin are head-spinning, as he is an honest and loyal person, even as he runs a vile organization.

"Perhaps the author's greatest talent is in revealing the background of his characters and how their historic identities shape their current temperaments and values. This is not a book for someone looking for the good guy wearing a white hat and the bad guy a black one. This is closer to reality, and it's left to the reader to discern, based upon his or her own perceptions, what is right and what constitutes wrong.

"Thumbs up for E. A. Coe, a novelist who takes us out of the chute with a jolt and gives us a spectacular ride around the arena of noir fiction."

—**Dana Hayward**, Author of *Entropy*

"*The Other Side of Good* pulled me in from the very first page with full, well-rounded, and realistic characters. As the story progresses, the line between good and bad begins to blur with good people doing bad things, and bad people doing good things, until there's a large, murky gray area.

"By crafting a story that leaves the reader feeling sympathy for characters you'd expect to loathe, the author demonstrates the complexities of human nature and how very little in real life is black and white. In the process, E. A. Coe has also masterfully shed light on the very real and disturbing issue of human trafficking, highlighting the deception and brutality of the involved organizations, as well as the difficulty they pose for law enforcement.

"Ultimately, many characters will have to adjust their definitions of good and bad in order to effectively make a difference in the world, a concept that translates well to real life. Intriguing, realistic, and ultimately beautiful, this is a book that will stick with you for the long haul."

—**Katherine Turner**, Author of *Resilient*

"*The Other Side of Good*, by E. A. Coe, gets your attention with the first chapter and doesn't let it go. It's a fast-paced, intelligently written story whose characters grow on you. There is sympathy for those you want to hate, pathos for those you should admire, and unforgiving anger for the conscienceless criminals who prey on youthful innocence. Coe masterfully weaves his characters into a thought-provoking story that rings true to the core of human debauchery while celebrating the power of human goodness. I highly recommend this book—it doesn't disappoint."

—**Brandon Currence**, Author of *Looking for the Seams*

"The new E.A. Coe crime story, *The Other Side of Good*, is a fast-paced drama set in inner-city Cincinnati. Woven together with well-developed characters and intricate plotlines, the author takes the reader from deep within two criminal enterprises and corrupt local government to redemption for a very bad man. When youthful past indiscretions come to light, a celebrated cop must reacquaint himself with an old friend, a businessman who happens to be a master of living on the other side of good. Circumstances throw the former friends together, and they soon collaborate to dismantle an international human trafficking syndicate. I can only hope that the protagonist, Theo Jackson, and his pal, righteous cop Denton Jones, will reappear in future E. A. Coe novels."

—**Jim Davison**, Author of *Bottom Feeder*

"I didn't think I would embrace one more novel filled with police corruption, crime, drug, slave trade, and more evils of street-life reality. But *The Other Side of Good* changed my perceptions. The reader is led through a series of coincidental connections that are made plausible by few authors with the skill of E. A. Coe. The research judiciously interwoven through the book is tantamount to its believability. Well-developed characters are entwined in real-life dilemmas, and the riveted reader will embrace and cheer for them. Is it possible to both loathe and love a main character? Coe makes that a possibility, leading thoughtful readers to pause in some self-reflection."

—**Trudi Van Dyke**, Freelance Contributor, Independent Fine Art Curator

"The fast-paced action of this crime novel was captivating from page one. Although a work of fiction, *The Other Side of Good* resonates with issues all too often in today's news. Worldwide trafficking, enslavement of women and children, corruption, dirty cops and politicians—Commander Denton Jones's city has them all.

"The story unfolds in Cincinnati, where crime has prospered since the eighteenth century. The author's characters swarm through issues black, white, and technicolor as the intrigue builds. Conversations bristle with emotional conflicts over loyalty, faith, and racial justice. Mild corruption morphs to dangerous greed as the tale evolves.

"Denton finds himself caught up with the leader of a powerful drug cartel, who is also a philanthropist and childhood friend. The reader is channeled to a love/hate relationship with the key characters. Truth looks like a hologram with a different version on each side.

"As the story concludes, the reader is challenged: Evaluate outcomes according to your own personal, long-held standards? Admit that it's a new world with new rules?

"Get ready to be immersed and engaged. A great read."

—**Annette E. Petrick,** Creator and Host of *Consider This with Annette Petrick* Podcast

"In *The Other Side of Good*, E. A. Coe takes on the question 'Can evil have a silver lining?' His quest begins with a pair of boys who grew up in the tenements of Cincinnati. The friends got involved with an unsavory person and experienced a brush with true badness that impacted each of them differently. Denton Jones becomes a police officer, and Theodore Jackson turns into a notorious drug kingpin. But when Jones gets involved in a complicated investigation, he finds himself needing the help of someone who is familiar with the seedy side of society.

"Coe takes on serious contemporary topics with a light hand. He lets his characters move toward each other in a way that does not feel forced or fanciful. Commander Jones struggles with not only his former friend but also evil that hits a lot closer to home. This is a great read that is well executed and worth your time."

—**Cindy Earehart Rinker,** Writer and Former Newspaper Editor

"E. A. Coe has a way with words, and reading his latest book *The Other Side of Good* was exciting. It's a real page-turning, 'don't want to put it down' kind of story that kept me trying to figure out exactly what surprise was going to pop up next!"

—**Sondra Baker Johnson**, Author of *Even Now*

"Historically, I am a person who champions good over evil, right over wrong, but what happens when your version of good is my version of evil?

E. A. Coe writes an intriguing story of two men who have known each other since childhood and have chosen different paths in life. Their lives intersect after many years have passed; Denton tries to uphold his version of good, and Theo tries to fight an injustice with his version of good. Coe brings the story together in a way that keeps the reader guessing about each character's intent and even wondering if trust can be placed in any one character. The story keeps you on the edge of your seat as you wonder which side of good will prevail, and it may change your opinion of where the line is drawn between good and evil."

—**Alice Wilcox**, Professional Editor

"Everyone has broken a law a time or two (who hasn't exceeded the speed limit on occasion?), but when is an illegal action really wrong and when can it be justified? These are questions E. A. Coe explores in *The Other Side of Good*. Dipping into noir fiction, Coe brings back endearing characters from his previous books—big-hearted 'Ten Ton' Denton (*Full Count*) and practical and wise Pastor Tom Burns (*The Road Not Taken*)—to help wrestle with where to draw the line between right and wrong.

"Together with a Cincinnati-based drug lord, this unlikely trio combines forces to combat an international human trafficking ring. Coe's well-researched and cleverly knit plot could be ripped from today's headlines. Its realism will leave readers grappling with the idea that criminal behavior may not be unethical if it achieves a greater good. With some baseball action reminiscent of *Full Count* tossed in, Coe's third book treats his fans to another good read."

—**Elaine Specht**, Columnist

"*The Other Side of Good* is a novel where the story is king. The plot brings out the contrasts between good and evil with the gray area in between and is written in an appealing colloquial style which makes the book difficult to put down. As Coe develops his characters, we begin to feel we know them. . . . An excellent and topical tale from an accomplished writer!"

—**P. E. Oberdorfer III**, Captain (USNR, Retired)

The Other Side of Good

by E. A. Coe

© Copyright 2022 E. A. Coe

ISBN 978-1-64663-559-7

Published by

köehlerbooks™

3705 Shore Drive
Virginia Beach, VA 23455
800-435-4811
www.koehlerbooks.com

Shane,

Thanks for the support!

Coe

THE OTHER SIDE OF GOOD

E. A. COE

VIRGINIA BEACH
CAPE CHARLES

To my wife, Jean, who makes me glad to get up each morning; my children, who make me want to live; and Jack, Alex, Sam, Jo Jo, Addy, and Hudson, who make me want to live longer.

CHAPTER 1

The three teenagers boarding the 747 were victims of an international human trafficking ring, but they didn't know that yet. Accompanied by an older woman, the girls didn't appear to be sisters, and the woman with them wasn't their mother. The escort was Asian, petite, and fit with the darting eyes of a fox seeking prey. She kept any womanly shape she might have possessed concealed beneath a plain business jacket and loose slacks.

The teens were well dressed and seemed shy, even nervous. Those observing the small group board the large aircraft might assume the girls were students, perhaps traveling with a teacher on an educational excursion to the United States. They would be terribly wrong.

"Keep your eyes down," the woman hissed. Her name was Mei Feng, and she didn't teach. She worked for a Chinese criminal organization, the Santu, and her role on this trip was to deliver the three teenagers to a United States destination. The girls came from Moldova, a small independent country formerly part of the Soviet Union.

Bordered by Ukraine to the north and Romania to the south, Moldova ranked as one of the poorest countries in Northern Europe. Desperate parents in the region often left children with grandparents or other relatives as they crossed their country's borders, searching for work. In many cases, these children resorted to begging on the streets for money or food to survive, and they became easy targets for human traffickers.

An employment agency specializing in placing Moldovan women into domestic-service positions in the United States recruited the girls. In return for passports and travel accommodations, the agency required recruits to reimburse the company for such expenses with a portion of earned income from United States employment. The business maintained just enough legitimate domestic-service relationships in the United States to assure a stream of success stories back to Moldova. Tragically, most of the agency's clients did not end up in domestic service.

On the previous day, the group had flown from Iasi, Moldova, to Frankfurt, Germany, staying at an economy hotel on the airport property. Ms. Feng instructed the three girls to wash their clothes in the room's bathtub and hang them to dry overnight. The teens had slept in one double bed and Ms. Feng in the other. After using the iron that came with the room to remove wrinkles from the hanging clothes, the girls dressed the following day and repacked their backpacks. They ate a loaf of bread with some cheese Ms. Feng purchased from the convenience store next to the hotel. Then they caught the shuttle for the airport. Ms. Feng warned the girls the flight to Dulles would be long, over nine hours; she also told the three not to talk to anyone.

———

As the aircraft began the boarding process, a pastor in the waiting area completed a short call on his cell phone. "Package on board. Three plus escort. They checked no luggage, and each carries a single backpack." An average-sized man, the pastor's friendly face featured eyes that danced with an untold joke. His clerical collar and tunic might present a comforting sight to any who sat near him on the flight, but the pastor's toned physique could have as easily fit into the uniform of a soldier.

"Roger," replied the Diplomatic Service Security agent. "Homeland Security will ensure the group passes through a specified passport checkpoint, and we'll follow them from the airport. Four agents will be in place inside the airport and six outside. Medical personnel will stand by to transfer the girls to a safe place for examinations and any treatment required. We plan to intercept the four females as they approach the vehicle sent to pick them up—but before they enter it."

"Okay," said the pastor, "but I thought you wanted to discover where Feng would take the girls."

"Yes, sir. We did, but the FBI's Human Trafficking Division folks convinced us that plan might cause unnecessary danger for the three girls. The escort will almost certainly be unarmed to pass through the security at several airports. However, the driver of the vehicle picking up Feng and her party will likely carry a gun. Therefore, arresting the escort and the driver of the car separately would be safer for the girls. With two gang members to interrogate, we hope to obtain almost as much information as we might have by following the vehicle to its first destination."

"I guess that makes sense, and our priority has always been to retrieve the girls safely."

"Yes, sir. We appreciate your assistance in this exercise but ask that you remain out of sight for its remaining execution."

"I understand. I'll call this number when we land at Dulles."

"Roger." The agent disconnected.

———

The pastor boarded and proceeded to a seat four rows behind Feng and her party. Placing the cell phone in airplane mode, he slid the specially equipped, encryption-enhanced secure device into his front tunic pocket. He removed from his briefcase one of the three paperback novels he'd purchased before boarding and mentally prepared for the grueling transatlantic flight ahead. Within two chapters, he realized he remembered nothing from the preceding pages and closed the book.

Barely fifteen feet away from the man of God sat a woman who personified evil. Between them were three young girls with innocence, if not lives, at stake. In preparation for the coming engagement, the pastor had prayed, but, taking no chances, he also enlisted the help of enforcement from the most powerful country on earth. Sleep would not be likely on this flight.

Hindered by headwinds over the Atlantic, the big 747 landed about forty-five minutes late in Dulles. The magic of flying west through six time zones caused ten hours in the air to add only four hours to the day started in Frankfurt. The Lufthansa flight left Germany at about 1 p.m., and the time now in the nation's capital was a little past 4:45 p.m.

He turned on his cell phone, glancing four rows ahead to ensure the three teen girls still sat with their escort. Then, speaking in a low voice so none around him could hear, he said, "We've landed. Our group is about two-thirds of the way back on the plane, so we won't be coming off for a little while. I'll loosely follow them to Customs. If I don't hear from you, I'll assume you picked up their trail from there."

"Roger. Will you be going home from Dulles?"

"Yes. My car's in long-term parking. I live in West Virginia, about two hours away. Would you call me when the exercise today is complete and the girls are safe?"

"Yes, sir. We will. The girls will never know your name, but you helped save them from something most would believe to be worse than death. Thank you."

"I'll sleep a little better tonight," said the pastor. "Will the girls be allowed to remain in this country?"

"That depends on many things. If we can locate parents or family in their home country, we'll provide transportation back. If we can't find family, or if the victims have bona fide reasons for not wanting to return to their home country, they may stay in the United States on a special T visa. They could also have individual mental health or medical needs requiring time at a facility in Florida before entering our foster care system in the United States."

"Okay, thanks. Our rows are moving now. Good luck!"

———

The pastor followed Feng and her small group to the customs area, where an agent directed passengers to six different lines to check passports. The pastor's line moved faster than the one Feng entered, but, following the Diplomatic Security Service agent's earlier instructions, the pastor didn't wait for them. After receiving his stamped passport back from the Homeland Security agent, he headed toward Ground Transportation and Baggage.

Before stepping on the escalator to go down, the pastor sat on a nearby bench, pretending to look at his cell phone. Certain that other agents now trailed Ms. Feng and her group, the pastor still wanted to ensure the group passed him one last time toward the airport exit area. Within a few minutes, Feng and the three teens came in his direction. The girls walked behind Feng as the escort talked on a cell phone. They went by the pastor's bench and then proceeded toward a passageway to the C gates instead of getting on the escalator to leave the airport.

The pastor kept other pedestrians between himself and Feng's group while following them. Feng looked around several times, and the pastor feared she might be searching for him; then, she quietly greeted another person coming from the opposite direction. The man handed Feng a small package and kept moving toward the pastor. The pastor turned toward the wall, feigning a gaze at an advertisement, and the man passed without glancing in his direction.

The pastor didn't see him well, but the stranger appeared to be Asian, wearing a brown, hooded sweatshirt. Checking the area where he last saw Ms. Feng, the pastor watched her party proceed toward the C gates.

When Feng stopped at C-21, the pastor kept walking toward the next gate. He took a seat on a bench and continued to monitor Feng's gate. The teenagers and escort seated themselves near the ticketing podium, under a monitor indicating that United Flight 237 would depart in thirty-five minutes for Las Vegas, Nevada. The pastor's phone chirped, and the screen showed an incoming call from an unknown number.

"Hello."

"Pastor, our agent has eyes on both you and Feng's party. We suggest you depart the area so Feng doesn't see you. The escort may become suspicious about a minister on her last flight showing up for another one leaving from a gate adjacent to hers. She might wonder why you didn't take a direct flight from Frankfurt to La Guardia rather than connect in DC."

"I'm sorry. I worried when Feng didn't leave the airport as we expected she would. I should have known you had the situation under control."

"Well, it's far from under control, I fear. The additional flight to Las Vegas surprised us, and we aren't set up for it. You may have witnessed the ticket transfer in the passageway. We checked with the airline, and United's manifest lists Feng and the three girls. Someone purchased the tickets last evening."

"Did you follow the guy who passed the tickets to Feng?"

"No. Our assets at the airport were in the wrong places to accomplish that. With one agent in the passport checking area, two near the exit doors to transportation, and six outside, only one remained to follow the group from Customs. That agent described the male who passed the tickets to our other folks at the airport, but we decided the guy delivering the tickets to Feng was a lessor priority."

"Can you set up a team in Las Vegas?"

"We could. The flight is over four hours long, which is plenty of time to coordinate an interception in Nevada. Our exercise would also be more valuable if we found out where the girls might end up in Las Vegas. We're not going to do that, though. Number one, these girls have already been through enough with the four-hour flight to Frankfurt from Moldova followed by a ten-hour flight to Dulles. Number two, we aren't risking more chances for additional surprises. We want to rescue the girls now while we can."

"Good," said the pastor. "I agree. Can I stay to monitor the arrest?"

"Yes, but find a more discreet location. We worry that other members of Feng's organization are monitoring Feng at the airport. The more invisible you remain, the safer you'll be. Our team from outside the building is on the way to C-21 as we speak."

"Understood. Thank you."

Within minutes, two lean and muscled young men and a fit-looking female, all with small suitcases and carry-on bags, sat in areas around Ms. Feng. Another male stationed himself just behind the agent at the entrance to the gateway. A public address announcement requested, "Passenger Mei Feng, please visit the ticketing agent at gate C-21. Mei Feng, repeat,

Mei Feng, if you are in the boarding area, please see the ticketing agent. Thank you."

Feng glanced around her and then at the tickets in her hand. She said something to the three girls before she left and rose to approach the ticket counter. She didn't notice a man and woman rise from their seats to follow her to the podium, but she did see the man near the jetway move closer to the ticketing agent.

"Is there a problem?" asked Feng, holding her four boarding passes out to the young agent. The agent didn't answer before the man behind her moved quickly toward Feng, presenting identification to the escort.

"Yes, we do have a problem. Mei Feng, you are under arrest for violation of the Trafficking Victims Protection Reauthorization Act of 2017, for transporting minors illegally into the country for exploitation."

Feng jolted into action, turning to run, but a man and woman blocked her exit. The man expertly locked Feng's right arm between both of his, and the woman performed the same maneuver on the other side. Feng kicked at the two officers, and they lifted her by her arms from the floor. The arresting officer, still standing at the ticketing podium, calmly said, "You cannot escape, Ms. Feng, but if you continue to resist arrest, we will use more extreme measures to subdue you."

Feng stopped kicking, and her captors lowered her to the floor. While the officer secured her wrists behind her, security personnel led the three teens away from the boarding area. The whole sequence lasted less than a minute, and the smooth choreography of the arrest impressed the pastor, watching from a gate away.

—

The pastor didn't follow the officers who took Feng, and he waited long enough at the adjacent gate to leave unnoticed. Back in his car after retrieving baggage, he dialed a number on his cell phone.

"How much did you witness, Pastor Burns?" asked the agent.

"Until your people took Feng. Did everything else go routinely?"

"Yes. Mei Feng is in custody but, as expected, not talking. We couldn't find the man who transferred the tickets to her. The three girls are safe and on their way to a medical facility nearby. While hungry and scared, they had so far experienced nothing more harmful than intimidation by fear."

"Thank you for that news," said the pastor. "I wish we could've gotten more from this, but we accomplished our main mission. We saved three young girls."

"Right," said the voice on the other end. "We may extract some information from Ms. Feng yet. She undoubtedly understands she's now useless to her organization, and cooperation with us may offer a better alternative than the one the Santu will have for her. Also, we achieved another small piece of intelligence that could prove useful later."

"Something you can share?"

"Yes, sir. Feng made two calls from Dulles. Her phone scrambled the numbers dialed and the voice transmissions' content, but our software mapped the general location of the satellite tower connecting her conversation. The area is one in which, to date, we have noted no other Santu activity."

"Where?"

"Area code 513, Hamilton County, Ohio."

"What's in Hamilton County?"

"Cincinnati."

CHAPTER 2

Denton Jones didn't wholly buy into the accepted scientific theory regarding a sixth sense that alerted animals to imminent danger. Most researchers believed the heightened awareness resulted from a combination of neurological signals from the other five senses. Over time, animals instinctively learned that specific tiny changes in smells, sounds, or vibrations led to problems. When these same changes recurred later, the animal adopted an alert status. Through evolutionary generations, animals developed their senses of sight, sound, smell, taste, and touch in ways that allowed them to detect things people couldn't.

Denton *believed* in the sixth sense that often warned him of impending danger, which he named the "bad feeling." The sensation saved his life on several occasions, and while it sometimes alerted him unnecessarily, it never failed when necessary. He had the bad feeling now and wondered if the internal alarm was false or warranted.

On the ground floor of one of the city's tallest buildings, Denton checked the area around the elevator for curious observers and then entered the elevator alone. Watching the doors close, he touched the button for the twenty-fourth floor. The elevator door opened to a spacious lobby with a reception desk immediately in front. *Theodore R. Jackson Investments*, printed in bold, gold-plated letters, adorned a mahogany wall behind the desk.

As the mountain of a man stepped from the elevator, the receptionist briefly admired the sight. His spotless police uniform contained enough material to make a tent for a rifle platoon, yet the cloth covered not an ounce of fat. All squares and straight lines, the man seemed chiseled from a large block of black granite.

"Hello. Are you here to see Mr. Jackson?" asked the stunning woman behind the desk.

"Yes," Denton answered. "I have an appointment."

"Fantastic! Then you must be Denton Jones. Follow me."

Walking past a series of plate-glass windows highlighting a beautiful and complete view of downtown Cincinnati, Denton followed the receptionist through the door to one of the most spectacular offices he had ever seen. A single oversized desk in the middle of the space commanded a panoramic view of the city. Two chairs faced the front of the desk, and behind it sat one of the country's most successful drug lords. Tall, handsome, and confident, Theodore Jackson could easily have been a male model for the Gucci suit he wore. With a skin tone like Derek Jeter's, Jackson also appeared as fit as the retired baseball legend. When he stood to greet Jones, Jackson's smile warmed the entire room.

"Denton! It's been a long time," he said, extending a manicured hand.

"Yes, Theo. It has."

"Sit down, sit down. I have an idea about the reason for your visit. In case I'm wrong, why don't you tell me."

"Thanks," said Denton. "I'm here about your offer to support the Victory Park Youth Center."

"Okay, what about it? Isn't five million dollars enough to make the facility one of the best youth centers in the country?"

"More than enough. The amount isn't the problem; *where* the money comes from creates the problem, and your condition that requires the city to name the center after me."

"I see," said Jackson, seeming undisturbed by the insinuation. "Let's discuss where the money comes from later and first address why I believe your name belongs on the building. You, Denton Jones, have single-handedly done more for our city's disadvantaged youths than anyone else in its history."

"Excuse me," interrupted Denton, but Jackson held up his hand.

"Other cities across the nation duplicate your tactics and strategies for youth programs, positively impacting many more places besides Cincinnati. You accomplished this through hard work, absolute determination, and extreme personal sacrifice."

Denton stared at his childhood friend in astonishment as Jackson continued.

"You deserve the credit for achieving this youth center for the city because *you* inspired me to make the necessary contribution. On a policeman's income, you may never afford the kind of financial commitment to the worthy causes you support that I can. Recognition of your efforts, such as a name affixed to a building, provides advertisement that might induce other well-intentioned people of means to make similar financial commitments."

Surprised by the speech and uncertain how to answer politely, Denton said, "I'm sincerely flattered and surprised you know anything about my work with the youth programs. The city appreciates your offer, but can't you understand how the mayor might feel about this? Products your business distributes destroy the lives of many parents of children who would benefit from this center. The community would label the mayor as the worst sort of hypocrite if she accepted such a donation from the city's most notorious drug dealer."

Mr. Jackson's nostrils flared almost imperceptibly, but with complete composure he answered, "Denton, you are a little dramatic. What makes you so certain of the details of my businesses?"

"It's common knowledge, Theo. You control most of the illegal drug trade in this city, as well as in several others. While drugs negatively impact many communities, poor neighborhoods suffer the most."

"Ah, yes. I'm familiar with the accusation, and it pains me. Is it true the police department refers to my business activities as the Evil Empire?"

"Yes," replied Denton. "I hear the term used."

"So unfair. Are you aware I have never been charged with a single violation for anything in the city? No drug offenses, no possession, no tax violations, not even a parking ticket. With my spotless record, how do you justify the allegations?"

Denton smiled for the first time in the meeting. "Because you're brilliant, Theo. You're smart, and you're careful, and you're meticulous. Those are all admirable traits for a business leader, and I don't doubt you're one of those. In your business, though, getting caught is always an eventual possibility."

"Hmm," Jackson answered thoughtfully. "Getting caught in certain businesses does sometimes result in nasty consequences. Do you remember Ray Hinton?"

"Of course I do," replied Denton, tensing. "He got caught stealing from the Whistler." Denton's mind flashed back to three decades earlier.

———

"Denton!" his mother called. "Someone left a package for you on the porch."

"What is it?" asked the nine-year-old, turning away from the small TV set in the den.

"I don't know. I didn't open it, but who's gonna be sendin' you a package?"

"Don't know, Ma," said the boy as he retrieved the small box. Sitting on the front steps of the dilapidated tenement porch, the boy opened the package. Inside, a handwritten note sat on top of something wrapped in toilet tissue. Even a third grader could understand the four words on the paper: *Don't steal from me!* When Denton unwrapped the tissue, he screamed as a small bloody finger rolled to the sidewalk.

His mother ran to the porch and grabbed her screaming child, not noticing the amputated digit on the ground. When her son pointed to it, she gagged, vomited, and brought her son inside. Denton withstood an intense hour-long interrogation, providing no shred of evidence for why he would receive such a gruesome warning. When his mother finally allowed him to leave his house, Denton went four doors down the sidewalk to his friend's apartment.

"I got the same package," said a grim Theo. "I didn't tell my mom about it."

"The Whistler sent it, didn't he?" asked Denton.

"Who else?"

"Do you think it was—was—"

"Ray's finger? Well, it wasn't one'a mine or one'a yours! And the Whistler only uses the three of us for local deliveries," said Theo.

"But why?"

"Most likely cuz Ray was stealin' from the bags."

"What did the bags contain?" asked Denton. "The Whistler told me I should never look."

"Well, probably not brownies," answered Theo.

———

"Denton, are we still talking?" Jackson asked, snapping Denton back to the present. "You seem zoned out."

"Oh, yeah. Sorry. My mind wandered off, thinking about what happened to Ray."

"I understand," said Jackson. "You went one way and I went another after that. I guess we learned different lessons from the incident."

"You think?" exclaimed Denton. "The whole episode horrified me. Someone amputated our friend's fingers with garden shears, and that was enough for me to decide I didn't want anything to do with that kind of life."

Raised by a single mother, Denton managed to escape his neighborhood's violence by leveraging his size and aggression successfully in high school athletics. His coaches helped him obtain a scholarship to Lefton, recommending to college officials that Denton play baseball and not football. His football coaches feared Denton's sheer size and strength, coupled with his fearsome aggression, might pose a safety risk for opposing players at the

Division III college football level. He became a successful relief pitcher on the baseball team at Lefton and helped the team win a national championship during his senior year.

Since graduating with a degree in criminology from Lefton College in Indiana, Jones had been in the Cincinnati Police Department. He finished a master's degree in criminal justice, going to night school at the University of Cincinnati. During college summer breaks, Jones helped the city organize a youth program for at-risk teens, and his pet project, named Elevation, achieved national recognition; as Theo had mentioned, many cities were duplicating its practices and procedures.

"I know. You got disgusted, and I, well, I got pissed off!"

"I was mad too, but—"

"Sure you were. But after you left my apartment that day, I went over to Ray's sublet. All bandaged up, he looked like he had white boxing mitts on. His mom threatened to call the cops, and Ray, well, Ray warned her not to."

"Why not call the police?" asked Denton.

"Ray was a coupl'a years older than us, and he *understood* the Whistler's message. Ray also knew if his mom went to the police, the Whistler would find out. Ray suspected the Whistler had no qualms about killing his mom, him, or anybody else who got in the way. The police wouldn't have either the resources or the incentive to prevent it. Ray's mom just hung her head and cried, but me and Ray went back to where he slept, and we talked. We decided the lesson the Whistler delivered wasn't 'don't steal'; it was 'don't get caught.' The two of us also vowed the Whistler would someday pay for what he did to Ray. I mean, who cuts off a kid's fingers?"

"You're right, Theo," said Denton. "I guess that's when we went different ways. What happened to Ray provided me a clear sign of what happens when you do bad things, and—"

"Bad!" exclaimed Jackson. "Bad? You, Ray, and I weren't doing anything bad."

"Well," answered Denton, fidgeting with his belt. "Maybe not bad, but—"

"We lived in a ghetto as three poor, hungry kids trying to get fed. When a man offers you twenty dollars to deliver packages a few blocks away, do you have a moral obligation to ask him what's in the packages?"

"Maybe not."

"But you and I reacted differently." Theo smacked the top of his desk with a flat hand. "Then Ray and I put a long-term business plan together that eventually worked."

"Whatever happened to the Whistler?"

"He and the kid who helped him work on Ray disappeared about two years after you and I got those boxes delivered to our porches."

"You and Ray have anything to do with that?"

Jackson didn't answer right away. "Here's the thing, Denton. I never lie. If I tell you something, you can take it to the bank and count on it being true. I'm not honest because some Bible tells me to be. Trust among partners and associates in my business sometimes separates the living from the dead. As you might guess, my activities in various enterprises aren't always protected by the law, so I'm forced to depend on a sense of trust. If I break this trust with even one tiny lie, I'm toast."

"What's your point?"

"You asked me a question I can't answer."

"You can't or won't?"

"Doesn't matter," said Jackson. "For your purposes, the word *can't* and the word *won't* mean the same thing. That could be because the answer might put me in trouble, but it could also mean I don't want the answer to cause *you* a professional problem. I can tell you that when the Whistler and his assistant went missing, nobody seemed to care. Nobody asked about them, and nobody investigated. His supplier found somebody new, and the market never missed a beat."

"I assume," said Denton, "you and Ray knew the supplier's new middleman?"

"Yes."

"And I'll take a wild guess you wouldn't want to share that information?"

"Right. Ray still works for me here at my investment company.

It's ironic, but his nickname is Pinky. He has a beautiful home over in Newport, and both of his sons graduated from Marquette."

"Fascinating," said Denton. "Your investment firm must pay well."

"We do, and we also reward loyalty."

"How noble, Theo, but let's refocus on the purpose of our meeting. While the city would love the funds to create a new youth center, the mayor won't accept them under the conditions you requested. If you made the donation anonymously and removed the condition relating to my recognition, the city might reconsider."

"Okay, Denton. I'll need to think about those changes. I wanted you to receive some credit for your charitable work, but maybe that isn't possible this time. I would appreciate one other small favor, though."

"What?"

"A name."

"What kind of a name?"

"The name of a child who possibly entered the foster care system about twenty-three years ago."

"Theo," said Denton, "there were dozens of those back then. With all your resources, can't you find the information on your own?"

"Not easily. In 1996, social services placed one hundred thirty-seven babies into the orphan system in the city. Most of those had at least one known parent and a recorded birthday. Some did not. I'm fairly certain the one I'm looking for was one of those who didn't."

"What's your interest in this child?"

"I can't tell you, but I know the mother's name. Mae Hamilton. And her baby wasn't with her at the time she died."

"Well," said Denton, "I'm not sure of my legal authority for this kind of a query, and these matters often take weeks to research. If I could help, or wanted to, I don't have much spare time now."

"I'm willing to pay you well for your time," answered Jackson.

"I'm sure you are, Theo, but you can't buy me."

"I'm certain of that, and I'm proud of you. Believe me, many in your position, and more important positions, are available for purchase. I'm asking you because I trust you and believe you will exercise prudence. I'm not out to hurt this young man in any way. My goal is to help him."

"Because you're his father?" asked Denton.

"Because I want to help him," answered Jackson.

"Okay. Let's agree to think about what we discussed today and meet again next week. Can you provide me a cell phone number I can call? I don't want my name to appear on your list of office visits too many times."

"I obtain a new cell phone number every single week of the year. In my business, I take extreme precautions. If you call the office number, Teresa can always find me. The proprietary software in my telephone system automatically encrypts calls coming to our location. While we can't hide the fact we receive an incoming call, my software makes the incoming number indecipherable on phone records."

"Wow," said Denton. "Our decisions years ago sure led us to different places, didn't they?"

"Denton, we both made good decisions back then, just different kinds of good. Your decision resulted in a fulfilling life of notable accomplishments, making you a beloved figure in our city. My decision led to a successful business resulting in fabulous wealth. Neither of us has reason to second-guess ourselves. You might be surprised, but I believe we're more alike than we are different."

"I think that's a stretch," said Denton. "We started in the same geography, and we share one awful incident, but beyond that, we aren't much alike."

"Sorry, friend, but we share more than that. Single mothers raised us in one of the filthiest parts of South Cincinnati. Neither of us knows our daddy or what our daddies did, but we sure enough know what our great-granddaddies did, don't we? They rode a stinkin' boat over from Africa in shackles and then worked on some Southern plantation in Alabama, or Mississippi, or Louisiana. Somehow, when freed, they found their way to Cincinnati. They looked for jobs, and some of them found those.

"They also found drugs and alcohol. Not all in this group gave in to addiction, only the ones who chose to. You didn't. I didn't. We lived around the problem the same as all the other idiots who did, but we made a different choice. To you, this may sound harsh, but I don't control the lives of the folks living in places like the one you and I came from. I'm not their parent, their teacher, or their god. I'm just a salesman trying to meet their demand for a product, no better or worse than a cigarette salesperson. Shit, Denton, cigarettes kill more people than my products, yet tobacco companies can advertise and promote. Nobody's trying to throw them in jail; in fact, Americans invest in their products through the stock market every day."

At the end of Jackson's speech, Denton said, "You can rationalize your business plan all you want, Theo. The fact remains, whether you like or agree with the laws we live under or not, you and I are on different sides of them. Whatever we may have had in common in the past, the respective lives we've each chosen make us adversaries now."

"My offer to the city has nothing to do with our respective professional reputations."

"Right, and don't think I'm not appreciative of what you're trying to do. Politically, your proposal presents public-relations problems. If you genuinely want to help the underprivileged kids in the area by creating a new youth facility, an anonymous donation will accomplish that, and my name on the building isn't necessary to ensure its success. Think about that, and we'll talk again next week."

CHAPTER 3

"**H**ey, J," called Denton as he came through the front door.

"Hey, T," replied Jessica. "Where have you been? I started to worry." Denton met Jessica while attending a college friend's nuptials. Almost as tall as Denton, she had blonde hair, blue eyes, and skin as light as Denton's was dark. A bridesmaid in her cousin's wedding, Jessica ensured she served as Denton's dance partner for most of the reception. She had graduated from Duke Law School and, when Denton met her, worked with a law firm in Indiana. The couple married a year later, and Jessica took a position as general counsel for the Law Department in Cincinnati.

Jessica's cousin, Jill, first introduced Denton to Jessica as "Ten Ton," a college nickname referencing his large size at six feet, nine inches, and almost three hundred pounds. Jessica continued to refer to him as either Ten or T for short, unless he irritated her. Then, she called him by his first name.

"I'm sorry," answered Denton. "I got held up at the colonel's office. Fitzpatrick wanted all the details of my meeting this morning."

Denton held the position of commander of the Cincinnati Central Business District police patrol, one of six such districts in the city, and he reported to Colonel Jack Fitzpatrick, chief of police.

"What meeting was that?"

"You better sit down for a minute." As the couple headed toward the den, Denton told Jessica about meeting with Theo Jackson.

"You met with whom?" she asked.

"Sorry I didn't warn you, but I didn't want you to worry, and I had no idea what to expect. Jackson and I grew up on the same block, and a long time ago, we were friends. We went through some rough times together."

"Okay, let me get this straight," said Jessica. "I'm in the solicitor's office doing everything I can to get people like Theodore Jackson off the streets and behind bars—and *you* cozy up to him for morning coffee? You must know he's the biggest and most powerful drug czar in this city *and* our part of the world, right?"

"Yes, and for the record, we didn't have coffee." Jessica's sour gaze prompted Denton to continue quickly with his summary. "He wants to make a five-million-dollar donation for a youth center on Victory Parkway. One of his requirements for the donation is that my name appears on the building. The mayor asked if I would discreetly meet with Jackson to inform him the city couldn't accommodate such a request."

"Whoa!" exclaimed Jessica. "When did all this happen? I haven't heard anything about it."

"A few days ago. The mayor kept Jackson's offer top secret to avoid alerting the press. The city would relish the money for such a cause, but not with those requirements."

"And not with Jackson's name associated with it," said Jessica. "My God, T, the man facilitates more crime in this city than any other single person, and he's half the reason we even need a youth center on Victory. He's the main one facilitating the addiction problem in that area. Accepting a donation from him would represent the pinnacle of hypocrisy!"

"I hear you, Jessica, and I'm not arguing. On the other hand, Jackson would say he has no control over what adults do with their lives. In his opinion, he's just a salesman filling orders based on demand. He reminded me that he's never been charged with anything, not even a parking ticket, in the city."

"Wow, honey. Honestly, you're starting to sound like his attorney. What happened between you and him this morning?"

"Nothing really, J," replied a thoughtful Denton. "We had a long conversation. I don't defend his career choice, and I certainly don't condone it. You know that. I ask myself how two people who started in the same place could take such opposite paths."

"But something about your meeting with him bothers you?" asked Jessica.

"Yeah, a little. Doesn't his clean criminal record astonish you? I mean, how can we all be so certain he's the biggest drug lord in the city, and yet he's never been arrested for anything? Is he that smart, or are we that inept?"

"Good question, T. I wasn't aware of his spotless arrest record. Do you have a theory?"

"No. Sorry to say, I don't. I also apologize that the meeting caught you by surprise."

"I'm letting you off this time with a warning, Officer. The next time you plan to hobnob with drug dealers, you better tell me."

"Deal," said Denton. "Fitzpatrick wants me to brief the assistant city manager tomorrow morning."

"Roberson?"

"Yeah. I guess Roberson has the point on this with the mayor. I'm meeting with him at ten o'clock."

CHAPTER 4

Denton arrived at his office early and went straight to the county mortuary archives on his computer. He typed in the name May Hamilton and waited a few seconds for the database search to complete. Two records came up, but neither death occurred in the right time frame. He clicked on the advanced-search icon and requested all records between 1993 and 1996 with similar spellings. Four names came up. *Bingo!*

According to the police report, officers found the body of Mae Hamilton, a Caucasian female estimated to be between sixteen and nineteen years old, at an apartment located at 117 Ridley Street on August 17, 1996. The fourth district police duty desk received a call from an unidentified person indicating someone possibly died at the location. When patrolmen arrived, they saw the body on the floor through the open door to the apartment. They didn't administer CPR because the condition of the body confirmed the death had occurred several hours earlier. Discarded needles and other drug-related paraphernalia littered the apartment, and medical personnel transferred the body to the county morgue. The county coroner determined an overdose of heroin administered by a needle to the left arm caused her death, and he classified it as an accidental overdose.

A purse found near the body contained a prescription with Mae Hamilton's name, several food stamps, and some loose change. She had no driver's license in her wallet or any other form of identification. The purse also contained two baby pacifiers, leading officers to believe the deceased was the mother of a young child. Nothing indicated a baby had been at the scene or on the premises where police discovered the body. Per procedures for unclaimed bodies, the county cremated and interred the body in section eighteen of the Ohio Pike Cemetery. The county marked the columbarium with a small metal ring stamped with the dead woman's name.

Unfortunately, the end of the report read like many others Denton had seen in his history with the police force. Denton grew up two blocks east of the area where officials found Hamilton's body. The apartment had no doubt been one of a dozen or so crack houses in the vicinity.

With a date of death for the woman, Denton could narrow the search for babies delivered to various social service–related organizations in the city around that time. Since Hamilton still had baby paraphernalia in her purse at the time of her death, she most likely had not given up her baby at birth. Denton accessed a different database and entered a date range of July through September 1996. The query generated information on seven infants identified by sex and a number corresponding to when they officially entered the city's social services network.

The infant Jackson sought stood out immediately on the short list. Someone deposited a male, biracial baby on the Southside Baptist Church's steps two weeks after Mae Hamilton's death. The baby represented the only Black or biracial male entered into social service records during the period with no known mother or father, no birth certificate, and no name. Hamilton had also died just one block away from the Southside Baptist Church.

Denton could discover the baby's history after leaving the church's doorstep by typing the baby's social service–system identification number into yet another database. The most secure of all the databases he had accessed so far, this one required his secret administration password and a one-visit-only password provided on request by the database administrator.

Denton had to complete a short questionnaire to access the site, which would go to the city's Department of Social Services. If officials deemed his reasons for desiring access urgent enough—and official enough—the head of the agency would provide a temporary password to view the sensitive information relating to foster care or adoption records.

Denton felt reasonably sure his position within the city's police force would earn him a peek at the necessary records. However, he took no chances, stating in the block requesting the necessity for viewing the file, *Safety of Individual.* When a ranking police officer indicated viewing a private record constituted a safety concern, Social Services personnel seldom denied the request. After he submitted the online form, Denton received an automated message informing him to expect a review of his query within forty-eight hours.

CHAPTER 5

After briefings with his sergeants, Denton checked his computer for messages. Seeing none, he started for the elevator bank and the office of the assistant city manager. There the receptionist told him to proceed back to Charles Roberson's office.

"Commander Jones!" the heavyset Roberson said cheerfully. "Thank you for making time for me this morning."

"No problem at all," said Denton. "I assume you talked to Colonel Fitzpatrick about my meeting with Jackson. I debriefed him yesterday."

"Yes, we talked on the phone. Fitzpatrick gave me the facts, but I'm interested in also getting the nuances of the meeting from you in person."

"Sure. Anything in particular?"

"Not really," said Roberson. "What about his demeanor? How did he respond to being turned down? Did you find him threatening in any way?"

"No. He acted cordially and businesslike. He dresses like the CEO of a Fortune 500 company, and he displayed no obvious emotion about anything in our discussions."

"Did you like him?" asked Roberson rather abruptly.

Denton paused before answering, looking Roberson in the eye.

"Knowing his history, I don't like him. His conduct during our meeting didn't change my opinion one way or the other. He is, however, articulate and presents himself well."

"Right. He's been a problem for me and the city for a lot of years. This latest idea about committing five million dollars to us sets off internal alarms."

"I can understand, sir. My meeting with him made me curious about several things too."

"Like what?" asked Roberson.

"Well, you've occupied the halls of this city for as long as any. You might have one of the best historical perspectives on our dealings with Jackson."

Roberson laughed. "Commander, you might be right about that. I'm the city's relic here. What would you like to know?"

"Though I know not to trust him, one of the things he told me checks out. Jackson says he has never been convicted of anything in the city. He told me he has no violations even as large as a parking ticket. When I pulled his name up in our records, I couldn't find anything either—so what he told me is accurate. If that's the case, how are we so sure about the things we *think* we know about him? It seems to be common knowledge on the force that Jackson is the city's most powerful drug lord."

"Well, without doubt, he holds that title," answered Roberson. "Our drug task force has a lot of information, and we work closely with the feds. Over the years, we have conducted numerous wiretaps to understand drug movements to and from our community. As a result, we built a rather good database that provides an idea of what his organization looks like."

"Then why can't we or the feds arrest him?" asked Jones.

"The man's too darned crafty, so far," answered Roberson. "As an example, we recorded countless hours of his voice on wiretapped telephone conversations perfectly matched through sophisticated voice-recognition software to his voice in various in-person conversations. We're sure it's him, but we can't trace the calls back to any of his offices or known locations because he only uses burner cell phones in these conversations.

As good as our technology is, we don't have enough solid evidence that would stand up in court. We acquire detailed information about various product shipments, but somehow, when our folks arrive to intercept them, we find nothing. He switches locations and times without us knowing."

"Wow!" exclaimed Denton. "So, how do we understand the size of his business without actual evidence?"

"By trying to follow the money," explained Roberson. "We're aware of most of Jackson's holdings in our city and quite a few of them in other parts of the country and offshore. He owns buildings and businesses worth hundreds of millions of dollars, and we're certain he didn't inherit the money for these investments from a wealthy relative. We have difficulty separating his illicit income from his legitimate income. He makes this a little easier for us by paying a substantial amount of federal and state income tax on his legitimate income."

"Is that unusual for a criminal?"

"Very. Most criminals employ as many ways to hide their legal earnings as they do their illegal ones. I think he enjoys toying with us at times, challenging us to match wits with him. That's partly why I encouraged the mayor to assign you to take the recent meeting with Jackson."

"Not sure I understand," admitted Jones.

"Jackson's latest charitable offer troubles several in the mayor's office. To build a substantial youth center in one of the city's most blighted areas and then name it for a popular citizen—you—appears to be a publicity stunt designed to endear him to the community and embarrass the city. It could also hint at Jackson's effort to legitimatize himself further and his legal businesses politically. At this point, we're not ready to accommodate those efforts."

"So, how did I end up in the middle of it?"

"Nothing much you could do to avoid it," said Roberson. "You can't help where you lived. How close were you and Jackson as kids?"

"Pretty close, and we went through some tough situations together. Our paths diverged when we turned ten or so, and I haven't had contact with him since then. Until the meeting last week, I hadn't seen Jackson or spoken to him in over twenty years. I had no idea he even knew where I was or what I had been doing."

"Strange, isn't it?" Roberson said. "Nothing much surprises me about him anymore, though. How did he leave your discussion?"

"He just said he'd think about the city's requirements and get back to me. I assume the mayor hasn't changed her position?"

"No," replied Roberson. "She would still feel comfortable with an anonymous donation, as long as your name or anybody else's name in the city administration isn't part of the deal."

"Okay. I'll alert you when Jackson contacts me. One last thing, though, sir. Have we ever suspected Jackson employed someone on the inside of our department?"

"Why do you ask?" Roberson questioned, seeming a bit annoyed.

"No reason, sir, except I think he's awfully lucky to have escaped charges all these years, given the apparent size of his operations."

"I would prefer to think him extremely cautious rather than believe he had assistance from someone on our side. His activities go back a long time, so it would have to be from multiple sources if he had help. Few public officials in our organization have that length of tenure."

"Yes, sir. I didn't mean to impugn our organization in any way, and you're probably right. Jackson is a dangerous man and an intelligent one."

"Right, Jones. Remember that in any of your dealings with him."

"After I complete the current negotiations you and the mayor asked me to facilitate, I don't plan any dealings with him. My duties seldom overlap with those of our drug task force unit."

Denton left the meeting feeling uncomfortable; he seemed to have irritated or rattled Roberson. Denton also thought Roberson's respect for Jackson bordered on admiration for the villain. The assistant city manager appeared resigned to Jackson's craftiness preventing his ever being caught.

———

While Denton met with Roberson, Jessica reviewed her caseload with her supervisor, Fred Gunnells. As the senior attorney on the Law Department's staff, Gunnells was the acting city solicitor while Jim

Hargrove, the elected city solicitor, recovered from a heart attack. Gunnells had served three different city solicitors in his fifteen-year tenure and enjoyed broad respect within the city's administration. Encouraged to run for the office himself on several occasions, Gunnells declined, preferring life outside the political arena.

Gunnells had acted as Jessica's unofficial mentor in the Law Department office since she took the job as general counsel for the city several years back, and the two worked well together. Jessica respected his experience and balanced judgment; Gunnells appreciated the younger attorney's extreme intelligence and work ethic. They frequently helped each other on cases, and Jessica often used Gunnells as a sounding board. While some attorneys on the staff harbored information as a personal asset for their own agenda, Gunnells did not. He performed at the highest possible level as a consummate team player with no ego.

After wrapping up an analysis on another case, Jessica asked the senior attorney if he knew much about Theo Jackson. Gunnells set his papers on the desk and told Jessica he didn't, except that most in the city believed Jackson held the distinction as the city's number one criminal. When Jessica told him she'd heard the same thing repeated around City Hall but recently found out he had never been charged with anything, not even a traffic ticket, Gunnells sat back down behind his desk, saying nothing. Uncomfortable, Jessica queried whether anyone in the Law Department ever expressed concern about Jackson having an inside connection at City Hall.

Gunnells had no response except to ask Jessica what made her suspect the possibility of corruption. When she tried to extract herself from the awkward conversation by telling Gunnells she was only curious, Gunnells told her others occasionally suggested the same thing. He also told her he didn't have an answer or an opinion. Gunnells appeared distracted, and Jessica, somewhat embarrassed, quickly gathered her papers and left the senior attorney's office.

———

After Jessica left, Gunnells waited a few minutes, thinking, before picking up his phone and dialing from memory.

"Hargrove residence," said a cheerful female voice.

"Hi, Jenny, this is Fred. How's Jim doing?"

"Oh, hi, Fred. He's doing pretty well. He's progressed from meek and mild to mean and ornery, and the doctors believe it will only be a matter of weeks until he's back to intolerable. When that happens, I'll send him back to you."

Jenny Hargrove had been married to Jim for forty-two years, and the couple's playful banter was at times downright comedic. Their two grown children, both attorneys, lived outside the area, so Jim and Jenny lived in the big house on the city's outskirts by themselves. Jim had served most of two terms now and would likely not run again when the current term ended.

"I'm aware he's not supposed to talk about work while he's recovering, but I have a fairly generic question not related to any specific case. Do you think I might earn an exemption this morning?" asked Gunnells.

"It would break the monotony of *General Hospital* and *Days of Our Lives*," said Jenny. "Hold on."

The next voice on the line said, "Hey, Fred, thanks for calling. I've decided dying of a heart attack is possibly more humane than dying of boredom. What's going on?"

"Not much, Jim. Everything's fine here. Something came up a few minutes ago, and I wanted your opinion."

"Great, Fred. I'm plum full of opinions today. Shoot!"

"Jessica Jones questioned me about Theodore Jackson. As you know, she's married to Denton Jones, and recently the mayor asked Commander Jones to meet with Jackson regarding a donation Jackson wants to make to the city. Jessica's question related to how it's common knowledge Jackson holds the title as the city's biggest criminal, and yet he has a spotless criminal record with us."

"Interesting," said Hargrove. "Do you think the query resulted from something Jackson said to Commander Jones in their meeting?"

"I'm not sure, and I didn't pursue the conversation with her. I told Jessica she wasn't the first who noticed the anomaly but that I couldn't explain it. I wondered if I should tell her about the joint task force?"

"No, Fred, I don't think so. The fewer aware of that, the better. We don't need suspicions aroused because of people asking random questions. Jessica's a good attorney, and the inquiry probably resulted from a meaningless passing thought. Alert Roberson, though, and if nothing else comes up, let it pass."

"I thought you might say something like that. I didn't want to appear evasive with Jessica. She asked a reasonable question, but I don't want Denton and her to get unnecessarily caught up in something which might become messy."

"Right," said Hargrove. "Keep me posted."

When Gunnells made the phone call to close the loop with Charles Roberson, the assistant city manager acted perturbed. "Her husband asked me the same thing," he fumed. "Do you think Mr. and Mrs. Jones are developing a conspiracy theory, or do you think Jackson told Commander Jones something to bait us?"

"I guess Jackson could have provided Commander Jones with information, but why would he plant a thought with a policeman which might potentially cause our administration to look harder for a connection he placed inside? *If* such a connection exists, Jackson wouldn't want someone to start research to expose it. As for Mr. and Mrs. Jones, I doubt either suspects a conspiracy. Both are outstanding city employees working in different departments with no past exposure to Jackson's history. I think their questions simply represent natural professional curiosity."

"You might be right," agreed Roberson, "but Jackson is crafty. We can never predict what's up his sleeve. At any rate, we already have a task force engaged on the matter, and we don't need to muddy their efforts with misguided collateral investigations."

"Understood," said Gunnells. "I'll call you if I hear anything else."

"Thank you," ended Roberson.

———

When Jessica returned to her desk from Gunnells's office, she passed her college intern, Jaden Stokes. "Are you okay, Mrs. Jones?"

"Yes, Jaden. Why do you ask?"

"Because you went into Mr. Gunnells office with a sheaf of papers that included things I worked on for you. Usually, when that happens, you come back to my desk to tell me what I need to do next. This time, you passed me without even saying hello. Did something I prepare upset Mr. Gunnells?"

"No. Not at all, Jaden. I'm sorry. Gunnells's reaction to a question I had surprised me, and I guess I'm distracted. The work you did on the sale of the Edelman property was perfect, and we can send the newspaper a listing right away."

"Okay. I have the draft for that ready. Once you approve, I can send it this afternoon."

"Excellent, Jaden. Why am I not surprised you're one step ahead on this? How are you enjoying your last summer as a student?"

"A lot, Mrs. Jones. Without having to study, I'm not sure what to do with the extra time. I ordered a study guide for the Ohio bar exam, which will give me some new evening reading material."

"Come on, Jaden! Lighten up. Take a breath and enjoy your free time. I doubt you'll have much of that once you're back for the final year of law school. How's the team you're coaching over in Avondale looking this season?"

"Currently, they look like a bunch of young hoodlums more comfortable with knives and rocks than baseballs and bats. They'll come around, though; the teams from the youth center always do. Junior is no better off with his team." Another city employee and a childhood friend of Jaden's, Junior Bridges, coached a youth baseball team in the same summer league.

Jessica laughed. "Do I need to send Officer Jones over to the field for a motivational lecture?"

"Not yet," said Jaden, chuckling. "We'll hold that card out another week or two. I think Junior and I will have a handle on these dudes in a few more days, but tell Mr. Jones he's welcome to come down to practice anytime."

"I'll do that, Jaden. You know his favorite times in the summer involve you and the boys down there."

———

Jaden Stokes attended law school at the University of Cincinnati, where he'd finished an undergraduate degree two years earlier. He sailed through his first four years at the school, graduating magna cum laude and now placed near the top of his third-year law class. At her husband's suggestion, Jessica had hired Jaden the summer before as an intern for the city solicitor's office, and he exceeded everyone's expectations. Now in his second summer as an intern, Jaden performed many tasks usually assigned to full-fledged attorneys. Jim Hargrove didn't mask his attempts to recruit the young man for a Law Department position after Jaden graduated.

A product of Cincinnati's successful social welfare system, Jaden was adopted as an infant by Alan and Sofia Stokes. Both Alan and Sofia worked as administrators for the Cincinnati Children's Hospital and raised Jaden in one of the nicer neighborhoods near the hospital.

As a light-skinned, mixed ethnic child, Jaden didn't learn what the term *biracial* meant until middle school. His White adoptive parents fiercely protected Jaden from prejudice through adolescence. The Stokeses attended a Baptist church in a predominantly Black neighborhood and participated in many multicultural community events. When Jaden turned eight, Alan enrolled him in Denton Jones's first inner-city youth summer program.

Now Jaden would soon become an attorney, and maybe more. Jessica believed the young man's combination of intelligence, personality, and work ethic would serve him well in places beyond the courtroom.

CHAPTER 6

Several days later, Denton received a cryptic email on his personal computer at home. The message requested that he call the telephone number listed in the email the following morning. When Denton dialed the number the next day, Theo Jackson picked up right away.

"Good morning, Denton," said a cheerful Theo. "Thanks for calling. Can we meet someplace more private than my office?"

"I'm not entirely sure that kind of place exists in either your business or mine. I can pick you up somewhere in my vehicle if you'd like."

"Good plan. How about in front of the Starbucks on Thirty-Fifth at nine o'clock?"

"Okay. That will give me time to check in at my office for a few minutes. Wait inside until you see my vehicle—I own a tan Yukon."

"I know what kind of car you drive," Theo said.

"Of course you do," replied Denton, somewhat alarmed.

At a little after nine o'clock, Denton pulled up in front of the Starbucks. Less than a minute later, Theo exited the small cafe and climbed into the car's passenger seat. "Thanks, Denton, for accommodating me."

"No problem. Did you think about the mayor's offer?"

"Yes, I did," replied Theo. "Honestly, I don't like it much. The city made no reasonable attempt to negotiate. The mayor gets a big donation, and I seem to get nothing. Why should I accept those terms?"

"You don't need to. If you wish to help a good program, your monetary gift will do that. However, if your goal relates to gaining positive recognition or linking your name to a reputable community citizen, the mayor isn't interested. She's willing to lose the gift."

"I see," said Theo. "She must realize the name of the contributor could leak out or be discovered sometime later anyway, right?"

"She knows, and she believes nobody would hold her responsible for researching the source of an anonymous gift. Alternatively, refusing a donation of funds for a project that would benefit so many in the community would not serve her city well."

"Okay," replied Theo. "This may surprise you, but I'll still contribute. The funds will come from an anonymous source with no conditions other than how the city uses the money. Every penny of it must be allocated to the youth center."

"Nothing about you surprises me, Theo, but thank you for your generous contribution."

"*You* earned it," replied Theo.

"You understand the city won't allow my name to be linked to the contribution?"

"I do, but that doesn't change the fact you're the one responsible for this gift to the city. I'm only donating because of your work in our community over the past three decades."

"How do you find out all this stuff?"

"In my business, knowing *stuff* keeps me alive. I admire what you do to better the lives of kids born into places like you and I were. I haven't done much to help so far, but I'm in a position I can now—if not through my personal efforts, then through my money."

"Do you think your contribution in some way atones for your career choices or for the way you made your money? Do you hope this sort of philanthropy will eventually buy you respect?"

Jackson laughed. "Denton, you don't quite understand me. I don't need to buy any respect. I get all the respect I need in all the places I need it. Neither do I feel the need to atone for anything. You operate within a strict framework of laws created somewhat arbitrarily by various governments. These laws change all the time, making them moving targets. For example, one product I import from the South was illegal in every state in the union until recently. Today, it's legal in some form in all but fifteen states and will probably be allowed nationwide within ten years. Was I wrong to import the product before it became legal, or just ahead of my time? This city, this state, and this country all institute laws—but none of these trump the law of the universe. If there's a demand for a product, someone will find a way to fill it, if not legally, then illegally. I simply choose to compete on all sides of the process."

"But what about the people you hurt or even kill in that process?"

"I don't physically hurt people. I also don't kill them."

"Come on, Theo! Let's not debate semantics here," said Denton. "You may not personally kill people, but you can't tell me you don't have others do it for you."

"Maybe, Denton. I told you—I never lie. Remember, though, no infrastructure of public safety protects me or many of my operations. Law enforcement officers like you try to corner me regularly in several states and at least three countries. Worse, lawless competitors with no morals or conscience come after me every day of the year. With no set of laws or regulations to protect me, I'm forced to improvise fair justice independently. Does the state of Ohio kill people?"

"If you mean does this state approve capital punishment, you know the answer. Yes, we do. We execute deserving criminals."

"No different from my system," said Jackson. "Deserving criminals are sometimes executed."

"Who decides if they're deserving?"

Jackson smiled a bit. "Well, we don't conduct trials with juries, but pretty much the same things get punished in my system as yours: murder, theft, dishonesty, and disloyalty. Innocent people aren't punished. Look, I enjoy this philosophical discussion, Denton, but neither of us will likely change our position on how we see things. I can promise you, on the scale of bad, there are many things worse than selling drugs to crackheads and addicts."

"I don't disagree, Theo, but on the scale of good, there are a lot of better things you could sell than products illegal in this state and much of the world."

Amused by Denton's response, Theo smiled and said, "Damn, Denton—you're quick. Somebody should write that in a book. We should move on from this debate, though. Take a right up here on Victory, and I'll show you the building I believe we could convert for the youth center."

As Denton drove through neighborhoods close to where he and Theo came from, Theo gazed out the passenger window in silence. Not much had changed in this part of town over the past decades other than older buildings. Few businesses remained, and of those, not many Denton remembered from childhood. Theo instructed Denton to stop the car when they arrived at the deserted former junior high school.

"Do you own this?" asked Denton.

"Let's say I have an interest in investments of the group of partners who own the property. You should be familiar with the property since the city owned it until a couple of years ago. Your administration wanted to sell it at public auction, but my friends bought it before that happened. The building's infrastructure is still solid, and you may remember the property already includes a baseball field."

"I do," said Denton. "So, you think the current owners would consider a reasonable offer from the city to repurchase the property?"

"Pretty sure they would," answered Jackson.

Denton's vehicle circled the old school. A chain-link fence surrounded the property, but that security had not prevented trespassers from covering the lower parts of the brick structure with graffiti. Vandals had also broken most of the windows on the two lower levels.

"Looks in sad shape," said Denton.

"True, but most of the damage is superficial. The city constructed this building almost one hundred years ago when lumber cost little. The frame consists of twelve-inch by twelve-inch beams, and the exterior walls were built with concrete blocks covered by a brick veneer. The roof is metal. To build the same-size structure today with similar materials would cost over five million dollars, but all this building needs now are new walls, floors, windows, and insulation. The property would also benefit from a pest control initiative. It's full of pigeons and rats."

"Interesting," said Denton. "Have you shared this part of your plan with the mayor?"

"Not yet, but I will. While the property seems perfect for the youth center, the surrounding neighborhood still needs a little work."

"What do you mean?"

"See the commercial building across the street?"

Denton observed a one-story concrete structure occupying about half the block, which appeared to house three different businesses. A tall cellular tower with various antennae, cameras, and satellite dishes attached to the frame rose from the building's metal roof.

"What about it?" asked Denton.

"Do you know anything about the owner of those businesses?"

"Nope. Do you?" Denton now regarded Theo suspiciously, sure that Theo *did* know something about the owner.

"Yes. A little. I followed the sale of the building closely. Rather arbitrarily, the city changed some restrictions in the original school-zone code to accommodate the buyer. I wasn't happy about that."

"So, one person owns the building and all three stores?" asked Denton. The storefronts advertised a tanning salon, a video store, and a photography studio.

"Yes, and if you go around the block to the other side of the building, I'd like you to look at something else."

Denton complied, and Theo pointed to a parking area servicing the stores fronting the street. Denton slowed the vehicle, and Theo asked, "Notice the Lexus on the right, the red one?"

"Yeah. Nice car."

"That's the owner's car. The dumbshit even has vanity plates identifying him as *sunny*."

"Okay," said Denton. "Why does that make him a dumbshit? Lots of people purchase vanity plates."

As Denton's car completed the circle around the block, Theo stared at the three businesses. "Doesn't it strike you strange someone would put a tanning salon in this neighborhood? Not too many around here want to get any tanner. And who buys videos anymore?"

"Well, judging by the owner's car, he must do okay with the photography business, then."

"Or something," replied Theo. "The tower on the roof is also curious."

"Theo, we have cellular towers all over the city. What makes this one special?"

"Utility companies own most cell towers. They need the towers to support their own electrical and communications infrastructure and then make some income by renting space on the towers to other companies. A private company owns the tower on this building. Like the utility companies, this tower's owner rents space to several cellular providers, at least one interstate trucking company, and a couple of internet providers. Hard to guess what the rest of the equipment does, but one thing is for sure: wires attach all those devices on the tower to some massive computers in the building which track more than photography and video sales."

"I see," said Denton. "Have you ever met the owner?"

"No, but I know of him through some peripheral business. Name's Sun Yi. I think he's Chinese. Not much paperwork exists relating to the sale of the building, and he purchased it with cash after no negotiation."

Denton whistled softly and glanced at Theo. "Drug money?"

"Nope, don't think so. I have ideas about where the money comes from, but the vanity plates don't make sense. Smart criminals don't generally do stupid things that might attract attention."

"Why does this bother you?"

Theo turned to Denton, smiling. "Denton, my friend, some of the things that bother me might surprise you. A conversation for a different day."

The bad feeling Denton had at the beginning of his drive with Theo had just elevated to badder, and Theo changed the subject. "Did you happen to look into the other matter we discussed?"

"Unofficially, yes," replied Denton, "but I doubt I found much more than what you may have discovered on your own."

"Which is about seven or eight babies entered various social service agencies around the time of Mae Hamilton's death?"

"Something like that," answered Jones. "Why send me after this stuff if you already have it?"

"Because the information I have doesn't tell me all I need to know."

"Well, so far, you already know all I've discovered."

"Meaning you aren't finished looking?"

"I didn't say that," said Denton. "You could have shortened the research a bit by providing all the pertinent information."

"What do you mean?"

"You didn't mention Mae Hamilton was Caucasian. Biracial babies are a subset of all babies. Knowing to look for a biracial one might have reduced the field to research."

"Denton, I'm not looking for a black baby or a white baby and don't care if it's something in between. I'm looking for one born to a specific woman who died around the period I provided you. How much more detail do you need?"

"Relax, Theo. That piece of information didn't hold me up. Just surprised you didn't share it with me."

"Honestly, Denton, I didn't think it would be important to you, of all people. It might surprise you, but I quit thinking in terms of black and white a long time ago. The rest of the world hasn't quite evolved to that, but I have, and I thought you had. Tell me this, do you think of your wife, Jessica, as White . . . or as beautiful?"

"Neither. I think of her as extraordinary, but I take your point. I'm sorry. Assumptions are dangerous, and I should know better. I don't have a lot of extra time, but I'm not done with my research yet."

"Okay, let me help you a little. Your analysis will most likely lead you to only one name meeting all the criteria, but even that name won't help me without something else."

"Like what?" asked Denton.

"Like some form of DNA testing," answered Jackson.

"Theo, if I *do* find a name, and if I decide to help you—which I haven't yet—how do you expect me to obtain a DNA sample?"

"I don't need to explain that to you, Denton. You can obtain a sample in several ways. If I'm making a five-million-dollar contribution to the city with absolutely nothing in return, couldn't you help me on this one little thing?"

"If you're willing to pay five million dollars for this *one little thing*, it must be damn important. I don't care how much you contribute—I'm not going to put a citizen in jeopardy."

"Okay, okay," answered Jackson. "Relax. I said the contribution had no strings attached, and there aren't. I want to help the person I'm looking for if I can, not hurt him."

"You're sure this person's a boy?"

"Yes."

"And you think this boy, now a man, is your son?"

"Maybe."

"Then tell me why it has taken you almost twenty-two years to decide you want to help him."

"Ya know, Denton, I'm not used to someone grilling me like I'm a third-rate pickpocket."

"And I'm not used to assisting a known criminal, so we're both on new ground here. Tell me why you want this information now, or I'm not lifting another finger to help. And even if you do tell me, I'm not guaranteeing anything."

"You're tougher than people give you credit for, Denton," Jackson said. He sat for a long minute, gazing out the window before speaking again. "I guess I'm softer than most people believe. In my business, I work about sixteen hours per day, seven days per week, year-round. I don't have time for a wife or kids or any other kind of personal relationship—nor would I ever consciously put someone in the dangerous position of being affectionately involved with me. Anyone with me or close to me becomes as much a target for violence as me. I have always been, and will remain, cautious in this regard."

"With only one exception?" asked Denton.

"Yes. One unfortunate exception—which at this point in my life I hope to turn into a *fortunate* one."

"How? By putting him into your organization?"

"No. Nothing like that. Just maybe helping a little from the outside."

"Okay," said Denton. "I'll think about it. No promises."

"I understand. Thanks. I'll make arrangements to deliver a donation to City Hall next week."

———

When Jackson returned to his office, he booted his desktop to life and searched for an advertisement he'd spotted on a storefront window during his ride with Jones. Finding it, he studied the ad for several minutes before pressing the intercom function on his desk phone to summon his administrative assistant. After huddling over the computer screen together for a few moments, Theo asked, "Teresa, would this advertisement attract teen girls?"

Teresa Adams had served Jackson as his primary assistant for nearly a decade, and he trusted her completely with all aspects of the complex organization of his diversified businesses. Mensa-level intelligent, loyal, and calm, she occupied the desk in front of the elevator. Content to allow visitors to believe she served only in a secretarial capacity, Teresa's responsibilities included much more.

The hard drives in the extensive network of fast, cutting-edge computers scattered throughout Theo's office contained few details of the inner workings of his operation. Teresa kept most of this information in her head and on several USB drives that she took with her wherever she went. Teresa enthusiastically, if quietly, encouraged Theo in his pursuit of legitimate business ventures but remained nonjudgmental of his less wholesome operations. Born on the streets of the inner city herself, she recognized the tough choices many with her background made to survive. She also shared Theo's lack of sympathy for those making poor life choices relative to drugs and addiction.

Attractive people of opposing sexes working together in a close office environment often creates sexual tension. Not in the case of Theo and Teresa, however. While each appreciated the handsome appearance of the other, Teresa didn't seem attracted to men. Their professional relationship depended only on mutual respect and trust.

"It sure would, Theo. A free photography session with no obligation to purchase anything? And you get to keep the digital files for the sample photos? What's the catch?"

"Don't know, but I'll bet there is one. I wonder how many girls in the neighborhood bite on this. A big sign on the store's window displays the offer, and the ad we're looking at runs on Facebook."

"Don't know," answered Teresa. "Also, not sure why you're interested. I can't help you with this unless you tell me what's going on in your mind."

Theo smiled and sat back in his chair. "Come on, Teresa. You're almost a mind reader."

"Yeah, well. Not in this case. What's bothering you about the photography store?"

"The guy who owns it. His name is Sun Yi. Chinese, I think. He paid cash and opened the photography store, a video shop, and a tanning salon in the three commercial spaces."

"Sort of an eclectic mix of poor choices for an area like Victory Avenue, but why should you care?"

"I shouldn't, but something isn't right about it, which gnaws at me. Yi now ranks as one of Reggie Lincoln's biggest customers."

"I'm aware," answered Teresa. "Reggie asked me last week if he could provide Yi a few of our burner phones."

"What did you tell him?"

"I said, 'No way.' Those phones only go to folks inside the organization."

"Good," answered Theo. "That's the right answer."

Teresa handled the weekly distribution and programming of seven disposable cell phones. Two went to Theo and herself. She placed the other five in a private mailbox maintained at the nearby UPS outlet. Strategic associates of Theodore Jackson Investments retrieved these phones at random times during the week. Quantity orders for the devices went to three different companies, including Nokia, LG, and TracFone. The four-hundred-plus phones purchased annually represented an expense of over fifteen thousand dollars, which both Theo and Teresa believed constituted necessary security.

"So, what's Mr. Yi doing with all the product Reggie provides?" asked Teresa. "He isn't reselling it on the street. We'd know about that if he were."

"I can't imagine where it goes. Someplace else besides here for sure. Interstate Transport, a local trucking company, owns one of the satellite dishes on the tower located on his building. I assume that might give Yi a convenient method for distribution to other locations."

"Theo, why don't you just tell me what you're thinking versus playing 'who's got a clue' with me?"

"Honestly, I haven't pieced it together, but a rich Chinese guy with three silly choices for businesses in the inner city, purchasing lots of drugs, is no coincidence. I'm curious about how all that relates."

"Then let's find out. Why don't I send Lucretia over there with a couple of her friends for a photo session?"

"No way, Teresa. Not a chance. Whatever this guy's doing, he's a criminal. I don't want your niece mixed up with him."

"She's not going to be mixed up in anything, Theo! She's just another good-looking, starry-eyed teenager from the hood interested in Yi's photography offer. She's gonna get her picture taken, not audition for his gang!"

Theo thought for a minute. "I guess that's easy enough. We'd at least find out what the catch is for a free photo session."

"Right. I'll talk to Luci this evening."

Lucretia Adams—or "Luci," pronounced with a hard *C*, to her aunt and close friends—was the nineteen-year-old daughter of Teresa's older sister, Estelle. When Estelle died from complications of HIV, Teresa took her sister's four-year-old daughter to live with her. Teresa had taken care of Luci for the fifteen years since. Luci's father was unknown, but her appearance hinted the man might have been Latino.

Estelle had many partners in the year before Luci's birth, all of whom paid Estelle for companionship. During this period, Teresa, only a teenager herself, watched in horror at her older sister's method to escape the family's poverty. One of Estelle's earlier boyfriends, a handsome man with some money, promised Estelle the world but instead delivered her into a life of prostitution from which she never escaped. Teresa could not forgive that man, or men in general, for her sister's tragedy. Since that time, she preferred the company of women for herself. She was, however, thankful her sister had not aborted Lucretia.

One afternoon after Theo's discussion with Teresa, Luci and two girlfriends visited GlaMore Photography and asked about the free photoshoot advertised. The owner, Mr. Yi, explained to the girls that such a session would cost them nothing except the opportunity for him to present a photo package, which they might optionally purchase later. He only needed them to complete a personal data form and provide an email address to send his finished photography's digital samples.

The girls completed the paperwork, and Mr. Yi told them they could begin a session right away. He led them down a short hallway and through a door labeled *Makeup and Wardrobe*, where they met a petite Asian woman named Lin Song.

"Oh, goodness!" exclaimed Lin. "Papasan, where you find these beautiful models? Look at them." Afterward, she directed each girl to a makeup counter. As the girls experimented with different eye shadows and lipstick, Lin darted in and out among them, offering suggestions and assisting. When each girl finished with makeup, Lin asked what kind of clothing they preferred for the photos.

"Well," said Luci, as she surveyed the lined racks of bathing suits, lingerie, and evening wear, "I thought I would just wear what I have on."

Lin acted disappointed. "You no want sexy, sexy? You so beautiful."

"No," said Luci. "My aunt would kill me. One of these evening dresses would work, I think."

"Yes, yes," said Lin. "We make you look very nice in one these."

During the photo session, conducted in another room in front of a bright-green screen, Lin snapped the photographs, directing Luci's various poses. While the evening dress Luci chose was modest enough, Lin consistently pushed the limit of Luci's comfort. She took several shots with the gown's straps pulled off Luci's shoulders, and she also insisted on a picture from a sitting position with the dress parted to show one of Luci's legs almost to the thigh.

Luci's girlfriends had similar sessions and seemed more comfortable with exotic poses, but the whole experience made Luci feel awkward. Using her cell phone, Luci took several candid shots of her friends as they posed, ensuring that she captured Lin Song and Mr. Yi in the edges of the frames. When the photoshoot ended, Mr. Yi told the girls he would send the digital samples shortly via email. The girls could then purchase from among a variety of options if they chose.

Several days later, Luci received a thick package in the mail from GlaMore Photography with a personal note from Mr. Sun Yi. Surprised the photography had not arrived digitally in an email, Luci reviewed the photos and called Yi as he had requested in the note.

———

"So, tell me about the next meeting with Yi," said Jackson.

"When I received the package, I called him right away. He asked if I liked the samples, and I told him I did but didn't think I could afford any of the packages he offered. He told me he understood but still had something to discuss in person and asked if I could come back to the studio."

Luci, Teresa, and Theo sat at a conference table in Theo's office several days after Luci's meeting with Yi. Theo wanted all the details.

"Is that when he informed you about the modeling opportunity in Las Vegas?" asked Theo.

"Yes. Yi and Lin Song were both at the studio when I arrived, and they showed me a whole wallboard display of my photos. Ms. Song raved about the pictures' quality and flattered me about my appearance when

Mr. Yi finally stopped her. He became serious and told me he shared my collection of photos with several modeling agencies. One of these, Foxee Modeling, requested that I fly to Nevada for an interview right away."

"At their cost?" asked Theo.

"Not exactly." Luci smiled. "Yi said the Las Vegas agency would require Yi to pay for my airfare but that the agency would reimburse him if the interview went well."

"What about the return airfare if the interview *doesn't* go well?"

"Funny thing about that," answered Luci. "He glossed over what might happen then, expressing confidence I'd do fine in the interview. He speculated I'd sign a contract for thousands of dollars and start professionally modeling immediately."

"Teresa?" asked Theo. "How do you feel about Luci going to Las Vegas?"

Teresa and her niece exchanged glances, and Luci fielded Theo's question before Teresa could. "I call her my aunt, but she's more like a mother. I love her and respect Aunt Teresa's judgment. She would prefer that I not travel to Las Vegas, but she left the decision to me. At nineteen, I haven't traveled anyplace more than a hundred miles from here. I'm not gullible enough to believe a high-priced modeling job awaits in Nevada, but my classes are over for the semester, and I think I'm smart enough to keep myself safe on this trip."

"Which puts the responsibility squarely on you, Theo," said Teresa, glaring at her boss.

"I don't want that kind of responsibility, and I agree with you, Teresa," Theo said. Then, focusing back on Luci, he said, "You already established what I needed to know about Yi's photography business, Luci. I don't want you to take additional risks. In fact, I already owe you for the work you've done. Pick any spot in the country you'd like to visit, and I'll buy the airline ticket for you. You can even choose Las Vegas, but I don't want you meeting with any of Yi's contacts if you go there."

Luci stared at Theo, reminding him of similar looks he had received from the girl's aunt on occasion. "I appreciate your concern—yours, too, Aunt Teresa. At what point do children grow up, though? When do we become adults allowed to make our own decisions? I have an offer from Mr. Yi that I can take with or without the approval of anyone here. I now suspect Yi of the same thing you do, Mr. Jackson, and I'm in a unique position to learn more. Do I have to do this on my own, or will you help me?"

Knowing Luci had outmaneuvered him, Theo said, "Teresa, take five thousand dollars from petty cash and bring it here. Luci—don't sign anything, no matter what kind of pressure you feel. The agency will probably allow you to stall for a while before they give up. During that period, find out as much as you safely can about the modeling requirements and the other models. Whenever you need to, you have the funds for airfare back here. Do you understand all this?"

"Yes, sir, I do. Should I call you with information?"

"No," said Theo. "For your safety, only call me in an extreme emergency. The less communication with anyone back here, the safer for you. We'll debrief when you return."

CHAPTER 7

"I can't really explain it well," said Denton. "The guy isn't just bright. He's extremely credible. Jackson says he never lies, and I believe him."

Jessica and Denton sat in the den, each with a glass of wine. This almost daily ritual represented a favorite part of their routine. Sometimes their conversations included stimulating summaries of their respective workdays. Other times, the discussions consisted of frivolous chatter about nothing in particular. This evening the discussion centered on Denton's meeting with Theo Jackson earlier in the day.

"Sounds like you're becoming a fan," Jessica said with a hint of sarcasm.

"Not at all, J. He's a known criminal, and I detest everything he stands for. While he may be a bad man, I don't think he's a purely evil one. He possesses a misguided sense of right and wrong, but some of his values have virtuous aspects."

"What are you going to do about finding his person? You *know* what could happen if anyone found out you were doing anything, no matter how insignificant, for Jackson."

"I'm aware, and I'm not sure what I'll do. Probably nothing. The contribution to the city doesn't depend on me providing him the information."

"I'll be glad when this little chapter of our lives closes. I'm not fond of you meeting with dangerous men, and I'm upset the mayor and the city manager put you in the middle of the negotiations. You risk enough in your job without this."

"I agree, but I don't think the mayor's the one who put me in the middle. Jackson did by placing a condition on the donation that my name appears on the building."

"Do you think he did that on purpose?"

"Do I think he sincerely wanted me recognized for my efforts with at-risk kids? Yes," answered Denton. "Do I think he wanted to irritate city officials or cause me some personal trouble? No. When we talk, it's like going back thirty-some years. I'm certain he wouldn't do anything to hurt me or us, Jessica. He provided me a hint today about something shady he thought was happening up on Victory Parkway. If you get a chance tomorrow, will you check the business licenses for the shops on Eleventh Street right across from the old junior high school?"

"Does he want you to shut down one of his competitors?"

"No. I don't think this has anything to do with drugs, and it's possibly nothing at all. I'd just like some basic information for now."

"If you say so," answered Jessica. "I still don't trust him, but I'll have Jaden pull the business licenses and tax records tomorrow. After you and I talked the other evening, I asked Fred if anyone ever suspected Jackson received help from inside the city administration or the police force."

"What did he say?"

"He asked me why I wanted to know," said Jessica.

"Roberson asked me the same question."

"I told him it seemed odd to me that a criminal like Jackson would not have any charges in over thirty years. After staring at me for a little too long, Fred told me I wasn't the first to notice that. He didn't seem to want to discuss the subject, so I dropped it."

"I think that was a good idea," said Denton. "In my first conversation with Jackson, I told him he couldn't buy me. He responded that others in higher positions than me were not so virtuous. Then, in our conversation this morning, Jackson related the importance of having lots of information from many sources. He said that's what keeps him alive. Those admissions would support our suspicion that he receives critical information from inside the city's administration. I wonder whether his sources are random, different ones at different times—or whether he has a more permanent and well-placed confidential contact."

"Oh, Denton, what are we doing? Why are we asking these questions, and what does any of this have to do with us? It scares me!"

Denton placed both arms around his wife. "Jessica, we're asking because it's what the citizens pay us to do. We're public servants, and the community expects us to do our best to keep them safe. I don't particularly like attending meetings with known criminals like Theo Jackson. Suspecting I may cross paths regularly with an unknown criminal within our administration concerns me more. Possibly, we opened Pandora's box with our questions, but we can't pretend we don't have suspicions."

Jessica sniffed lightly into Denton's chest, and both stayed silent for a long time. Jessica finally pulled away, putting her hands firmly on Denton's shoulders. "Okay, T," she said, "but we do this by my rules, together. No secrets on this subject between us—ever! We will also share everything and not take any action without the other's approval. And we'll be careful. If Theo Jackson is a dangerous man, someone who works for him inside our city organization is even more dangerous. We should be cautious about our questions and cautious to whom we direct them—if it isn't already too late."

Denton agreed. But it was, unfortunately, too late.

CHAPTER 8

Roberson accepted the evening call on his cell phone gruffly, expecting another solicitation about his expiring car warranty. "Roberson here."

"Mr. Roberson," said a silky-smooth voice with a hint of an accent. "We seem to have a problem."

"What kind of a problem?" asked Roberson as he left the den for the privacy of a different room.

"Someone from your city attorney's office called my business today about missing paperwork for a permit. Your administration currently cannot find all the information required for our filings relating to the antenna tower."

"I don't know why someone would call about that now. Your tower has been in place for over two years. Who called?"

"His name was Jaden Stokes, and he said he worked as an intern in the city's Law Department. He told me his supervisor, a Mrs. Jones, requested he track down the missing paperwork."

"Shit!" exclaimed Roberson. "You know very well what happened to that paperwork."

"I am aware of the history, Mr. Roberson, and we appreciate your past accommodations. It appears, however, that an overzealous city employee noticed the incomplete permit document. You must now do some additional work. Mr. Stokes requires me to provide copies of the previously filed permit or face more serious inspections that could negatively impact my operations. I'll need your assistance to handle these filings."

"I'm not sure what more I can do for you, Mr. Yi, and I'm sorry I ever assisted you in the first place."

"And I promise you will be even more sorry if you refuse to help now. We know many things about you, Mr. Roberson, and you are not in a good position to refuse my request. We now require something simple, and your assistance will allow you to remain healthy and well employed. Do you understand?"

"Yes. What is it you want?"

"When I provide Mr. Stokes a downloaded file tomorrow, it will contain some tiny bits of computer code which will protect my company's interests."

"You propose to infect our computer systems with a virus?"

"No, Mr. Roberson. This code will only alert informed people to the file's location. One of these informed people, namely you, can then execute a command that will make both the code and parts of the attached file disappear. The proper documentation, when it is refiled and archived, will satisfy your city employee. Our concerns will subside when certain personal information in the file disappears again. Everyone will be happy."

"I'm no computer geek, Yi, and our IT department will certainly suspect me if I make an unusual request to delete files from our servers."

"You can execute the necessary commands from your desk. I will call you when I have provided Mr. Stokes with the requested files."

———

Charles Delwray Roberson, one of two appointed assistant city managers, worked for elected city manager Haley Doolittle. Starting nearly four decades earlier with the city as a patrol officer in the Cincinnati Police Department, Roberson methodically graduated through the ranks to become a commander of the second district. After twelve years on the police force, Roberson earned a promotion to a management position in the city manager's office. Four years later, the mayor appointed him to assistant city manager. As one of the city's longest-tenured employees, Roberson's performance was never flashy but usually consistent and professional. Roberson represented a comfortable bridge between the past and the present for Cincinnati, an uncontroversial "old shoe" with no political ambitions or apparent prejudice.

His relatively mild corruption began not because of excessive greed but through naivete. Early in his career as a patrolman, a chance acquaintance with a street delinquent helped him resolve a personal family issue. When the youthful offender who assisted him later encountered a minor legal problem, Roberson successfully vacated the charges from juvenile records.

In the years since, Roberson's little bits of assistance graduated to more significant bits, and his rewards for the help also grew. Roberson owned no secret bank accounts, and any investigation into his personal finances would reveal nothing unusual. The assistant city manager participated as a silent partner in several investment groups in the city with sizeable real estate and business holdings, and both of his sons had benefited from college scholarships awarded by out-of-the-ordinary organizations. Roberson and his wife, Carmen, could also access various Caribbean vacation locations for the most nominal of fees.

While Roberson's occasional assistance to a single criminal over a long period provided him benefits, the help was so obscure that Roberson doubted authorities would ever discover his role. Then, he made a mistake. He performed a seemingly insignificant task for a different kind of criminal, which changed his life—for the worse.

Several years before, Sun Yi approached the assistant city manager to discuss the city's zoning relative to a distressed property Yi desired to purchase on Victory Parkway. The property sat across the street from a deserted junior high school. While both the property Yi wished to buy and the old school occupied a zoning district labeled "Urban Mix," additional restrictions applied to zoning in the immediate area due to the school's presence. The code didn't allow adult-oriented businesses, and it limited the height of new construction or permanent structures in the immediate area. Yi planned to open an adult video store on the property, and he also wanted to place a communications tower on the roof of the existing structure. Yi argued that the current zoning was obsolete since the school located in the vicinity had been long closed.

Roberson agreed to review the zoning and potentially bring the issue to the zoning board's attention. On the day the board published the planning meeting's agenda, Roberson received a call on his personal cell from Theodore Jackson. Mr. Jackson expressed concern about the Victory Parkway property and strongly encouraged Roberson not to support a change in the existing zoning. When Roberson reminded Jackson the school in the vicinity had not operated in years, Jackson informed Roberson that his investment company had a financial interest in the partnership owning the old school property. He told the assistant city manager the group planned to rehabilitate the junior high school as a community center and hoped Roberson would not allow a zoning deviation that might discourage such a development. Roberson's argument with Jackson escalated during the phone call, and Roberson finally told Jackson he could feel free to attend the zoning board meeting to share his concerns.

"Mr. Roberson, as you are well aware, I can't do that," Jackson had replied. "I'm unhappy with your response and disappointed that our long-standing relationship must end in this fashion. Goodbye."

When Roberson disconnected from that call years ago, he rationalized that the time to sever ties with Jackson had probably come anyway. The zoning change to accommodate Yi proved a relatively easy and noncontroversial matter, and the initial consulting work Roberson performed for Yi afterward was straightforward—and lucrative. Adjusting the original paperwork for the obscure antenna tower permitting wasn't tricky and posed little risk of exposure. However, Roberson balked at later requests from Yi, and Yi threatened to expose the assistant city manager's earlier corruption.

—

Now, after this evening's communication with Yi, Roberson's mind rumbled in turmoil. Yi's organization, whoever they were, scared him, and he regretted his association. Roberson did not doubt Yi's ability to hurt him both professionally and physically; he would have to find a way to accommodate Yi's latest request.

He struggled to understand why somebody at the Law Department would suddenly check detailed information from a permit completed years earlier. Then dots began to connect in his mind. Jaden Stokes, a summer intern, worked for the city's general counsel, Jessica Jones. Her husband, Central Business District commander Denton Jones, had just met with Theodore Jackson about the donation Jackson wanted to make to the city. When the mayor mentioned the offer from Jackson to Roberson, Roberson recommended that she appoint Denton Jones to provide the city's response to Jackson. That, Roberson now realized, was a mistake.

No doubt Jackson desired the youth center at the property he and his partners owned across the street from Yi's building. Roberson and Jackson had discussed that very thing in their ill-fated argument about zoning years before. Unlike Sun Yi, Jackson had not once in their relationship used intimidation to achieve a favor. Was it possible now that Jackson wanted to retaliate for Roberson's poor zoning decision? Did Jackson perhaps provide hints to Jones about Roberson's past improprieties, possibly prompting his wife to direct her intern to dig up information about an ancient incomplete permit? Commander Jones had also recently asked the strange question about whether Roberson believed Jackson ever benefited from help inside city administration. What the hell had Jackson told Denton Jones?

Bastard! thought Roberson, overwhelmed by the suspicion he might be on the wrong side of not one but two criminals. The danger from Yi represented a more imminent problem, and Roberson's professional survival depended on his ability to dilute his exposure. Fred Gunnells didn't mention anything about Yi when the acting city solicitor called several days earlier; he seemed only concerned about Mrs. Jones's inquiries relative to Theo Jackson's arrest record, or lack thereof. Perhaps Gunnells knew nothing about Jones's request to her intern for information about Yi's business. Still, the call from Gunnells provided an easy opportunity for Roberson to follow up with the attorney. Removing Mrs. Jones from the current equation for a short period could interrupt her department's further efforts to discover other issues about Yi.

The assistant city manager also knew things about Denton Jones's past that could negatively impact the popular police officer's credibility. Neutralizing Officer Jones's role as liaison between Jackson and the city might at least temporarily block efforts Jackson might make against him through that convenient line of communication. If Roberson could then doctor the antenna-permit file as Yi instructed, he could get himself almost back to even. After that, he would concentrate on ridding himself of Sun Yi.

As he sat in his den, Roberson wished he'd never met Sun Yi. He couldn't go back in time to fix that, though, and had plenty of motivation for accommodating Yi now. He hoped to retire soon, ideally with both his reputation and health intact. After the call with Yi this evening, neither seemed assured.

Roberson made two calls from his office the following morning: one to Fred Gunnells in the city's Law Department, the other to Jon Franks, the Internal Audit Division manager. In the assistant city manager's mind, the danger presented by Sun Yi mandated expediency. More careful consideration might have resulted in a different course.

———

Denton had three interesting messages waiting for him when he arrived at his office on Wednesday. An email from the Department of Social Services approved him to view the records he requested. A second email from the mayor's office addressed to all department heads and ranking police officers reported a large cash donation received over the weekend. A box delivered by FedEx to the mayor's receptionist's desk contained five million dollars in large-denomination bills. The anonymous donor left a note inside the parcel, requesting the city use the funds to construct a new youth center on Victory Parkway. Denton laughed, thinking the FedEx box was a classic touch from Theo Jackson.

The third message was not as positive as the first two. From Dan Simski, one of the investigators assigned to Cincinnati's Internal Audit Division, the memo requested that Denton call him. Since Simski and he were friends, Jones hoped that the call had more to do with the lunch-break basketball game than with anything official. Simski, a large man of Polish heritage, played like a beast on the basketball court. Years earlier, he had been a spot starter at center for Marquette University, where he performed the role of "hatchet man," inserted into games at critical times when strategic fouls to opposing players benefited his team. The ironies of life found him now serving as a hatchet man for the city as a member of the always unpopular Internal Audit Division.

Internal Audit had few fans among city administrators, but Denton was one of them. He thought all large organizations needed a watchdog unit to ensure that good guys remained good and bad guys got weeded out. Employees with nothing to hide usually had no reason to fear Internal Audit. Denton punched Simski's number on his cell phone with only minor concerns.

"Morning, Denton," said Simski. "Thanks for calling."

"No problem, Dan. What's up? Can't make the lunch game today?"

"No, probably not, but that isn't why I wanted to speak to you." Simski now spoke hesitantly. "This morning, we received an assignment to conduct a short interview with you."

Denton's shock precluded a quick answer to his friend, and he waited for Simski to start laughing at the practical joke. When Simski remained silent, Denton said, "I'm obviously surprised. What would your department want with me? Who requested the interview?"

"I'm confused, too, and not sure who made the request, but it came from upstream. It has nothing to do with any other investigation we're conducting. I can't tell you much more right now."

"Wow," said Denton. "So, how does this work?"

"Any interviews we conduct," said Simski, "are strictly confidential. Nobody but our office, your chief, and the city manager's office will be aware of the discussions."

"So, the city manager directed this investigation?"

"The call to us came from the assistant city manager's office, and our instructions require us to report information from the interviews directly to Mr. Roberson. Also, Denton, our department currently classifies these discussions as interviews. This isn't an investigation. The technical term is *interrogatory questioning.*"

"Okay. I'm still a little shocked. What's the subject of the questioning, and when does it start?"

"Mr. Franks will meet with Mr. Roberson this afternoon to receive a briefing on the nature of the interviews. I would guess we'll want to get it done as soon as we can after that. We will make ourselves available at your discretion and, naturally, will work around your schedule."

"Thank you, Dan. Give me a call after the meeting today, and we'll go from there, I guess."

"Okay, Denton. I'm sorry about this and doubt if it's anything important. Don't worry about it."

"Easier said than done," replied Denton.

Denton hung up the phone, confused. He knew he had done nothing to earn the attention of Internal Audit, but that someone *thought* he had bothered him. Furthermore, in his meeting with Roberson several days earlier, the assistant city manager didn't hint of a potential probe. That could only mean this pending interview related to something discovered since that meeting. As he replayed the events of recent days in his mind, he could think of nothing.

Then, another thought occurred. Perhaps the meeting with Roberson triggered the need for the interview? Maybe something Denton said about Theo Jackson started questions in Roberson's mind. As he considered this, he turned back to his computer, looking at the three messages displayed. Was it a coincidence all three had a common thread: Theo Jackson? Still considering this, he called the archives manager for the Social Services Division.

After the third digital rerouting, a female came on the phone to provide Denton the needed password and some additional instructions.

She told him the password would work for twenty-four hours after the first time he used it. He could not download examined information, and the woman reminded Denton of the sensitive and highly confidential nature of archived documents. Denton provided a voice signature to acknowledge he understood the instructions, thanking her as he hung up.

Denton glanced at the clock on the wall and the password written on a tablet in front of him. He could not imagine the records now available to him would take him more than a few minutes to review. Still, with the potential for an Internal Audit interview later in the day, his schedule threatened to become cluttered. Since he had at least an hour this morning with no other commitments, he decided to pull up the Adoptive and Foster Care Services archives. Within seconds of entering the required password, a short record appeared, providing the disposition of the unidentified baby left on the Southside Baptist Church's steps years before.

An elder of the church discovered the basket containing the infant as he prepared to unlock the church's doors. The man called the fourth patrol district's duty desk, and a police officer accompanied by an EMT arrived to take custody of the child. The officer in charge filed a written report indicating he delivered the baby to the Cincinnati Children's Hospital on Albert Sabin Way. The basket contained blankets and a short note written on a piece of torn cardboard that read, *Baby's mothur died. We can't take care a him.*

Examining physicians at CCH found the baby mildly dehydrated but otherwise healthy. The hospital contacted the Hamilton County Department of Job and Family Services, and a member of that organization came to the hospital the following morning to pick up the child. The baby went to the St. Joseph Orphanage on Edalbert Drive for temporary care while authorities tried to locate relatives. DNA taken during the initial examination didn't prove helpful in this attempt, and after a month of searching, the agency abandoned the effort. In October, the baby entered foster care.

When Denton read the names of the foster caregivers, he needed no further details. He stared at the computer for several minutes as if the information might change if he watched long enough. It didn't. He closed his search and exited the confidential archives. Glancing at the wall clock, he realized he had only needed the password for a total of ten minutes of the twenty-four hours allowed.

Denton had known the boy for many years, just not the circumstances of his first several. He felt sure he also knew the identity of the child's biological father. In retrospect, the discovery didn't surprise him.

Between the information Theo provided Denton and that retrieved from the social service archives, little doubt remained for Denton about the boy's lineage. Without DNA comparisons between the father and the child, a 100 percent–guaranteed determination could (or would) never be absolute. Still, the facts surrounding the time and place of the baby's discovery provided the most compelling circumstantial evidence. Denton was at this moment the only person in the entire world with this knowledge, and he planned to keep it that way—with one exception: Jessica.

CHAPTER 9

Denton received a call from Dan Simski just before five o'clock. The Internal Audit officers had finished a briefing at the city manager's office, and Simski said Denton's interview could start any time after nine o'clock the following morning. Denton suggested ten o'clock after his sergeant's briefing. Simski surprised him by indicating the preliminary interview would take no longer than thirty minutes.

"Preliminary interview?" questioned Denton. "You mean this will take multiple interviews?"

"Not necessarily, Denton," answered Simski. "It sort of depends on the results of the preliminary. Once we send an analysis of our findings on the initial interview back to the city manager's office, the assistant city manager will determine the necessity for follow-up interviews."

"And what about Colonel Fitzpatrick?" asked Denton. "I think he would want to review any information about one of his officers before other departments do."

"He'll receive a copy of what we send to Roberson's office," explained Simski, "but he has no official function in this type of inquiry. He's not the one who requested the interview, and unless the discussions result in information requiring a formal investigation, we require no involvement from him."

"Okay," said Denton. "I'm new to this. I have no experience with Internal Audit interviews, but I don't like the mechanics so far. If someone in the city has questions for me serious enough to arouse Internal Audit's interest, I'd feel more comfortable if my boss were the one asking the questions. Colonel Fitzpatrick should be in the room to hear my answers if he can't ask the questions. If that isn't possible, I think he'd at least want to know my answers before his superiors did."

"I understand," said Simski, "but I don't make the rules. I don't think anyone would try to stop Colonel Fitzpatrick from attending the interviews. Do you want to check with him before we confirm the time for tomorrow?"

"Yes, Dan, I would. Give me a few minutes and let me see if I can still catch him this evening."

Denton hung up and immediately dialed the chief of police's office number. Fitzpatrick's assistant told Denton the chief had just left but that she would try to contact him. About three minutes later, Denton's phone rang. "Commander Jones speaking."

"Denton, Jack. Cindy said you called. What's up?"

"Well, Colonel, I'm not sure. Are you aware of the Internal Audit interview I'm supposed to attend?"

"Yeah," said Fitzpatrick. "I heard about it about a half hour ago when Roberson's office called me. Sounds like a bunch of bullshit to me and a waste of several people's time, but it's an interrogatory interview, not an investigation. I don't have official status in one of those."

"Dan Simski told me the same thing," said Denton. "Can you speculate the reason for the interview?"

"I can now, but someone instructed me that information was confidential until the interview."

"Okay, but wouldn't you want to know my answers before they go to some other department?"

"Denton, I'm not worried about your answers to their stupid questions. You aren't going to tell them anything I don't already know, and I'm telling you this whole thing's a waste of valuable time. Don't concern yourself."

"Thank you, sir. I appreciate your confidence," answered Denton. "Internal Audit scheduled the interview for ten o'clock tomorrow, and Simski says it shouldn't take more than thirty minutes. Could you possibly attend?"

Fitzpatrick didn't speak for a few seconds, then said, "Absolutely, Denton. I can rearrange a few things."

"I appreciate that, Colonel."

"No problem, Denton, but do yourself a favor and don't worry about this tonight."

"Thanks. I'll try not to."

———

When Denton arrived home, he had much to share with Jessica. She met him at the door with a glass of red wine as if she knew he needed it.

"Thanks, J. It's been a long day."

"I thought that might be the case. I saw the memo about the big contribution."

"Yep. The notice represented the best part of the day. It deteriorated after that."

"Oh, T, I'm sorry. Sit down and tell me about it."

The couple made their way to the den, where Denton set his glass on the side table and sighed. Looking at his wife, he said, "Inspectors from Internal Audit are interviewing me tomorrow morning."

Jessica set her glass on the table in front of the sofa. "For what?"

Denton gave Jessica a summary of what transpired during the day relative to his pending meeting with Internal Audit. When he finished, Jessica asked, "Could this have something to do with Jackson?"

"I don't think the timing of the interview and my recent meetings with Jackson are a coincidence. I can't imagine what Internal Audit's questions could be, though. I didn't initiate the meetings with Jackson. The city manager's office did. I only did what they told me to do."

Jessica thought for a moment. "T, don't worry about this. You haven't done anything wrong. Maybe the meeting has to do with the note accompanying the donation this morning."

"What note?"

"You got the message about the five-million-dollar donation delivered in a FedEx box to the city manager's office this morning, didn't you?"

"Yes, but nobody mentioned a note coming with it."

"Okay," said Jessica. "I didn't personally see the message about the donation. That only went to Fred. Let me think . . ." She paused. "Fred didn't mention the note when he told the staff about the donation, but when I went to his office later in the day, I heard him talking about the gift on the phone. He asked whoever he was speaking to about the contents of a note in the package. I sat down at his desk to wait for him to finish his call, but he motioned for me to wait outside."

"Was that unusual?" asked Denton.

"Yes. Fred involves me in everything going on in the Law Department, no matter how sensitive. I didn't think much about it this morning, but when he came to get me after the call, he didn't say anything more about the note."

"Well, if the note had anything to do with me, it might explain why he wouldn't want you listening in on the call."

"Possibly," said Jessica, "but we're reaching here, aren't we?"

"We are, but the day was a strange one with too many mysteries. I guess I'll find out soon enough. Colonel Fitzpatrick's going to sit with me during the interview."

"Great!" said Jessica. "Was that his idea?"

"No, mine. If someone's trying to start something with me, I want the colonel with me in the interviews."

"You're smart," agreed Jessica. "Let's put this behind us for the evening and enjoy some dinner. I picked up some barbecued ribs from Tony's on the way home."

"Tony's ribs would normally stop all conversation from me," said Denton, "but not tonight. Not quite yet. I have something else to tell you."

"It must be serious because I'm not sure I've ever seen anything get between you and a plate of ribs before."

"Oh, those ribs won't cool much in the next few minutes, and believe me, they're toast then. I need you to know what else I found out this morning. I finished the search for the name Jackson wanted."

"About the baby?" asked Jessica.

"Yeah, the baby. I tracked the child from the steps of the Southside Baptist Church to the Children's Hospital, to the Hamilton County Department of Job and Family Services, to the St. Joseph Orphanage, to the child's foster parents, who ended up adopting him." Denton stopped talking and looked at Jessica.

Jessica now stood at the end of the sofa. When Denton didn't say anything more, she asked, "So, you know the baby's identification?"

"Yes, I do," said Denton. Then, he told her.

Jessica sat back down on the sofa, astonished. "Are you sure?"

"Am I sure this is the child found abandoned on the steps of the church? Yes. Do I think this is Theo Jackson's son? Pretty sure. Without specific DNA sampling, one hundred percent confirmation isn't possible, but both the facts and the timeline led to only one likely conclusion."

"My God," said Jessica. "What now? Will you tell Jackson?"

"No," answered Denton. "Not yet, anyway. I don't think telling Jackson would benefit this young man, and at this point, Theo hasn't convinced me he deserves to know."

"But now that *you* know, will someone else be able to find out?"

"Not without the information Jackson gave me, and I don't think Theo would give that to anyone else."

"So, you may end up the only one who will *ever* know?"

"Nope. One other person knows now."

"Right," said Jessica, "and that person agrees that you should share the information with nobody else."

"OK. I'm ready to eat then," said Denton.

"Good idea."

The couple shared a delicious dinner, but their preoccupied minds precluded enjoyment to the extent the ribs deserved. They then shared a sleepless night, mercifully ended by the sound of the alarm clock at five thirty the next morning.

CHAPTER 10

Denton conducted the daily sergeant's review meeting without his usual enthusiasm. If his team noticed, nobody said anything. After the briefing, all his officers departed, and Denton returned to his desk to wait for ten o'clock. Colonel Fitzpatrick poked his head into Denton's office a little before ten, and the two left together for the Internal Audit Division offices.

When Fitzpatrick and Jones reached the reception area, Simski greeted them and led them back to one of the private conference rooms. The space seemed simple enough, but Denton knew the city had equipped the room with the latest audio and video recording devices. Fitzpatrick and Denton seated themselves at the table across from Simski, and Mr. Jon Franks, manager of Internal Audit, joined them, sitting next to Simski.

"Good morning, Commander Jones, Colonel Fitzpatrick. Thank you for giving us some time this morning," said Franks.

"Did Commander Jones have a choice?" asked Fitzpatrick bluntly.

"Actually, sir, he did," answered Franks. "We categorized this interview as an interrogatory questioning, which means Commander Jones participates voluntarily."

"I'm not sure anyone told me that," said Denton, glancing at Simski, "but we're all here now, so let's do what we need to do."

"Right," said Franks. "This shouldn't take long. The city manager's office requested we review your history with Theodore Jackson, Commander Jones. When we start the interview, we will ask you a list of questions. We request you answer them simply and truthfully. You should not add statements of your own not related to the specific questions asked. Additionally, these interviews are one way, meaning you may not ask questions of us. Do you understand the protocol, Commander? If so, we will begin."

"I understand," said Denton.

"Okay, then," said Franks. "From this moment until the end of the interview, we record our discussions."

Franks then stated the date, time, and names of participants in the interview. He also noted for the record the classification of the discussion: *voluntary interrogatory questioning*. Franks then asked his first question.

"Commander Jones, are you acquainted with Theodore Jackson?"

"Yes," answered Jones succinctly.

"Okay," said Franks, sounding irritated. "Could you elaborate on your answer? When did you meet Jackson, and what's the nature of your relationship with him?"

"We grew up on the same block in Avondale and were friends until around ten or eleven years old. Other than that, I have no relationship with him."

"You aren't still friends with him?" asked Franks.

"No."

"Did you not recently meet with Jackson at his offices?" asked Franks.

"Yes, at the request of the mayor's office, I met with Jackson about ten days ago."

"And why did the mayor pick you to attend that meeting?"

"The fact a meeting occurred, the subject of the meeting, and the reason someone asked me to attend are all classified, sir. I would need direct approval from the mayor's or city manager's office to answer questions relating to these subjects," said Denton.

"Okay, Commander," said Franks. "We can arrange to meet your conditions, but in the interest of time, let's move on for now. Are you aware of a large donation received by the city this week?"

"Yes."

"Do you know the amount of the donation?"

"A message from the mayor's office indicated five million dollars."

"Yes, your information is correct," answered Franks. "Do you have an idea who donated this money?"

"The same message also indicated an anonymous donor made the gift."

"Correct again, but you didn't answer my question. Do you suspect the identity of the donor?"

Denton thought for a moment. "I can make a guess, but no, I don't know for sure."

"So, who do you *guess* the donor is?"

"I'm sorry," said Denton, "but I believe the same confidentiality covers the answer to that question as your previous one. I would need permission from the mayor to provide my opinion as well as the reason for that opinion."

Franks sat for a moment and said, "We may need to reconvene this interview once you receive the necessary permissions you cite, but let's see if we can cover some other ground before that. Did you know the donation we're discussing came with a typewritten note?"

"I heard a rumor to that effect, but, officially, no. I'm not aware of a note," answered Denton.

"Well, the fund's anonymous provider indicated the reason for the donation was your work in the community. The only demand was that the city uses the money for constructing a youth center on Victory Parkway," ended Franks.

"Fascinating," said Denton, "but you're the first to tell me what the note said."

"But why, in your opinion, would this anonymous donor want to recognize you in such a way?"

"I'm not a mind reader, sir."

Colonel Fitzpatrick could sit quietly no longer. "What part of this relates to the stated reason for the interview, Mr. Franks?"

Franks glared at the chief of police. "Colonel, I respectfully ask that you adhere to the protocol for the interview. Unless we ask you to respond to a question, you are not to speak, and under no circumstances can anyone in this room except Mr. Simski or me ask questions. Do you understand, sir?"

"Yes," answered a steaming Fitzpatrick.

Turning back to Denton, Franks said, "To move beyond the facts surrounding the donation, let's go back to your earlier relationship with Jackson. What kinds of things did you do with Jackson as a young boy?"

Denton looked at Franks, then Simski, and after a pause answered, "The same kinds of things any kids born in the hood did. We played stickball, threw rocks at cans, and played basketball with an old volleyball using a basket made from a cardboard box held to a pole by duct tape."

"I see," said Franks. "What about jobs? Did you and Jackson work at any part-time jobs?"

Denton now felt something moving beneath his skin, and his heart rate increased. "I bagged groceries at the co-op a couple of days per week when the owner would let me. Nobody paid me, but sometimes customers would tip me."

"What about you and Jackson? Did you not also conduct a delivery service together?"

The question infuriated Denton because he suspected where Franks was heading in this part of the interview, and the only ones who could have provided the pertinent information were Theo Jackson or Ray Hinton. He couldn't imagine what Jackson's strategy might be in providing such information to officials in the city, but, at this point, answering the question honestly was Denton's only option. "I wouldn't call it a job. A couple of us made some money occasionally by delivering packages around the surrounding blocks."

"What did the packages contain?" Franks continued.

"The person who provided the bags told me never to look, and I didn't, so I'm not sure," said Denton.

"How well did you know Julian Stenson?" asked Franks.

"Who?"

"Julian Stenson."

"I didn't know him at all. Who's Stenson?" Denton asked.

"For the protocol, Commander Jones, remember that only Mr. Simski and I can ask questions in these hearings. I'll make an exception this time to answer yours. Stenson had a nickname in your old neighborhood. People called him the Whistler."

Denton froze in his seat, doing all in his power to hide the rising anger and fear working its way from his heart to his face. "Yes," he replied calmly. "I remember the Whistler, but not by any other name. He was a scrawny little man with a space between his front teeth that caused a whistling sound when he said some words. That's why we kids called him the Whistler."

"And this man gave you and Theodore Jackson the packages to deliver?"

"Yes."

"Why did you stop delivering packages for him?" asked Franks.

Denton suspected Franks knew the answer to this question before he asked it, so he replied, "Because he did something bad to one of my friends."

Denton expected Franks to now attempt to extract the entire ugly incident from him a piece at a time, but the investigator didn't. "Whatever happened to Stenson, or the Whistler as you called him?"

"I have no idea," Denton said. "He just disappeared."

"Right, Commander," said Franks. "He did disappear one day—he and another man named Lucien Short. Nobody can tell us where they went or what happened to them. Can you?"

"I already said I couldn't," said Denton.

"Okay," Franks said. "Let me put it another way. Are you acquainted with someone else who might know about what happened to these two?"

"Yes."

"Who?"

"Theodore Jackson," answered Denton.

Franks made some notes, looked at his watch, and said, "For now, we have completed our list of questions, Commander. Depending on what we hear from the city manager's office, we may require additional follow-up later. We may also need to revisit the questions you were unwilling to answer."

"The commander was not unwilling!" Colonel Fitzpatrick said. "He was *unable* because of the mayor's required confidentiality."

"Sorry, Colonel," said an icy Franks. "My mistake. If the city manager's office or the mayor desire to lift the confidentiality for these interviews, we'll alert you, Commander."

The interview concluded, and all four officers exited the room. Simski caught up with Jones and Fitzpatrick at the elevator. "Denton, I'm sorry about this. I don't enjoy these kinds of interviews, especially when they involve people like you."

"Thanks, Dan," said Denton. "I appreciate that, but you're just doing your job."

"Mr. Simski, maybe you should consider a transfer," interceded a still-fuming chief of police. "The air in here stinks from all the horseshit thrown around back in the interview room." The elevator doors opened, and Fitzpatrick entered before a stunned Simski could reply. Denton quickly followed him.

Fitzpatrick followed Denton into his office but didn't sit down. "I've got another meeting to attend, Denton, but as soon as I'm out of it, I'll call Roberson. This interview was an ambush, and I'm pissed! The note didn't surprise me, but all that history about you when you were ten did. Where'd they get that from anyway? Not that it means a thing."

"I'm glad you attended with me, Colonel. The stuff relating to the Whistler could only come from Jackson, I think. He and Ray Hinton are the last ones still alive who would remember anything about it. Those things happened over thirty years ago."

"And why would Jackson want to throw you under the bus now?" asked the chief.

"I'm not sure, sir. When I met with him, he seemed only interested in placing my name on a building, and he bragged about the good stuff I had done over the past decade. I don't get it."

"Well, I don't either," said Fitzpatrick as he walked to the door, "but Jackson hasn't succeeded in his profession by being predictable. Stay in touch on this. If the mayor escalates this by a millimeter, I'm going to jump all over her skinny little body!"

"Thanks, sir," said Denton, glad for the chief's sake that no recording devices existed in his office.

After Fitzpatrick left, Denton leaned back in his chair and stared at the ceiling for a few minutes. The bad feeling he had trusted in life to warn him of danger now sounded mild alarms, and he felt something unraveling. As he mentally traced his steps back to determine where the problem started, his gaze passed the ceiling, passed the wall, and stopped on the plaque across the room from him. He didn't have to read the words inscribed; he could recite them by heart.

> *Do all the good you can,*
> *By all the means you can,*
> *In all the ways you can,*
> *In all the places you can,*
> *At all the times you can,*
> *To all the people you can,*
> *As long as you ever can.*
>
> *John Wesley*

For most of its existence, the plaque occupied an office wall of Denton's old college baseball coach, a man named Stewart Blevins. Besides being an outstanding and successful Division III coach, Blevins acted as a mentor to Jones. The coach delivered his lessons through actions, not words, and Jones realized Blevins coached lives, not baseball.

Two years earlier, Blevins died, and Denton went to the man's memorial service in Indiana with Jessica. The reason for the event was sad, but the service wasn't. Many of Blevins's former players attended, including nearly all from the team that had captured a Division III national championship Denton's senior year.

Coach Blevins's best friend stopped Denton after the service to give him the box with this plaque in it. The man told Denton the coach insisted from his hospital bed several days before he died that Denton receive it. When Denton removed the box's plaque at home, he found a short note folded beneath it.

Denton,

If Claude is giving you this plaque, it means I ran out of time in the game and ran out of resources to continue the mission. I hope you will keep it up!

Stewart

"I'm trying, Coach," said Denton to the plaque. "I'm trying. Somebody's messing with our plan, though."

CHAPTER 11

Denton, still upset from the interview when he arrived home that evening, wanted to review the meeting with his wife. But coming through the door, he realized other priorities existed. Jessica sat at the dining room table, surrounded by spiral notebooks, empty drink cups, and two take-out food containers. She had connected her home desktop computer to a dining room outlet, and it sat next to her laptop on the table. To the side of the two computers was their laser printer, also connected to a nearby outlet. The dining room looked like a candidate's campaign headquarters, and Jessica a frazzled news reporter.

"What's going on, J?" asked Denton tentatively.

"What's going on? What's going on is the start of a war!" she said dramatically. "My boss gave me two weeks of compensated administrative leave for reasons undisclosed. I can take business and personal calls from my home phone or personal cell phone, but I cannot go to the office until the end of my leave. Additionally, I can't talk to anyone—including my husband—about past or pending cases in the city's system until further notified."

"Who ordered this?" asked Denton.

"My friend, mentor, and immediate supervisor, Fred Gunnells," screamed Jessica.

"Okay, okay, let's sit in the den, and you tell me everything about this. Gunnells loves you. He would never do anything to hurt you."

Jessica's eyes appeared red and swollen from crying, but now no tears remained. She seemed a committed and driven woman. Responding calmly, she said, "Okay, we can sit for a few minutes, but I'm in the middle of some important research."

"I understand, but let's compare notes. My day was a little rough too."

At that moment, Jessica blinked and remembered what had been on Denton's schedule. "Oh, T, I'm sorry! Of course you had a difficult day. In all my self-pity, I forgot about the Internal Audit interview. I'm so sorry. Sure, let's sit down. I need a break anyway."

Denton took a place on the sofa and said, "First, you. Tell me what happened."

Jessica related how Fred Gunnells called her to his office after lunch. He seemed flustered and beside himself but explained she needed to take some time away from the city offices. A sensitive issue had come up, requiring her to recuse herself for at least two weeks. She questioned why, but Gunnells couldn't tell her, citing confidentiality.

"Fred appeared upset, and I could tell he wasn't comfortable with the decision. It obviously came from a higher level in the city."

"Strange," said Denton. "So, what have you been doing here all afternoon?"

"I may be blonde, but I'm not dumb! Something happened when I asked Fred about Jackson's criminal record the other day, and things haven't been the same in the office since. That stupid question flipped a switch someplace leading to here, and it may even be partly responsible for your interview today. Rather than sit still on the sidelines, I'm getting myself ready for whatever's next and researching every single drug bust conducted in the city for the past ten years."

"That's a lot of work," said Denton. "If Jackson has no record, what will all the other drug incidents he had nothing to do with tell you?"

"I'm not sure," she answered. "Maybe if I see what those other cases have in common, I'll get a picture of what's missing with Jackson. At a minimum, I'll begin to develop knowledge about Jackson's competitors and know the mechanics of how the city orchestrates drug busts. I'll also gain information about who on our staff plans the busts and then executes them."

"Seems like enough work to keep you busy for two weeks," said Denton. "I'm surprised that when Gunnells removed you from the office, he didn't revoke your access to city records."

"Believe me, that surprised me as well. Since it wasn't Fred's idea for the administrative leave, I think he did the bare minimum somebody else asked him to do. Fred knows that with my password I can access anything from home available to me at the office."

"Right." Denton thought for a moment and said, "I guess you better work fast before someone changes their mind about the access. Can anyone tell what records you examine?"

"I don't think so," she replied. "For the most part, these are public records. I only need a separate login to access confidential records. So far, nothing I checked required a password."

"Okay, just be careful." Denton then gave Jessica a summary of his day, concluding with how irritated Colonel Fitzpatrick acted throughout the process. "Whoever's directing this, the chief isn't involved. He's on my side, and I'm glad he attended the interview with me."

"So," said Jessica, "you think the mayor's office is behind the questioning?"

"No, I think the city manager's office—more specifically, the assistant city manager, Charles Roberson—is."

"Why would he want to do this?"

"I'm not certain he does. He might be getting stirred up by Jackson, somehow."

"Why Jackson, though?" asked Jessica. "What does Jackson gain by having you come under suspicion?"

"I'm not sure," answered Denton. "Mr. Franks had information about me that only Theo would know, and, like you, I don't want to sit still. We promised each other we would keep each other informed, so I'm telling you now—I'm going to confront Jackson about this, face-to-face."

"Oh, Denton. No! If anyone in administration finds out, it will make things worse—and Jackson is dangerous. You did nothing wrong, and once Internal Audit finishes questioning, this will probably go away."

"Why work so hard on your research, then?"

Jessica sighed and said, "So that I'm ready in case it *doesn't* go away."

CHAPTER 12

The following morning, Denton placed a call to the Theodore Jackson Investments office. He hoped Theo's presumption that software scrambled the telephone number of incoming calls was correct, but today, that wasn't his primary concern. A female, probably the attractive Teresa, answered the phone after the first ring. "Theodore Jackson Investments. How may I help you?"

"Hello," said Denton, not sure whether to give his name or not. In a split second, he decided Jackson wouldn't take a call from an unidentified caller and said, "This is Mr. Jones. Would Mr. Jackson be available this morning?"

"Hi, Commander Jones, this is Teresa. I'm sure Mr. Jackson is available for you. Hang on."

The next voice on the line was Jackson's. "Hey, Denton. Good to hear from you. Is the city going crazy about the donation?"

"Hey, Theo," replied a more somber Denton. "I think people are pleased with it, but some things came up since you—or somebody—delivered that package. I need to discuss something with you."

"Sure," Theo said with some concern. "Is everything all right? I put a little note with the cash, indicating you were the reason for the donation, but I didn't make any demands about your name going on the building. The note didn't cause a problem, did it?"

"I'm not sure, but something did. Can we meet where we can talk face-to-face privately?"

"Absolutely! When? I'm available now. If you don't want to meet here, tell me where."

"Are you familiar with the storytelling circle in Friendship Park?"

"Yeah, I think so. Maybe twenty or thirty yards down the path when you enter?"

"Yes," said Denton. "The park is never busy, and benches face the river next to the path. I'll meet you there in thirty minutes."

"Okay," said Jackson. "I'll see you at the park."

———

Denton parked and walked to the storytelling area, picking one of the many empty benches facing the Ohio River to sit. Named by the city's first African American mayor, Theodore Berry, the park opened in 2003. Mayor Berry was beloved in Cincinnati but especially by the city's minority community. Many poorer households, including Denton's, hung framed pictures of the man on a wall somewhere. Berry performed as Cincinnati's mayor from 1972 until 1976, and Denton still remembered how the older folks carried on when the man died. At the time, Theo and Denton discussed their mothers' grief on Denton's porch.

As he reflected, Denton became mesmerized by the Ohio River's beauty from this spot on the Cincinnati side. Three of the four large bridges connecting Ohio to Kentucky rose above the waterway, which today bustled with commercial activity. A powerful tug pushed a small train of connected barges piled with rock northward against the current. Coming south at a lazy pace floated the largest of the Bernstein paddleboats, the *Belle of Cincinnati*, packed with over five hundred passengers enjoying a day of fine dining and sightseeing. Flitting between these larger vessels, a half dozen small motorboats took advantage of the warm and glorious day.

When Denton saw Theo strolling toward the bench, he rose and greeted him. "Thank you, Theo, for meeting me on short notice, but I'll warn you. I'm not happy."

Theo's smile disappeared. "Okay, sit down. Tell me what's going on."

"I got called in by Internal Audit. They questioned me yesterday, and investigators had one piece of information that could have only come from you. What the hell are you trying to do to me, Theo?" Denton's voice rose as he relayed this information, and he shouted the last words.

Theo didn't react and sat thinking for a few seconds. Finally, in a calm voice, he said, "Denton, I told you I never lie, and I don't. I gave nobody, anywhere, at any time, anything about you. This concerns me, but I promise you, I'm *not* your enemy."

Theo's demeanor and sincerity surprised Denton, and for a moment, Denton could only stare at him. "Then how would the Internal Audit investigator know anything about the Whistler?"

"Tell me what he asked," said Theo.

"Jon Franks, the manager for Internal Audit, was trying to establish my childhood relationship with you—I assume because *someone* is concerned that we might still have a connection. Anyway, he asked about things we did together as kids and suddenly brought up the name of someone I never heard of—"

"Julian Stenson?" Theo interrupted.

"Yes, who I now know to be the Whistler. So, how would Franks know about my history with the Whistler if it didn't come from you?"

"Other people besides you and I knew about the Whistler, Denton."

"Not many, Theo, and how many people other than you and Ray Hinton knew we delivered bags for the man thirty years ago? I can't think of anyone."

"I can," said a quietly contemplative Jackson. He sat with his fingers pressing the bridge of his nose and his face down. When he looked up, his eyes burned darkly, and his mouth formed a straight line that barely moved when he spoke. "I didn't provide anyone information, but I'm quite sure of who did, and I'm not happy about it. Your assumption is correct.

You have a problem, but it isn't from me. I want to help, but as you can understand, my options are limited. My notoriety and lack of popularity within the city administration pose challenges for me to assist you."

Listening intently, Denton asked, "Do you think Ray did it?"

"No, it wasn't Ray."

"Who then?"

Again, Theo thought for a long time before answering. Finally, he said, "Denton, trust me on what I'm about to tell you. I don't believe it's in my interest, or your interest, to inform you about what I think. On the other hand, you *should* find out who provided the information. You're a smart officer with the necessary resources to figure this out. Now you should also be motivated."

Denton listened, but Theo's cryptic explanation confused him. "Can you tell me where to start looking?"

"What's the one piece of information you learned from the Internal Audit interrogation you didn't know before the interview?"

Denton thought for a few seconds. "Only the Whistler's real name."

"Right," said Theo. "Why don't you start there?"

"Okay, but I'm not sure how much time I have to figure this out."

"I think you have enough," said Theo. "Just be careful with whom you confide."

"You think my wife is safe?"

"Yes, I do," said Theo seriously. "I also think she's in a good place to help with your research."

"Okay," said Denton. "Thanks. Sorry for jumping to the wrong conclusion."

"No apologies necessary. You reached a logical conclusion, just not the correct one. I'm not going to do anything to hurt you purposely. We were close friends a long time ago, and I'm sorry our respective careers preclude a friendship now. I admire what you do, though, and I want to help a little with your causes. I hope the mention of your name in my note wasn't responsible for the questioning."

Denton rose to leave when something Theo said struck a nerve. The word *questioning* reminded him that he had *questioned* someone about Theo's spotless criminal record—and his wife had done the same thing in her department.

"Maybe it wasn't my name in your note that generated the Internal Audit interview, Theo. Based on something you told me in our first meeting, I shared my surprise at your clean criminal record with the city's assistant city manager. I asked him if he believed it possible someone inside our administration assisted you. I didn't know it at the time, but Jessica asked her boss, acting City Solicitor Fred Gunnells, the same question. These were innocent questions from both Jessica and me, but perhaps they touched off some sort of alarm."

Theo listened without emotion. "I suggest you and Jessica be smart from here on out. Those kinds of questions would certainly rattle certain people." Changing the subject abruptly, Theo asked, "Do you remember sitting with me on your porch after Ted Berry died?"

"Yes, I do."

"A great man, and our moms loved him," said Theo.

"They did."

"See ya, Denton."

"Right, Theo. Thanks." Denton remained on the park bench for a few minutes after Jackson departed, thinking of Theo's last few words. Indeed, there was a time when Theodore Jackson and Denton Jones breathed the same air, shared the same life, and were very much alike.

———

When he returned to his desk after the park meeting with Jackson, Denton saw the pink slip. The message came from Sonny Wilkins, the city's sanitation department manager, and Denton returned the call.

"Hey, Commander Jones, thanks for calling me back. I'm sorry to trouble you. I hoped you might help me a little with Junior Bridges. I'm aware of your relationship with him."

"Certainly, Mr. Wilkins. What's the problem?"

"Junior found out a couple of days ago he didn't get a position he applied for. He hasn't been himself since, and I'm not sure what to do. He's one of the best employees I have, and I don't want him to hurt himself now over something like this."

"Thank you for calling. What's he been doing?"

"Frankly, for the last few days, he's done exactly, *and only*, what he's supposed to do—which probably doesn't sound like much of a problem. For Junior, though, doing the minimum required represents about twenty percent less than his normal production. Over the past couple of years, he's established quite a reputation in this department, and his potential is, I think, unlimited. Being passed over for the job opening in the recreation department was a letdown for him, but I hope it doesn't permanently change his work ethic and attitude."

"Damn! I'll talk to him. Thanks for your concern and for alerting me. What job in Rec came up?"

"Assistant director, with a pay rate around five grand more than he makes here in sanitation. With his volunteer work at Elements, Junior seemed more qualified for the job, but Human Resources ran the interviews, and they picked someone else."

"I didn't know the city was interviewing for positions in Rec, but I can understand Junior's disappointment. He's one of our most respected coaches at Elements, and he loves working with kids. Who got the job?"

"Well, that's part of the problem, I think. A peer in Sanitation got the position, and it's someone who isn't anywhere near the caliber of employee as Junior. I provided references for both candidates and a strong recommendation for Junior. Human Resources picked Jack Rollston for the position, though. He runs the route five sanitation crew here."

"Is Jack related to Bill Rollston, the deputy comptroller?"

"Yep. His son."

"Do you think Jack's father's position influenced the decision?" asked Denton.

"Commander, I can't answer that. Maybe it did, but Jack also finished Cincinnati Central Junior College and hasn't spent any time in a corrections facility. Rollston's work over here isn't superior, but it's at least consistently average."

"Right, Mr. Wilkins. I understand. I'll try to provide some counseling for Junior."

"Thank you, Commander. I'd appreciate your help."

What a day, Denton thought as he hung up. Glancing at his desk calendar, then the clock, he decided the counseling session with Junior was as important as anything else today. The sanitation department's offices were inside the city's water treatment facility near the river, and Denton headed from his office to his car. As a younger police officer, Denton had years before played a part in sending Junior to the Cuyahoga Hills Juvenile Correctional Facility in Highland Hills. Since then, he and Jessica were most responsible for preventing Junior's life from spiraling further downward. Denton didn't plan on losing the young man now.

Like Jaden, Junior was adopted by foster parents as an infant. Tunisa and Jaelyn Bridges raised Junior, whose given name was Julian, in a modest neighborhood north of Avondale. They did their best to shelter him from the surrounding neighborhoods' evils, and these efforts were successful through Junior's grade-school years. Out of high school, Junior passed on college opportunities for the lure of easy money made on the streets. Denton's intervention in an incident with the Evil Eyes ended Junior's short tenure with the local gang. He had just turned seventeen.

Junior's involvement resulted in a two-year sentence that proved costly, not only for Junior but also for his foster parents. Outraged by Junior's participation in a drug-gang shootout, Jaelyn Bridges blamed both his wife and Junior, and the couple separated and divorced. Tunisa moved back to Minneapolis to live with her mother; Jaelyn remarried and remained in Cincinnati. When Junior returned to Cincinnati after his release, his adoptive father told Junior he could no longer live in Jaelyn's home.

Denton heard from another officer that Junior lived at a homeless shelter operated by the Salvation Army. He found the young man and offered him the opportunity to stay with him and Jessica until Junior could find a job and afford an apartment. Junior started working in a low-level city sanitation position and soon saved enough to afford an efficiency apartment over a convenience store. Since then, Junior had become the sanitation department's star employee and now served as the crew chief for sanitation route number three.

———

"Hi, Mr. Jones," said Junior. "What brings you down to the river?"

"Well, I guess you," said Denton. "I got a call from Mr. Wilkins a little while ago."

Junior avoided Denton's gaze. "Am I in some kind of trouble?"

"No, I don't think so. Wilkins says you're doing average work recently. I didn't know about the rec department position you applied for."

"Yeah, well, I didn't get it, so no big deal."

"If you say so, but Mr. Wilkins believes it *was* a big deal for you. Are you aware he provided a reference and recommended you for the job over the other candidate?"

Junior raised his head. "No. I didn't know that. I'll thank him. He's always supportive of me, and I appreciate it."

"Right, but I doubt average work here will earn you any other recommendations from him."

Junior's eyes darkened. "Mr. Jones, I don't think you understand how all this went down. It was a railroad job and completely unfair!"

"Explain it to me, then."

"Jack Rollston runs crew five, and his trucks are the filthiest ones in the fleet. We receive more complaints from people who live on his route about incomplete pickups than any others. Besides that, he has never even seen a youth rec program, much less managed one. I have almost five years of experience with similar programs at Elements. You already know Jack's father is the deputy comptroller, so what do *you* think?"

"You think nepotism's a factor?"

"Isn't it obvious, Mr. Jones? I'm a better employee with more relevant experience for the position than him."

"It *might* be nepotism, but maybe it's because Jack obtained a community college degree and never spent time in jail. Some citizens might question the city's judgment in placing a former criminal in charge of their recreation programs."

Junior sat stunned and didn't speak. After a long pause, Denton continued. "Look, Junior, Jessica and I are your biggest fans, and I'm sorry to be harsh. I can't go back and undo your life, though. You can't either. Your past is history, and we can't change it, but all of us can do things to impact our future. Your commitment to overcoming poor choices made earlier in life has put you in a far better place than many who made similar mistakes. Now isn't the time to quit."

Junior sat for a long time in quiet contemplation. At last, he said, "I'm sorry, Mr. Jones. You're right. I just, well, Rollston ranks as one of my least favorite people. Do you know his nickname for me?"

"No."

"He calls me Big House, and not because of my size. He thinks the reference to jail is funny—even after I told him it isn't funny to me."

"I understand, but you don't beat people like Rollston by giving up or giving in. You beat them by outperforming them—which you *will* do over time. You're still young with a long way to go in the race."

"Okay. I understand. Thanks for coming down. I guess I need to catch up on some work around here. Mr. Wilkins isn't so skilled with spreadsheets, and I can prepare the week's route schedules way faster than him. I usually help him with the schedules but haven't yet this week."

"Sounds like a good idea. I won't hold you up. See you down at the ball field next week."

CHAPTER 13

When Denton arrived back at his office, he expected to see a message from Internal Audit. There wasn't one, but it would likely come later in the day. The message from Jessica surprised him, however. She never called him at work, but then, she usually stayed busy at her own office.

Jessica picked up before the first ring ended. "Hi, T. How did the meeting with Jackson go?"

"It went well, J. I have a lot to tell you, but not on the phone. Can you wait till I'm home?"

"Of course I can, as long as you tell me you think everything's okay. I worried about you today."

Denton thought for a second before answering. "I'm fine, but everything *isn't* okay. I don't think Theo is our problem, but I can't give you more details until we talk later."

"What time do you think you'll be home?"

"I'm not sure," said Denton. "When I leave here depends a little on whether Internal Audit wants a second interview today. In the meantime, while you're researching this morning, see what you can find out about Julian Stenson."

"That's the name the Internal Audit investigator asked you about yesterday. What should I look for?"

"I guess anything you can find. An arrest record, liens, driver's license, birth and marriage records. I'm not sure exactly what we're looking for, but Jackson gave me a strong hint to find out what we could about him."

"Wow! Okay. I'm interested. This will keep me busy until you get home. Also, I glanced at the files from the USB drive Jaden brought to me yesterday. Those included the information you wanted about the stores on Victory, which isn't much, I'm afraid. I'll show you when you get here, but the guy who owns the stores is named Sun Yi, and he seems to pay his real estate taxes. His three business licenses for the shops are also in order. Jaden found an old permit file missing some information, but the owner sent him a digital file with the corrections. Jaden included that file on the flash drive, but I didn't open it."

"Okay. Thanks. I'll look through that with you later. I warned you it was probably nothing." As he hung up, Denton thought perhaps the bad feeling about the businesses on Victory Parkway was a false alarm.

Later in the day, Denton received an envelope through the inter-administration mail from the assistant city manager's office. When he opened it, he found a short, handwritten note from Roberson. Internal Audit had been officially "read-in" to the events relating to the anonymous donation to the city, including Denton's meeting with Jackson. Roberson cleared Denton to discuss the details with Internal Audit interviewers.

Denton suspected the note meant another round of interviews soon. The city manager's office was obviously driving this initiative, not the police department, and he wondered what Roberson hoped to accomplish. He called Colonel Fitzpatrick's office to alert the chief of the possibility of additional interviews.

"Fitzpatrick here," said the gruff voice.

"Hi, Chief. Denton Jones. I just got a note from Roberson's office instructing me I could share any of the confidential information surrounding my recent meeting with Jackson. Will you sit in with me for any additional interviews?"

"I insist on it," said a clearly irritated Fitzpatrick. "This appears to be some kind of rogue investigation of one of my best officers by the city manager's office, and frankly, I object. Neither of us has time for this, and I doubt the mayor or city manager does either. Text me if you get a notice."

"Thank you, sir. I will."

Denton hung up, relieved the city's police organization had no enthusiasm for the interviews. He also felt confident Theo Jackson had nothing to do with starting them. The city manager's office and, more specifically, the assistant city manager's office provided the energy.

Later in the day, as he headed for the door to leave the office, Denton received a call from Dan Simski. As expected, Franks wanted to schedule another interview at Jones's earliest convenience to finish the first interview discussions. Jones read between the lines and presumed Franks hoped Jones would make the time right away, but Jones didn't feel so accommodating.

"Okay, Dan," he said. "I'm tied up all day tomorrow. Can I give you a call back with a time for Friday or Saturday?"

"Yes—I guess," said Simski. "I think Jon wanted to finish this tomorrow, but Friday will probably work. Just call me with a time."

Before Jones left the office, he sent a quick text to Fitzpatrick, asking him to pick the most convenient time for Friday.

———

When Denton came through the door, Jessica greeted him with a glass of wine and invited him to join her at the dining room table. Piles of paper and several directories, in addition to the computers and printers, hid the table's surface.

"My Lord, Jessica! Do we need to build you an office?"

"No, T, I already have one, and it isn't here. For now, though, this will do." Jessica seemed energized, and the clutter on the table provided evidence she had spent the day in this room. "I discovered some interesting things to share with you. Sit down, Officer." Denton took a sip of wine and obeyed his wife. "As you requested, I did a lot of research on Julian Stenson today. The analysis took a while because, as you might expect, he had a colorful history. Stenson achieved an extensive arrest record from about eighteen years old, including petty theft, breaking and entering, possession, unregistered firearm, and drug trafficking. Mostly small stuff, but he served time in the county jail a couple of times. When he went missing, he was in violation of parole."

"No real surprises there," said Denton.

"A check of his driver's license produced nothing unexpected—a couple of traffic tickets and one DUI. His birth records also presented nothing out of the ordinary for the area. Born at the Children's Hospital to an unwed mother, Dolores Stenson, and an unknown father, he was about fifty-two when he went missing—or, I should say, when his public records quit producing results. No record exists of a missing person report for Stenson, and there's no record of any investigation into his disappearance. Suddenly, he ceased to exist—and nobody cared."

Denton started to ask a question, but Jessica held up her hand, smiled, and continued. "The last records I checked were the county marriage records. Julian Stenson married twice. His first, to a woman name Cicely Beech, at about twenty-two years old, lasted only three years. The court granted Cicely a divorce on the grounds of adultery. Cicely also cited verbal and physical abuse in her request for the divorce. Julian's second marriage could interest you more. It occurred about five years after the end of the first one when he married a woman named Claudia Jean Roberson."

Denton stared at her in amazement. "Don't tell me Claudia is related to Charles Roberson!"

"His sister."

"Oh my God!" said Denton. "Theo told me the truth. Somebody else *does* know about the Whistler and me—Roberson."

"The story becomes even more interesting if you want to hear the rest," said a self-satisfied Jessica.

"Yes, J, go on."

"How much do you know about Roberson's background?"

"Not very much. I think he served on the force for a long time before receiving an appointment to the city manager's staff. He's been the assistant city manager for my entire career so far."

"Right," said Jessica. "His last job on the force was commander, second district, and the city promoted him to chief performance officer in charge of data analytics in the city manager's office. He became an assistant city manager about eight years ago, but he began his career in the city as a patrolman assigned to the third district."

"The third district serves Avondale and Victory Parkway," said Denton.

"Exactly," said Jessica.

"I'm not sure what all this means, Jessica, but it's scary."

"I think so. At a minimum, we know Roberson had more than a casual relationship with Stenson. We're also certain he knew the streets around Avondale—which means there's a good chance he and Theo Jackson were acquaintances a long time ago, too."

"And ever since," said Denton.

"Yes, ever since."

Jessica and Denton talked throughout dinner, and Denton congratulated his wife on her investigative skills. Jessica elaborated on her discoveries and told Denton that Claudia, still alive, had a home in Columbus. Stenson and Claudia had no children, and Charles Roberson had no other siblings. They discussed how to utilize this information and their next steps.

"I'm thinking," said Denton, "I might get a chance on Friday at the Internal Audit interview."

"Okay," said an uncertain Jessica. "How? I think we're both in dangerous territory here."

"I agree," said Denton, "but things shifted in our favor with what you found. I have a different idea about what Roberson tried to do with the Internal Audit interviews now, and I think he made a mistake."

"I'm listening."

"Well, I don't have everything worked out yet, and we're still missing some important pieces. Based on what we know or suspect, though, Roberson might be afraid of what he *thinks* Jackson is telling me about him. He became alarmed by your question to Gunnells and my question about whether Theo Jackson received help from inside the city. Those questions may have struck too close to home. So he panicked and initiated the Internal Audit investigation. He steered the interview questions about my childhood relationship with Jackson on purpose, to make me believe Jackson provided the information. He wanted me to distrust Jackson, and his strategy worked. I wrongly concluded Jackson was the only one who could provide the detail Franks had in the interview. Roberson made a costly mistake, though, when he gave Stenson's name to Franks. He didn't calculate on somebody discovering his own family relationship to the Whistler."

"How will you use the information now?" asked Jessica.

"Not sure yet, J, but if I find a way to slip it into the interview, it would be a game changer. I doubt either Internal Audit interviewer knows Stenson was Roberson's brother-in-law. Fitzpatrick doesn't either."

"You think a relationship like that from thirty years ago would mean something to them?" asked Jessica.

"Maybe. No statute of limitations exists for murder."

"Denton! You don't think Roberson had something to do with Stenson's disappearance, do you? You said you thought Theo might be responsible."

"Now I'm not sure. I *did* assume Theo and Ray Hinton were involved, but maybe not. Or maybe they had help. Roberson hoped to accomplish something else with the interviews, I think. He wanted to highlight, even exaggerate, my past relationship with Theo. He didn't want me to continue as a source of communication between the city and Jackson and hoped the results of the Internal Audit interviews could expose my possible conflict of interest in representing the city."

"Roberson's panic might also explain my administrative leave," said Jessica.

"It might, but that one's more of a stretch. I can't think of a reason the assistant city manager could give the city solicitor good enough to warrant a two-week leave of absence for the city's general counsel."

"How did we ever get into all this?" asked Jessica. "It seems like the good guys are chasing us while the bad guys try to help us. What kind of world is this?"

"The world hasn't changed," said Denton. "It's still spinning the same way as always. Someone told me that good and bad are just meaningless adjectives in the absence of perspective. The more we know, the more perspective we have, and the better chance to reach the right conclusions."

"The whole thing scares me," said Jessica. "I'm not sure who to trust anymore."

"I think our best bet might be to trust nobody but each other."

CHAPTER 14

O n Thursday, Denton checked with Colonel Fitzpatrick, and they agreed that late afternoon on Friday would be the best time for the interview. The time slot would do two things for them: it would ensure no follow-up from the meeting until after the weekend, and it would irritate the Internal Audit inspectors, who liked to clock out early on Fridays.

At a little before four o'clock the next day, Fitzpatrick stopped at Denton's office, and the two proceeded to the elevators. Both officers went back to the same interview room they used before, where Dan Simski and Jon Franks waited for them. Simski respectfully stood when the senior officer entered the room. Franks remained seated.

After reviewing the interview rules, Franks began the questioning in the same manner he did in the previous one, stating the date, the time, and the participants in the room. He then asked Denton whether he had received the correspondence from the city manager's office. When Denton replied affirmatively, Franks said, "Good, then we're no longer precluded from keeping certain critical information about your recent meeting with Theodore Jackson confidential?"

"Apparently not," answered Denton.

"Okay," said Franks. "So, can you explain to us why Mr. Jackson, reputedly one of the most powerful criminals in our part of the world, would want a youth center on Victory Parkway named after you?"

Denton answered, "No."

The short answer irritated Franks, so he asked a more provocative question. "Do you think it was just because of your friendship?"

Again, Denton answered succinctly. "We aren't friends."

"Sorry," said Franks. "You aren't currently friends, but you were at one time, right?"

Denton felt anxious because he was about to set his trap for Franks. His wording had to be exactly right to induce the right question from the investigator. "Yes," he replied, "a long time ago."

"Yes," said Franks, "but back then, I understand you did many things with each other. Not only did you play together, but you also shared a part-time job. Am I correct?"

Franks's questioning edged ever closer to the trap, but he wasn't there quite yet. "I wouldn't call it a part-time job," said Denton, purposely evasive. "We occasionally delivered some packages around the neighborhood for someone."

"Yes, we talked about this in the last interview. You and Jackson delivered an unknown product for a Mr. Stenson, correct?"

Bingo. I have you! thought Denton. He hesitated before answering, thinking carefully of everything he needed to include in this answer. "Yes, Mr. Franks, we *did* talk about this. I told you I didn't know the Whistler by his proper name, Julian Stenson—and learning that Stenson was also Mr. Roberson's brother-in-law shocked me."

Franks looked confused and, before thinking, said, "Excuse me?"

Bonus! thought Denton. This time, to benefit the video and audio recording, Denton made sure to enunciate as clearly as possible. "I *said*, I had no idea Stenson and Charles Roberson were acquainted, much less related. But, of course, I didn't know Mr. Roberson back then either."

Franks looked stunned, and Simski fidgeted uncontrollably in his seat. Fitzpatrick gazed at Denton, wide-eyed and confused. Franks finally regained his composure and said, "I'm sorry, gentlemen. I need to stop the interview momentarily and check on something. We'll reconvene in a minute or two."

He left the room, and Denton shook his head ever so slightly to warn Fitzpatrick not to speak. Simski had the appearance of someone enduring a colonoscopy, but he said nothing. After several awkward and quiet minutes, Franks reentered the room and concluded the interview for the day. When all rose to leave, Colonel Fitzpatrick said nothing until he and Denton stood together in the elevator.

"What the hell just happened?" Fitzpatrick asked.

"A bomb went off, I think, sir. Let's not talk until we're back at my office."

Once the two officers were behind Denton's closed office door, Fitzpatrick asked, "So, Roberson's related to this guy Stenson?"

"Yes," said Denton. "Stenson married Roberson's sister, Claudia."

"When did you find that out?"

"As I said in the first interview, I had no idea of the Whistler's proper name and never would have if Franks hadn't told me. Once I had the name, I became curious, and Jessica did some research. Stenson had an interesting history in the city that stopped when he disappeared suddenly. Everything we found, including his marriage to Roberson's sister, came from public records available to anyone."

"My God, Denton! I'm speechless, but why would Roberson want you to know Stenson's name?"

"I'm certain he didn't. He made a tactical error, I suspect, by dropping the name to Franks before the interview. Roberson wanted Franks to press me about my early relationship with Jackson—and I believe he wanted me to believe Jackson created Internal Audit's interest in me. The strategy worked for a while because I thought only Jackson and Ray Hinton knew what we did for the Whistler. I was wrong."

"So, Roberson's misguided interview backfired. What happens now?"

"My guess, Roberson is furious and probably also concerned. I'll receive a call pretty soon from the assistant city manager, I think."

Almost on cue, Denton's desk phone rang.

"What the fuck do you think you're doing, Commander Jones?" asked the voice on the line.

Denton nodded to Fitzpatrick, and the colonel signaled he would wait outside for Jones to complete the call. "Mr. Roberson," said Denton politely. "I'm not sure how to answer your question because I'm doing my best to answer Mr. Franks as completely and as truthfully as I can in the Internal Audit interviews. What *is* it you think I'm doing?"

"You're up to your eyeballs with your old friend, Theodore Jackson, causing people in this administration to ask questions. Because of your excellent service record and other good work, I suggested Internal Audit conduct an informal interview to clear the air and preserve your good name. And how do you reward me for this effort on your behalf? You associate my name with criminals. I am stunned and beyond disappointed."

"I'm sorry you feel that way, sir," answered Denton, "but my only contact with Theodore Jackson since our childhood friendship over thirty years ago occurred in a meeting with him which the mayor's office asked me to take. I'm insulted you would say I'm 'up to my eyeballs' with Jackson. Mr. Franks shocked me when he brought up childhood events that I thought only Jackson and I knew about. I assumed Jackson provided the information to somebody inside the administration to hurt my career, and I couldn't understand why. I presumed incorrectly, of course, because somebody else knew the connection between the Whistler, Jackson, and me. You. And now I'm equally confounded to understand your motivation to try to hurt me, Mr. Roberson."

"Jones," spat out Roberson, "you are insubordinate, and I will have your badge. I started serving this city before your mother delivered you, and my reputation is beyond reproach. I won't allow some impertinent, full-of-himself, from-the-hood riffraff impugn the stature I spent most of my life building. You don't know who you're messing with, but you're about to find out."

"You do what you need to, sir. I'll do the same." After Denton hung up, he checked the scan disk in his receiver to ensure he had successfully recorded the call. With a couple of quick commands on his handset, he sent the audio transcript to his computer. He then joined Colonel Fitzpatrick in the lobby.

"Colonel," said Jones, "we should discuss some rather urgent developments. Would you join Jessica and me this evening for dinner?"

"I have no other plans," said the colonel, "if you're sure your wife won't mind."

"She has much to add to our conversation, so she isn't going to mind at all."

Denton surprised Jessica with the dinner invitation to the police chief, but she knew Jack Fitzpatrick well and liked him. Single and sometimes a bit gruff, Fitzpatrick provided good company at the many job-related social functions high-profile administrative officials had to attend.

———

"Jessica," exclaimed the chief as he came through the door, "I'm sorry your husband provides such dull company he needed me to come along to amuse you at dinner. I hope I'm not imposing."

"Colonel Fitzpatrick," said Jessica, "I *wish* he were duller. For the last few weeks, that hasn't been the case. Thank you for coming."

"Let's go with Jack, Denton, and Jessica tonight," said Fitzpatrick.

"Deal!" said Jessica. "Sit in the den for a few minutes until I'm ready in the dining room. Can I bring you a beer, some wine, or a cocktail?"

"A double scotch if you have any," said Fitzpatrick. "Double bourbon if you don't. Anything close or as potent is a close third choice."

"No problem, Jack," said Jessica. "Will Cutty Sark do?"

"Perfect."

While they waited for drinks, Denton related the events of the past two weeks to his boss. When Jessica brought the chief's double scotch and Denton's wine, Fitzpatrick stopped her before she could escape back to the kitchen. "Jessica," he said, "you did some good research on Stenson. Tell me why you're on administrative leave."

Jessica, embarrassed by both the question and her current professional situation, quickly briefed the chief. Fitzpatrick listened intently and when

Jessica finished asked, "Was the leave Gunnells's idea, or do you think he called the city solicitor, Hargrove?"

"I'm not sure, Jack. Fred seemed uncomfortable with the decision, but he didn't elaborate on either its reason or originator."

"But this happened after you asked about Jackson's arrest record—or lack thereof?"

"Yes. Denton told me about the mayor's request to take the strange meeting with Jackson. When he told me about Jackson's reputation versus his arrest record, the anomaly piqued my interest."

"Right," said a perplexed Fitzpatrick. "Fred Gunnells and I aren't close, but I'm friends with Hargrove. I'm sure his wife doesn't want anyone to interfere with his rehab, but I may give him a call tomorrow."

"We're so sorry to involve you in this," said Jessica, "but thank you, Jack."

"Jessica, I'm the chief of police of the city. Don't be sorry to involve me. In fact, you both are a little derelict in reporting some of this to me so late. I don't like what I have seen or heard recently—and I'm a little behind. I can catch up fast enough, but we need to ensure an open line of communication from here forward. Do I make myself clear?"

"Yes, sir. You do," said Jessica. Denton nodded.

Jessica returned to the kitchen, and Denton brought Fitzpatrick up to speed on the rest of his wife's research. He also confided to the chief of police about other parts of his past two conversations with Theodore Jackson. By the time Jessica called the two policemen for dinner, Fitzpatrick had all the relevant information Denton and Jessica did. During dinner, the three collaborated on strategies to deal with Denton's and Jessica's current career calamities and the city's possible administration issues.

CHAPTER 15

On Monday morning, the police chief arrived at his office earlier than usual, amused to find he already had a message from Charles Roberson. *That can wait*, he thought. He had another call to make before talking to Roberson.

The chief made the call, and a cheery voice answered on the second ring. "Hargrove residence."

"Good morning, Jenny. Jack Fitzpatrick. I'm sorry to bother you so early in the morning."

"This isn't early for us, Jack," said Jennifer Hargrove. "What can I do for you?"

"I feel terrible about interrupting Jim's rehab, but something reasonably urgent came up that I want to discuss with him if possible."

"I'm still screening his calls, but I'm sure Jim would want to talk to you. Hold on."

"Chief," said the next voice on the line, "thank you for interrupting the goddamned boredom of rehab. Only three more weeks of this, and the doctors think I'll be eligible for parole from house arrest."

"Sounds like it can't come too soon for you, Jim. Thanks for taking my call," said Fitzpatrick.

"What's up? Jenny said it might be urgent."

"Possibly. I'm not sure yet, but Jessica Jones's administrative leave is relevant to the problem."

"Oh—well, Jack," said Hargrove, "nothing in Jessica's case should cause alarms. She's one of the best attorneys on the staff and certainly not in trouble. Jessica became curious about sensitive topics. Considering her husband's position, some in the administration thought a short break for her would keep both her and Commander Jones from getting mixed up in things which might impact an ongoing investigation."

"Well, Jim," said Fitzpatrick, "I'm not sure to which investigation you refer. As chief of police, I'm fully aware of all active investigations. Which one of those might either Commander or Mrs. Jones impact?"

Hargrove didn't answer right away, and when he did, he seemed unsure of himself. "Jack, at the chamber's annual First Citizens Awards Banquet last August, someone from the city manager's office told me our task force had made significant progress in building a case against Theodore Jackson. The official told me the task force initiative had reached a sensitive and critical stage that mandated airtight security in administrative communications to avoid accidentally alerting Jackson to our progress. I considered this good news and shared it with key members of my staff, including Fred Gunnells. Since then, I haven't heard anything about it until Gunnells called me last week to tell me Jessica Jones asked about Jackson's arrest record. I'm aware of the mayor's recent negotiations relative to a certain donation for the city. Based on Commander Jones's involvement in that matter, Fred and I thought we should protect Jessica. We took her out of the line of fire, so to speak—until the dust settled a bit."

"I see," said Fitzpatrick. "But here's the thing. Our drug task force is no closer to having anything solid on Jackson now than we've had in the last twenty-plus years. If we were getting close to something good enough for court, I'd be the first to know it—and believe me, you'd be the second. Jackson has been a problem for me for most of my career, and

I'm ashamed by our inability to find a reason to arrest him for anything as minor as jaywalking. Let me take a wild guess, though. Did this confidential information you received come from Charles Roberson?"

"Yes," said Hargrove. "It did. What's going on, Jack? Did someone mislead me? I should have thought to confirm the information, but, my God, tell me what's going on!"

"I'm not sure yet, Jim, but I'm going to find out. Don't say anything to anyone about this, and don't bring Jessica back in yet. I'll get back to you before the end of the day unless you prefer I talk to Gunnells."

"No," answered Hargrove. "Call me. I'll brief Fred when you tell me I can. For now, I'll keep what you told me between us."

"Okay, but two others share the information besides you and me. Denton Jones and Jessica uncovered this."

"Got it," replied Hargrove. "I'll talk to you later today."

Fitzpatrick had what he needed from Hargrove now, and his next call went to Assistant City Manager Charles Roberson. The phone rang on the other end, and Roberson picked up immediately. "Roberson here."

"Charles, this is Jack Fitzpatrick returning your call."

"Thank you, Chief," said Roberson. "I want to discuss an issue I have with one of your officers."

"Would the officer be Denton Jones, commander of the Central Business District patrol force?"

"Yes, in fact," said Roberson. "Commander Jones recently spoke disrespectfully to me and is spreading malicious rumors designed to impugn my reputation. I'm aware of his otherwise excellent record but believe his recent actions warrant a severe reprimand, if not a suspension."

"Can you enlighten me on the rumors you say Jones is spreading?" asked Fitzpatrick.

"Yes. Jones told other city employees I consort with criminals."

"And how do you know he made these accusations to others?"

"Because I have a transcript of his testimony to Mr. Franks and Mr. Simski," said Roberson. "Internal Audit also videotaped the interview. Would the recording provide you enough proof?"

"Yes," answered Fitzpatrick, "but as you know, I also attended Mr. Franks's questioning. The only time Commander Jones mentioned your name related to your brother-in-law. Julian Stenson *is* your brother-in-law, correct?"

"*Was* my brother-in-law. I don't know whatever happened to him and don't care. He was a low-life criminal, and I had as little association with him as possible. I'm infuriated by Commander Jones's insinuation."

"Again, Charles," said Fitzpatrick, "I attended the interview, and I witnessed no insinuation from Jones other than his discovery that the man was your brother-in-law. The past relationship isn't a rumor."

"Fine, Colonel Fitzpatrick, but Commander Jones had more to say to me than what you heard in the interview. We talked on the phone after the interview, and his insolent remarks crossed the line from simply offensive to intolerable."

Fitzpatrick had waited for this and paused before answering. "Yes, Charles. I'm also aware of the telephone conversation between you and Jones. Would you like to hear the recording of it?"

"Are you telling me your department tapes my calls?" exclaimed Roberson. "I'm outraged!"

"Excuse me, Mr. Roberson!" said Fitzpatrick. "Do you not remember that you are the one who initiated the recording of incoming calls to city administration numbers? You received a ruling from the city attorney that allowed such recordings. Since incoming calls are voluntary on the caller's part, our attorney determined we may record them. We can't use the recording feature on outgoing calls unless the party we call grants permission. Nobody from our department purposely records calls, but all calls to each other, including this one, are automatically saved on our system hard drive."

Roberson didn't speak for a long time, and Fitzpatrick began to think he had hung up. Finally, Roberson said, "Colonel, I'm sorry to have disturbed you. We have nothing more to talk about."

"Actually, Charles, we do," said Fitzpatrick. "I'm meeting with the mayor late this afternoon, and the city manager will join us. As a courtesy, I invite you to attend. The meeting starts at five o'clock in Mayor Guzman's office."

"Okay, Colonel. I'll plan on coming." Then he hung up.

Fitzpatrick called Denton and reviewed his conversation with Roberson, telling Denton about the meeting scheduled with the mayor in the afternoon. "I'm not sure of everything that may result," said the chief, "but I doubt Internal Audit will require additional interviews."

"Thank you, sir," said Denton. "The interviews worried me, but what about the larger concerns you and I discussed over dinner relative to Roberson? Do you plan to discuss Roberson's possible collusion with Theo Jackson with the mayor?"

"No, Denton. Until I accumulate more information, I won't."

CHAPTER 16

Denton decided to avoid the vicinity of his office around the time of the mayor's meeting with his boss. He knew Fitzpatrick would fill him in on the details after. To clear his head, he went to one of his favorite places in the city: the Avondale High School baseball field.

He pulled up to the diamond and saw Junior Bridges and Jaden Stokes striping the base paths. When they saw Denton's car, both young men stopped what they were doing and walked to the chain-link fence to greet him.

"Hey, Mr. Jones," said Jaden. "Are you here for the game?"

"No," said Denton. "I still have some other appointments. I just wanted to stop by and see how the camp was going so far—and get a breath of clean, fresh, neighborhood baseball air."

The boys laughed, and Junior said, "We have a scruffy lot this year and maybe the laziest bunch ever. We're making some headway, though. Jaden's team and my team play each other for the first time today."

Denton smiled. "I'm a little out of touch, so I haven't seen the neighborhood betting line. Who's favored?"

Jaden answered, "I don't think there is a favorite, Mr. Jones. I just hope we settle it out here on the field and not after the game with guns and knives. As Junior said, the group is rough this year."

"We've had our share of those sorts of groups over the years," reminded Denton. "I wouldn't characterize the summer you two started here as a picnic!"

The two looked at each other and laughed. "You're right about that, Mr. Jones. Some bad dudes played on that team."

"Including you two," said Denton. "But look at you now. Good luck today. I need to go, but maybe we can get together at the end of the week. I want to review the list of participants this year and hear your evaluations."

"Sure thing, Mr. Jones," said Jaden. "See you later."

As Denton drove back downtown, he reflected on the two young men he had just left. Both attended the first youth summer camp Denton ever conducted, and both developed into outstanding ballplayers. Each earned starting positions on their respective high school baseball teams, and Jaden received a partial scholarship to the University of Cincinnati after high school. Junior went in a different direction.

After playing varsity baseball for the Bearcats for all four years of his undergraduate years, Jaden earned a degree in economics. Accepted to the university's prestigious law school after that, he now attended his final year there. The internship at the city's Law Department provided a real-world experience for Jaden before taking the bar exam the following summer. Denton knew the young man's successes were only starting.

Like Jaden, many of Denton's former summer-camp participants parlayed athletic talent into college degrees. His programs produced several Division III and Division II players and at least two Division I athletes besides Jaden. Some achieved "star" status as collegiate players, but the fact that all earned degrees gratified Denton more than the athletic achievements. Academic accomplishment represented a giant step in breaking from the generational cycle of poverty existing in the environment where most of Denton's camp participants were born.

Despite the successes of his youth programs, Denton regretted the failures. Unfortunately, no matter how much he might try, he couldn't make all kids choose a better path. He understood the factors working against him and the dilemma children of the inner city faced better than most. Born into poverty and neglect, these children learned at an early age to adapt to their adverse environments to survive. Hunger could blur the sense of right and wrong, and when it came time to choose a vocation, the easy money in the lower hierarchy of drug trafficking could be compelling. The income was lucrative, the risk of getting caught statistically low, and the punishment was not much of a deterrent. Jail time—with guaranteed meals, a warm place to sleep, and reasonable safety—represented not an entirely unpleasant alternative.

Junior gave in to these temptations. He enjoyed the local street action's excitement, and his innate intelligence made him a savvy asset in the lower levels of narcotics distribution. The Evil Eyes, the neighborhood gang he joined, worked for a mid-level supplier named Thorn Silver, who paid the gang members reasonably well out of his profits. Silver also supplied Evil Eye members with various weapons to "protect their turf."

On a fateful summer day six years prior, three squad cars surrounded a group of Evil Eyes gang members as they retrieved a supply of product from Silver. Ignoring the warnings from the policemen, five of the gang members jumped into a vehicle, firing several shots from their departing car. Under a barrage of bullets, the gang members' car crashed through the blockade, speeding down a side street only to slam into the front door of a nearby tenement. The gang members fled the vehicle and barged through an open door on the first floor of the building. A woman with two young children crouched near one of the apartment's walls. The Evil Eyes raced to the front windows and fired their guns as police cars arrived in front of the building.

The gunfire stopped the police officers' advance temporarily, and the gang members held their fire, motioning the terrified young woman to sit on the sofa with her children. Soon, hostages and gang members heard a bullhorn from one of the police vehicles announce, "Gentlemen, please put down your weapons and proceed through the front door of the building. We know five of you are inside the building, and so far, nobody has gotten hurt. Let's leave it that way. You cannot escape."

The senior member of the gang yelled back through the window, "You're wrong about that, five-O. We've got plenty of ammunition, and this ain't over. We also have three hostages!" He directed one of the other gang members to give his gun to a younger member. "You two stay here," he told the youngest members of the group, "and guard the hostages. If the police start advancing toward the apartment, shoot at them. The three of us will search for a back exit from here. When we find it, we'll come back to get you." Then they left.

The lady and both children cried, and the young man holding the gun tried to console her. He told her nobody would hurt them and that they planned to leave as soon as they could. Both gang members watched the police cars in front of the building, hoping they would not have to fire the gun before the others in their group returned for them. A fourth police car arrived at the building within ten minutes, and a tall policeman stepped out of it. Both gang members recognized him.

Through a bullhorn, he said, "Boys, this is Officer Denton Jones. You're in a bad situation, and I don't want you to make it worse by getting someone hurt. I'm leaving my weapon here on the car and coming into the building to talk to you."

The two young men didn't know what to do. It appeared the other Evil Eyes had deserted them. Neither wanted to harm the young lady and her kids, and they also didn't want to hurt the familiar policeman heading in their direction.

When Officer Jones entered the apartment, he said, "Hi, Junior, K-Man. We need to talk. First, give me that gun and let these nice people leave the room."

The two nodded, and K-Man handed the pistol over. The lady and her two children quickly escaped the apartment toward the safety of the police vehicles outside. When Officer Jones received the weapon, he expertly retracted the ammunition magazine. After a quick survey, he showed it to the two teenagers in front of him.

"Empty," he said. "Junior, K-Man, don't look so surprised. I'm certain you two boys knew this weapon had no more ammunition. You never intended to hurt those hostages or the policemen out front, did you?"

Junior picked up on the officer's strong hint and said, "No, Officer Jones, we didn't. We didn't expect any of this to happen this way. I'm sorry, sir."

"Me too, Junior," said Jones, "but it could have been a lot worse. Let's make the best of the situation we can now. We're all going to walk out the front door together, and you're going to surrender to the officers out front. Where are the other three?"

"They left us," said K-Man. "They said they were going to try to find another exit and that they'd be back for us."

"Right," said Denton. "So, they had you cover their retreat with an empty weapon."

"I guess that's right," admitted K-Man. "They probably never intended to come back for us."

"Nope," agreed Officer Jones.

The two teenagers walked through the building's first-floor door with their hands up, accompanied by Officer Jones. Two policemen outside cuffed them and placed them in a police vehicle for the trip downtown for booking. Charged as juveniles with various felonies and misdemeanors, the court sentenced them to detention terms at the Cuyahoga Hills Juvenile Correctional Facility in Highland Hills. The state reduced sentences for the two for cooperating in the investigation of the Evil Eyes and with details of Silver's drug operations. Their excellent conduct during incarceration further reduced the time required at the correctional facility. Both teenagers left Cuyahoga Hills after serving two years.

K-Man went to live with relatives in Chicago after his release. Junior Bridges stayed at the Joneses' home for a short time until Denton helped him obtain a low-level position in the city's sanitation department.

Jones's brave action during the short hostage crisis earned much publicity and resulted in a Civilian Service Medal of Honor. Deflecting the praise he received for his role in the event, Jones told reporters who interviewed him, "I was never in danger as I walked into the building. I knew both boys on the other side of the wall and felt certain they wouldn't hurt me. They weren't bad people. They were just people from bad environments who, in bad circumstances, did some bad things."

CHAPTER 17

When Denton came through the door, Jessica greeted him with a glass of wine, a warm smile, and a message. "Colonel Fitzpatrick just called for you on our home phone. He told me he also left a message on your cell phone and that you could call him anytime this evening."

"Drat!" Denton retrieved his cell. "I see the missed call here. I had my phone plugged into the vehicle's system when I stopped to talk to Jaden and Junior at the ball field. I didn't hear the ring."

"It must have been *some* meeting because right after I hung up with the chief, I got a call from Fred Gunnells. I'm now officially invited back to work."

"Great!" said Denton. "The meeting didn't last long either. It started at five o'clock, and it isn't even six yet. Let me call the chief to find out what happened." Denton took his glass of wine to the den and dialed the chief of police's number.

"Fitzpatrick here."

"Colonel, sorry I missed your call. It seems your meeting didn't last long."

"No, it didn't, Denton. In addition to Mayor Guzman, City Manager Doolittle and Roberson attended. The mayor also asked acting City Solicitor Fred Gunnells to sit in."

"Why Gunnells?" asked Denton.

"I think because Shirley figured this had something to do with your wife," answered Fitzpatrick. "I wouldn't be surprised if the mayor got a call from Jim Hargrove before the meeting."

"Oh, right. You talked to Jim about this, didn't you?"

"Not much, but I don't think he liked what I *did* tell him." The chief then summarized the discussion. "I didn't get into any detail of our suspicions about Roberson. I simply expressed some outrage at the nature of the Internal Audit discussions. I also shared my belief that the service you performed for the mayor in taking the meeting with Theodore Jackson seemed to have contributed to your wife's temporary dismissal from her office."

"What did the mayor say?"

"She said volumes with her eyes and her demeanor, but she spoke very little. She asked Doolittle if he had anything to add, and the city manager almost choked. He told the mayor someone had informed him of the Internal Audit inquiry only that morning and that he didn't know about Jessica's situation. He halfheartedly tried to cover for Roberson, saying he believed the whole thing a misunderstanding with Roberson only trying to protect the city."

"Sounds weak," said Denton. "Did Roberson say anything?"

"Not a word. My impression is that Doolittle told him to say nothing. Fred Gunnells also remained quiet during the meeting, but he had plenty to say to me after it. He and Jim Hargrove suspect Roberson purposely misled them. They're angry!"

"So, what now?" asked Denton

"I'm not sure," said the Colonel, "but I don't see a reason to hurry. We neutralized Roberson for now, and perhaps permanently. He can't go anywhere. I want to do a little more research before going back to the mayor with anything more serious."

"Understand, sir," said Denton. "Thank you for this."

"No thanks required, Commander. The situation should have never escalated to the level it did."

After hanging up, Denton reviewed the results of the meeting with his wife. Jessica listened intently and when Denton finished asked, "So, you aren't going to pursue Roberson's possible connection to Jackson aggressively?"

"I think the colonel would prefer to wait until we collect more concrete evidence. We're currently only sure that at one time, long ago, both Jackson and Roberson knew the same criminal."

"I may know a little more than that," said Jessica. "My time to research this will become scarce when I return to work the day after tomorrow, but today I scored. Sit at the table."

Jessica recovered a yellow legal pad covered with her neat handwriting from several piles of stacked papers and labeled boxes. "Yesterday, I downloaded a complete list of every employee who ever worked for the city of Cincinnati in the past twenty years."

"My Lord, Jessica! How did you find out such a list existed?"

"It didn't, until now. I had to download twenty separate lists consisting of each specific year. Human Resources maintains these as a public record, and they include names, job functions, and compensation levels."

"So, anyone in the world can find out what any employee of this city makes, anytime they want?"

"Correct, Denton. That isn't unusual for a municipality. As part of the Freedom of Information Act, we try to ensure that citizens understand how we spend tax dollars."

"Okay, so why did you need all these lists?"

"By loading the information into a Microsoft Access database, I could eliminate duplicate names from year to year and track the employment history of people who had worked for the city for at least twenty years. Guess how many there are."

"Well, twenty years is a long time. The city employs over two thousand, so maybe a hundred worked here that long?"

"Eighty-five," said Jessica. "Some of the names on the list fascinated me. Bunny Conrad, the mayor's secretary, has worked for the city for almost thirty years. Her husband, Dennis, became a city employee twenty-five years ago. He's the manager of the water plant."

"Wow! Bunny's mother and my mother were friends," said Denton. "She was just a little girl from the hood."

"Maybe so, Denton, but she's done all right," said Jessica. "She started in the Human Resources Department secretarial pool at $5.25 per hour, and now she makes over $70,000 per year. Her husband makes more than that."

"Good for her," said Denton. "Their two boys both went to the university, and I think Bunny and Dennis live over on Riverside. When they retire in a couple of years, they'll receive Social Security and a pension from the city."

"Right," said Jessica. "It's a nice story with a good ending."

"But I assume that isn't the only thing you discovered. Why did all the folks who worked twenty years or more for the city interest you?"

"Because twenty years represents the approximate period Theodore Jackson has ranked as Cincinnati's most successful criminal. If someone inside our government helped him all that time, I wondered who."

"Well, it could be more than one person," said Denton, "and I doubt Jackson could obtain anything useful from secretaries or water plant personnel."

"No, you're right. So, I applied some additional filters to the access list, eliminating all but police personnel or high-level administrative managers."

"That would shorten the list for sure. Who made the new list?"

"Only three people," said Jessica. "Jack Fitzpatrick, Charles Roberson, and James Kilroy. Since Kilroy worked for fifteen of his twenty-two years in public works before coming to the assistant city manager's office, I eliminated his name as well."

"Interesting," said Denton. "Sometimes, when we *think* we already know the answer we're seeking, that's the answer we find. Could that be the case in this research?"

"Maybe, but the facts are still the facts. I learned something else I think you'll find interesting."

"Which is?"

"Jackson has no arrest record as an adult, but the city keeps juvenile records separately. When I checked those, Jackson's name appeared on an arrest occurring almost twenty-five years ago. Charged with possession with the intent to distribute, Jackson was only seventeen at the time. The charges were later dropped in juvenile court for unspecified reasons."

"Is that such a surprise?" asked Denton.

"No," said Jessica, "but the officer who made the arrest, and then had the charges dismissed, was Sgt. Charles Roberson."

———

Teresa and Theo both waited at the arrival gate as Lucretia came through. Theo told her to leave the airport with her aunt. "Give me your baggage claim ticket, and I'll retrieve your luggage. We'll meet later at my office."

"It's okay, Mr. Jackson. I didn't check any bags. When things started looking dicey in Las Vegas, I went straight to the airport without packing anything. That's what you told me to do, right?"

"I sure did! Good girl. I seriously doubt anyone would already be looking for you here, but let's not take any chances. We can talk at the office."

When Teresa and her niece arrived, Theo had a table full of food and drinks set up for Lucretia. "Lordy, Mr. Jackson. Do you think I'm going to live at your office? I'm a little hungry, but you brought more food here than I could eat in a week!"

Theo laughed and said, "I didn't know what you liked, so I got a little of everything. You can take what you don't finish home. Since you left the rest of your clothes in Vegas, Teresa also needs to take you shopping on my credit card."

"Oooh, that sounds fun because I don't think I'm going to try to collect any fees from Foxee Modeling."

"Do they have any way of contacting you? You didn't provide personal information, did you?"

"The agency doesn't. I gave them fake numbers and addresses except for my cell phone—which I also left in Vegas. GlaMore Photography here in Cincinnati has my home address, though."

"Okay, since you'll get a new cell phone number soon, Yi won't know how to contact you by phone. He'd be stupid to try to reach you at all, but if you receive anything in the mail, let me know. After you eat, fill me in on what you learned about Foxee Modeling."

Luci settled back on the couch with her aunt after making a dent in the fast-food buffet Theo provided. Pulling a pocket-sized notebook from her purse, she gave Theo a detailed chronology of her three and a half weeks in Las Vegas.

An agency representative had picked Luci up at the airport and taken her to the Dice 'N Fun Casino. She stayed for two evenings in a luxurious room with a view of the city. Foxee Modeling maintained a modest office in the hotel's basement, and Luci met the agency's owner there on her first morning. Gerald Story—around forty years old, Luci thought—seemed cordial. He flattered her with compliments about the photo spread from GlaMore Photography and predicted great success for Luci in Las Vegas. Story needed additional photos of Luci for her modeling profile and directed her to visit the agency's photo studio next door after lunch.

Things went downhill at the studio when the female photographer requested that Luci remove her clothing. Luci balked, asking the lady what other clothes she was to wear for the photo session. The photographer appeared surprised and said she needed nude photos. When Luci refused, the frustrated photographer eventually agreed to pose Luci in a variety of swimwear.

After her second night in Las Vegas, the agency moved Luci from the hotel into a small apartment with two other girls, Sissi and Lila. These girls were about the same age as Luci and both pretty. According to Lila, they joined the agency about a month before and, so far, had done no modeling. Foxee provided female hostesses for functions sponsored by hotel guests, and both Lila and Sissi had attended several of those.

"Did they perform only as hostesses, or did the clients expect more?" asked Theo.

"Believe it or not, these girls only hosted, nothing else," answered Luci. "There was a bit of a catch, though. The girls kept only the tips received from guests at the functions—no other compensation. The agency retained all earned wages derived from the event to reimburse itself for expenses such as apartment rent, photography spreads, makeup, and some other stuff."

"Like what other stuff?" asked Teresa.

"My roommates liked cocaine," said Luci. "Wherever they came from, they could never afford the drug before, and the Foxee Modeling agency made it easy for them to obtain in Las Vegas."

"Did they make decent tips at the hotel functions?" asked Theo.

"They learned how to—and they gave me advice on their best methods. They earned anywhere from two hundred to four hundred dollars per event by standing close to men, allowing occasional gropes, and teasing them. After my first week, both Sissi and Lila got different jobs with Foxee and moved from the apartment. My new roommates were both brand-new employees."

"Did you stay in touch with Sissi and Lila?" asked Theo.

"I tried. Sissi went to a complex called the Ranch, where she lived with eight other women. We talked a few times after she left. The last time, right before I came back here, she complained about her workload and warned me the Ranch wouldn't be a place I'd want to work."

"I assume her job there didn't include things like gardening?" asked Theo.

"She didn't say, but we both knew her responsibilities. The last time we talked, she had difficulty maintaining a normal conversation because of the drugs."

"What about the other girl, Lila?" asked Teresa.

"Lila joined the company's dating service, and I never heard from her after she moved. I saw her picture in one of the company's ads on a local tabloid's back page. The ad left no question about what she sold."

"So, how did you avoid an assignment to one of those other divisions of Foxee?" asked Theo.

"Probably because during my initiation or trial as a hostess, I never took the bait of free drugs. I also didn't exhibit a genuine interest in doing what other hostesses did to earn additional money. I think new employees with Foxee tend to promote themselves into the company's more lucrative work lines. As hostesses, the girls gradually become used to doing more provocative things to earn better tips, and the money finally trumps any morals they once had. Going to the next level of service no longer takes a leap, just a short hop."

"So, as a hostess, nobody forced you to do something you didn't want to do?" asked Theo.

"Not until this week. I guess Mr. Story realized my progress lagged that of other recruits, and Foxee hadn't earned much money from my efforts so far. He called me for a meeting and told me he needed to sell my contract to another company."

"Your contract?" asked Theo. "I thought you didn't sign any contracts!"

"I didn't," answered Luci. "I reminded Mr. Story about that and told him I had no interest in working someplace else. I also told him if he found my work performance disappointing, I would just return home."

"Good!" said Teresa. "Did you go to the airport then?"

"Not quite. Mr. Story yelled at me when I told him my plans and said things didn't work like that in Las Vegas. He said I owed him over two thousand dollars for room and board, modeling commissions, and photo sessions, which I had to pay before leaving the city. Then, he bragged about how he had negotiated an excellent deal for me with another modeling agency which would clear my debt to him."

"What was the name of the new agency?" asked Theo.

"I didn't find out, but I met the owner. She waited in Mr. Story's reception area until my meeting with him concluded. Her name was Madeline Horn, maybe in her mid-forties, bleached blonde, and a little overweight. Friendly enough, she acted excited about my potential with her company. By then, I knew I should leave Las Vegas, but I didn't want Ms. Horn to suspect anything. I played along with her and said I could move from the apartment the following day. That seemed fine with her, and she said she would return to help me. When I got back to the apartment, I called an Uber for the airport. Sorry I couldn't find out more, but you told me I should leave whenever I started to feel uncomfortable."

"Luci, you stayed longer than I would have preferred under the circumstances," said Theo. "I'm glad you left when you did and feel guilty for putting you in danger in the first place."

"Honestly, Mr. Jackson," replied Luci, "until yesterday, I don't believe I was ever in much danger. Nobody threatened me while I performed as a hostess or pushed me into things I didn't want to do. I think Foxee's strategy for recruits entails exposing them to opportunities to make more money. The financial rewards associated with the racier temptations cause the employees to make poor career choices that later benefit the company. When recruits don't naturally gravitate quickly to activities creating better profit margins for the agency, Foxee has a way to cut losses by selling nonperforming assets to a different kind of organization."

"Right," said Theo. "I'm glad you didn't wait around to find out what sorts of work Ms. Horn expected or her methods to ensure performance."

"I am too, but I wish I could have done more to help girls like Sissi and Lila."

"You did plenty," said Theo. "You gave me what I needed to know."

"I'm glad I could help, but can I share with you a potential problem you might have?"

"Certainly, Luci. I appreciate any insights you can offer."

"I'm not exactly sure how to explain this, but I don't think you'll ever get much help from victims like Lila and Sissi. Maybe you don't need it, I don't know, but if you do ever need them as witnesses or as resources, you might be disappointed."

"Why?"

"Well, like Sissi. I told you about our last conversation. I felt bad for her, and I asked her why she just didn't stop—you know, walk away from her current situation. Despite being high on drugs, her answer made some sad and awful sense. Sissi told me if she quit what she was doing, she'd end up back where she came from. She said the hell she was in wasn't as bad as the hell that was behind."

"I see," said Theo, understanding the logic only too well.

CHAPTER 18

Roberson reacted with surprise when he received the next call from Yi. "What now, Yi? I deleted the file less than an hour after I received your message two weeks ago. I also managed to have the city employee responsible for making the request placed on administrative leave for a short time. She's not in a position to make additional inquiries for a while."

"Yes, Mr. Roberson. We can confirm you successfully deleted the information from the city servers. The file, however, still exists on another computer somewhere in the city. We must ensure you eliminate all traces of it."

"How am I supposed to do that?" yelled Roberson. "Who else has the file?"

"Calm down, Mr. Roberson, and I will tell you what you must do. The signal alerting us of the continued existence of our sensitive information on another computer is intermittent. We can only discern an alert when a host computer holding the file connects to the internet. Your servers in the city are continuously connected, and we see no alert coming from them. The computer still containing the file isn't always online. I suspect the city employee who downloaded the file from me may possibly have it on a home computer. I can provide the address for where the alert originates."

"Fine, but if the file isn't on city servers, how can it impact you?"

"In its current location, it probably can't, but we take no chances. Whoever has the downloaded file could easily upload it to the city servers again in the future."

"Jesus, Yi! You aren't paying me for any of this, and your requests are unreasonable."

"Oh, but I disagree," said Yi coldly. "You still have a high-paying job with your city, and you and your family also remain healthy."

"I don't appreciate your threats, Mr. Yi!"

"And my organization does not appreciate your laziness. I work for people who value privacy and go to great lengths to ensure that identities and business affairs remain confidential. They do not accept failure and levy extreme punishments for it. For that reason, I must exercise persistence to ensure you meet their requests. Do you want the necessary address so you may complete your work, or would you prefer my organization finish it for you?"

"What's the address?" asked Roberson.

"Twenty-Two Fleming Drive, in the city."

"Okay. I'll check. The address seems familiar to me. Once I know who lives there, how do you expect me to access the computer?"

"That isn't my problem, Roberson. You figure it out. The exercise isn't as critical as the other one, so you may take a little time. Make sure you do the job in a way that raises no additional suspicion." He hung up before Roberson could respond.

Roberson accessed the city's Geographical Identification System from his home desktop computer and entered the address Yi provided. He expected to find an apartment building at the location, most likely home to the summer intern, Jaden Stokes. He guessed wrong.

Roberson cursed silently when the listing indicated a single residential home; he cursed loudly when he read the owners' names: Jessica and Denton Jones. Punching the keyboard harder than necessary to close the program, Roberson tried to figure out why the downloaded files existed on Denton Jones's home computer—and how they got there. He began to panic but stopped as he pieced together the most likely scenario.

Assistant City Solicitor Fred Gunnells placed attorney Jessica Jones on administrative leave at Roberson's request. Gunnells did this right after Yi informed Roberson of Jessica's request for information relative to Yi's business. Roberson pretended to Gunnells that Jones's innocent question about Theo Jackson's criminal record in the city constituted the reason. In fact, Roberson just wanted Jessica Jones iced for some time to ensure she didn't cause him additional headaches with legal curiosity relative to Yi's business. Her intern, Jaden Stokes, most likely brought a flash drive with the data she requested to her home.

While attorney Jones now worked back at her office, the files provided by the intern likely remained archived on her home computer. The realization caused some comfort, but Roberson knew he had little time to figure out how to remove the file. The assistant city manager had created enough trouble for himself with his boss and the mayor because of his ill-advised Internal Audit request on Denton Jones. He didn't need more trouble from Yi.

———

Several days after the mayor's meeting with Chief Fitzpatrick, Denton's cell phone vibrated, indicating a call from an unknown number. Despite suspecting a solicitation, he answered.

"Denton Jones here."

"Hey, Denton," said the familiar voice. "What's going on?"

"Hi, Theo. Too much to talk about on the phone. Can we meet someplace?"

"Sure. When?"

"I suggest as soon we can, and preferably away from your office again, if possible."

"Okay," said Theo. "How about the Catholic church on California Street, Church of the Resurrection, in about an hour?"

"Won't people be there?" asked Denton.

"Not today, and not at this hour. Father O'Dowd's a friend of mine, and he'll let us use one of the parish meeting rooms. Go in the side door of the right wing of the church."

"Okay, see you in an hour."

When he hung up, Denton shook his head, wondering how Jackson might surprise him next. Denton knew the church's location north of Victory Parkway, and while he had never met Father O'Dowd in person, he was familiar with the priest's reputation. Catholic membership had been declining for many areas, but in O'Dowd's church, it rose, primarily from among the city's minority populations. The *Cincinnati Enquirer* had done a story on the popular priest, which appeared several months back in a Sunday edition of the paper. The article portrayed O'Dowd as a singularly charismatic leader and a near-legendary humanitarian. Denton wondered what the priest's connection to Jackson could be.

———

When Denton entered the side of the church, Theo greeted him just inside the door. He led Denton down the hallway, where the two came to a small meeting room. When they sat, Denton said, "Theo, you certainly have a diverse and unusual mix of friends. Should I ask how you know Father O'Dowd?"

"You can, but the answer is unimportant and irrelevant to our meeting. Let's say I'm an equal-opportunity friend and don't discriminate based on race, color, sex, religion, or age. Father O'Dowd is a good man, and we help each other when we can. So, tell me what's going on in the city."

Denton gave Theo an update on all that had happened since they last spoke. Theo listened intently and when Denton finished asked, "Have you had any other contact with Roberson since Fitzpatrick met with the mayor?"

"No. Things got quiet, and Jessica returned to work. Why do you ask?"

Instead of answering the question, Theo said, "As a police officer, you're in a rather dangerous line of work. I assume you take appropriate precautions to protect yourself, your family, and your property?"

Denton, confused by the question, said, "Yes. I'm generally armed, and I try to remain alert to everything happening in my environment. What exactly are you asking?"

"Does your home have a reliable security system?"

"No. It doesn't, and you're scaring me, Theo. What's going on? Can you quit beating around the bush?"

Jackson sat for a long time without answering. After reaching a mental decision, he said, "Someone approached my organization recently with a request I would not accommodate. The request had to do with you and Jessica."

"Jesus! Does this have to do with Roberson?"

"I can't answer that question, but you should take the information seriously. Desperate men take desperate measures, and just because I wouldn't accommodate the request doesn't mean others won't."

"Can you tell me what I should look for—what I should expect?" asked Denton.

"You should go to Costco and look for the best home security system you can buy. Beyond that, I'm not sure what you can expect. For the record, I'm sorry if I'm responsible for this, and I'm trying to help the best I can."

"I understand, Theo. I appreciate it. What about you? Are you okay?"

"What do you mean? Of course I'm fine."

"If one of your sources inside the city administration becomes obsolete or compromised in some way, won't that hurt your business?"

"You're making assumptions again, Denton, which you know is dangerous. You don't know if I have—or ever had—sources inside the city. And *if* I do or did, I'll worry about that. You don't need to. Also, depending on the strategy I decide for the future of my various enterprises, sources inside the city may no longer matter at all."

"Can I ask why? Or is that another one of those questions you can't answer?"

After a few moments Theo finally said, "Something you don't realize— most likely nobody realizes—is that most of my business enterprises are legitimate. The total of my, shall we call them, *politically correct* enterprises don't earn as much as the relatively few businesses I own that you and others might judge less lawful. Collectively, however, they do very well. Despite what some might think, I'm not a greedy person. I can live well on what I make from my legal businesses. I can also do other things with the money I make from those businesses: I can take care of my employees, and I can help causes I think worthy."

"Like the youth center."

"And others," said Theo. "You're making positive differences in people's lives by your efforts, Denton. I'm able to do that with some of my money. I could do this easier if I owned fewer businesses that were unpopular with various enforcement agencies."

A bit stunned by Theo's plan, Denton said, "We've talked a little about this before. Given your reputation, I'm not sure you'll ever become a respected philanthropist."

"It isn't important to me to become respected. Believe it or not, my ego doesn't require that. The only thing important for any charitable causes I might choose is my money—not my name. Just for the sake of argument, though, have you read the history of this country's first multimillionaire, John Astor?"

"I know the name, but no, I don't remember much about him."

"He's famous for his generosity, including large contributions to the Metropolitan Museum of Art in New York City. His heirs and descendants continue to be both rich and generous. The Astor name is as well known for its great wealth as for the many good causes the family has supported over time. However, Astor's original wealth resulted from profits made illegally in the Chinese opium trade. He became even wealthier later in life, establishing a profitable fur-trading business. Some historians believe he built this business by swindling our country's indigenous people with whiskey."

"I had no idea," said Denton.

"Early members of the Forbes family, brothers John and Robert, also successfully participated in the opium trade. The Delano family, too. Specifically, Franklin Delano Roosevelt's grandfather. Have you heard of the Rockefeller Foundation?"

"Of course," said Denton. "Don't tell me the Rockefeller fortune originated with opium too."

"Nope. The Rockefeller Foundation donated over five hundred thirty million dollars to various charities during John D. Rockefeller's lifetime. Since then, the total donations exceed a billion dollars. According to many credible historians, Rockefeller created the foundation to offset negative public relations against himself and his company, Standard Oil, in the early nineteen hundreds. Our federal government pursued Rockefeller through the judicial system for using illegal business practices to build his company, including pricing out competition, controlling railroad transport, and manipulating supply, in violation of the Sherman Antitrust Act."

"Theo," said Denton, "are you some kind of history buff? When do you have time to study all this?"

"I like to read, but that isn't the point. Lots of great fortunes got their start with activities considered questionable. The French novelist Honoré de Balzac wrote, 'Behind every great fortune is a great crime.' While I believe his statement exaggerates, our world's lifeblood is money. In the end, how we use it seems more important than where it comes from."

Fascinated by Theo's knowledge of history and his eloquence in stating it, Denton realized he wasn't academically equipped to compete in this debate. After a brief reflection, he replied, "You've thought a lot about this. You may or may not be right, but your recent donation to the city will result in good things for kids who need some good things."

"We can agree on that. The capital for the youth center comprises my largest contribution for such causes yet, but it isn't my first."

"No? Would I be familiar with others?"

Theo smiled. "Oh yeah. I think you would. Remember when you started the youth summer camps during your breaks from college? You created a spectacular program for poor kids in the neighborhood with practically no funding from anyone."

"Yes, of course I remember," replied Denton, now gazing at Theo suspiciously. "The high school allowed me to use the field and the locker rooms. The city rec department gave me a bunch of mismatched uniforms and a truckload of old equipment that had cluttered the lost-and-found bins for years. That's all the help I got."

"Right," replied Theo. "Then you recruited some civic-minded teachers on summer break to help, and you allowed kids to attend the camps for free."

"Correct."

"Didn't you also provide participants with lunch?"

"Yes, I did. I went around to several of the area restaurants willing to help. The city contributed two dollars per kid from their community-relations fund, and I asked each participating youth to bring their drinks from home. With all that, I normally provided around thirty lunches per day for the length of the camp."

"Do you remember which food establishments helped you?"

Denton began to suspect where Theo's conversation was headed and looked at him curiously. "Yes. The Chicken Little on Twenty-Third, the Alfie J on Elm, the Ben and Julius Deli on Victory, and sometimes the Burger Barn on Twenty-Fifth. The Co-Op grocery would also contribute cheese and cold cuts once per week."

"How did you pay these businesses?"

"Different ways," said Denton. "The Co-Op would settle for any money I had; the Chicken Little and Burger Barn only charged me for raw food cost, which I paid with cash; the Alfie J and Ben and Julius gave me charge accounts and charged a dollar fifty per meal."

"And you paid them at the end of the month, or the end of the camp?" asked Theo.

"I was supposed to reimburse the businesses at the end of the camp," answered Denton.

"Supposed to?"

"Yes. For the first three years of the camps, when I requested the final charges from those two businesses, the managers always acted like they couldn't find the invoice. I never understood whether this was just the managers' decision or some corporate charitable initiative."

"Probably a corporate decision," said Theo.

"Were you in some way responsible for the decision?"

"Maybe. Ya see, Denton, as I told you before, I own many legitimate businesses around this town—and others. Nobody would ever know because, in most cases, no paperwork exists that would link me."

"What kind of contracts do you have, then?"

"The only kind worth anything: a handshake between two people who trust each other—and the handshake is optional. You can cover a business deal with all the contracts you want, created by the smartest attorneys in the country, and in most cases, all you have in the end is an expensive pile of paper. The same lawyers who create these fancy contracts are the ones educated in the ways to break them. They're for hire by the folks on both sides of contracts, and most don't care which side they work on."

"I'm not sure what to say, Theo," said Denton, still trying to grasp all the nuances of Theo's revelations. "Thank you, I guess, for helping me with the youth camps."

"No thanks necessary. Back then, I could only afford to help in small ways. Now my resources allow me to do bigger things."

"Like the youth center."

"Yes, like the youth center." Then Theo changed the subject. "Any progress on the name I'm looking for?"

Denton felt guilty since he now knew the criminal had apparently helped him significantly in past years. He wasn't ready to share the information, though. "Some work remains on that," he answered honestly. "Whatever I find on my side won't be one hundred percent certain, though, without a DNA sample from you to confirm, Theo."

"I'm certain you can guess why I'm not able to meet that requirement. If you give me a sample from the young man, I can arrange to analyze it privately."

"If we ever get to that point, your suggestion won't work for me, I'm afraid. Both of us will know this information or neither of us will. We don't have to decide now, but think about it."

"Okay. I will. I have one other thing I want to share with you before you go."

"What's that?"

"Remember those shops we looked at across from the old junior high school?"

"Sure," said Denton. "The ones the Chinese guy owns? Jessica had her intern pull some tax and license records, and she didn't see anything weird. Some paperwork was missing on an old permit, but the owner provided it to Jessica's intern."

"Huh. When did that happen?"

"Probably three weeks ago. I asked her about the businesses right after you and I drove by the junior high school. Why?"

Theo became suddenly distracted in thought, then said, "Oh, no reason. Just, well, I researched the photography studio, and I think I found out yesterday the business strategy for the video store."

Denton waited patiently. "Are you going to tell me, or should I guess?"

"I'll tell you what I know, but it isn't anything you can act on yet. I'm not done. GlaMore Photography lures young females for free photo sessions to further create fake modeling positions for them. The modeling positions, at least some of them, turn into entry-level prostitution employment."

"Jesus, Theo! How do you know? Are you sure?"

"How I know isn't for publication, but yes, I'm sure. I can't give you what you need to make any arrests yet—but I will eventually. The video store connection is even more disgusting."

"I can hardly wait."

"In one of my business lines, I deal with a relatively low-level, degenerate bunch of scumbags. I made some quiet inquiries among this group about the video store on Victory, and a contact provided a clue. I'll have some physical evidence, a video, soon."

"The internet's full of every sort of pornography you can imagine these days. Nobody needs to go to a video store for that."

"In our country, we're pretty permissive about what we allow, but the United States still bans one kind of pornography."

"Please don't tell me Yi's store deals in child pornography."

"Sorry. Even worse. Besides that, exclusive memberships in sex clubs specializing in the most depraved activities imaginable."

"That occur in Cincinnati?"

"No. Not Cincinnati—at least, I don't *think* the events take place here. The members come from all over the United States, and they attend junkets to Latin America and the Caribbean. Administration for the club, or some part of it, occurs here. Also, this store and others scattered around the country like it deal in illegal videos for their *select* membership."

"Shit!" exclaimed Denton. "You were right about Yi, I guess."

"No. I wasn't. I suspected Yi to be a penny-ante, low-life criminal. He's much worse than that."

CHAPTER 19

While the Avondale Youth Center would not open until the following year, contractors finished the stadium and ball field located on the property by mid-July. The playing field required additional funding, and Denton was perhaps the only one in the city not surprised by the corporate sponsorship providing the capital: Independent Avondale Restaurant Associates, LLC, owners of the Chicken Little, Alfie J, Ben and Julius Deli, and Burger Barn franchises nearby.

The city announced that since the field was completed in time for the citywide AAU championship, the mayor would unveil the sign over the press box with the field's new name in a ceremony before the first game. The mayor kept the name a secret from everyone except her staff, and Denton presumed it would be some marketing-oriented combination of the four sponsoring fast-food restaurants' names. The mayor tasked Jones, as commander of the downtown business district of the police department, to present the city flag and a new American flag to the color guard on the field in the pregame ceremony.

After finding seats behind the plate with Jessica, Denton gave his wife a quick hug. "I'll be back in a few minutes. This shouldn't take long."

"I'll wait right here," she said with a sneaky smile. "I'm so proud of you, T."

"Jessica, I'm delivering two flags. That isn't such a big deal."

"I'm not referring to the flags. You started all this years ago, and I'm not the only one in the stands today aware of that."

"I might have played a small role in what happened here, but this resulted from many people's efforts, not just mine. Even if you *are* the only one who knows my part, I'm happy. I don't need anything else."

"Go deliver those flags."

Standing near the first-base foul line, Denton watched the mayor approach the podium set up near second base. A color guard representing the Army, Air Force, Navy, Marines, and Coast Guard marched to a position behind the podium where several city council members and other dignitaries sat. Colonel Fitzpatrick occupied one of those seats with others Denton presumed represented the sponsoring restaurant businesses.

Denton's role was simple. When requested by the mayor, he would march to the podium and hand the two flags to a corporate-sponsor representative, who would then follow the color guard to the open gate in the outfield fence. The representative would then attach the flags to two flagpoles beyond center field and raise them as the national anthem played.

Denton listened as the mayor began her speech, introducing the audience to the dignitaries seated near the podium. She then talked about the youth center's importance and thanked the various contractors and organizations involved in the construction. She spoke briefly about the anonymous donation that facilitated the financing, and thanked the Independent Avondale Restaurant Associates LLC for funding the stadium. Then, Mayor Guzman talked about the name of the field.

"After the horrific war between our states, newly freed men and women swarmed to the Northern and Western cities. Our city received its share of these people, who were willing to do anything to support their newfound freedom. Unfortunately, these new citizens of our city had little training for anything beyond hard, manual work. However, we in Cincinnati had plenty of this sort of work available because of our presence as a port on the mighty Ohio River. Many of the strong and able men who began to populate the neighborhoods near the river like Avondale found work on the riverfront docks and piers.

"Unloading the smaller vessels required no additional labor for vessel owners, but the larger ones, the ones carrying ten tons of cargo or more, required many strong arms. When these bigger ships arrived at our docks, the ships' captains felt relieved to see the swarm of muscled men assembled on the shore to assist them. As a group, these men became known as the Ten Ton Men. They were the great and great-great-grandfathers of most of the children who now live in this neighborhood, and we dedicate this field to their continuing legacy. Welcome to Ten Ton Field!"

This piece of history was new to Denton, and the apparent coincidence in similarity between the field's announced name and his old college nickname stunned him. Loud applause occurred as two men pulled the gigantic tarp away from the colorful metallic sign over the scoreboard that read *Ten Ton Field*.

When noise from the crowd died, the mayor finished her speech. "The seeds of progress planted long ago shouldn't be forgotten, and we honor those responsible for the legacies created. We also understand our shared responsibility to add to these legacies by doing all the good we can, for all the people we can, for as long as we can. The Ten Ton Men began a journey that doesn't end with this beautiful stadium. We are only getting started—in this town, in this country, and in this world. Thank you, citizens, and thank you, Independent Avondale Restaurant Associates."

Denton's mind whirled in confusion as the mayor finished a speech entirely too personal for him. Someone had to lightly nudge him when the time came to deliver the two flags to the color guard in center field. Coming out of his daze, Denton marched toward the Restaurant Association representative waiting for him near the color guard. The man looked familiar, but Denton could not place him until the man reached to receive the two flags from Denton. Each of the man's outstretched hands had only four fingers. When Denton glanced up, the man smiled, winked, and did an about-face to head toward the flagpoles.

After the national anthem, the mayor and the city council members began to vacate the playing field. The day had been full of surprises, and Denton had many questions. Before heading back to his seat in the stands, Denton found the mayor still near the podium.

"Mayor Guzman," called Denton to the retreating woman.

Guzman stopped and turned toward Denton. "Commander Jones. Thank you for taking care of delivering the flags for us. I'm glad to see you today."

"Yes, ma'am. You as well. I found your speech most interesting because even though I'm from this neighborhood, I didn't know the history about the Ten Ton Men."

"Thank you, Commander," the mayor replied. "That little nugget was news to me, too, but the partners of the Restaurant Association provided the information. Those gentlemen all grew up around here, and according to them, the Ten Ton Men constitute an important part of local lore."

"I see," said a skeptical Denton. "So, *they* came up with the idea for the name of the field?"

"Yes. The Association asked for nothing else in return for funding the project other than the name. They also insisted we keep the name secret until the ceremony. I'm astonished, however, if any of this surprised you."

"Why is that?" asked Denton.

"Because, Commander, the partners of the LLC suggested my office coordinate with your wife in preparing remarks. They said Jessica would prove a valuable resource for background material because of your history in the neighborhood. The look on your face makes me think Jessica concealed her participation from you."

Denton tried to hide his shock. "Oh, well, Jessica would make an excellent resource. I have told her much about the neighborhood history, so she didn't need to ask. She probably wanted this to be a surprise for me—which it was."

"She's a lovely woman and very articulate. I hardly changed a word of the remarks she wrote."

"Yes, she's quite the writer," Denton agreed as he turned to head to his seat.

As he climbed the bleachers, Denton began prioritizing the questions he had for Jessica. He realized the conversation would have to wait, however, as he advanced closer to his seat. An assembly of old college friends now sat next to Jessica, including Jill and Shane Reynolds. Jill was responsible for introducing Denton to his wife. The three men in the group played baseball with Denton at Lefton College, and all knew Denton's nickname at the school: Ten Ton.

Shane spoke first when he saw Denton coming toward them. "Ten Ton! You old dog. You finally got a stadium named after you. Way to go. You deserve it!"

As the others in the group laughed, Denton tried to deflect the attention. "You must not have listened to the mayor's speech, Shane. The Ten Ton Men she talked about had nothing to do with me—and what the heck are you all doing here?"

"Right," said Shane sheepishly, glancing at Jessica. "We heard the speech, but we're not buying it. One of your closest friends sent us an invitation to this event, and there was no way we were going to miss it."

Denton looked at his wife with some intensity. "Hmmm—wonder which friend that would be. Probably the same one who provided the mayor all that horseshit she put in her speech. Jessica, do you have any idea how the mayor got that ridiculous story?"

Jessica blushed. "Sorry, T. I *did* assist the mayor a little with her comments, but the story about the Ten Ton Men came from the Restaurant Association guys. They're from the neighborhood, and they swear the Ten Ton Men are legends among local folks around here."

"Jessica," said Denton. "*I'm* from this neighborhood! How come I never heard of these guys?"

"Don't know, T. Maybe you didn't meet the right storytellers as a kid. The mayor didn't much care about the stadium's name as long as the partnership paid for its construction."

"So you just threw a few extra things into the speech? You're too much. All of you. I have a field named after me thanks to my wife and some poorly researched history—but only a few people in the world will ever know that. The rest will all believe a fairy tale someone made up!"

"So what?" said Jessica. "The tale was a nice one, and the people who know the truth are the ones who care about you the most. Doesn't that count?"

Denton hugged his wife. "It's the only thing that counts, but what happens when the mayor finds out the truth?"

"Who's going to tell her? Not Theo Jackson, I bet," she said quietly.

Denton looked at his wife and could only smile.

CHAPTER 20

This year, the seventeen-and-under championship came down to two teams Denton knew well. Both Junior's summer camp team, the Garbage Men, and Jaden's, the Law Dogs, had survived the thirty-two-team bracket tournament and would now meet for the city championship. Denton had seen many of his teams make it to the championship game in his history of conducting youth summer camps. Today would mark the first time both squads vying for it originated from the Victory Parkway Youth Program.

After the excitement of the opening ceremonies, Denton and his friends took little notice of the player warm-ups on the field. When he could refocus on the upcoming game, Denton observed the two opposing coaches laughing together near the third-base dugout. With unusually low humidity on this beautiful summer day in July, the sky was high and blue, and a pleasant breeze blew toward the outfield fence. The day presented a perfect one for baseball, and Denton relished the short respite it provided from the pressures of his job. He had no favorite team in the contest and hoped only for a well-played game. Glancing around the stands, Denton saw two familiar figures seated along the left-field foul line. He nudged his wife and said, "See the two men sitting behind the dugout over there, about three rows up? One has a clerical collar."

"Yes," said Jessica. "I think that's Father O'Dowd, isn't it?"

"Yes. The man sitting next to him is Theo Jackson."

"You're kidding! What's he doing here?"

"I don't know," answered Denton. "I'm curious. I may ease over there for a few minutes and see if I can find out."

"Do you think that's wise? Won't people wonder why you're speaking to him?"

"Not if I happen to be talking to Junior near the fence at the dugout. Today, we're just a couple of baseball fans who bumped into each other. I know of O'Dowd, so nobody would find my greeting him unusual."

"Okay. I'll stay here. Wish Junior luck for me. If Jaden comes near the fence, I might go down and say hi to him."

"Great!" said Denton. "If that happens, tell *him* good luck for *me*."

"I will."

Denton took a circuitous route to the end of the third-base side dugout to avoid early contact with either Jackson or O'Dowd. When he got there, Junior came over, extending his hand to Denton over the fence. "Thanks for coming, Mr. Jones. This will be a good game, I think."

"I'm counting on it and bet both coaches have some tricks up their sleeves."

"Maybe," said Junior, "but I think both of us are aware of each other's tricks by now." Noticing several of his players watching his conversation with Denton, Junior called to them, "Hey, guys! Come over here, and I'll introduce you to a baseball legend."

When six or seven of the young ballplayers reached the fence, Junior made the introduction. "This is Commander Denton Jones. He's in charge of the downtown business district patrol force now, but not that long ago, he was the Lefton College Monarchs' star player. An exceptional college hitter and pitcher, Commander Jones pretty much carried his team to a national championship."

Several of the boys hooted in admiration and stuck their hands through the fence to shake Denton's. The embarrassed police officer tried to correct Junior's exaggerated story. "I'm afraid your coach here has inflated my baseball history, boys. I was a relief pitcher in college and a below-average hitter."

"Guys, don't even be listening to this man's garbage," said Junior. "He's just modest. As a boy, I watched him play in a game right across the river against Mount St. Joseph College. He struck out the side in relief in a close game and then hit one of the longest home runs recorded at that field. Now, you guys better get back to the dugout because the game's about to start."

When the boys left the fence, Denton protested, "Junior Bridges, I can't believe you! I only batted about six times in my entire college career, and I got one hit. The hit became a home run because of a fortuitous collision between a large bat and a baseball thrown over my head. The homer may have been the *highest* ever hit in the stadium, but it certainly wasn't the longest. The ball landed only a few inches over the center field fence."

"Mr. Jones," said Junior, smiling, "I'm sorry, but this isn't your story anymore. It's mine. If I want to use it to help inspire a bunch of hard-luck boys to do a little better, I think you should let me."

At that moment, Theo Jackson and Father O'Dowd approached and stood behind Jones. Junior motioned the priest closer. "Father, maybe you can help with a little philosophical debate between Commander Jones and me."

O'Dowd stepped to the fence cheerfully, extending his hand to the young coach. "Sure, Junior. How can I help?" The two were obviously acquaintances.

Junior said, "Officer Jones here challenges my memory of his baseball career as I have related it to members of my team. He seems to think I'm misleading them with an exaggerated version of his success. I, on the other hand, believe I'm using the *legend* of his success to provide a benchmark and worthy role model for my players."

Staring at Denton, O'Dowd asked, "Is this correct, Commander?"

Smiling, Jones answered, "Yes, more or less. I'm not sure the coach should so blatantly misrepresent the facts of history to accomplish his mission in this case."

O'Dowd thought for a moment. "Sorry, Commander, I think I have to side with the young minister. Sometimes too many facts ruin a story, and constructive fables often teach better lessons than factual history. Wouldn't you agree?"

Denton chuckled. "I agree that I'm probably not going to win a debate on ethics with a priest, Father. Did you just refer to Junior as a minister?"

"Yes, as a matter of fact, I did. He is, and you are, whether either of you knows it or not. I refer to all those who preach the gospel as ministers."

"Excuse me?" said a confused Denton.

"St. Francis of Assisi instructed his ministers to 'preach the gospel at all times, using words when necessary.' When people provide good role models and useful benchmarks for living, they perform the best sort of ministry."

"Thank you, Father," Denton replied. "I appreciate your perspective." Seeing Theo Jackson behind O'Dowd, Denton said, "Mr. Jackson, I didn't know you liked baseball."

Jackson laughed. "Oh yeah, Commander. I'm a huge fan, and this is like the World Series for amateur baseball in the Queen City!"

"I guess so," said Denton.

"Nice to see two teams from our old hood get to the finals, isn't it?"

"Yes," Denton agreed. "Both teams originate from the Victory Parkway Youth Program."

"I'm aware," said Jackson. "You know both the coaches well, don't you?"

The question seemed innocent, but Denton sensed meaningful intent. "Yes, I do. Both participated in the first youth program I ever conducted—a long time ago."

"You should be proud, Commander Jones," said Jackson. "Who do you want to win?"

"Both!"

"A diplomatic answer, indeed," said Father O'Dowd. "Looks like they're ready to start. I'm going to head back to our seats."

As the two retreated to the stands, Denton shook his head. So much confused him recently. When he returned to his seat with Jessica and his old friends, the umpire announced, "Play ball!"

Fans enjoyed a thrilling game between two exceptional youth teams. The coaching was excellent, as Denton expected it would be, and at the end of the regulation seven innings, the game remained tied at four to four. Junior's team managed the winning run in the bottom of the ninth inning when their cleanup hitter dropped a surprise bunt with a man on third base.

Players for the winning team raced from the dugout to celebrate; then, Denton saw something happen he had never seen after a baseball game before. Jaden organized the losing players in a line in front of the first-base dugout while Junior did the same with his jubilant players on the third-base side. As this took place, a chant from the crowd behind the third-base dugout began. Several fans, including Theo and Father O'Dowd, stood, and fans around them also rose. At first, Denton couldn't understand what they chanted, but as more voices joined, he heard, "Good game! Good game! Good game!"

In seconds, all in the stadium stood and joined in the chant. On the field, the losing players walked over in a line to the winning players. In a display of sportsmanship undoubtedly orchestrated by the two coaches before the game began, losing players shook winning players' hands. As the single file of losing players moved down the line of winning ones, occasional fist bumps and even light hugs occurred. This caused the chant from the fans to grow even louder and more enthusiastic.

Denton glanced across the stands in Theo's direction, where his childhood friend smiled and gave Denton a thumbs-up. Denton returned the signal and looked back at his wife, who had tears streaming down her face.

"T, I have never seen anything like this in my life! Isn't it wonderful?"

"Yes, Jessica. It is. If we can make this happen in Cincinnati, why not the rest of the world?"

"We can," she said. "We just can't ever give up."

Denton hugged his wife, gazed at the cloudless sky, and thought back to what Father O'Dowd said before the game. When his eyes returned to the field, searching for his two "ministers," he found them together among the team members. The orderly lines of players had disintegrated, with the field a blur of intermixed uniform colors. Many of the players stared upward into the stands in awe of the continuing applause, wondering what they had done to cause it. No matter the reason, the attention felt good, and they would remember the ovation for the rest of their lives.

CHAPTER 21

Theo entered the church and followed the hallway to Father O'Dowd's office. The priest sat behind his modest desk but rose to greet Theo as he reached the doorway. "Theo, my friend, how are you? Your message sounded urgent."

"I'm fine, Father, thank you. I appreciate your accommodating me on short notice. I'm in a bind and need some advice."

"Sit down and tell me your problem."

Theo sat and related to the priest the research Lucretia provided on Foxee Modeling and shared his suspicions about Sun Yi. Theo never shared information with anyone about the parts of his business less popular with enforcement agencies; on this occasion, however, he gave the priest an estimate of the quantity of illegal drugs purchased by Yi. Theo also told the priest that he believed Yi's organization utilized the drugs to enslave prostitutes through addiction.

"Theo," said O'Dowd, "while we usually avoid the details of your various business enterprises in our discussions, on several occasions you shared with me your opinion of those who purchase illegal drugs. You compare them to those who use alcohol or tobacco products, and you have no sympathy for their poor health choices. What makes this different?"

"Addicts and crackheads choose their lifestyles and bear the responsibility for their health just like people who smoke or drink. The line separating enforcement of the sale of certain drugs versus the sale of alcohol and tobacco seems arbitrary. Mr. Yi, though, isn't using the drugs he purchases to satisfy the demand of crackheads. He employs drugs as a tool for enslaving women."

"I see," said the priest. "Your problem isn't the product, but the use of the product?"

"Exactly! Father, do you know the number one contributing factor to death in the United States?"

"Is it tobacco—smoking?"

"No. That's number two. Obesity is number one. Should we outlaw food?"

"That might be a bit extreme."

"Of course, but my point is, food isn't the problem. It's how certain people use food. The same for tobacco, alcohol, guns, or drugs. We could continue this part of the debate for hours, but I'm here for a different kind of advice."

"Okay, Theo. I'm not sure I can help, but I'll try."

"My research into Sun Yi has opened a hornet's nest of sorts, beyond my capability to manage. I believe Yi manages a part of a much larger organization involved in human trafficking. While enslavement is the worst crime anyone can commit against another human, I don't have the resources to stop an organization like Yi's. I need help."

"Like, from local or federal law enforcement?"

"Yes. I'm willing to help, but policing agencies most likely would not want my assistance."

"I understand. A problem for sure. Give me a day or two, and I'll think about this. I know someone who might have ideas if you allow me to share what you've related."

"I trust your judgment, Father, and I'm sorry to burden you. When I began my research on Yi, I didn't expect to uncover something as bad as I did."

"I'll call you within a day or two."

After Theo departed, O'Dowd dialed a number in Compton, West Virginia.

"Pastor Burns speaking. How may I help you?"

"Hello, Tom. This is Tim O'Dowd in Cincinnati."

———

O'Dowd first met Tom Burns when Burns worked with the priest for a summer in Cincinnati. Burns attended Gettysburg College and came to Cincinnati to assist O'Dowd with a summer-long community outreach program. The two became friends, and O'Dowd traveled to Pennsylvania for Burns's convocation when the young pastor completed seminary. Since then, they remained in touch, with their professional paths occasionally crossing over youth-related initiatives.

A Lutheran minister, Pastor Tom Burns also worked with the International Children's Ministry, a sizeable organization that assisted worldwide humanitarian issues. Inevitably, the ICM mission intersected with one of the world's fastest-growing criminal endeavors, human trafficking.

Perhaps the most repulsive area of worldwide trafficking involved the enslavement of women and children. The ICM worked with enforcement agencies in many countries to collaborate with local governments to control and hopefully curb the trade. While much of the ministry's humanitarian efforts were well known and publicized, a vital area of their work occurred clandestinely. Behind the scenes, specially trained clerics wearing collars and robes worked closely with elite undercover commandos. When he wasn't leading his church in West Virginia, Pastor Tom Burns assisted in these sorts of unusual coalitions.

———

"Hey, Father. Nice to hear from you. What's going on in Cincinnati?"

"Nothing good, I'm afraid." O'Dowd then related the pertinent parts of his recent conversation with Jackson to the minister.

"I'm glad you called," said Burns when O'Dowd finished. "Back in March, I assisted in an operation that successfully rescued three young

Moldovan girls from a trafficking ring. A member of an international crime organization, the Santu, escorted the girls, and we intercepted them at Dulles Airport. We hoped to learn more about Santu trafficking operations into the United States, but our tactical plan at Dulles fell apart. We arrested the escort but learned little from her. The only useful evidence from the case came from an intercepted cell phone transmission from the escort's phone just before her arrest. The phone's encryption software effectively scrambled the voice message, but our techs pinpointed the receiving cell tower's area code to Cincinnati."

"Do you know where in Cincinnati?"

"No, just the area code. Enforcement here in the States has no other record of Santu activity in your area. The organization mostly operates out of places like New York, Miami, Houston, and Las Vegas. That's why I didn't call you earlier. I had no other leads to provide. Can you give me additional detail about Yi or his operations in your area?"

"My contact here might," said O'Dowd. "One of our problems is my contact's reputation as a local criminal. He wants to help, but he's not the most popular guy with the Cincinnati Police Department."

"Hmmm. Too bad. That complicates things. Can we obtain a picture of Yi? One of our international sources will run it through their database."

"I'm sure we can do that. Anything else?"

"Not now, but, Father, let me warn you. If the Santu *does* operate in your community, be careful. The group is well organized, well financed, and efficient. They are also brutal. Don't do anything to arouse Yi's suspicions, and you should warn your friend."

"Thank you, Tom. I will."

When O'Dowd reached Jackson and requested the photographs of Yi, Jackson asked if he could speak to Tom Burns personally. "I would prefer that," said O'Dowd, "but I didn't mention your name to Pastor Burns and presumed you wanted to remain anonymous."

"What I prefer and what's realistic are two different things at this point, Father. I'm concerned we don't have much time. Dealing directly with Pastor Burns may expedite the additional research we need."

O'Dowd provided Theo with Pastor Burns's private business number, and Theo called. After a brief introduction, Burns said, "Mr. Jackson, I appreciate your call and your willingness to help. Your sense of urgency is, I believe, well founded. My schedule doesn't become cluttered until Friday. Can I meet you tomorrow at your office?"

"Sure, Pastor. Anytime. I'll clear my schedule. Can I pick you up at the airport?"

"I'm driving," replied Burns. "You're about five hours away, so if I leave this afternoon, I'll arrive in Cincinnati tonight. I can meet as early as you like tomorrow morning."

"Fine," said Theo. "Plan on coming at eight thirty. We'll have breakfast and coffee when you arrive."

"That sounds good. See you then."

As Theo replaced the handset in the cradle, he smiled. Pastor Tom Burns presented himself as a no-nonsense, action-oriented individual, and Theo looked forward to meeting him.

———

When the elevator doors opened at eight thirty to the Theodore Jackson Investments lobby, Pastor Burns's eyes lingered a moment on the vision before him. Teresa greeted him with a radiant smile. "You must be Pastor Burns. Good morning. We don't see too many from the clergy here."

"Well," said Burns, nodding toward the sign on the wall, "most ministers have just enough money to invest in the next meal. Mr. Jackson probably deals with a different level of investors."

"Or something," she said, rolling her eyes. "He's waiting for you. I'll bring some breakfast and coffee in a few minutes."

"Excellent. Thank you."

"Follow me," she said, which Burns did gladly.

"Pastor Burns," said the tall, handsome man at the desk. "I'm Theo Jackson. Thank you for driving from West Virginia for this meeting."

"My pleasure," said Burns. "I like driving, and it gets me here faster than flying out of Dulles would."

"Where are you staying? I insist on covering your accommodations."

"I'm at the Hyatt on Fifth Street. Thank you for your offer, but another agency already covered the cost for my accommodations."

The two men sat at a conference table to eat the hot breakfast Teresa delivered. Saving the business part of their discussions for after the meal, the men engaged in introductory small talk. Burns caught Jackson off guard when he asked if Jackson knew a police officer named Denton Jones.

Dropping his fork to the plate, Theo answered, "Denton Jones commands the business district of our police force here. He and I also grew up together in a housing project not far from where we sit. How do you know Mr. Jones?"

"Sort of an unusual coincidence, I guess," said Burns. "Jones and I played on opposing teams for the Division III college baseball championship back in 1998. He hit me with a pitch during one of the games, and I went over to his dugout afterward to introduce myself. I wanted to meet him because I had heard his name mentioned by someone else I worked for one summer. That was your friend, Father O'Dowd."

"Wow," said Theo. "Sometimes I wonder if life just enjoys playin' with us. Twenty years after our paths unknowingly crossed the first time, we're involved in a completely different game."

"Except this time, I'm on the same team as Denton. You are too, I think."

Theo squirmed in his seat. "Denton doesn't even know about the game we're here to discuss yet, I'm afraid. We haven't played on the same team since childhood."

"I'm aware," said Burns. "I did some research before coming down. I also talked for quite a while with Father O'Dowd. Besides my duties as a minister in West Virginia, I have expertise that takes me worldwide to assist with efforts against human trafficking, particularly related to children. In some foreign countries, the enforcement agencies are only slightly more ethical than the organizations I'm trying to stop. Still, no worse crime exists on the planet, and those of us committed to stopping it accept assistance wherever it's offered."

"Thank you for the explanation. We agree on the scale of the crime."

"I must warn you that your help won't buy you a pass from legal enforcement relating to other crimes. You understand that, right?"

"Yes, Pastor, I do."

"Okay. Then call me Tom, and I'll call you Theo. Let's get to work."

After almost two hours of discussion, Jackson and Burns rose from the conference table. Burns had copies of Lucretia's pictures of Yi and Lin Song, and he had taken several pages of detailed notes. Jackson also shared with the pastor his suspicions about Yi's video stores.

"I believe I'll have some evidence, a video, from my contact soon. I'm working through a confidential intermediary for this research."

"Okay. As we discussed, in the criminal world, and particularly with the Santu, pornography relates closely to prostitution. A collaborative relationship between Yi's photography shop and the video store would not be surprising," said Burns.

Before leaving, the pastor gave Theo a USB drive containing exhaustive research about human trafficking. "The second folder in the drive contains an extensive file on all we know about the Santu organization," said Burns. "When I return to West Virginia, I'll provide the photos you gave me to our international sources. They maintain much larger databases than ours in the States. I'll call you if we get any hits on the pictures."

"Thanks, Tom. Teresa can print off the files on the flash drive if you can wait."

"Is that your receptionist's name—Teresa?"

"Yes, but she's much more than a receptionist. She's like my right arm."

"Well, thanks, but I don't need the drive."

When Burns exited Theo's office, he stopped and extended his hand to Teresa. "I didn't introduce myself earlier. I'm Tom Burns."

Teresa shook Burns's hand. "Oh, thank you. My name is Teresa Adams."

"I appreciate the coffee and breakfast this morning. Both were excellent. Mr. Jackson and I will conference again soon, so I'm certain I'll see you again. It was nice to meet you."

"You too, Pastor."

"It's Tom."

"Good. It's Teresa."

"I know," he said with a wink.

CHAPTER 22

Denton arrived at the church and went through the side door he had used in his previous visit with Theo Jackson. He found the office with Father O'Dowd's name on the door and softly knocked. Footsteps approached on the other side, and seconds later, Father O'Dowd appeared.

"Commander Jones. Come in."

"Thank you, Father, and thank you for taking this meeting with me."

"I'm delighted," said the cheerful priest. "Is this official or social?"

"It isn't official. When I saw you at the game last week, I became curious about some things."

"Great, but before we start, was that not one of the best ball games you've ever seen?"

"It was right up there, Father," answered Denton. "What happened after the game made a memory I'll keep forever."

"Me too, Commander Jones. I related the event in my sermon last week and believe the story will be central to many future sermons."

"It was special," agreed Denton. "How do you know Junior so well?"

"Junior began attending mass here a little over a year ago. His girlfriend, Lissy Brown, started bringing him. Do you know her?"

"No," said Denton, "but I've seen her picture on Junior's desk in town. She's a beautiful young lady, isn't she?"

"Yes, she is that—inside and out. In such a large city administration, I'm surprised the police department would have much interaction with the sanitation department."

"We don't, Father, but my wife and I have known Junior for a long time. I try to check in on him every week or two."

"I know you are close. Junior speaks of you often."

"I'm flattered, Father. Thank you for telling me. Is he in one of your Bible classes or meeting groups?"

"No," said the priest. "But he's active in many of our outreach initiatives. I see Lissy and him on weekends during our clothes drives, habitat programs, and youth-mentoring missions. He's an impressive young man on many levels."

"He is," said Denton. "I'm proud of him. Are you aware he got off to a rather rough start?"

"He told me his history—and your history with him, Commander," said O'Dowd. "The path to good isn't always straight and narrow."

Denton gazed at O'Dowd for a long moment. "That's a wonderful quote. Is it yours?"

"I haven't seen those words written precisely as I said them," said O'Dowd, "but the concept isn't unique among clerics and scholars. As humans, we are weak and subject to all varieties of temptations. Often, we can only learn from our mistakes. Sinners who repent are the most credible teachers for other sinners."

"That makes sense. Sometimes we have difficulty relating to people we think are better or smarter than we are. We tend to listen more carefully to people who we think are more like us."

"Exactly!" exclaimed the priest. "Two of the most common themes in almost every major religion, not only Christianity, are forgiveness and redemption. We who do wrong and repent can be forgiven, and when we are forgiven, we regain the power and ability to accomplish good."

Denton smiled. "Father O'Dowd, I can understand your success in growing this ministry. You appear to have a private hotline to God."

"No such thing, Commander. Honestly, I wouldn't trust anyone who says they're connected in such a way. I don't believe God or Allah or Buddha or Zeus or Ha-Wen-Ni-Yu ever speaks to anyone personally. That just isn't how God usually communicates."

"Who is Ha-Wen?" asked Denton.

"The Iroquois peoples occupied Cincinnati for hundreds of years before European-based American settlers started arriving. In the Iroquois culture, Ha-Wen-Ni-Yu was the ruling God."

"You study all these other religions?"

"I do when I can. I'm a Christian and a Catholic, but I believe a common thread of truth runs through all religions. When we seek to understand the similarities, we equip ourselves to address the differences."

The philosophical discussion stimulated Denton, but looking at his watch, he realized he was running out of time to question the priest about Theo. "Father O'Dowd, I have a question."

"What is it?"

"You appear to enjoy a close relationship with Theodore Jackson. Given Mr. Jackson's reputation, this seems odd to me."

"I would guess it would," said O'Dowd, smiling. "Is your interest professional or personal?"

"Given Jackson's background, I certainly maintain a professional interest in his activities, but that isn't why I'm talking to you. As you may be aware, Mr. Jackson and I grew up together, and he is somewhat of an enigma to me. I thought you might be able to provide some insight."

"I see. Is he a friend of yours?"

"He was—a long time ago. Now we operate on two different sides of the law. It would be difficult for me to call him a friend."

"We could debate your assumption, Commander, but in the interest of time, let's not. I'm aware of both your past and current relationship with Theodore, and you should know you are one of his heroes."

"Excuse me?"

"Yes, a hero," answered O'Dowd. "He's in awe of what you are accomplishing to change the culture of so many troubled young people in our community. At the end of the game last week, when the losing team so graciously advanced across the field to congratulate the winning team, Theodore said to me, 'Denton is responsible for that.'"

The priest's remark surprised Denton. "Father, I would love to take credit for what happened at the end of the game—because it was remarkable. I can't, though. The two coaches came up with that awesome display of sportsmanship."

"Coaches who are both products of your past youth programs and who you continue to mentor in different ways." The priest continued, "Commander, when we plant an oak tree in our front yard, the tree doesn't become mighty and beautiful in a week. It takes years and years. Your many small and continuous efforts over time create a cumulative effect that is both important and impressive. Last week, few in the stadium may have realized your role in creating the miracle they witnessed, but one man did. Theodore Jackson."

"I'm not sure what to say. Until recently, I wasn't aware Jackson knew much about my life other than I was on the police force."

"Oh, he's kept track of you," said O'Dowd. "For many years, you served as an essential part of his rationalization for the reason he chose the career path he did."

"I'm not sure I understand."

"Theodore is a complex man, Commander. He's one of the most intelligent people I ever met, but he has a generally low opinion of humanity, and he maintains a fatalistic outlook for our world. For him, you represented his example of the good person who worked tirelessly for good causes but achieved minimal results for all the effort. The collective accomplishments over the past decade with your youth programs made him rethink his rationalization."

"You're aware of his reputation, right?" asked Denton.

"Of course I am," said the priest. "I also believe a portion of that reputation to be well earned. I don't support many of his career choices or condone all his activities, but I enjoy our thoughtful discussions."

"I do too," Denton admitted. "Some of his theories are just downright crazy, but others contain elements of logic not easily ignored."

"Part of his problem," said O'Dowd, "is his intolerance for those who are weaker or less intelligent than himself. Because *he* avoided the temptations of drugs and alcohol, he believes others who grew up in the same environment should also. In his opinion, addictions are a choice, and he's unsympathetic. Ergo, he feels no guilt in supplying weak people with the products they desire."

"He's made that argument to me too."

"It's one of his favorites," said O'Dowd. "I continually try to make him understand not all are born with the same great gifts as his and recite to him the passage from Luke in the Bible which states, 'To whom much is given, much is expected.' My mild success in convincing Theo to *share* his gifts is fairly recent."

Denton considered the priest's words and felt he could easily spend the rest of the day with this perceptive and compassionate man. However, his schedule wouldn't accommodate such a wish, so he reached to shake O'Dowd's hand. "Thank you for meeting with me, Father O'Dowd. I think you've helped me understand Theo—and myself—a little better. I hope we will have other opportunities to talk."

"You are welcome," said O'Dowd. "Don't give up on Theodore. He has qualities that might surprise you. I would, in the same breath, also warn you never to underestimate the man."

"Thank you, Father. I'll take your advice on both counts."

———

Jackson called Pastor Burns's private number. "Hey, Tom. Did you have any luck with the photos?"

"Yes, Theo. We put them through an international database and got a hit from a friendly collaborator in Cambodia. Sun Yi's real name is Lei Zheng, born in China and without a doubt a Santu member. He's an upper-echelon leader who came up through the ranks as an enforcer. He's brutal, sadistic, and heartless. His assistant, Lin Song, which is her real name, is a Vietnamese orphan adopted by the Santu when she was thirteen.

In Cambodia, where Zheng hired her, she's called *Tufu*, which translates to 'the butcher.' She is an expert in long and excruciating torture."

"Well, Pastor! That isn't news I'm happy to hear. Lucretia said Ms. Song seemed so sweet and friendly."

"The truth is, Theo, she might be that. Raised by the Santu, she's a soldier and does a specialized job the Santu trained her to do. She knows no other life and understands what would happen if she didn't perform to Santu expectations. With this new information, you should be motivated to be extra cautious. The worst thing that can happen to you is not to die quickly inside Mr. Yi's business."

"I understand, Pastor Burns, but if I needed additional motivation to pursue initiatives relating to Yi and his organization, I received it yesterday. The contact I mentioned to you in our last meeting provided the evidence relating to the video store."

"A video?"

"More like an abomination—but, yes, a video. I also learned this part of Yi's business provides a select group of customers other services besides videos."

"Perhaps I should make another trip to Cincinnati," said Burns. "I have additional information to share with you, and I believe I should visit Mr. Yi's buildings. I failed to do that last week. Have you shared what you discovered about the photography shop and the video store with anyone else?"

"Father O'Dowd knows about my research, and I told your old athletic adversary, Denton Jones, a little."

"I'm surprised by your apparent line of communications with local enforcement. Do you speak with Commander Jones often?"

"No," answered Jackson. "The city assigned Jones to be a liaison of sorts relative to another matter involving the city and me. As you and I discussed in our last meeting, Denton and I grew up in the same neighborhood, and I trust him."

"Does Commander Jones have plans to initiate an official investigation into Yi's activities?"

"Not yet. I told him my information wasn't complete."

"Good. It might be important to schedule a larger meeting soon to ensure our efforts remain coordinated. We can talk about that when I'm in town. What does your schedule look like this week?"

"This issue has become my priority. Tell me when you'll be here."

"How about the day after tomorrow? I'll drive down in the morning, and we can meet sometime after lunch."

"That will be fine. Why don't you plan to have lunch here? I don't mind if it's late. I'll have Teresa pick up some sandwiches and drinks."

"Sounds good. Is your assistant informed about your research into Yi?"

"Teresa knows everything. I told you Lucretia is her niece, didn't I?"

"You did mention that," said Burns. "Why don't you have Teresa join us for lunch? I would be interested in her perspective."

"That would be great!" answered Jackson. "I should have thought about that myself. Teresa is brilliant."

"Then I'll see you on Thursday." As Burns disconnected from the call, he smiled. He didn't need Teresa's perspectives on the Santu, but he could darn sure use her company for lunch—almost made him look forward to the five-hour drive.

———

"Hello, Pastor Burns—I mean, Tom," greeted Teresa when he stepped from the elevator. Burns noticed another young woman sitting across from Teresa at the receptionist desk.

"Hey, Teresa. How are you? Good to see you. I warned you I'd be making additional visits here but didn't think it would be this soon."

"We're glad, and thank you for inviting me to lunch. Tom, meet my niece, Lucretia."

"Lucretia, I have heard much about you." Burns extended his hand.

"My aunt has also told me about you," Lucretia said, winking at Teresa. "My friends call me Luci."

"Good. Luci. My friends call me Pastor—but your aunt calls me Tom, so you can too."

Hearing the chatter near the front, Theo appeared at the doorway. "Welcome, Tom. I hope you don't mind if Luci joins us for lunch too. Since she saw Foxee Modeling firsthand, I thought you might like to meet her."

"Absolutely! Thank you for inviting her."

"I hope you're hungry, Tom, because Teresa made the lunch and brought it from home—and there's a lot of it."

"My goodness, Teresa," said Burns. "You didn't have to go to that trouble, but thank you."

"I get tired of all that fast-food crap Theo gets from the restaurants he owns. I thought you should try a Cincinnati specialty."

"Can't wait! I didn't know Cincinnati had a food specialty."

"Oh, we do! It's called Cincinnati chili," said Teresa.

"And Aunt Teresa's recipe for it tastes way better than either the Skyline's or the Gold Star's," interrupted Luci.

When Burns appeared confused, Theo explained, "Skyline and Gold Star are Cincinnati-based restaurants that specialize in chili, but I agree with Luci. Teresa's should be in the Chili Hall of Fame. But see for yourself. Come on back to the conference table."

Theo's office smelled of fresh cornbread and a spice, maybe cinnamon. Teresa set the conference table for four diners; three crockpots steamed in the middle. A large bowl of mixed salad sat next to the crockpots, and each place mat already held a small plate with a section of cornbread. As Burns neared the table, he saw one crockpot was filled to the top with spaghetti, another had a soupy-looking sauce with small particles of beef in it, and the third one held . . . "Are those sliced hot dogs?" asked Burns.

"Correct," answered Teresa. "Put the spaghetti in your bowl first, then some hot dogs. Pour the sauce over the spaghetti and hot dogs, then put your choice of cheese, onions, or beans over the sauce."

"Wow! I've never seen anything like this," said Burns.

"Since you're from West Virginia, that doesn't surprise me," Teresa teased him. "But today is a good one to expand your culinary horizons."

Burns found the unusual meal delicious and rewarded the hostess by loading his bowl for a second helping. "This was worth the drive down here all by itself, Teresa. You shouldn't have gone to all this trouble."

"I couldn't stop her," said Theo. "When I told her about the meeting, Teresa insisted on preparing the lunch. Makes me think I should invite clergy for lunch meetings more often."

Playing along with Theo's joke, Teresa said, "*All* clergymen wouldn't work. Just ones from West Virginia."

As the group finished lunch, Burns asked Luci several questions about her experience in Las Vegas. The young woman's answers were concise, intelligent, and unemotional; Burns marveled at what a good witness she would make in a courtroom. "Do you believe the women at the Ranch were enslaved or imprisoned?"

"Yes," she answered, "but most didn't know it. They were addicted, economically deprived, and educationally disadvantaged. Their prison was having no better place to go, and their captors kept them in that condition."

"Sorry, Tom," said Theo. "That description may not be the one you wanted to hear. Many people might argue that what Luci describes doesn't equate to slavery."

"Which partially explains why the worldwide totals for human trafficking aren't higher," answered Burns. "Trafficking, as a crime, ranks third beneath illegal drugs and the illicit arms trade. The statistics don't include the cases like Luci just recounted. That doesn't make the crimes against these women more forgivable or less important. Thank you, Luci, for your help."

Luci and Teresa left Theo and Pastor Burns after lunch, and the two men exchanged new information relative to their respective discoveries about Yi and the Santu. Once Burns was alerted to a Santu cell's potential existence in Cincinnati, he had asked other agencies about possible Midwest connections. A relevant response came back from the FBI field office in Miami.

"During a federal sting operation focusing on prostitution," said Burns, "a coordinated sweep in Miami resulted in the closure of a dozen businesses.

The raids also produced hundreds of arrests. During the arrests, agents recovered sixteen fake passports, and three of those originated in Cincinnati."

"Yi's operation sent that many ladies from here to agencies in Miami?" asked Theo.

"Not at all. Most United States women employed in prostitution don't need or have a passport. All the fraudulent passports collected in Miami came from illegal immigrants."

"I'm not following."

"Many females employed in this country for prostitution come from other countries. Organizations like the Santu bring them here using false passports. The new holograph technologies employed in most official documents make it more challenging to print off a bunch of credible passports, so blanks are stolen from passport offices. For example, the three girls we rescued at Dulles earlier this year traveled on documents originating in Iraq."

Burns continued, "As you can imagine, some countries have more lax controls than others or are more susceptible to corruption by employees. Iraq is one of those countries, which means inspectors examine Iraqi-based passports more closely than others. Controls in the US are better, so blanks coming from US locations have greater value to criminals. While the sample size is minimal, to have three out of sixteen fake passports in a single sweep originate from Cincinnati is significant."

"So, somebody in the passport office here steals passport blanks?"

"All it takes is a secretary with the keys to the supply closet."

"Is the FBI investigating this?"

"Probably, but it isn't the easiest thing to track. Legitimate reasons also exist for discarding unused passport blanks. If authorities don't properly shred misprinted passports, they can be recovered from trash baskets. Regular audits expose unusual numbers of missing blanks, but thieves also steal many authentic passports after issuance. The discovery in Miami represents a small piece of evidence corroborating our very recent suspicion of a local Santu cell operation. You told me you had additional evidence in the form of a video."

Theo then related to Burns how he had discovered this seedy part of Yi's business plan. With deference to Burns's profession, Theo warned the pastor about the video, apologizing in advance for its indecent content. After viewing the first several minutes, Burns said, "You can turn it off."

"I'm sorry to share something so disgusting with you, Pastor. I thought I had met some bad characters in my line of work until I viewed this. The video created a new low, and I lose sleep over it. It gives me a perhaps rash desire to punish Sun Yi myself."

"I understand completely, Theo, and sympathize. Through my work with the Children's Ministry, I'm more familiar with these types of depravities inflicted on children than you are. However, the frequency with which I encounter things like this never numbs my sense of outrage or commitment to eradicating the responsible criminals. I share your impulse relating to Yi, but punishing him alone would do little to impact the world problem. Significant forces worldwide are aligned to address the larger mission. Now you, perhaps unknowingly, are a part of the coalition. For that reason, I hope you will be patient."

"Thank you, sir. I hear you, but please keep me informed."

"I will. Would it be possible for me to borrow the DVD?" asked Burns.

"Yes. I made a few copies on USB drives for other law enforcement to examine."

"I would prefer the original copy in the case from the video store. The evidence might be important in a peripheral initiative relating to Yi."

"Sure, Pastor. I don't need the original and will be glad to have it out of my sight forever."

"I head back to West Virginia tomorrow. We'll be in touch again shortly."

Theo walked Pastor Burns to the door of his office, watching him depart. Burns stopped briefly at Teresa's desk to exchange a short laugh, then stepped into the empty elevator. On the way to the bottom floor, Burns decided not to return immediately to his hotel room.

———

At five o'clock, the video store employee began to reverse the paper sign hanging in the door from *Open* to *Closed*. Before he could lock the door, a customer approached.

"We're about to close," said the employee.

"I'm aware," said the customer, "but I'll only be a minute. I have something to return."

Reluctantly, the employee held the door for the customer, a White man wearing a clerical collar. "Are you sure you're in the right place?" asked the employee. "We don't see too many priests in here."

The customer smiled pleasantly and said, "I'm not a priest. In my faith, we are called pastors, but I'm not surprised members of the clergy don't represent a large portion of your customer base."

"How can I help you?" asked the employee, anxious to rid himself of the annoying customer.

"I want your total inventory of videos similar to this one," said the pastor, holding up a DVD case.

"I'm not familiar with that video. It didn't come from this shop," lied the employee.

"Yes, I'm afraid it did. If you turn the case over, you will see a website address to benefit customers who desire additional videos. The website provides information about locations where people can purchase such videos. Since this video and any like it violate Section 2256 of Title 18 of the Federal Code, the advertisement seems to be a careless lapse in judgment by someone in your organization. At any rate, I'm here to do your shop a favor. Please give me your inventory of videos like these, and I'll destroy them for you."

The employee stared at the pastor quizzically, moving to a position behind the counter. Retrieving something beneath the countertop, the employee turned to face the pastor, holding a small pistol in his hand. "I don't know who you are, mister, but you should leave the store now."

"Unbelievable!" shouted the pastor. "Now you're going to hold a gun on a customer! My role in this community is to attempt to keep it clean, wholesome, and moral. In the process, I'm also attempting to keep your shop from more serious problems with enforcement. I'm disappointed you don't appreciate my efforts."

At that, the pastor delivered a powerful upward karate chop to the employee's wrist, causing the gun to fly into the air. The employee's head instinctively dropped as he surveyed his broken wrist, colliding violently with the pastor's knee. The employee fell against the wall, unconscious. As the pastor recovered the handgun, he heard steps coming from a hallway behind the counter.

Yi burst through the door, yelling, "What's going on in here?"

"Your employee and I had a disagreement, and he pulled this gun on me," answered the pastor, pointing the pistol loosely in Yi's direction. When Yi reached around his back with one hand, the pastor fired the gun he held, sending a bullet into the wall behind Yi. On the way to the wall, the bullet passed within millimeters of Yi's right ear. "I didn't miss, Mr. Yi. That bullet went exactly where I planned. The next one will go three inches to the left unless you drop the gun you were retrieving to the floor. Don't hesitate. My last shot will attract police soon, which could leave you in a difficult position."

"What do you want?" said Yi, dropping his handgun to the floor.

"I want a cleaner neighborhood, Mr. Yi." The pastor retrieved Yi's revolver. "That's all. I'm a good man and do my best to spread goodness globally, but sometimes appearances can be deceiving. And sometimes, good men, when we become frustrated, show a different side. Get rid of the illegal videos you sell, Mr. Yi. It would also be best to take your employee to a hospital. He has a broken wrist and suffers from a concussion. Goodbye."

After the pastor departed, Yi locked the front door and returned to the employee, who began to stir. Confused and still dazed, the employee asked, "What happened? Did a minister just knock me out?"

Yi replied, "I don't think he was a minister."

———

Burns tossed two pistols in the dumpster near the hotel's food-deliveries bay and then went to his room. Still somewhat exhilarated by his visit to the video store, Burns knew he had done the very thing he had warned Theo against.

Well, he thought. *I'm not perfect*. Nothing Burns accomplished in Yi's shop would impact Santu activities much, but the pastor's actions didn't expose elements of the larger plan relating to Yi either. He'd done nothing but hurt an employee and scare Yi. The pain in his hand from the blow to the employee's wrist brought a smile to the pastor's lips; the bit of fear in Yi's eyes during the encounter created a satisfying memory. Burns wanted to share the relatively insignificant punishment he inflicted on Yi with Theo Jackson but knew this wouldn't be prudent. The only ones who would ever know about the incident were Yi, the employee, and himself—and Burns and Yi would likely never meet again. *Every once in a while, we deserve to treat ourselves*, thought Burns.

CHAPTER 23

Denton accepted Theo's cryptic invitation to join him and Father O'Dowd for a meeting at the Catholic church. He assumed this conference might relate to the discussion Denton had with O'Dowd the week before. When he entered the conference room, the group assembled surprised him. Next to Father O'Dowd sat Theo Jackson. Another man wearing a clerical collar occupied the chair next to Jackson's. This man stood when Denton entered the room and said, "Ten Ton, you may not remember me, but the last time we met, you were throwing baseballs at me. I'm Tom Burns."

"Oh my God—I mean, gosh. Sorry! Tom Burns! It has been a long time. Nobody around here calls me Ten Ton except my wife occasionally. I can't believe it. What on earth could put you three in the same room together?"

"Commander Jones, I think you're the common denominator," Father O'Dowd answered. "Can you join us?"

Still looking from one face to the next, Denton said, "Sure. This will undoubtedly be interesting."

"Before we start, Pastor Burns," said Father O'Dowd, "tell me about the baseball incident. I thought you knew about Denton through his work with the youth programs here."

"Right, Father. You're the one who told me about Denton's programs for disadvantaged children years ago when I came down here on college breaks. But as a junior in college, I met Commander Jones in person when he hit me with a pitched ball in the Division III college championships. After that game, I introduced myself."

"I remember that," said Denton. "You hinted our paths might cross again, and here we are. But why?"

O'Dowd interjected, "We live in a small world, it seems, Commander Jones. Through his work with the International Children's Ministry, Pastor Burns developed an expertise in human trafficking, especially as it relates to children. Next to illegal drugs and arms sales, human trafficking is the third most lucrative criminal activity globally. Sadly, it's also one of the fastest growing."

"Do we have a problem in Cincinnati with trafficking that I'm not aware of?" asked Denton.

"No," said Pastor Burns. "Statistically, the level of human trafficking in Ohio, and specifically Cincinnati, is low. The hot spots in our country remain in the big cities like Atlanta, Miami, Las Vegas, and Houston. The incidence of trafficking children in the United States also remains modest. Most of this type of criminal activity occurs in Eastern, Middle Eastern, and African countries."

"And yet here you are."

"Correct," answered Burns. "Worldwide, human trafficking activities aren't well organized. Various criminal entrepreneurs ranging from small mom-and-pop operations to local gangs to some larger criminal organizations engage. Of these larger groups, the legendary Chinese gangster fraternity known as the Santu is the most organized. Large, well funded, and completely ruthless, they currently control much of the trafficking in the Eastern and Middle Eastern countries and look to expand. We have evidence the Santu has established a presence in Cincinnati."

Denton held up one hand. "This sounds serious, and I'm concerned, but why do I sit here and not my chief of police?"

"That's a fair question," said Father O'Dowd. "You're here informally and unofficially because all at this table know you personally and trust you. We want your opinion and your advice on how to proceed. If we're to maximize the results of our current knowledge, we'll need to move quickly and quietly. If the Santu suspects even a nuance of our effort, their operation will vanish overnight into thin air and to a different location. We will have learned little."

"So, why is Theo Jackson in the meeting?" Denton pushed.

O'Dowd and Burns glanced at each other, fidgeting, and Theo, who had said nothing so far, answered for them. "I'm the connection, Denton. Doing my own research, I found the link, and the discovery horrified me. So I came to Father O'Dowd for advice. He told me about Pastor Burns, and I suggested you attend our first meeting—because I trust you, and I don't trust everyone in our city administration. You and I may not agree on everything that constitutes good and bad, and I respect your opinion. However, when it comes to slavery, particularly to hurting children, there's no gray area. Trafficking isn't just bad. It's evil. You may believe me to be a criminal, which I accept, but what we're talking about at this table represents something worse than criminal. I'm not sure a word bad enough exists yet."

Paster Burns interceded. "I understand this might be an awkward team for you, Commander. Nothing discussed here changes your responsibility for upholding other laws, and I don't believe Mr. Jackson seeks a waiver for anything. As he said, everyone in the room has a common goal to stop something beyond just criminal, using whatever resources we have and doing whatever it takes."

Jones sat at the table. "Until someone briefs me on what we're dealing with, I can't make promises for either myself or my department. I'm okay with participating in the meeting, as long as everyone here understands I will share whatever I learn with whomever in the city I believe I should."

"I'm fine with that," said Theo.

"We are, too," said O'Dowd as Burns nodded.

"Denton," said Burns, "so that I am as transparent with you as you've been with us, I can also access some specialized enforcement resources. Your department would not need to handle this alone."

"What sort of resources?" Denton asked.

"I can't provide specifics," answered Burns, "but, as a global problem, trafficking receives attention at the highest levels of our government as well as other democratic governments across the globe. Several countries, including ours, have established joint child-exploitation task forces. All the governments involved prefer the operations of these organizations to remain confidential and undercover."

"So, are you a Lutheran minister who works with the International Children's Ministry, or do you do something else?" asked Denton.

"I'm a minister, and I collaterally assist the work of the International Children's Ministry," answered Burns. "Through the ministry, I'm familiar with the unusual enforcement assets just referenced."

"But if I'm not familiar with the capabilities of these resources, how can I coordinate any work between our police force and other assistance?"

"When you hear what we're dealing with, you can determine what parts your group can handle. After that, I'll request help in the areas beyond your scope. We hope we can capture a Santu resource here, which might help us impact the larger organization. Cincinnati's police department certainly would not be expected to assist in national or international initiatives that might follow."

"Then start by telling me how we got to this table and what we know. I'm taking a wild-ass guess, Theo, that it has something to do with the block of buildings on Victory Parkway."

Theo smiled. "Very perceptive, Denton. Two months ago, I told you I couldn't figure out why someone would open a tanning salon, a photography studio, and a video store in our old neighborhood. The man paid for the building in cash, and I suspected he was a criminal. For reasons I won't explain, I learned he purchased products from the illegal drug trade but didn't participate in this business commercially. The photography store didn't take much research to understand, and, not long ago, someone helped me figure out the angle on the video store. I shared my suspicions with you several weeks ago. I don't know how the tanning salon fits in yet."

Theo then shared the results of his investigation into GlaMore Photography. He explained how the photography business lured young women into fake modeling opportunities, eventually leading to prostitution in larger cities. While the total number of new working women created in this fashion from Cincinnati might be small, Theo expected the Santu organization employed the same formula at many other satellite photography studios.

"So, how does Mr. Yi sustain a thriving criminal business providing such limited product to the larger organization?" asked Denton.

"Because Mr. Yi is diversified. New female recruits don't represent his only business. I'm familiar with a certain seedy group of folks in the surrounding neighborhoods through other business activities, and I initiated some inquiries about Mr. Yi's video store. One degenerate in the group finally gave a contact of one of my contacts the answer. While Yi sells few retail videos, he maintains a select and extremely exclusive membership-only club for specialized products. He can access pornographic videos too disgusting to be legal in this country. He also sponsors special events for members of his club that include the most depraved activities imaginable. I saw part of a video this no-load had, and it made me vomit."

"When we spoke about this earlier, you had not yet acquired the video. I assume you have it now, and it's the one that caused the physical reaction?" asked Denton.

"Yes, I do. Because the evidence came to me in the most circumspect manner, I can't yet prove it came from Yi's store. I also don't have the name of the person who purchased it. I only know my intermediary in the exchange."

"Do you believe the activities you describe occur here in Cincinnati, like the 'special events'?" asked Father O'Dowd.

"I don't know for sure, but I think most of these occur offshore someplace. A few members in the club come from here, and they have the funds to travel."

"I'm sorry to tell you, Denton," said Tom Burns, "what Mr. Jackson described occurs in too many places in the country. Our Jeffrey Epstein was perhaps the most famous of the United States scum promoting this sort of deluded entertainment, but he wasn't and isn't the only one. More recently, our federal court indicted the Canadian fashion industry mogul Peter Nygard for sex trafficking. For the most part, citizens in our country remain appropriately outraged when they find out about these types of crimes. In other parts of the world, local populations have become numb to them, causing the criminal activity to become more prevalent."

"Hopefully, our citizens never become desensitized. How do we stop this in our community?" asked Denton.

"The problem in your city isn't the humans enslaved or children abused," answered Burns. "Those numbers are relatively small. Of more concern, the Santu appears to be making Cincinnati a clearinghouse for administrative functions relating to their growing presence in the country. When Father O'Dowd called me with the information he received from Mr. Jackson, I contacted an international resource that maintains a massive database relating to human trafficking. I asked my contact to check on whether anything popped out relating to Cincinnati. It was a long shot, but I thought one worth checking."

"Did she find anything?" asked Denton.

"Yes. During a recent federal sting conducted by the FBI's field office in Miami, targeting a national prostitution ring, agents recovered several fraudulent passports. Three of those originated in Ohio. When my source expanded her search to similar sweeps conducted in Houston, Las Vegas, and Atlanta over the past year, she found a total of eight fraudulent passports that came from Cincinnati's federal office. That represented almost fifteen percent of the fake passports collected during those sweeps."

"All those women came from here?" cried Denton.

Burns reiterated what he had told Theo.

"So, somebody stole a set of passport blanks from here in Cincinnati?" asked Denton.

"More likely someone on the inside provides the blanks, I'm afraid," answered Burns. "Criminal organizations once had to hire corrupt immigration officials in several international airports to stamp poorly counterfeited passports. An easier method now involves recruiting dishonest employees who have access to the storage places for passport blanks. Mr. Yi's photo business may complement this part of the counterfeiting, although document technology has made photo swapping on passports much more difficult."

Burns continued, "Cincinnati has a centrally located international airport convenient for distribution. Banking, record keeping, mailing lists, promotional materials, and internet-related communications can be conducted from anywhere in the world with good internet access. Cincinnati's other advantage for a group like the Santu is that your city flies under the radar as a location for criminal gang activity compared to places like Atlanta, Miami, and New York. Gang operations often go unnoticed in places where not as many enforcement agents look."

"I'm sickened by the thought this goes on right under our noses," Denton said with a grimace. "Recognizing the need for extreme caution and secrecy, I still need to bring my police chief and our mayor up to speed. While we're here, can someone tell me what your next steps include?"

"Of course," said Tom Burns. "Let me tell you about a strategy Mr. Jackson and I think might work."

CHAPTER 24

When Roberson's cell phone rang at 7:30 p.m., the incoming call came from an unknown number. He suspected the identity of the caller. It had been over a month since Yi last spoke to him, but Roberson had not yet determined a method for accessing the Joneses' home computers.

"Roberson here."

"Mr. Roberson, you disappoint us by not completing the work relative to the computer file."

"You told me I had time to accomplish this. I have not yet found a convenient opportunity to access the necessary computers confidentially."

"When I indicated you had time, I meant days, not weeks. My management now becomes impatient, and I insist you finish this work within the next two weeks, or we will do it ourselves. If my organization must take care of the problem, you may not like how we accomplish the work or the consequences for yourself. Did you talk to your son in Paducah today?"

"My son in Paducah? How do you know I have a son in Paducah?" Roberson's gut roiled in fear as he recognized the extent of Yi's grasp.

"The sensitivity of my operations requires me to know much about my business partners. You should call your son because I understand a minor tragedy occurred in his family recently." The phone went dead as Yi disconnected.

Roberson, angry and terrified, immediately touched a single digit on his phone to access the stored quick-dial number for his son's home landline. Within seconds Roberson's daughter-in-law, Marguerite, answered. "Hello, Charles. Maurice isn't here right now. We've had a rough day."

"I'm sorry to hear that, Margie. What's going on?"

"We're so afraid, Charles. Maurice is with a police detective downtown. Somebody came into our house last evening and killed Mittens."

Mittens was a female Maine Coon cat and the Roberson family's only pet. "My God!" exclaimed Roberson. "Were you away? How did this happen?"

"No, Charles. Somebody broke into our home while we slept. Maurice found the cat on the couch in the living room this morning with her throat cut."

"Jesus Almighty! Did Maury or Steffi see this too?" Roberson's grandchildren, Maurice Junior and Stephanie, were nine and seven.

Marguerite sniffed now as she answered. "No, they hadn't come downstairs from their rooms yet. Maurice put the cat in a box in the garage and cleaned the couch before the kids got up. We told them their cat died during the night, but we didn't tell them how."

"Why would someone do this?" asked Roberson, feeling guilty for knowing the answer. "Did the intruder take anything?"

"That's one of the strange things. Nothing else in the house was touched, and all the doors and windows were still locked when we got up this morning. Maurice and I are terrified. He's been with the police for most of the day."

"I'm sorry, Margie—and at a loss for words. Was your security system engaged?" Marguerite didn't answer right away. "Margie, are you still there?"

"Yes, Charles. Sorry. I'm just a little emotional. Our security system consists of some ADT signs posted in several places outside, *warning* potential intruders the house is protected. We never installed an actual system. Our neighborhood is so safe a full security system seemed like a waste of money."

"Damn," Roberson said. "That apparently isn't the case. I hope Maurice plans to remedy the security situation soon."

"He does. He purchased cameras and monitors at Costco today and will install them tomorrow morning."

"What about Perry and Beth? Does their house have a system?" Perry, Roberson's second son and Maurice's younger brother, also lived nearby in Paducah.

"I think they do," replied Marguerite. "I've seen Beth enter some numbers on a wall panel when we come back from shopping sometimes."

"Okay. I'm sorry this happened to you, and I'm extremely concerned for your safety. None of this makes any sense, but we need to take it seriously."

"Believe me, Charles, we are. I'll tell Maurice to call you back. Can I tell him why you called?"

"Oh. Oh, nothing in particular. I was just checking in. No need to call back, but alert me if the police find out anything."

As Roberson disconnected the call, another wave of guilt rolled over him, mixed with raw, undiluted fear. Since he never called either of his sons randomly without reason, Roberson suspected Marguerite would connect the coincidence of his call and their cat's misfortune. He couldn't worry about that and had to find a way to get to the Joneses' computers before anything else happened. How he might accomplish that came to him as he gazed at the weekly calendar on his desk. The annual Chamber of Commerce Gala honoring Cincinnati's leading citizens was on Saturday evening, and Roberson assumed both Denton and Jessica Jones would attend the event.

———

As Jessica adjusted the bow tie on Denton's tuxedo shirt, she apologized for not accompanying him to that evening's gala. "This is the first one I've missed since we've lived here. I'm sorry to send you off alone tonight."

"It isn't a big deal, Jessica," answered Denton. "I know you've got work to catch up on. Everyone will miss you, but I'll make the appropriate apologies."

"Thank you, T. I'm sort of curious this year about who will be selected. Do you have any idea?"

"Not really. They've done a good job of keeping it quiet. If it's someone from our administration, I'd guess Shirley Guzman. She's had a good year as mayor and gets most of the credit for the funding for the new youth center."

"Why? Because she sent *you* to negotiate with Theo Jackson? Which has caused *you* one of the most stressful years in your career? Give me a break!"

"Jessica! I'm surprised at you. The mayor did what she had to do, and her strategy succeeded. She had nothing to do with what happened to me, and whether she planned it or not, I now have a stadium named for me. Did you forget that?"

"No, I didn't," answered Jessica, laughing. "I'm sorry. I hope Shirley *does* get the award."

"I'll let you know, and I'll call you when I'm on my way home. It shouldn't take long. I'll leave right after the presentations. Will you be okay here by yourself?"

"Yes, T. Fort Knox's security system probably isn't as complete as the one you installed here. I'm sure I'm safe."

"Yeah, maybe I went a little overboard," Denton admitted. "Theo scared me with his warning, though."

"Me too," said Jessica. "I'm glad we bought it. Anyway, don't worry about me this evening."

Denton had recently installed the most complex home security system he could find online, from a specialized company named Security Plus. One of its unique features was that its presence around the house's exterior was virtually invisible. Ten miniature cameras attached to the house looked like decorative molding beneath the dwelling's eaves, and Security Plus concealed the wiring behind the home's guttering system. The Joneses could view or review video on any of their three TVs by merely selecting channel sixty-eight. The computer responsible for controlling the system came with a massive memory, enabling the storage of months of video history if necessary.

The only downside to the system was the number of evenings it took for Denton and Jessica to learn how to use it efficiently. The design provided an audible notification anytime one of the ten cameras detected movement and automatically turned on all three household TVs to channel sixty-eight. The TV's noise kept Denton and Jessica up most of the first night after installation until Denton eventually turned the system off in frustration. It turned out that the movement created by insect-eating bats flying past the cameras continuously activated the security system at night.

After a few evenings of testing different sensitivity settings and alternative options for receiving notifications, Denton now had the system set so that only the outside movements of something as large as a raccoon would activate the cameras. He further adjusted the system so no audible notification occurred unless the operator specifically selected one. When outside motion caused system detection now, the automatic alarm was silent and visual, in the form of a blinking red light on the monitoring computer's front.

The videos of a raccoon family that regularly visited their house entertained the couple on many mornings. Relieved by the absence of anything more threatening on the tapes, Denton joked with his wife that he would thank Theo for insisting on the security system. They now seemed safe from attacks by local wildlife.

The couple was, in fact, still in danger from other types of wildlife. As Denton closed his car door and backed away from the driveway, someone two blocks away lowered a pair of binoculars.

———

"Hey, Commander Jones," exclaimed Colonel Fitzpatrick. "Where's my favorite attorney this evening?"

Denton had been at the Marriott for over an hour, making the rounds among guests at the cocktail reception. He talked to Mayor Guzman and several of the city's council members but didn't see Charles Roberson.

"Colonel Fitzpatrick," replied Denton, "how are you? Jessica begged off tonight to catch up on some work projects."

"Our loss. The evening won't be quite as grand without her."

"Thank you, but we'll survive. Have you seen Roberson?"

"Yes, about fifteen minutes ago, but as you can imagine, he didn't seem anxious to visit with me. He went to the other end of the room. There he is, talking to Dooley near the shrimp display."

"Yep, I see him. I'll stay in this area with you. Roberson wouldn't have much interest in talking to me either."

"But just as you say that, he's heading our direction. I'll talk to you a little later."

Fitzpatrick ducked away, and Jones followed Roberson's careful movements through the crowd. When Roberson stood in front of Jones, he spoke without offering the customary handshake. "Commander Jones, we haven't yet had the opportunity to finish our discussion of last month."

"I assumed we *did* complete those discussions," replied Jones.

"Not even close, Officer! But perhaps a conversation for a different time. Does your wife not join you this evening?"

"No, she couldn't attend. I'm by myself tonight."

"Too bad," said Roberson. "Well, I must excuse myself and mingle with other guests."

Finding Roberson's quick conversation and abrupt departure strange, Jones watched him cross the room. Roberson reached into his tuxedo pocket to retrieve a cell phone, and Jones intended to follow him to determine whether Roberson was making a call or receiving one. However, his own phone vibrated with an incoming call.

"Jessica! What's going on?"

"T," she said calmly, "you need to get home right away. I'm fine, but leave now!"

Denton ended the call and left the room—in a hurry.

CHAPTER 25

After Denton departed, Jessica took her laptop to the den. She planned to wade through the stacks of paper on the coffee table this evening. Darkened except for a single lamp in the den, the house appeared empty from the outside.

Jessica initially ignored the blinking red light on the security monitor beneath the big-screen TV. When it continued to flash, she entered a code on her laptop to connect to the security monitor. She expected to see the visiting raccoon appear on one of the split screens. Instead, her eyes froze on the dark figure on the third screen. The image looked like a person leaning toward the front bedroom windows.

Jessica isolated the video to that screen and observed as the intruder tried to peer through the shuttered windows. The figure moved along the wall of the house toward the next set of windows. Through these, he would be able to see into the living room.

Taking her opened laptop with her, Jessica hurried to the kitchen, continuing to monitor the person skulking along the back wall outside. The living room was dark, but Jessica feared the light from the den's lamp might be visible through the windows the intruder approached. Jessica wanted to get to her small office on the other side of the living room without being seen. Using the computer screen for minimal lighting, she went through the side hallway and entered the office, where she set down her laptop and retrieved a miniature bottle of pepper spray from the top desk drawer.

She switched the video on her laptop to a different view. The intruder now approached the back porch. He opened the unlatched (*Damn it!*) screen door and placed a hand on the sliding glass door that led into the living room.

Jessica had no time to call 911, and she now had choices to make. She felt confident the intruder still believed the house was empty. If she turned on the lights and went to the sliding glass door, the stranger would no doubt bolt and disappear. Most women would probably choose this option. Jessica was not like most women, though, and now she was mad!

Clutching the pepper spray in her hand, she slipped back to the front of the house, where she retrieved a thirty-six-inch aluminum baseball bat from the coat closet. She returned to her office and saw the intruder at the sliding glass door, apparently working with small tools to pick the lock. She moved to a position behind the pantry door next to the outside door. With pepper spray in one hand and a bat in the other, her heart beat fast.

The man concentrated on the door handle, holding a small flashlight between his teeth. He seemed unconcerned about his tools' soft tinkling noises.

After several minutes, he slowly began to slide the door open. When it had opened about an inch, he stopped and put his ear near the opening to listen, probably for an inside alarm. Hearing none, he stepped back and slid the door wide enough to pass through it. Jessica tensed, now only about four feet away from the man. The room's only light came from his small directional flashlight and the soft glow from the adjoining den's lamp. Jessica planned to wait a few more seconds, but when the intruder pointed his flashlight toward her hiding place next to the pantry, she reacted instinctively.

Bringing the container of pepper spray up, she pointed it above the flashlight beam and pressed the release button. The intruder immediately yelped and dropped the light, moving both hands to his face. Jessica advanced toward him, continuing to release the pepper spray, arcing her arm around slightly to ensure maximum mist coverage. The man screamed now, not in surprise but from pain. He attempted to go back through the sliding door but, temporarily blinded, couldn't find the handle. Dropping the pepper spray bottle and using both hands, Jessica swung the bat wildly in the dark at an area she hoped might contain the intruder's head. The bat connected solidly with something, and the man's screaming stopped at about the same time. Jessica stood in place for a few seconds, listening and afraid to move. Hearing nothing, she reached over to the pantry wall and turned on the lights for the living room.

On the floor next to the sliding glass door lay a man who Jessica hoped wasn't dead. Fear suddenly caused her body to tremble uncontrollably. After standing still for nearly a minute, she approached the sprawled body—tentatively, and with the aluminum bat in her grasp. The man didn't move, and Jessica stooped to feel his neck for a pulse. She exhaled in relief when her fingers picked up the steady beat of blood. A large bruise on his forehead was already turning purple against the man's black skin.

Now thinking more calmly, she retrieved a roll of silver duct tape from the utility drawer in the kitchen and secured the man's arms and legs. While she did this, she sensed a vibration coming from one of the man's trouser pockets and realized the man was receiving a cell phone call. She considered retrieving the phone but decided she shouldn't. After a few seconds, the vibrating stopped, and Jessica picked up her cell to make a call.

"T, you need to get home right away!"

———

As Denton entered the front door, Jessica called to him from the back of the living room. He raced there and found a scared and shaken wife holding a baseball bat over a body lying on the floor.

"Oh my God, Jessica! What happened?" said Denton as he embraced his wife.

Still trembling, Jessica gave her husband the abridged summary of her evening. Denton knelt next to the body and felt the man's temple for a pulse when she finished.

"Heartbeat's good," he said. "He's just unconscious. Is this where you hit him?" He pointed to the bruise on the man's forehead.

"Yes, I think so, but honestly, it was dark, and I swung the bat blindly at a place where I thought his head might be. I only knew I connected when the bat stopped moving."

"Wow!" said Denton. "This guy's lucky to be alive, then. Did you say you hit him twenty or thirty minutes ago?"

"Yes, about that. I called you right after I put the duct tape on him."

"He looks pretty well wrapped. I'm glad we had enough tape."

"Yeah, well, we're out of it now," said Jessica.

"Did you call anyone else? Like 911?"

"No, T," answered Jessica with a hint of attitude. "I called the only policeman I needed to call."

"Right. You did the smart thing. Nobody could get here faster than me, and this gives us a few more minutes before we need to call other officers to the scene. Do we have any ammonia or smelling salts?"

"Smelling salts?" she exclaimed. "I don't even know what that is. I have some ammonia in our first aid kit, though."

"Okay. Ammonia will work. Bring me some, and let's try to wake this guy up."

Denton held the cotton soaked in ammonia near the unconscious man's nose, and after ten to twelve seconds, the man's eyelids fluttered. A few seconds later, he gasped, coughed, and started to regain consciousness. When the stranger opened his eyes, he reacted violently, trying to move—an action made difficult by the three-hundred-pound man sitting on top of him. Confused and frightened, he finally asked, "Where the fuck am I? What happened? Oh, Jesus! My head hurts! What's going on? What did you do to me?"

"Sorry, mister, but I'll ask the questions for a bit," said Denton. "You currently lie inside the back door of the home of Denton and Jessica Jones. You broke into this house and collided with a baseball bat held by Mrs. Jones, and you're fortunate you aren't dead. Now, what is your name, and why are you here?"

The relatively small Black man listened and started to absorb his surroundings. "Yeah, I'm starting to remember now. Look, this was just a mistake. I thought my girlfriend lived here, and I forgot my keys. When it looked like she wasn't home, I decided to come in the back and wait for her inside."

"Really?" said Denton. "What's your girlfriend's name?"

"Uh, oh, well, Sylvia Drake. That's her name. You mean she don't live here?"

"Nope," said Denton. "What's her address?"

"Well, I thought it was this one," said the man.

"Really? And since you said you forgot the keys to her house, you must have visited your girlfriend at her home before?"

"Well, maybe I got confused. I'm not sure."

"T," said Jessica, "he received a cell phone call right after I hit him. I didn't want to touch his phone, but it's in his right front trouser pocket."

"Go bring me a plastic baggie from the kitchen."

"Now, you wait a minute," said the intruder. "I don't want you touching any of my private shit."

"That so?" answered Denton. "I'm a police officer, and you're a criminal who just broke into my home. Your rights are understandably minimal."

When Jessica returned with the baggie, Denton slipped it over his hand and retrieved the stranger's cell phone. While he still had the baggie on, Denton checked the man's other trouser pocket and pulled out a small, .38 caliber, snub-nosed pistol.

"Well, well, you escalated from simple breaking and entering, a misdemeanor, to breaking and entering with a firearm. If this gun is loaded, you're up to a felony." Denton checked the revolver's chambers and, discovering them full, said, "Congratulations! You did it! If you weren't before, you are now a felon."

Denton put the gun on the living room table and refocused on the cell phone. Sure enough, the screen showed a missed call, and Denton recognized the number. He hit redial. On the second ring, someone answered.

"Shorty Roland, where the hell are you, and what's going on? I called you over thirty minutes ago!" said the irritated voice on the other end of the line.

"Hello, Mr. Roberson. Denton Jones here. Did you say the man on the floor of my living room is Shorty Roland?"

"What the . . . what's going on? How did you get this number? I don't know what you're talking about!" said a frantic Charles Roberson.

"Thank you," Denton said. "You gave me what I need for now. I'm sure we'll talk again later." Denton ended the call and placed the phone back in the stranger's pocket. The man on the floor, now presumed to be Shorty Roland, remained quiet, and Denton asked Jessica to call 911. While she did that, Denton called Chief Fitzpatrick's cell phone number. After a short conversation, he returned to the man on the floor.

"Okay, Mr. Roland," said Denton, "we now know your identity and who you work for. The police will arrive in about ten minutes, and they'll take you into custody for further questioning. Before you go, though, I'd like you to answer some questions for me."

"I ain't telling you shit."

"Okay," said Denton. "Have it your way. Perhaps you'd rather talk to my wife while I use the bathroom? She's somewhat upset with you."

Jessica approached the prone man, and Denton winked at her while handing her the empty canister of pepper spray he found on the floor. Shorty's eyes widened, and he started yelling, "Hold up there. Hold up! What you think you doin'? That bitch is crazy! You can't leave me alone with her and that pepper spray. She gonna hurt me."

Denton stopped momentarily and looked knowingly at his wife. "Shorty, you might be right about that. She's pretty mad at you, with good reason, I think, but here's the thing. I have sort of a weak stomach and don't think I want to witness what she might do to you." At that, Jessica gave her most sinister smile as she stalked toward the intruder.

"Okay, okay. What you wanna know? But keep that bitch away from me!"

Denton smiled, got his cell phone out, and touched the record button. He then asked a series of questions, which Shorty Roland answered reluctantly. The doorbell rang almost on cue with Shorty's final reply. Jessica answered, and two uniformed patrolmen entered to take Roland into custody. Denton provided the officers with some information, gave them Shorty's revolver, and asked them to notify him after Roland's interrogation.

When the officers left with Roland, Jessica hugged her husband and asked, "Is it over now?"

"I think we're out of immediate danger," said Denton, "but we're going to have to work fast to find out what else Roberson might know. That's why I needed some quick answers from Roland before the officers took him downtown. Nothing he told me here can be used in court, but hopefully he won't change his answers at the station. No matter—he gave me what I need to corral Roberson this evening. I already talked to Fitzpatrick, and sorry, honey, but I have to leave again. Will you be okay?"

"I have my aluminum bat and an empty canister of pepper spray. What more would I need?" she said, smiling.

"*And* that evil smile you showed Roland. I hope I never see you look at me that way."

"Yes, T," she said sweetly. "You *should* hope you never do."

"I'll be back as soon as I can."

CHAPTER 26

As Denton got into his car to head back to the Marriott, his cell phone vibrated.

"Hey, Colonel," said Denton. "What's up?"

"Roberson left the function in a hurry about ten minutes ago, and I followed him. He appears to be heading home."

"He lives on Riverside, right? What's your plan?"

"I'm making it up as I go," said Fitzpatrick. "For the time being, I'm planning to follow him loosely and see what he does next."

"He may just hole up there and start calling attorneys. He's going to need them."

"He'll need more than attorneys. I would prefer to talk to him before lawyers do, but I'm not sure exactly how to accomplish that."

"Well, wait until I get there. I made a recording with his perp that might be useful," said Denton.

"Okay. I didn't plan to confront Roberson before he got into his house. I worried that he might head straight to the airport."

"Maybe not the worst idea he ever had."

"Agree," said Fitzpatrick. "Buzz me when you're on Saluda Street, and I'll tell you where I'm parked."

When Denton pulled in behind Colonel Fitzpatrick's car, the chief got out and entered the passenger side of Denton's car. "Roberson knows my car. Let's use yours if we need to follow him."

"That's fine, Chief, but if he comes out the door looking like he's going to leave, I don't think we should let him."

"Probably right. Let's pull up across the street."

After about ten minutes, Roberson and his wife, Carmen, came out the front door, heading toward their car. They each had a suitcase and a duffel bag. Chief Fitzpatrick and Denton got out of Denton's car and casually walked up the sidewalk.

"Evening, Charles," said Fitzpatrick. "Planning on going somewhere this evening?"

"None of your business, Chief," answered Roberson. "What are you two doing in my driveway?"

"Charles," said Fitzpatrick, "I think you know the answer to that question. Would you like to discuss it inside or out here?"

Roberson's wife, looking uncomfortable, demanded, "Charlie, what the hell's going on? Why are the chief of police and Commander Jones in our driveway? And why is it necessary for us to go to the airport?"

"Carmen, let's not discuss this now. Just go back inside for a few minutes. I'll handle this."

Carmen left her suitcase on the sidewalk. When she disappeared inside, Roberson tried one more act of bravado. "I'm not sure what this concerns," he said, "but you embarrassed me in front of my wife. Now leave my property!"

Fitzpatrick turned to Denton and said, "Looks like I was wrong, Commander Jones. Mr. Roberson doesn't want to talk to us. Go ahead and call the squad car."

As Denton faked a call on his cell phone, Chief Fitzpatrick began to recite the Miranda rights: "Charles Roberson, you have the right to remain silent—"

"Wait a second, wait a second! Don't make that call yet," Roberson yelled.

Denton told the imaginary person on his phone to hold for a moment.

"What do you want to talk about?" asked Roberson.

"You're in a lot of trouble, Charles," said Fitzpatrick. "We have the person you hired to break into Commander Jones's home in custody and under interrogation downtown as we speak. He already told Denton about your involvement, which Denton recorded. At a minimum, you're an accessory to a serious felony, and we think you're involved in other more serious crimes that we will actively investigate."

"What do you want if you think you know all those things?" asked Roberson.

"We'd like to talk to you about your potential cooperation relative to your knowledge of larger crimes against the city," said Fitzpatrick. "We can promise you nothing this evening other than the delay of a public and embarrassing arrest tonight. Your cooperation tomorrow morning with the mayor, myself, and the acting city solicitor will determine what happens after that."

"It's Saturday night, Jack," said Roberson. "Can this meeting wait until Monday morning?"

"No," answered Fitzpatrick.

"Can I at least talk to my wife about this inside before giving you an answer?" asked Roberson.

"No, Charles, you can't. We require your decision now," said Fitzpatrick. The chief then looked at Denton and asked, "Do you carry cuffs in your vehicle, Commander Jones?"

"Yes, Colonel. I'll get them."

"Never mind," said an angry Roberson. "I'll take the meeting tomorrow. What time?"

"Ten o'clock at my office," said Fitzpatrick. "For this meeting, you'll come alone. We make this accommodation as a courtesy to you, and the meeting will be both private and confidential. If you bring legal representation with you, the meeting's no longer private. At that point, our only alternative is to arrest you and place charges before further discussions. Do you understand?"

"Yes."

"Good," finished Fitzpatrick. "Commander Jones, for the safety of Mr. and Mrs. Roberson, I believe we should staff a patrol car here for the evening."

"Yes, sir. I'll call one in."

"Goodnight, Mr. Roberson," said Fitzpatrick. Roberson turned and left without responding.

After Roberson entered his home, Denton asked Fitzpatrick, "How much of what you told Roberson is in the works? Did you call Mayor Guzman about the meeting?"

"No," Fitzpatrick admitted. "I was operating completely on the fly. I'll call the mayor and Gunnells, and I'm certain they'll make time for the meeting. I feared if we arrested Roberson tonight, he would lawyer up and then clam up. He still might, but if he doesn't, we may have a small window to learn some things we might not otherwise."

"What do you think the mayor and the city solicitor will offer him?"

"Not a clue," replied Fitzpatrick, "but we should contact both right away to make them aware of what we've gotten them into. I'll make those calls. You radio the squad car to watch the house."

When Denton arranged for the surveillance, he returned to Chief Fitzpatrick's vehicle. Fitzpatrick ended his call and said, "We're meeting the mayor and Gunnells back at the Marriott now. They'll arrange for a private conference room. I think Jim Hargrove may also come in."

"Okay," said Denton. "I'll head there after the squad car arrives."

———

City Manager Haley Doolittle joined Mayor Guzman, Fred Gunnells, Chief Fitzpatrick, and Denton for the Marriott meeting. City Solicitor Jim Hargrove arrived for the last hour. By the time the group parted, well after midnight, all believed they had a game plan for the next day's discussions with Roberson.

———

When Assistant City Manager Charles Roberson walked into the chief of police's private conference room on Sunday morning, about fifteen minutes late, he saw the chief, the mayor, the city manager, the acting city solicitor, and Commander Jones seated at the table. Only one chair, at the end of the table, remained unfilled. Without greeting those present, Roberson went to the unoccupied seat. He avoided eye contact with anyone and pulled a yellow pad and a pen from the briefcase he brought with him.

Mayor Guzman started the meeting. "Gentlemen, it's ten fifteen, and I will open by saying our discussions this morning are unofficial and confidential. We will not record anything or otherwise publicly disclose our comments or opinions. Our purpose is to determine the disposition of potential charges against a high-ranking official of the city, Mr. Charles Roberson."

The mayor stopped talking and glanced around the table. She briefly put her head down, then raised it, glaring at Roberson, who could not hold her stare. "Charles," she said, "it goes without saying how disappointed— no, how *disgusted* I am with you. You betrayed everyone in this room, and your community, by what you did last evening. More seriously, we have evidence that you may have been disloyal to this city for many years. Based on what I now understand, I opposed offering leniency and would have pursued the maximum possible punishment for your actions. However, others here counseled that you may assist our efforts in stopping even more dangerous activity. Mr. Gunnells, would you care to explain Mr. Roberson's current options?"

"Yes, ma'am," said Gunnells, appearing nearly as irritated as the mayor. "Today, Mr. Roberson, we can charge you with accessory to breaking and entering with an armed weapon. Our evidence is sufficient, and your partner confessed to both his role in the crime and yours. The maximum sentence for an accessory is half that awarded the felon committing the actual breaking and entering. Mr. Roland's maximum sentence will be twenty years, so yours could be ten. I promise you'll serve all ten years, with no eligibility for parole, and that your incarceration will begin at once if you decline the offer made this morning. Do you understand so far?"

"Yes, Mr. Gunnells, but am I not allowed representation here by an attorney?"

"Yes, sir, you have that right during any discussions relating to crimes for which you are charged," said Gunnells. "No charges have been filed yet. If you desire legal representation, we'll conclude this unofficial and confidential meeting. You'll then be notified of your Miranda rights and arrested. After that, Chief Fitzpatrick will take you to a holding facility downstairs to await transfer to the city jail, where you may meet with an attorney. Once you're charged, we'll no longer consider other options for leniency, and the city will aggressively pursue both the current charges relative to accessory and potentially the other charges involving corruption."

Gunnells stopped and glared at Roberson, and Roberson somewhat defiantly returned the stare. "You're conducting a totally illegal railroad job!"

"No," said Gunnells, "we are not! You voluntarily chose to attend this meeting last evening. It earned you an additional evening of freedom—which may end soon. To this point, the meeting has been unofficial and off the record, but we'll go on record anytime you wish after you're booked. Would you still like to call an attorney?"

"Yes, I would," said Roberson.

"Okay then," said Mayor Guzman. "I'm sorry I troubled everyone this morning. We can conclude this meeting. Chief, you may take Mr. Roberson into custody."

"Whoa, whoa!" said Roberson. "You just said I could call an attorney."

"Yes, Mr. Roberson," said Gunnells, "I did. Before that, I explained to you in detail when that could be—which, to reiterate, is after you're arrested."

"Fine, fine. Goddammit! What do you want from me? What do I have to do?"

"We want your full and honest cooperation into the investigation of corruption in the city," said Gunnells. "We request that you provide evidence helpful in the apprehension of certain crime figures in this community as well as full disclosure of your illegal activities in the city for the past thirty years. If we receive your cooperation in these three matters, the charge against your partner will be reduced to simple breaking and entering, with a jail sentence of one year. Your sentence as an accessory would then amount to six months, which we would suspend, pending your continued cooperation. We will seal these legal actions and not disclose them to the public. Additionally, we would further agree to suspend legal remedies for other unlawful activities in which you participated discovered as a result of your cooperation."

"How do I know you'll keep your word?" asked Roberson.

"Because we prepared a legal draft, from you to the city, for your consideration. The document stipulates what we must do in return for your cooperation. If we sign this document, federal anti-crime statutes mandate that we adhere to the provisions."

"You've done a lot of work in twelve hours," commented Roberson. "May I have an attorney at least look at the document you propose?"

"Yes," said Gunnells, "but again, that would take place *after* an arrest. All the stipulations and provisions would still apply, but you would first be officially arrested and charged. If we agree to the document's requirements now, you would not be publicly charged but placed under house arrest with nothing more than an ankle bracelet to monitor your movements."

"Clever," said Roberson. "So, basically, my choices consist of leaving this meeting in handcuffs, or not?"

"Yes, Mr. Roberson," said Mayor Guzman, "and I can tell you the 'or not' part disgusts every person at this table except you. While we may not get the information we want if you choose not to accept our offer, I would personally prefer to see you leave here in handcuffs. I doubt anybody at this table believes you deserve the leniency of our proposal."

Roberson put his head down on one hand and thought for a few moments. When he raised his head, tears filled his eyes. "Mayor Guzman, I'm sorry you feel that way. I made mistakes and am ashamed, but there is much none of you currently understand. Allow me to read the document, and I'll give you a decision."

The group gave Roberson the room to himself, and Chief Fitzpatrick told him to dial eight on the phone on the conference table when he was ready to reconvene. Fitzpatrick's intercom light blinked almost thirty minutes later.

When all had settled around the conference table, Roberson spoke, referring to notes he had made on his legal pad. "I can comply with everything in this document with two exceptions. I want to change the period of activities you review. This document details thirty years; I propose a revision to twenty years. I would also like to stipulate that my assistance precludes the necessity of providing specific names. In other words, I will provide information on dates, procedures, activities, and processes involving illegal or unethical activities to the extent I can. Still, I will not implicate specific people, either inside or outside of this organization."

Gunnells reacted first. "We might accommodate the time revision, but your second request troubles me. The whole reason for this potential and, I might add, extraordinary leniency is to help our administration apprehend criminals. Allowing you to keep names confidential defeats the purpose."

"But if I inform you about dates, procedures, processes, leaks, and voids in security systems, you have the means to investigate past crimes better and prevent future ones. Giving you names equates to a death sentence, not just for me but also for my family. And the execution would occur whether I was incarcerated or free. Providing names simply isn't a viable option for me."

Chief Fitzpatrick said, "Roberson, step outside for a few minutes, and let us discuss your counter."

When Roberson left the room, Gunnells asked Fitzpatrick, "Why do you think he wants to reduce the time period?"

"Most likely to get any involvement with Julian Stenson's sudden departure off the table. You'll recall that during an Internal Audit investigation ordered by Roberson, Commander Jones surprised Roberson by identifying Stenson, a drug dealer known on the streets as the Whistler, as Roberson's brother-in-law. Stenson disappeared a long time ago, and Roberson possibly had something to do with that. No statute of limitation exists for murder. I don't have a problem shortening the time frame for the deal with Roberson because I'm not interested in Stenson. Nobody else was when he went missing either."

"What about the name thing?" Mayor Guzman asked.

"That one bothers me a little more," said the chief, "but I'm not sure we have the leverage to negotiate. Frankly, I'm more interested in *how* he's helped than who he's helped. I can't figure out the former and think I already know the latter. Even if Roberson were to implicate Jackson, finding corroborating evidence might be difficult, if not impossible. Jackson's ability to cover his trail defies the odds of logic."

"I think you're right," said Gunnells. "We have an opportunity to learn when and how someone breached our systems for over twenty years. If Roberson gives us enough information, we may still find evidence that ties back to Jackson. I'd vote to accept his changes."

"Any opposed?" asked the mayor. "Hearing none, let's bring Roberson back in."

———

When the meeting resumed, Fred Gunnells reviewed changes to the document. The proposed new agreement provided Roberson the same leniency for his cooperation, except for the requirement to provide specific names. It also precluded investigation into events that may have occurred over twenty years prior. When Roberson signed the paper, he turned to Fitzpatrick.

"Chief, it's in the city's interests, my interests, and the interests of specific people at this table that I access the home computers of Denton Jones immediately."

"Excuse me?" asked Fitzpatrick.

"You are already aware Shorty Roland attempted to break into the Jones home at my request. The idiot wasn't supposed to be armed, and he had no intention of harming either Mr. or Mrs. Jones. His sole mission was to retrieve any computers found in the house."

"Can you tell us why?" asked Mayor Guzman.

"You'll understand that when I can access the computers," answered

Roberson. "Nobody outside of this room currently knows my status with the city as a government witness, so the sooner I can do this, the better. Until I execute a command on one of the Joneses' computers, their lives, my life, and the lives of my family are in danger."

"Does this have to do with Theo Jackson?" asked Gunnells.

"Your legal document stipulates I'm not obligated to provide specific names," answered Roberson. "In this case, I will make an exception. The issue with the Joneses' computers has nothing to do with Mr. Jackson."

"Okay," said Denton. "Must we bring the computers to you, or can you make the necessary adjustments at our house?"

"Either would work, but I suggest you bring the computers to my office. The wrong people might become suspicious if someone saw me visiting your home. If you have more than one computer, I'm certain it is Mrs. Jones's computer that contains the information I must delete."

"We own two," said Denton. "I'll bring hers to your office right after this meeting."

———

Fred Gunnells, Chief Fitzpatrick, Jessica Jones, and Denton watched Roberson boot up Jessica's personal computer two hours later. Roberson said nothing but allowed all in the room to watch him work. When he entered the *Find Stryker* command, Jessica noted the files highlighted.

"Those are the forms for the antenna tower permit on Victory Parkway," she said. "Denton wanted some history on the sale of that building, and I asked Jaden to pull any information he could find. In the process, he discovered the tower permit lacked some information. He called the owner, who seemed irritated but sent a file of the permit to download. Jaden used the file to update the city's servers and brought me a copy on a flash drive. I reviewed the licensing and tax information but never opened the file containing the tower permit information. What makes it so important?"

"You may judge for yourself by comparing the file that currently exists on your computer to the one that will remain when I execute the requested command," said Roberson. "The extra bits of computer coding in the download delete parts of the file, not all of it, when I provide a specified command. Until then, the coding acts as a beacon, identifying its location whenever the host computer connects to the internet."

"A beacon for whom?" asked Fitzpatrick.

"Per my legal agreement, I won't provide that information, Chief. However, by noting which files the changes impact, I think you can figure that out. I can't emphasize enough that deleting the specified files only protects myself and others from danger *if* my cooperation remains confidential."

"We understand," said Gunnells. "The only people privy to our agreement, or even to the circumstances surrounding our discussions of last evening and today, attended the meeting with you yesterday, plus City Solicitor Hargrove. Your associate who broke into the Joneses' home isn't aware of your status with us."

Jessica stopped Roberson before he could initiate further activity on her desktop. "Chief," she asked, "can we connect the desktop to a printer? I want to make a hard copy of the files Mr. Roberson accesses before he executes the command to delete portions."

"Certainly," answered the chief. "Just give me a second."

"Wouldn't we already have hard copies of these records in our files for the permit?" asked Gunnells.

"We should," answered Jessica. "Someone so concerned to delete the digital files, however, might already have ensured the destruction of paper files as well. Also, as I examine the files displayed here on the computer, they appear to be documentation provided to the FCC, relating to a bond required for satellite communications infrastructure. As it relates to antennae tower placements, our role in the city is to ensure compliance with commercial zoning codes and applicable environmental ordinances for the structure and placement. We only ask potential permittees to prove that the FCC approved the use of equipment attached to the tower. If we see a check in the box from the FCC, I'm not a hundred percent sure we would file information as obscure as the name of a banking entity backing a federally-required bond."

"That might be the case, but we probably need to tighten our record keeping," said Gunnells. "Go ahead and print off the information on the FCC permit."

When Jessica and Gunnells compared the printed before and after documents, they were nearly identical. "Look at this," said Jessica. "In a complicated document containing over two hundred lines of information, mostly boilerplate, the second document—the one printed after Roberson executed the *Find Stryker* command—lacks only three lines from the original. Right here, under the block *Satellite Communications Infrastructure Bond Issued*. The block is clearly checked, but the original document contains several lines under that, listing the business entity to whom the bond was issued, the bond's amount, and the banking entity securing the bond. Those lines don't appear on the new document, and unless you knew what to look for, I doubt you would miss them."

"Does anyone know anything about Jet Sun Capital out of Newark, New Jersey? Roberson?" Gunnells asked.

"No. Nothing," said Roberson. "I only know someone didn't want this information on file."

"I'll do some research," said Jessica. "We can also call the International Fidelity First Bank in the Caymans about the bond. I doubt we'll get much from them, though. International offshore banks generally don't accommodate enforcement in matters like this."

"What are we dealing with here, Roberson?" asked Chief Fitzpatrick. "You must have some idea, and whoever it is, they've scared you enough to do some crazy things at this point in your career and life."

"If I knew the answer to that question, Chief, I would surely tell you—because you're right. I'm terrified. These aren't small-time hoodlums."

The chief stared at Roberson, then looked at each of the other three individuals in the room. "Mother of God!" he said. "When we finished our conversation last night, I felt relieved that we possibly closed the book on a long, bad nightmare for our city. Now it seems we might have just opened one."

CHAPTER 27

Jessica arrived home before Denton and waited for him in the den. As he came through the door, he was relieved and surprised to see a glass of red wine waiting for him on the coffee table. Jessica had also prepared a small plate of cheese and raw vegetables.

"Are we celebrating?"

"Hardly," his wife replied. "We're getting fortified for round two, but first, tell me what you're thinking."

Denton sat on the couch next to his wife, sipping the wine before he spoke. Relaxing back into the sofa's cushion, he said, "This tastes good. Thank you. I intended to ask you the same thing, but as usual, you're a step ahead of me."

"Sorry. But you go first."

"Okay. I feel completely bushwhacked. I'm so proud of my investigative skills and that sixth sense that's supposed to warn me of danger, but I've been operating in the wrong universe relative to Roberson. All this time, I thought Roberson tried to hurt my credibility because he suspected I might know something about him helping Jackson—and that wasn't it at all! I feel a little stupid."

"Well, don't beat yourself up too much. I think he *has* helped Jackson for a long time, but our problems with Roberson started because of a stupid little file I asked Jaden to get. That's my fault, not yours."

"How do you figure that? I'm the one who asked you to look into Yi's licensing and permits."

"Right, and instead of doing it myself, I assigned the summer intern. When Jaden received the file and brought it out here, I didn't even open everything in it. Instead of researching something important, I foolishly stayed busy finding information to support my own theories. We did just what we warned each other not to do."

"J, we were wrong about Roberson's agenda, but I believe we followed the most logical clues. Theo Jackson told us early on that we wouldn't uncover anything connecting him to Roberson. The warnings seemed self-serving at the time, and neither of us felt we could trust him. How could we have guessed this all started because of some missing information on an ancient antenna permit?"

"But where do we go from here? I still can't understand why Roberson drove the Internal Audit investigations against you. What would that have to do with Yi?"

"I haven't figured that out either," answered Denton. "When Yi bought the building, Theo became upset that zoning restrictions were changed to accommodate Yi. Maybe Roberson feared that Theo wanted to retaliate against him for assisting Yi and hoped the Internal Audit discoveries might eliminate further communications between Theo and me. I think Theo knows more about Yi than he told me."

"Why?"

"Remember when Theo warned me to get a good security system for the house? Well, that happened right after I accused him of causing the Internal Audit interview. He said he had nothing to do with that, but he *did* believe I had a reason for concern. He alluded to a proposition he received from someone that involved us. He confirmed he'd have nothing to do with anything that would hurt you or me, but he cautioned that other nefarious organizations existed in the area that might."

"Right, and you assumed it was Roberson who tried to recruit Theo."

"That seemed logical, but perhaps Yi approached Theo, or Yi tried to recruit someone in Jackson's organization. Either way, Theo worried enough to make me go online that day to get our security system."

"So, we're in sort of the same place as the city. We thought once we caught Roberson, we solved our problem. As it turns out, Roberson was only a part of the problem—and maybe the smaller part," said Jessica.

"Unfortunately, I think you're correct. I believe it's time for another short conversation with Theo."

———

"I understand the predicament, Denton, and hesitate to offer my advice because I believe you will think it self-serving," said Theo.

"Try me," answered Denton.

"Okay. You discovered a rat in your organization, and the man tried to hurt you professionally. If the same thing happened to me, I'd have difficulty concentrating on anything but vengeance and justice."

When Theo didn't continue, Denton asked him, "And you think I should react differently? The man didn't just try to hurt my career. He sent a thug to my house who threatened my family."

"I'm not telling you how you should react, but I hope you'll consider why I think Roberson may not be the city's top priority right now. He initiated a regrettable and stupid incident at your house, but you told me Roberson didn't intend to harm anyone physically. He wanted his good-for-nothing gopher to retrieve a computer from your home at a time he presumed neither you nor Jessica would be there. Roberson had no idea the idiot would carry a gun with him. I understand your outrage and agree that both Roberson and his accomplice deserve to spend time in jail, but you and the city already bartered away that chip for a chance to catch a bigger fish."

"And you don't think we should have done that?"

"I understand your choice under the circumstances—and with the limited knowledge you have about Roberson's prior connections with other criminals. If a chance exists to solve bigger problems by making concessions with Roberson, you should. I'm trying to tell you, though, that if the city believes I'm the bigger problem, people will waste valuable time in the research. If I ever received favors from Roberson—and I emphasize *if*—I'm smart enough not to leave a trail. Trust me, Denton. Roberson *can't* help the city relative to me, but he may prove valuable in other ways. I'm certain he's now well motivated to assist with a problem that also presents a tremendous danger to himself and his family."

"Jesus, Theo. That *does* sound self-serving. I'm still listening, though."

"The information I gave you earlier about Sun Yi and what you heard a couple of weeks ago in the meeting with Burns and O'Dowd *is* real. You also now know Yi applied pressure on Roberson to instigate the attack on your home. I've done enough research to understand Yi isn't a simple criminal with a few fake businesses. A large organization backs him. I'm certain of that, and after the meeting you attended at the church, I believe you also have a strong suspicion about that organization, don't you?"

"Santu?"

"Yes."

Theo left his desk for his administrative assistant's area outside the door. When he returned, he had a small binder in one hand and a USB drive in the other.

"I had Teresa put together some information I hope you'll review. The drive contains the video I mentioned in our meeting with Father O'Dowd and Pastor Burns. I apologize in advance for the video's content, and you will not need to view the entire thing. I hope you won't."

Denton accepted the two packages, and Theo continued.

"I'm at a point in my research that I can do little more by myself. I don't have the resources or the necessary authority to address criminal activity of this nature or magnitude. Cincinnati doesn't either, Denton. This problem will require assistance from the federal government, and I'm not exactly able to request that. We need help, though, and fast. Burns told us he can access some resources, but we need to start getting organized.

"Yi is part of one of the largest and most dangerous criminal organizations in the world. I appreciate the city's outrage with things Charles Roberson might have done over the past twenty years, but that's history. Those things can't be undone, and your current and future problems are potentially more serious. The time to figure out who the last person to leave the toilet seat up isn't when somebody's about to come through the front door with a bomb."

"I hear you. I'll look this stuff over and get back to you."

"Thank you. We need to bring Chief Fitzpatrick into the next meeting with O'Dowd and Burns—and Denton, don't show Jessica the video on the flash drive. It's too disgusting."

"Okay. Thanks."

CHAPTER 28

"Theo," said Teresa over the intercom. "Reggie Lincoln's here to see you."

"Thank you. Send him in."

Reggie Lincoln was one of four managers in Theo Jackson's "retail" operations. Each of these men had defined areas of responsibilities, and Jackson trusted all four implicitly. No job descriptions or employment contracts existed in Jackson's organization, but everyone knew what they were to do and when to do it.

All managers owned and operated a full-service, legitimate small business in the community. Jackson established these for the four and insisted each manager provide hands-on and engaged oversight. While none of Jackson's lieutenants possessed college degrees, all had an excellent knowledge of general business practices and expertise in the QuickBooks accounting platform. Jackson believed the skills and discipline required to operate a successful small business honed the similar ones needed to handle other parts of his larger enterprise's delicate matters.

The privately owned shops and stores also created safe retirement plans for his key people. Jackson stipulated that their work in the less politically correct parts of his operations was voluntary. Managers could leave those responsibilities at any time, but while they participated, they understood Jackson exercised complete control.

"Hey, Theo," said Lincoln. "What's up? It's unusual for any of us to meet in this building."

"True, Reggie, but my concern couldn't wait, and I thought it important enough to risk less discretion than usual."

"Since I'm the only one here, the issue must relate to me."

"It does. Several weeks ago, we discussed one of your larger customers, and I told you I wanted no more deliveries to him. Did you follow my directive?"

Lincoln squirmed in obvious discomfort, avoiding Jackson's eyes. "I'm sorry, Theo. I made another delivery last week. Can I explain why, though?"

"Go ahead."

"Forget that Yi ranks as my biggest customer in the city. I think he's also dangerous. He scared me. He reacted aggressively when I informed him I could deliver no more product and threatened to expose me."

"How could he do that? You're using an intermediary in your dealings with Yi, aren't you?"

"Up until a few months ago I did. When his account became so large, I decided I should handle it personally."

Theo dropped his head into his hands and stared at the desk before responding. "Reggie, not only did you violate an order, you broke one of our strictest rules. I don't require key people to use lower-tier intermediaries because I don't trust them. That requirement protects you. How much does Yi know?"

"Nothing more than my name. I provide him the telephone number of my burner phone for him to place orders."

"If he knows your name, don't you think he's smart enough to find your address or discover that you own the Burger Barn?"

"I guess so, but I always figured with all the purchases he makes, I have a lot more on him than he would ever get on me. I never imagined Yi would be bold enough to threaten me."

"Jesus, Reggie! You need to close shop here and find a new place to live. I'm not sure what else to tell you except that I hope you learned a lesson—and that it isn't the last lesson you ever learn in life."

"What?" exclaimed Lincoln. "You're firing me for one mistake? Come on, Theo! Our friendship goes back a long way, and I've helped you a lot."

"This isn't baseball, where you're allowed three strikes. This is life, and I'm not firing you for a mistake. I'm trying to protect you. I'll buy the Burger Barn, which will provide plenty of money for you to establish yourself someplace far from here."

Lincoln sat in shock, speechless. Finally, he said, "Theo, again, I'm sorry. I'll do what you ask, but this seems like an overreaction to me. Why wouldn't we just keep providing Yi the product he wants? He'd be happy then, and we'd be richer. Everybody wins."

Jackson slapped the desk and responded to Lincoln sharply. "No, everybody doesn't win, idiot! Yi uses the product we provide in ways I disapprove. My role is to tell you what to do, and your role is to follow instructions. You blew your cover to Yi, which means he has a tunnel into our business *and to me*. If he desired, he could even provide information to law enforcement. That makes you vulnerable. Correction—that makes *us* vulnerable. You have a valid reason for concern. If you don't disappear from this community, Yi might accomplish it for you, and his way might include leaving little pieces of your body scattered all over Cincinnati."

"Holy hell! What did I step into?" asked Lincoln.

"Nothing good, and it's something bigger than *our* organization. Quit while you're ahead and get out of here. That's the last advice I'm going to give you."

"Okay. I'll do what you ask. Thanks . . . I guess."

"You're welcome, Reggie. I'm sorry we had to part this way. I'd appreciate one last favor from you if you're willing."

"Sure, Theo."

"The name and address of the contact who provided you the disgusting video from Yi's video store."

"Okay, but he doesn't know anything about you. He only thinks I'm interested in joining the same depraved club he's in. He asked me last week if I'd return the DVD he loaned me."

"Returning the DVD isn't possible anymore. Don't worry about it. I'll explain all that to him when I talk to him."

"His name is Soloman Stubbs, and he goes by Sol. He owns some vending machine routes and lives in a nice house over on Robin Hood. I'm not sure of the street address, but he owns the large A-frame at the end of Robin Hood Court."

"Married? Family?"

"Divorced, I think. He lives alone at the house. Terrible poker player."

"Is that how you know him?"

"Yeah, but he's also a customer."

"Okay. Thanks, Reggie. Good luck, and don't take too long to get yourself gone. Yi isn't someone you want to fool with."

———

After Lincoln departed, Theo asked Teresa to bring him parts of the Santu file left by Pastor Burns. He extracted several photos and took them to the copy machine.

"I can make those for you," said Teresa.

"Not these," said Theo. "They're too gross. I don't want you looking at them."

"Oh—then I know which ones they are. Thank you. Why do you need copies of those awful pictures?"

"People say a picture is worth a thousand words, and I'm not going to have much time for words in the next meeting. I'll see you tomorrow morning."

———

On his way to Robin Hood Court, Theo stopped at a nearby Walmart.

Robin Hood Avenue passed through an affluent area of the city north of the hospital, and the court Jackson sought was near the end of a street with many large houses. The A-frame-style house at the back of the circular court stood out, and Jackson drove by it once before parking his vehicle half a block away. As he climbed the short level of steps to Stubbs's front door, Theo pulled on the mask he'd purchased at Walmart.

When Sol Stubbs answered the doorbell, the force of the door opening knocked him backward and to the floor. Looking up, he saw a tall man with a gun who wore a cheap, plastic, department-store clown mask. "What's this about?" Sol demanded. "Who are you? I don't keep any money in the house."

"I'm the Lone Ranger," answered the intruder. "Lost my other mask. Who I am isn't important, Sol. What's important is that I know who you are. Something else you should consider—if I have this mask on, it means you will live through our conversation. If the mask comes off, it means I'm no longer worried about you ever identifying me. Do we understand each other?"

"Yes. What do you want?"

"Two things, and I have little time and zero patience, so don't test me. First, I want the password for admission to the dark website Romper Room."

"Come on. Why that? You can make your own membership application online. The group who runs that site is serious about security, and I don't know what they might do if they found out I let someone else use my password."

"Last warning, Sol. Your answer contained about forty words too many, and I warned you of my limited time and patience. Give me the password now, or I'm going to let you see my face."

"Okay, okay, but the password is long and complicated. You'll never remember it."

"Yes, I will," said the intruder, holding up a cell phone with his left hand. "Speak in this direction."

"Capital letter *V*, five, five, six, exclamation point, dollar sign, small *e*, small *n*, small *d*, small *o*, small *r*, capital letter *C*."

"Good, now let's try it on your computer over there to make sure it works. Do you want to double-check that you got it right before we enter it? If it isn't right, I think you can guess what will happen."

"Oh, let me think—the symbol in the middle might be a question mark instead of an exclamation mark."

"Okay, Sol. Your first lengthy answer was strike one. Your mistake on the password is strike two. What do you suppose happens on strike three?"

"Sorry."

"Go to your computer and access the website."

Once Sol demonstrated the password worked, the intruder told him to close the computer.

"Part two of my request," said Sol's guest, "is a little more complicated and will require trust on both my part and yours. Tomorrow, you'll call Commander Denton Jones at the Cincinnati police force headquarters to request an appointment with him. You'll admit to being the person who provided the password for the Romper Room website. Jones will most likely invite you for an immediate meeting at his headquarters."

"Why would I do that?" asked Stubbs. "You're asking me to turn myself in for some pornography violation."

"Correct, and likely, with the information you could provide, the legal system will offer a reduced sentence, perhaps even immunity. I don't know and don't care. If you decide not to take this course or change your password when I leave, I'll make certain the video store owner becomes aware you provided your old password to law enforcement. By the way, Commander Jones already has the password and probably accumulates the evidence he needs from the Romper Room website as we speak. I sent it anonymously while you checked your computer."

"Jesus Christ!" Stubbs screamed. "I'm not sure what the guy at the video store might do to me, but he's scary. Why are you doing this? Are you police?"

"Far from it. If I were, I couldn't collect evidence in this manner. I'm a much bigger criminal target for Commander Jones than you, so my risks for this visit today are great. As you suspect, the man at the video store *is* dangerous. He works for an international criminal organization called the Santu. I brought a small file of pictures along with me that I'll leave with you. The photos depict victims of people who threatened the Santu, and I apologize for their grisly nature."

"So, my choice is to talk to the police and potentially go to jail, or take my chances with this Santu group?"

"Yes, and I don't care which. You represent the lowest level of human scum to inhabit the earth, and I can't guess how many showers I might need to rid myself of the stink from standing near you for so long. Whatever punishment you might receive from our government will be far less than you deserve, and I have not an ounce of sympathy for whatever grotesque or painful punishment the Santu inflicts on you."

Stubbs dropped his head into his hands. "What the hell did I get into? Why me?"

"I'm not a religious scholar, Stubbs, but if Hell exists, that's exactly what you got into. When you play in the Devil's domain, you must accept the Devil's rules. I'll check with my contact at the city tomorrow to confirm your decision."

"How do I know you'll hold up your end of the deal?"

"You don't, but if you decide to cooperate with enforcement, I gain nothing by exposing you to the Santu. On the other hand, if you choose a different course, I won't lose a minute of sleep worrying about your fate. Goodbye, Sol."

———

When Denton saw that the incoming call to his cell phone originated from an unknown number, he suspected it might be Theo Jackson. "This is Commander Jones."

"Hey, Denton. Theo. Did you get the text a little while ago?"

"Yes. The things I reviewed on the website violate at least two local statutes and probably several federal ones. I plan to review what I found with Chief Fitzpatrick and decide how to proceed. Currently, I'm only aware of the existence of a very dark web pornographic site. I don't have evidence the site has any relationship to people or businesses in my jurisdiction. I'm fairly certain our IT technicians would not be able to determine the owner of the password. You're the one who sent the text, I assume?"

"I can't answer that, Denton," said Theo. "How important is it to know where the tip came from?"

"Not important enough to stop the research."

"Good. I called because a rumor on the street suggests you might receive a call tomorrow from a witness able to provide more information relating to the password. I can't speculate on the accuracy of the information, but I wanted to give you a heads-up."

Denton sighed heavily. "Thank you, Theo—I guess. Something tells me all this relates to Sun Yi, and that bad feeling I get is sounding full alarms."

"I believe you should trust your instincts. Has Roberson's status changed any?"

"You aren't supposed to know about anything to do with Roberson, Theo. I can't answer questions like that."

"Except that I probably know more about Roberson than you do. My concern is Yi, not Roberson. Do you have any reason to believe Yi might suspect you compromised him?"

"No. Yi hasn't communicated with Roberson since Roberson removed the file from Jessica's computer."

"Good. Will Chief Fitzpatrick join the meeting on Thursday evening?"

"Yes. I briefed him on everything, and he plans to attend."

"I'll see you there."

CHAPTER 29

Lucretia ignored the first notice from GlaMore Photography. The invoice listed charges totaling $2,789, including $2,200 from Foxee Modeling for apartment rent, photo sessions, and wardrobe, and $589 from Mr. Yi for her airplane fare from Cincinnati to Las Vegas. A note at the bottom of the bill specified payment due within ten days. After that, penalties, interest, and late charges would accrue. Luci threw the correspondence in the trash as Theo Jackson had advised her to do.

The second notice was more demanding. The total due jumped to $3,789, including a late charge of $1,000. Mr. Yi also warned if she didn't pay the bill promptly and completely, he would place liens on her belongings, including her car. Frightened by these threats, Luci accompanied her aunt to Theo Jackson's office the following day.

Jackson reviewed the bill stoically and asked Teresa to make a copy of it for him. "He's trying to scare you, Luci, but I understand your concern. He can't place a lien on things you own without going to court, and he wouldn't risk potentially exposing his scam by doing that. I don't want you to stress about this, though. Teresa, provide your niece the funds to cover this invoice from petty cash."

"No, Mr. Jackson!" said Luci. "Not yet. This might be his last threat, so why not wait another week?"

"I doubt he would do anything more extreme than send harassing mail for such a relatively small amount of money, but I don't trust him. We shouldn't take any chances."

"Thank you, but I live in a secure apartment and take the public bus to and from work. I feel safe. Aunt Teresa has a friend who's an attorney, so if I receive another bill in the mail, maybe I'll have the attorney write Yi a letter."

"Good idea, Luci. Teresa's attorney friend is also my friend, so let me make those arrangements."

"If we need to send a letter, that will be fine," said Luci, "but we should wait to see if we receive additional notices. If the one you copied is the last, we shouldn't escalate anything."

"Okay," said Theo, "but keep me informed and take no chances. Be careful."

———

The next meeting between Father O'Dowd, Pastor Burns, Denton Jones, and Theo Jackson included Chief Fitzpatrick. Again, the group met in an empty classroom inside the Catholic church. Each participant shared new information relative to their joint endeavor, providing input on possible next steps.

When his turn to speak came, Colonel Fitzpatrick's news wasn't as positive as others'.

"Recognizing the necessity for the highest level of confidentiality, the mayor and I engaged as few people as necessary in our administration on this initiative. I appreciate the energy of all in this room to terminate possible Santu operations in our city. I'm shaken by the prospects of their presence and as committed as any here to address the issue as forcefully and as quickly as possible.

"However, after reviewing the documents provided to me by Commander Jones, this is beyond our capabilities to handle ourselves. In fact, the biggest crime we believe the Santu orchestrates here is also out of our jurisdiction. Trafficking isn't a local crime. It's a federal one. I understand the urgency to do something before our opportunity vanishes, and I'd like to talk to Special Agent in Charge Randall Warren, who oversees the FBI's Cincinnati field office. I will share with him what we know, most of what we suspect, and some of the identities of people here who contributed to our efforts. I don't believe it necessary for me to share the names of all who have assisted. Does anyone object?"

"No, sir," said Pastor Burns. "My sources inside another federal agency involved with trafficking issues in this country made the same suggestion. I doubt we could enlist other undercover federal assistance for the initiative we propose without first coordinating efforts with the FBI."

"What about the timing, though?" asked Jackson. "How long would all that coordination take?"

"I can't answer that, Mr. Jackson," said Fitzpatrick, "but I assume Santu activities concern our federal agencies as much as they do us. The feds also know better than we about how quickly the organization can disappear. I will find out soon, but in the meantime, Jim Hargrove expressed concerns about the evidence we have accumulated to date. Most of it is circumstantial. Hargrove doubted a judge would grant a search warrant for the property based on what we currently have. Identifying Song and Yi as dangerous people isn't enough to link the two to crimes in the Ohio jurisdiction. To our knowledge, these two have no criminal record in our city.

"On a positive note, I provided my federal contacts our suspicions about the passport blanks. After a little research, they called me and are certain they can identify the corrupt employee responsible."

"Will they arrest this person?" asked Burns.

"No. I suggested they keep the employee under surveillance but not alert her to any suspicion. They agreed to hold off on arrest for thirty days, but no longer."

"Okay, so what do we do?" asked Theo. "The longer we wait, the more the risk Yi may become alerted to our efforts."

"I understand," said Fitzpatrick, "but I can't condone illegal searches or improper arrests."

"Of course not, Chief," agreed Burns. "Nobody here would suggest that, but I also feel the same urgency as Mr. Jackson. Could we intercept some of Yi's communication legally? Perhaps we might obtain more usable evidence in that way."

Fitzpatrick appeared uncomfortable and looked around the room. "Based on new evidence we received this week, we already initiated that. Our efforts in this area need to remain confidential. Complex software codes encrypt voice and text communications entering and leaving Yi's buildings, and our team has been unable to break through these so far. We're still working on it."

"No surprise there," said Jackson. "What if I could somehow manage a conversation with Yi that would encourage him to talk?"

Fitzpatrick reacted harshly to Jackson's suggestion. "If this group suggests some kind of torture to extract information, I'll excuse myself from further discussions."

Jackson's nostrils flared, and he placed his hands on the table in front of him. For a tense few seconds, nobody spoke. Jackson at last broke the uncomfortable silence. "Chief, I respect your position in that regard, and I believe you misunderstood my suggestion. I can't and wouldn't attempt to abduct or subdue Yi to use extreme means to extract information. I believe other ways exist to encourage his cooperation."

Fitzpatrick relaxed back into his seat, and everyone else in the room took a long, relieved breath. "Explain, then, what other methods might work."

"The worst thing that can happen to Yi is *not* to be caught and incarcerated or to die quickly by gunshot in a shootout. For Yi, the absolute worst thing would be for his organization to believe he betrayed them. He knows what the Santu would do to him because earlier in his professional history, he himself acted as an enforcer in the organization. Any alternative to that outcome would be preferable to him, I think."

Everyone around the table absorbed the information, and Pastor Burns spoke first. "Your strategy is interesting, Theo. Our enforcement agencies may not have sufficient or strong enough evidence to arrest Yi now. Still, if the Santu believes Yi provided the evidence we *do* have, he might be in serious trouble with them."

"Precisely," replied Jackson. "Fear is often as powerful a motivator as a well-placed stick. We only need to show Yi how easily we can provide his organization with proof of his disloyalty. I believe we can accomplish that in a short meeting where both his resources and his time to react are restricted." Glancing around the room, Theo caught Denton's eye ever so briefly before continuing. "Without alerting Yi, I recently conducted a small experiment to test the potential of this tactic. Using only the fear of exposure to Santu punishments as the motivator, I attained valuable evidence from one of Yi's customers."

"What evidence was that?" asked Burns.

"I would prefer not to identify it specifically," said Theo, "but it's represented within the full body of evidence we, as a group, have seen or will review later today."

"This could be a strategy to consider, but I would like to discuss the legal nuances with Jim Hargrove and Fred Gunnells," said Fitzpatrick. "Our file against Yi grows daily, and I wouldn't want to waste any of that by an entrapment issue. I'll also call Agent Warren to meet with him as soon as possible. He may have ideas, or he may request to meet with this group. Mr. Jackson, I'll understand if you wish to avoid that meeting."

"Maybe, but I'll most likely want to attend. When you speak with Mr. Warren, I advise you not to detail how we achieved all the evidence. My participation could prejudice him against the effort. What's Roberson's status? Do we know if he has had further communications with Yi?"

"The assistant city manager is a beaten man," said Fitzpatrick. "He's also terrified of Yi, and his reasons for removing that information from Mrs. Jones's computer suggest Yi threatened him or his family with something terrible. He says he has had no contact with Yi since removing the file."

"Can you find out if Roberson has a private way of reaching Yi if we should need that?"

"I can check," answered Fitzpatrick.

"I suggest," said Pastor Burns, "that Colonel Fitzpatrick assume the lead in scheduling additional meetings and further planning. He will determine the types of enforcement coordination required once he meets with Agent Warren. Since calls to or from me arouse little suspicion, I'm happy to facilitate times and locations for any meetings. My cell phone stays connected twenty-four hours a day."

"Thank you, Pastor Burns. I'll call you after my conference with Agent Warren," said Fitzpatrick.

———

When the participants rose to leave, Denton stayed behind with Pastor Burns. "Tom, our plan appears to contain little downside for any of us, except Theo. His role seems risky."

"Yes, but nobody else in our current group could schedule a meeting like the one he suggests. I can't see Yi inviting a police officer back to his private office."

"No, but what happens if things go the wrong way?"

"I'm certain the federal government will have clandestine support in place during the operation. Colonel Fitzpatrick will confer with the local FBI field office soon and should be able to answer your question after that better."

"If we succeed, what happens to Theo? The Santu will likely discover his role, and he'll be subject to the same danger he proposes to use as a threat to Yi."

"Possibly," agreed Burns, "but don't get too far ahead of yourself. Let's first ensure a successful mission with Yi, then worry about Mr. Jackson. If everything goes as planned, the feds might figure a way to protect Jackson into the future too."

Denton didn't respond, suspecting Burns knew more details about the impending operation than he presently shared.

CHAPTER 30

Teresa sat behind Theo's desk when he arrived at his office, clearly upset.

"Have you heard?" she asked.

"Heard what?"

"About Reggie?"

"No. What about Reggie? I told him last week to find a new place to live. You know that. He was supposed to give me last year's accounting for the Burger Barn, but I haven't seen that yet."

"He's dead, Theo. Meera at the Burger Barn found him in his office this morning. I just got off the phone with her."

Theo collapsed into a chair across from Teresa. "How?"

"Someone cut his throat."

"I assume it wasn't part of a burglary or something?"

"No. Cash in plain sight on his desk. Each cash register in the store also contained the starting banks for the next day. And there's something worse, Theo."

"What?"

"Meera believes someone tortured Reggie. She found him tied to his chair with a pencil sticking out of his right thigh."

"Jesus!" said Theo. "Has Meera called the police?"

"Yes. Officers arrived while she talked to me."

"Did she happen to retrieve Reggie's phone?"

"She couldn't find a phone. She looked for it before calling the police."

"I'm sorry for this news, Teresa. Reggie and I have a long history. Besides our work relationship, we were friends. Hell, the friendship preceded our business relationship. I want to stop time to mourn him properly, but we can't afford that simple luxury right now. You, me, all our employees, and a major part of our business are in danger."

"Because of what Reggie might have said to whoever shoved the pencil in his leg?"

"Yes. The fact it was only one pencil means Reggie didn't wait for additional pain before providing the information the intruder wanted."

"You think Yi did this?"

"I can't imagine anyone else. Reggie angered Yi when he wouldn't provide additional product to him, so Yi came to ask Reggie who could. While he was at it, he sent a nasty message for what happens to suppliers who disappoint him."

"You think Reggie gave him your name?"

"I would bet on it. Yi will probably contact me sometime today. In the meantime, get the word out to everyone else to shut down. No orders, no supplies, dump product, close out everything."

"Theo! Isn't that an overreaction? You're talking about a huge investment."

"And I'm telling you, I'm *not* overreacting. We've done well with this business, but now somebody bigger than us knows too much. So far, Yi's information is restricted to my name because he believes that's all he needs. Make everything else disappear, Teresa, and I'll take care of myself."

"Is this a temporary situation, or are we leaving this part of the business forever?"

"I can't say yet. For now, that isn't important. Tell the others the same thing. We need to worry about tomorrow before planning next week."

———

At around noon, Teresa approached Theo's desk. "The call you're waiting for is on line two."

"Did Yi identify himself to you?"

"No, but the incoming number comes from Reggie Lincoln's last burner phone."

"Thanks, Teresa," Theo said. He took a deep breath. "Here goes. We'll see what kind of an actor I am." He answered. "This is Theodore Jackson."

"Yes, Mr. Jackson. This is Mr. Sun Yi. I own several stores on Victory Parkway, and I'm a customer of yours."

"I'm sorry. Could you repeat your name? I'm not aware of any customers on Victory Parkway."

"Nice try, Mr. Jackson, but you can cut the charade. I'm a busy man and don't have time for games. One of your salespeople, Reggie Lincoln, told me he could no longer provide the product I usually purchase from your business. I would like to appeal to you directly to reconsider that decision. You are Mr. Lincoln's supervisor, aren't you?"

Theo paused before answering, hoping to convey a sense of concern. "I'm not certain to what you refer, Mr. . . . did you say Lee? But perhaps you should pursue the matter with Mr. Lincoln."

"The name is Yi, which I believe you know, and unfortunately, Mr. Lincoln was involved in a serious accident. He can no longer help me. I found the product Mr. Lincoln provided satisfactory, and I never negotiated price. I am in fact, Mr. Jackson, a good customer, and only want to remain one. Our mutual interests would be well served to continue our business relationship."

Now Theo only desired to fortify his ruse with Yi. "I see, Mr. Yi. Perhaps we should continue the conversation on a different telephone line than the one for my investment company. If you provide a number, I will return your call from a different phone."

Yi told Theo the number of Reggie Lincoln's burner phone, which of course Theo already had; Theo promised to call Yi back in minutes. After disconnecting, Theo went to Teresa's desk with a short list of things he needed. Returning to his desk, Theo punched in the number of Lincoln's burner. Yi answered immediately.

"Mr. Yi, I must keep certain parts of my business extremely confidential, so I insist that you never use my business line to contact me again."

"I understand, Mr. Jackson. I can accommodate that request if you provide a safe number where I can reach you when I need you."

"I will text the cell phone you are currently using with a new number to reach me each week. This text will occur every Monday by ten o'clock in the morning. The number provided in the text will be the only one to use for that week to make orders. I reiterate you should never call my listed business telephone number."

"Okay. I'll only use this cell phone for orders. Since Mr. Lincoln's recent failures to deliver have put us behind, we'll need ten kilos this week."

"That's a large order, Mr. Yi. I will notify you where to retrieve it later in the week."

"I would prefer you deliver the product, and I would also pay you at that time," said Yi.

"That isn't how I work. I will *not* be at the location where you receive product, and I will never publicly meet with you. You will pay by leaving cash in a prescribed locker at the YMCA on Bunning Street. Each week that you receive product, I'll arrange the delivery of an unlocked combination lock to your business to secure the locker where you leave cash. Only I will have the combination for this lock, so take care not to inadvertently close the lock before you need it for the locker."

"These precautions seem extreme, Mr. Jackson. Are they necessary? And what if I decide not to make the required payment after receiving product?"

"Do you jest with such a question? My organization deals with failures the same way yours does. Also, you would never receive additional product again. I'll contact you shortly on this phone with the location to retrieve your product. Goodbye, Mr. Yi."

When Theo finished the call, he called for Teresa. "Did you get it?"

"Yes. I recorded the whole call."

"Good. Convert the recording to an MP4 file and give it to me on a flash drive. We may need parts of it later. Keep enough supplies to fill two weeks of orders for Yi."

———

Theo's next call went to Denton Jones. When Jones picked up, Jackson asked, "Hey, Denton. Theo. Do you know if Fitzpatrick met with the FBI guy?"

"Yes. The chief met with Special Agent in Charge Randall Warren the day before yesterday. Warren told him he wanted to look over the information and make a few calls. Fitzpatrick thought he'd probably hear back from Warren today or tomorrow. Why?"

"I may need to call Warren and update him with something myself."

"Anything you need to share with me or the chief?"

"Not yet, Denton. I don't mean to sound mysterious, but the information I have should probably go directly to Warren. Thanks."

———

Within thirty minutes, Theo drove his Prius north on the Northeast Expressway to the Cincinnati field office of the Federal Bureau of Investigation, located on Ronald Reagan Drive. When he passed the airport, Theo touched a single digit on the car's front display, sending a text notification to Special Agent Warren's telephone number. The agent had promised to meet him in the lobby for a quicker escort through several security checks.

Mr. Warren had been surprised by Jackson's call but cleared his late-afternoon schedule to accommodate Theo. Theo figured the special agent probably didn't receive too many requests from criminals for office visits. As Theo's small car rolled to a stop in front of the large, modern, steel-and-glass structure, a security officer directed Theo to a parking space next to the building. Before Theo reached the first set of revolving doors, a tall, fit-looking man, perhaps fifty years old, came outside to greet him."

"Theodore Jackson?" asked the man.

"Yes. Are you Agent Warren?"

"Yes. We keep security tight here, so I thought meeting you downstairs might expedite the journey to my office."

"Well, thank you, sir. Have we met before?"

The man smiled and said, "No, Mr. Jackson, but I recognized you from a few pictures in our files. You look much better in person, I might add."

"Thank you, sir. I would guess the lighting was less than ideal when someone took the pictures you have in your file."

The big agent laughed. "Could be right."

After bypassing several security gates and metal detectors, Jackson and Warren arrived at an office on the building's fourth floor. Warren greeted a secretary near the door to the office and picked up several pink sheets of telephone messages on his way to his desk. "Sit down here," invited Warren, indicating one of two chairs in front of the desk. As Jackson sat, Agent Warren stared across at him for a few moments before speaking again. "I'm sorry, Mr. Jackson, but this sight is *almost* like a dream come true for me."

"How's that?" asked Theo.

"You can't imagine the number of nights over the past decade I dreamed of you sitting across from me like this in my office."

Slightly embarrassed, Theo smiled and said, "Well, I guess the dream has come true."

"I said almost. In my dreams, you wore handcuffs."

Theo laughed. "Sorry."

"It's okay, Mr. Jackson. You have been a thorn in my side for a long time. What did you want to speak to me about?"

"Sorry about the thorn part, but maybe I can make up a little by helping you with something else you're working on."

"I can hardly wait," said Warren a bit sarcastically.

"I'm here about the Santu situation in our area."

Warren didn't immediately respond as he attempted to melt Theo with a firm stare. "What Santu situation?"

"I'm aware Chief Fitzpatrick briefed you, sir. He may not have mentioned my name, but I'm the source for much of the material collected relating to Sun Yi."

"Yes, the chief visited here two days ago. How well do you know Fitzpatrick?"

"I attended a meeting which included the chief on the day before you met with him. I also know Pastor Tom Burns. Have you met him?"

"No, but I'm aware of his reputation. How is it you keep the company of people like Fitzpatrick and Burns?"

"Perhaps the subject for a different day when we both have more time, sir. Today, I need to discuss important new information that I can only share with you."

"Relative to the Santu case?"

"Yes."

"Why me?"

"Because if I share the information with either Fitzpatrick or Commander Jones, their professional responsibilities may compel them to take action that might impede or delay initiatives against Yi and the Santu in Cincinnati."

Warren absorbed Theo's last statement quietly and sat thinking. "I'm lost, Mr. Jackson. I can't figure out your angle, but I'm aware of Yi's activities through a source other than Chief Fitzpatrick. Our agency is close to possibly capturing a high-level Santu target, and I don't want to blow it. You and I operate on different sides of the law, but will you just put your cards on the table? Tell me what you know and what that might cost me."

"We share the same goals relative to Yi, Mr. Warren, so my cost is minimal—only a few days of time. First, if you can, tell me your evaluation of the information Mr. Fitzpatrick provided you."

"Okay, but before I do, what exactly do you hope to accomplish, and why?"

"Human trafficking stands alone as the vilest crime committed on the planet. When it also involves atrocities against children, all decent humans should rise in disgust. Yi participates in such a crime, and I want to help stop both him and his organization."

"I can't adequately convey how strange I feel to admit that you and I share the same view on something. To answer your earlier question,

Jackson, the evidence your group has is compelling but in many ways weak. I want to learn more about Yi through on-site electronic surveillance, a bug, but no judge would grant the request with the evidence available. We might arrest Yi on trumped-up charges and strong suspicions, but the Santu attorneys would quickly arrange for his release. Assuming we found a way to hold Yi for a period, Santu members generally don't talk. They understand democratic governments like ours won't use extreme measures to extract information. Santu members are also aware of their organization's severe punishments for providing damaging testimony against it. Yi represents too important a target for us to waste on a weak case."

"That's what Chief Fitzpatrick summarized in fewer words earlier this week," said Theo. "I requested our meeting here today to provide you unusual evidence that you might use to establish bona fide reasons for an on-site listening device."

Warren looked skeptical. "What kind of evidence?"

"Yi killed a man in Cincinnati yesterday."

"What? How do you know that?"

"Right now, *how* I know isn't as relevant as my proof of the murder."

"I'm interested, Mr. Jackson, but need to warn you a murder inside the city limits is not an FBI responsibility. That falls under the jurisdiction of the city or state."

"I know that. I came here today to provide you a tip *you* can share with Chief Fitzpatrick. I have evidence to prove the connection between Yi and the man killed, Reggie Lincoln."

"Why not share this information with Fitzpatrick yourself?"

"Because my evidence could create a professional obligation for Chief Fitzpatrick to research *my* association with both Yi and the deceased. He might even arrest me as a suspect or as an accessory to the murder, which could derail the urgent actions required to arrest Yi."

"Were you involved in the murder or its planning?"

"No, but that's an investigation you or Fitzpatrick could pursue after resolution of other more urgent issues involving Sun Yi."

"What's your evidence?" asked Warren.

"What's your commitment to me if the evidence is good?" asked Jackson.

"If what you say is true, and we can confirm it, then I can share a tip with other law enforcement, redacting certain parts of it to protect the identity of the provider. Local law enforcement—in this case, Colonel Fitzpatrick—can then act on the discovered evidence to solve the immediate crime without having the information to pursue other actions against the party responsible for the evidence."

"That will work. Would you like to see my documentation?"

"Do you trust me to honor the provisions I just specified?"

"Yes, Mr. Warren. We don't have a lot of time."

Theo opened the file folder he brought and gave Special Agent Warren copies of several phone records from his office. One file contained evidence of numerous calls from Reggie Lincoln's burner cell phone to Theo's office and to another number, which Theo proved to Warren was a burner phone owned by Theo. Another file contained evidence of two calls involving the burner phone once owned by Lincoln, one incoming to Theo's business line and one outgoing to the same burner phone from Theo's office line. These occurred after the time of Lincoln's death, proving someone else used the phone. Concluding his presentation, Theo gave Warren a USB drive containing MP4 recordings of both Lincoln's and Yi's voices.

Warren reviewed the well-organized evidence and listened to the MP4 recordings. "Very thorough, Mr. Jackson. Should I ask why both Lincoln and Yi would communicate with you on the same burner phone? What was your relationship to Lincoln?"

"You can make your own assumptions," said Theo. "To know that relationship *could* help you in future investigations relating to me. Does it not also give you what you need to show the chain of custody of Mr. Lincoln's phone? He had the phone. He died, then someone else had the phone."

"Does Yi still have the phone?"

"You could determine that through on-site electronic surveillance. Eavesdropping conversations coming from Yi's office could also corroborate other aspects of Reggie Lincoln's murder. Just out of curiosity, Agent Warren—I'm certain you maintain an extensive database about me. Why don't you query Reggie Lincoln's name? See if you get any hits connecting Lincoln to me or any illegal activities."

Warren made a few keystrokes on his desktop computer and watched for results. After a few minutes, he said, "Nothing there. Who was Reggie Lincoln?"

"A friend of mine who owned a Burger Barn restaurant."

Warren smiled. "I'll share this tip with Chief Fitzpatrick. Thank you. He'll be able to obtain a court order for electronic surveillance based on the evidence. The surveillance might help to solve a murder, but how does it impact our efforts to find more about Yi's Santu activity?"

"Allow me to explain my plan," said Theo.

Thirty minutes later, Warren still had a question. "This might work. Interesting approach. What do you gain from this?"

"Nothing more than satisfaction for perhaps negatively impacting the Santu. As I see it, you have minimal downside if I'm unsuccessful, with potentially great upside."

"I agree, Jackson. You, on the other hand, have a more severe downside, whether this works or not."

"Such as?" asked Jackson.

"At some point in your proposed meeting with Yi, he will most likely pull a gun on you. He could shoot you. To me, that's a fairly severe downside."

"I agree, but the odds of Yi doing that are low. Killing me inside his building would gain him nothing and potentially cost him plenty. He *has* acted rashly lately, but he isn't stupid."

Warren replied, "Maybe, but realistically, we must consider all possibilities. Perhaps more important to you, whether our efforts with Yi succeed or not, your legal status doesn't change. You might end up as the subject of an additional investigation relating to Lincoln's murder. During any such investigation, the nature of your relationship with Yi and Lincoln might be discovered, and I speculate this could prove legally damaging to you. So far, neither you nor I talked about immunity or protection in return for your assistance."

"I haven't asked for any," said Theo. "I have another proposal to present, but nothing in it depends on what we have already agreed. So far, you only agreed to stall local law enforcement in Cincinnati from pursuing additional investigations about Reggie Lincoln's murder until after we complete our efforts with Sun Yi, right?"

"Yes," answered Warren. "I will honor that commitment."

"Good. If that part of our discussion is finished, my other proposal might address the thorn in your side, which you referred to earlier. Do you have a few more minutes?"

"I'm all ears," said Warren.

Almost an hour later, Warren prepared to wrap up their discussion. "Do you require a document to confirm this arrangement?"

"Documents are nearly worthless around smart attorneys. If you shake my hand, I'll trust you."

Jackson and Agent Warren stood and shook hands.

CHAPTER 31

He saw her walk from the back door of GlaMore Photography toward her car in the rear lot. It was after eleven o'clock in the evening, and he motioned his driver to intercept her in the parking lot. The driver accommodated Jackson, leaving the headlights off. Song never looked up to see the car beside her and was surprised when a man pulled her into the back seat.

She barely resisted Jackson as he held her tightly. With one hand over her mouth, he whispered softly in her ear, "Lin Song, I know who you are and what you do. Other people also have this information. You have served a terrible master for a long time, and you need a new one. I will help you and take care of you, but you must agree to my terms. If you don't, I must turn you over to authorities in this country along with Mr. Yi. Can we talk?"

The small woman nodded, and Jackson took his hand from her mouth and released her from his hold. Song sat without speaking for some moments, glaring at Jackson with dark eyes. Finally, she asked, "Who you? What you want?"

"For now, I'm nobody," answered Jackson. "And what I want is your cooperation. For that, I can give you a new life somewhere the Santu will never find you or be able to reach you."

"You not know Santu. They everywhere, and they can find anyone."

"If you don't accept my help, the Santu will find you in an American prison with Mr. Yi. If you try to escape here before authorities arrest Yi, the Santu will also track you down. To me, it appears you have a choice between the Santu finding you or trusting me to hide you as I promised. You are nothing to the Santu, Ms. Song. They didn't even bother to protect you here with fake identification like they did for Mr. Yi. You are the same Lin Song, born in North Vietnam thirty-four years ago. Cambodian mercenaries murdered your parents when you were three. These mercenaries sold you into slavery to the Santu at age nine, and your Santu masters trained you in specialized skills you have employed ever since. By following the Santu's orders, you have survived the past twenty-five years. I'm not a policeman and not interested in your crimes against members of competing gangs, but I need your answer."

"Yi no friend, only boss. He a pig. You want me cut his throat, okay, but how I live then?"

Theo smiled and spent the next fifteen minutes explaining his plan to Song. When he finished, he pulled an envelope from his coat pocket. "This is your first payment, Lin—ten thousand dollars in cash. If you accept it, you're my employee; in my business, I deal strictly in trust, not contracts. Do you understand?"

"Yes," answered Lin, taking the envelope and leaving the car. On this dark and rainy night, little vehicular traffic and no other pedestrians traveled the streets. The slight figure of the dangerous Lin Song disappeared quietly and entirely into the shadows.

———

At Colonel Fitzpatrick's request, Pastor Burns hosted what most thought would be the last planning meeting before the joint effort to arrest Sun Yi. He reserved a small meeting room inside the Hyatt Hotel where seven men and a woman sat around a circular table. Denton knew all in the room except the woman; Father O'Dowd wasn't present.

"Thanks for coming this evening," said Burns. "I thought moving our meeting to a neutral location might be prudent. You'll also notice Father O'Dowd isn't here. We appreciate his past accommodations and liaison, but his participation is no longer necessary. The less he knows about our operation now, the safer it will be for him. My role going forward may also be limited, but two additional guests join us for our preparation tonight. Their groups will play a key role during the day of Yi's arrest.

"Some of you may have met Special Agent in Charge Randall Warren, who commands the FBI's field office here. Next to him is Mary, who represents a different agency reporting to the Department of Justice. To my right is Fred Gunnells, assistant solicitor for Cincinnati, and his boss, Jim Hargrove, the city solicitor. To my left is Commander Denton Jones of the Cincinnati Police Department and his supervisor, Chief of Police Jack Fitzpatrick. Sitting next to you, Mary, is Theodore Jackson, a local Cincinnati businessman."

"Nice to meet you all," said Mary.

"And you," said Fitzpatrick. "I missed your last name, I'm afraid."

"Mr. Burns didn't give it," answered Mary.

Agent Warren filled the uncomfortable pause. "Sorry, Chief. Mary works undercover in an extremely confidential capacity for one of our federal enforcement agencies. I can vouch for her credentials and the merit of her attendance in this meeting."

Glancing around the room at the others present, Fitzpatrick answered, "Thank you, Agent Warren. Mary, I assume you're ICE, ATF, or DEA?"

"Something like that," she answered. Mary didn't waste time with extra words, and her demeanor suggested further efforts to find out more would be fruitless. Small and petite, with the frame of a marathon runner, Mary possessed a quiet air of confidence that garnered respect in the male-dominated room. She had the look of a poker player who knew she had the best cards in the current hand, other than perhaps Special Agent Warren.

With introductions out of the way, Burns turned the meeting over to Warren.

"Thank you, Pastor Burns, and thank you to all in this room who helped to create a unique opportunity to severely impact one of the most dangerous criminal organizations in the world. I met with Chief Fitzpatrick earlier and several others of you here. I believe most of the pieces are in place for an exercise that will begin in less than forty-eight hours. I'll answer any questions I can."

Jim Hargrove spoke first. "Agent Warren, Fred Gunnells and I reviewed the original plan proposed by Mr. Jackson and have some legal concerns. We believe using Yi's fear of his own organization to encourage his cooperation with us is brilliant, but Mr. Jackson's suggested method for generating Yi's fear seems to depend on manufactured evidence. If one of us were to do this, it would not be legal, and evidence derived in such a fashion would be deemed inadmissible. Does the employment of a third party to accomplish the same thing excuse us from the legal requirements for gaining evidence?"

"No, Mr. Hargrove. Certainly not. I reviewed the evidence Mr. Jackson proposes to present to Mr. Yi. I also asked our department's legal counsel to assess the premise and general outline of the interview Mr. Jackson expects to conduct. None of the evidence Mr. Jackson suggests using to intimidate Mr. Yi is manufactured. All of it exists. We agree with your appraisal that the evidence is collectively weak for a possible legal proceeding against Yi. However, the sheer volume could concern Yi if his organization believed he was responsible for providing it to law enforcement. The only part of Jackson's original proposal that seemed deceptive was Jackson's *threat* of a text message to Chief Fitzpatrick. That needn't be a deception if Jackson can really send the text message. None of the information in the proposed text includes information we don't already know."

"Good," said Hargrove. "Wouldn't we still need a way to listen to Jackson's conversation with Yi? Our current evidence probably isn't enough to warrant a judge's authorization for an on-site listening device."

"Correct," answered Warren. "As you know from the last meeting, your police force currently monitors digital information going into and out of Yi's building. We received permission for the surveillance based on probable cause that one of Yi's businesses purposely violates certain pornography statutes. To date, enforcement IT experts have been unsuccessful in decoding or unscrambling these digital communications. More stringent surveillance types, such as on-site listening devices and bugs, require a different court warrant relating to a different kind of crime.

"As of this morning, Chief Fitzpatrick has bona fide evidence about Sun Yi's involvement in a recent murder in the city. If enforcement can establish Yi's possession of a specific cell phone by privately listening to Yi's office conversations, we could arrest him for suspected murder. With probable cause for Yi's participation in this murder established, Chief Fitzpatrick feels confident a judge will grant the necessary approval for the requested electronic surveillance."

"That's good news, sir," said Hargrove. "How will that help your office to acquire the information needed to pursue the Santu for federal violations?"

"In the pursuit of evidence of Yi's involvement in the murder, enforcement may learn of other unrelated criminal activity conducted by Yi. We can listen to any conversations Yi has, not just ones relating to a murder. As you know, we can pursue legal remedies for *any* criminal acts discovered due to legal surveillance."

"Clever," said Hargrove.

"Not clever," responded Warren. "Legal. Bluntly, and only for this group, Mr. Jackson's bold strategy to achieve the information we all desire is also risky. If Yi had the time to carefully consider Jackson's threats to expose him, he might realize his position remains the same whether Jackson sends the text to Fitzpatrick or not. Whether Jackson alerts Chief Fitzpatrick—or anyone else for that matter—of the list of things known about Yi's operations during his meeting with Yi or later doesn't change Yi's potential problem with the Santu. If Yi ignores Jackson's threat, he gains some time to contact important members of his organization to warn of the security breaches."

"So, why wouldn't he do that?" asked Hargrove.

"We hope the pressure on Yi will cause him to panic and make a bad decision for himself. His recent action relative to your city official indicates he can occasionally act rashly," said Warren.

"Not everyone here knows what one of our city employees attempted at Yi's direction. You may reveal that if you wish, Mr. Hargrove," said Chief Fitzpatrick.

"Sure, Chief," said Hargrove. "Sun Yi recently instigated an ill-fated attempt, through a corrupt city employee, to eliminate obscure information from an application for a permit. This information wasn't a big secret; Yi filed it earlier with the city and the FCC. The form included the name of an investment company responsible for financing a portion of Mr. Yi's businesses and the name of a Cayman Islands banking entity that secured the bond required for the FCC tower permit.

"After Yi filed the original paper documents several years ago, he succeeded in having a city employee doctor the recorded paper permits and alter the digital records, eliminating the lines listing the two businesses. We believe an FCC employee did the same thing with the documents on file at the FCC. When someone from my office alerted Yi that he needed to resubmit the missing information, he panicked. Using unnecessarily extreme measures to replicate the same doctoring of the permit file he accomplished years earlier, he managed to expose both himself and the corrupt city employee who assisted him."

"At this point, the city employee involved continues to work for us under an agreement of immunity in exchange for his cooperation as a government witness," said Fitzpatrick. "We don't believe Sun Yi is aware of that status."

"Thank you, Chief and Mr. Hargrove. The city employee's participation in our plan may prove important even after the arrest of Mr. Yi. Any other questions?" asked Agent Warren.

"Yes," said Pastor Burns. "You said Yi panicked in the case of the information listed on the permit. Why is that your evaluation? Details about investment partners and banking entities seem fairly critical."

"The names are important," said Warren, "but they weren't new to us. If Yi needed to post these organizations' names to a public permit years ago, the investment company and the bank permitted that in advance. These businesses wouldn't allow their names on a legal document without confidence that their business relationships with the Santu were well covered or too difficult to track. That is, in fact, the case. Both Jet Sun Capital and International Fidelity operate fully legitimate corporations with excellent Dun and Bradstreet ratings. We *suspect* their ties to the Santu but, to date, have proved nothing. Yi's exercise to doctor old documents seems silly under the circumstances and to some extent resulted in our considerations today."

"I see," said Burns. "Thank you. So, now we hope Yi may overreact again in his conversation with Mr. Jackson?"

"Yes," answered Warren. "We can't estimate the odds for that but feel the effort is worth a try. We know for certain the chances of choreographing a similar conversation using law enforcement would be nil. If Mr. Jackson is unsuccessful, we're no worse off than when we started, and the city may at least prosecute Yi for the murder of Reggie Lincoln. It's possible that during the murder investigation, Yi could provide information relating to Santu activities, but that isn't likely."

"Does Jackson have a list of information he will try to obtain from Yi?" asked Hargrove.

"Since the authorization for electronic surveillance pertains to the pursuit of evidence relating to the murder of a city citizen, Chief Fitzpatrick will discuss those needs with Mr. Jackson."

"We did create a brief," said Fitzpatrick, nodding at Agent Warren. "We understand Jackson's time with Yi may be limited, so we'll keep the list short, restricted to the essential items relating to our murder investigation. For example, we want to know the location of the cell phone we think Yi took from Lincoln. We also are interested in Yi's upward chain of command to determine if others above him ordered this murder. The passwords for any computers located on Yi's property could be important for checking digital records relating to the murder. The records of banking accounts and activity can determine the extent of significant transactions of money before or after Lincoln's murder."

Pastor Burns smiled and glanced at Mary and Agent Warren. "That's a thorough list. I like it. Can Mr. Jackson ask other questions of his own?"

Agent Warren fielded the question. "Chief Fitzpatrick can provide Mr. Jackson suggestions about certain information that we believe is valuable, but Jackson isn't employed by either him or me. He's a private citizen, and what he chooses to discuss with Yi is ultimately his choice. Enforcement can use and act on any information acquired because of our legal surveillance."

"Can Jackson employ any means necessary to derive the information he wants in the meeting?" asked Hargrove.

"I'm sorry, Mr. Hargrove," answered Warren, "but I stand by my previous answer. As a private citizen, Mr. Jackson's activities with Sun Yi and his conversation don't fall under police control. Once inside, enforcement will record Mr. Jackson's actions and statements, the same as Mr. Yi's. If Jackson admits to past crimes or attempts to commit a crime while with Mr. Yi, he's as vulnerable to legal action due to the surveillance as Mr. Yi. Do *you* have a better candidate for this exercise?"

Hargrove recognized the reproach and apologized. "No, sir, and you misunderstand my question. I reviewed the documentation provided by Pastor Burns about Santu world activity and saw a disgusting video clip relating to the atrocities imposed on children by the organization. I hoped that you might say Mr. Jackson could use any means necessary to get any information needed. Jackson's reputation in our community makes him a natural adversary to my department, but I appreciate his efforts for this mission. He appears to be putting himself into a dangerous situation, and I commend his bravery."

"Thank you, Mr. Hargrove," said Warren. "I, too, apologize for misunderstanding the nature of your question. I share your sentiment and passion, but like you, I represent law and order. We will use every possible rule we can to get all the things we can, legally, but we won't break any laws or knowingly allow others to."

"Mr. Hargrove, Agent Warren, thank you for your comments," said Jackson, trying to break the tension in the room. "Could you put a couple of the things you just said about me in writing? I might need a reference someday."

When the nervous laughter subsided, a more serious Jackson continued. "Chief Fitzpatrick, I may have a way to place the necessary listening device in Yi's office, but we can discuss that separately. Agent Warren, can Mary discuss her role in the exercise?"

Since her introduction, Mary had not spoken. She now answered before Agent Warren could. "Yes. My team controls three areas. We provide undercover secondary security in the immediate vicinity of Yi's shops during the proposed arrest period. We're backup to the Cincinnati Police Department, who owns primary responsibilities for keeping the area secure. Second, we will provide immediate IT support on the day of the arrest. Contingent on the information we may learn during Mr. Jackson's conversation with Yi, specially trained agents will enter the building after the arrest to quickly recover as much information from the computers as possible. Third, once enforcement arrests Yi and places him in a police vehicle, our group will meet at an arranged location to transfer Yi into a federal vehicle. We'll take him to a secure and confidential government facility for further questioning. Of course, this depends somewhat on what Yi reveals during his meeting with Jackson. We need evidence of a federal crime."

"Thank you, Mary," said Fitzpatrick. "Will your group and my department have the ability to communicate with each other during the exercise?"

"Yes. The radios employed by your department have the most recent stealth capabilities, and we will provide you an encrypted channel for communications. We hope our presence on the scene and in this effort will remain confidential. We also encourage you to keep your department's efforts as covert as possible. The longer we keep Sun Yi's arrest unknown to his organization, the better our chances to recover meaningful information about the Santu. On the day of his arrest, we'll coordinate strategic enforcement sweeps in five other locations in our country and three locations internationally. These initiatives naturally depend on the quality of the information we achieve following Yi's arrest."

"I had no idea of the scale and complexity of this mission," said Fitzpatrick. "Thank you for sharing."

"What you and your group uncovered here," said Agent Warren, "represents one of our biggest potential breakthroughs in impacting Santu activities in the country. We appreciate your cooperation. Our shared mission is important."

"I wish I could take more credit," said Fitzpatrick. "Our accomplishments result from the combined efforts of a strange coalition, including priests, ministers, corrupt political officials, suspected criminals, and unnamed enforcement agencies of our government—besides our department."

"This group represents the sort of unusual collaboration necessary to take down an organization as large and as organized as the Santu," Warren said. "Thank you, all."

"Well," answered Fitzpatrick, "thank you, Agent Warren and . . . whatever your real name is besides Mary."

The woman who called herself Mary smiled politely.

———

As the meeting broke up, Denton caught up to Theo at the door. "Theo, can I talk to you a minute before you leave?"

"Sure, Denton. What's up?"

"This has been a long summer, and I'm going to be glad when it's over."

"You and me both, brother! Sun Yi shook my universe."

"My universe started shaking before I ever knew anything about Yi. I thought Roberson caused the quakes, but it turns out Yi was responsible all along. That isn't the only thing that blindsided me this year, though."

"What else?" asked Jackson.

"You, Theo. You're an enigma to me, and I'm conflicted about how I should feel. Despite your spotless arrest record with the city, I'm certain you are a criminal—and yet, at great risk to yourself and your business, you're the team leader in this exercise. You helped to protect Jessica and me this summer, you donate to good causes, and you have earned the respect, if not the friendship, of clergymen like Father O'Dowd and Pastor Burns. I feel like I'm proficient at figuring out what's 'good' and what's 'bad,' but you make the lines a little blurred. In my profession, that sort of confusion can be dangerous—perhaps even unacceptable."

"Aww, Denton. Don't overthink everything. No sane person would identify human trafficking as anything but the worst crime in the universe. It's up there at the top of any list for 'bad.' On the other end, few would argue that the kind of things you and Father O'Dowd do for underprivileged kids represents the best sort of 'good.' The wide area between those two creates the problem. Some of the gray areas are almost black, and some are close to white, but it gets really confusing in the middle. And that's where most of us live much of the time."

"I don't like gray," said Denton.

"I understand, friend. And for that reason, we *can* be on the same side in the Santu issue."

"So, why should you assume the greater risk?"

"Because I'm the only one with a legitimate reason to be allowed in Yi's office for a private meeting. I think our plan is decent, so don't be concerned."

"If you say so. What about the other thing we discussed in our first meeting? You haven't asked about the unidentified baby for a long time. Did you find the answer yourself?"

"Nah. I narrowed it down to the same two names I had when I first asked you. I still don't know which one it is."

"Do you want to know?"

Theo stared at Denton for a few seconds. "You thinkin' you might tell me now?"

"Maybe. I think you've earned the right."

Theo didn't answer, sitting in quiet contemplation. Finally, he said, "I don't want you to tell me. I did quite a bit of research on both young men, and they are each outstanding citizens with nothing but great things ahead. I'd be proud to know I had something to do with either one. If they ever found out about their real daddy, it wouldn't help 'em any—and it might hurt. That doesn't mean I can't try to help behind the scenes when it's possible. Thanks, Denton. I apologize for putting you in an uncomfortable position with the request in the first place."

"No problem, Theo. I'll say nothing more, other than you have every reason to be proud. Your son will accomplish great things for this world."

CHAPTER 32

O n the morning after the meeting at the Hyatt, Jackson arrived early
to his office. All partners in the task force had agreed the previous
evening to waste no further time, and they scheduled the complex operation
to arrest Sun Yi for the following afternoon. Theo had many things to
accomplish during the next thirty-six hours, including loose ends to tie up.
When Teresa arrived at eight o'clock, she ducked her head into Theo's office.

"You must have gotten here early and started the coffee. The first pot
is half empty."

"I did, Teresa. I have much to do today, including things to discuss
with you. Our exercise relating to Mr. Yi will begin tomorrow afternoon,
and something came up in the planning last night I need to discuss with
you and Luci. Could you possibly ask her to visit us this morning?"

"Yes. She doesn't work on Fridays and could take the bus downtown
at ten. If you need her now, she'll have to drive down."

"Ten o'clock is fine if that works for her. Let me know. Did Ray say
whether Yi picked up the package at the dock?"

"I'll call Luci when I get back to my desk. Ray says someone retrieved the package. He also checked the locker at the Y. An envelope is inside the locker, but Ray didn't remove it."

"Excellent. Leave it there. I don't want anyone near that locker for the next forty-eight hours. What's our status on supplies?"

"Ray says that after Yi's order, we have none left. They dumped everything we had in inventory. If we need more product for Yi next week, we don't have it."

"I don't think we'll need more after tomorrow," said Theo. "How are our people taking the new business plan?"

"They're rattled, Theo. Our employees trust you, though, and understand that if you're concerned, they should be too. Nobody asked for a reference to work someplace else," Teresa said with a smile.

Theo laughed. "Good. I think the time's right to adjust our strategies. The discoveries about Yi shook me, I admit, and I just don't want to compete with organizations like his anymore. We've done fine, so let's relax a little."

"You're the boss, Theo. You know the new plan isn't going to bother me. I've advocated it for years."

"That's the subject of a longer conversation between us later today. If my role changes, I need you to understand your responsibilities."

"Okay, Theo, but now you're making me nervous. Anything else you need this morning?"

"Yes. I don't think Pastor Burns has left the city yet, and I need to talk to him. Could you call him at the Hyatt Hotel?"

"My pleasure," said Teresa, with a bit more enthusiasm than Theo expected.

———

When Lucretia arrived, Teresa brought her to Theo's office immediately. "Hi, Luci. I changed my mind about what we should do about the invoice from Yi."

"It's only been eight days since I received the second notice," said Luci. "I thought we agreed to wait to see if Yi would send additional bills."

"We did. I have a different reason for wanting you to take the money to Yi—if you're willing."

After a short conversation with Luci, Theo picked up the handset for his desk phone and dialed Fitzpatrick. At the end of his brief discussion with the senior officer, Luci heard him say, "Lucretia Adams will be at your office within the hour."

———

Teresa called Theo on the intercom at eleven o'clock to tell him Pastor Tom Burns waited in the lobby. Jackson told his assistant to keep the pastor entertained for a minute or two while he finished reviewing a file. After a few moments, Theo placed the stack of papers in the front drawer of his desk and headed for the lobby to greet Burns. When he arrived, Theo found Teresa and Burns in a lively discussion—about major league baseball. The two seemed oblivious to Theo's presence at first as they continued a polite but animated argument.

"You're on, buddy!" said Teresa. "You sure you don't want to make that twenty dollars?"

"I feel bad enough about taking ten dollars from you, Teresa. The Reds are a three-run underdog. You know that, right?" asked Burns.

"I don't pay any attention to betting lines when it comes to Cincinnati Reds baseball, Pastor. When it comes down to *heart*, odds don't mean anything."

To announce his presence in the lobby, Theo finally interjected, "Do I need to referee this debate?"

Burns laughed. "No, Theo. Unfortunately for Teresa, the debate will finish at a stadium in Pittsburgh this evening. It seems your assistant and I share a passion for baseball, but for different teams. The Reds and the Pirates play each other this evening."

Theo acted surprised. "Teresa, we've worked together for almost ten years, and I didn't know you were a baseball fan."

Teresa shot her boss a withering glance. "Oh yeah, Theo. Big-time fan."

"Well, if you two have finished your wagering, I'll take Pastor Burns on back to my office."

"I think so," replied Teresa, winking at Burns. "He's afraid to go more than ten dollars. Do you drink coffee this late in the morning, Pastor

Burns? I need to make a fresh pot, but I can bring some into Theo's office in a minute or two if you'd like."

"That would be terrific," said Burns. "Thank you!"

Once seated at Theo's desk, Burns opened his briefcase and handed Theo several files. "The folders contain the additional information we pieced together on Lin Song and Sun Yi—or Lei Zheng, as we now identify him. It details some of their earlier histories with the Santu. The background might help establish credibility with Yi in your interview tomorrow if you need to."

"Thank you, Tom. Can we talk a little more about the timing for the extraction?"

Teresa entered with Burns's coffee. "I didn't ask if you used cream and sugar, so I brought some of each."

"Thank you, Teresa. I like a little cream," said Burns.

"Just like me." Teresa smiled. "Glad there's something we can agree on. Call me if I can get you anything else."

Theo observed the short exchange with amusement. When Teresa left, he asked Burns, "Am I imagining things, or were you flirting with my administrative assistant?"

"What? No. Why would you think that?"

"Well, last week, when we met at the church in O'Dowd's office, you told me you didn't drink coffee after the first cup in the morning."

"Oh, yeah. That's usually the case, but occasionally I break the rule."

"Like today?"

"Like whenever your assistant offers to bring me some," Burns admitted.

Theo laughed and slapped his desk. "I love it, Tom! Teresa can certainly impact males that way, but I need to warn you—she doesn't like men. She prefers the company of women."

"Good to know," said Burns. "That's something else we have in common."

Jackson and Burns completed their meeting, and Burns wished Theo luck on the following day's mission. On his way out, Burns stopped at Teresa's desk with a question. Whatever the inquiry, Teresa's answer resulted in a smile on the pastor's face as he entered the elevator.

———

At the end of the day, Theo leaned back in his chair, mentally progressing through the checklist he had created for himself that morning. The most challenging task had been the lengthy afternoon meeting with Teresa. The nature and subject matter of the discussion concerned her.

"Are you worried about tomorrow?" asked Teresa.

"Not really. I just want to prepare you for all contingencies. You know our businesses better than anyone else besides me."

"But why you? Why not law enforcement? You know, the people paid for this sort of thing?"

"Just something I need to do. I can't tell you how many times in the past few months I wished I'd never become curious about Yi. But then, if I hadn't, who would have? And when? Yi isn't another common criminal; he's a leader in one of the world's most dangerous organizations. He doesn't distribute and sell mood-enhancing medications and recreational drugs for willing users like some criminals we know. He deals in human trafficking—modern-day slavery—including children. On the sliding scale between good and bad, that's as bad as bad gets. I'm no martyr, Teresa, and certainly no saint, but in this case, I think it's my turn to help."

"But why not just let the police force handle it?"

"Because circumstances make it easier for me to facilitate critical parts of the plan. I'm not in this by myself. The effort involves several levels of support from a host of other competent folks."

"Don't you think once this is over, the same people you're helping now will turn back into adversaries?"

"I don't think it. I know it. That's the main reason we're meeting, Teresa. I have ideas to share and documents for you to review."

Teresa and Theo spent several hours poring over files Theo had prepared. By the end of the meeting, Theo felt confident his assistant could handle whatever happened after the next day's mission—with Theo or without him. Feeling this satisfaction, Theo could now enjoy the sense of anticipation and excitement for the next day's adventures.

———

Pastor Tom Burns's heart experienced a different kind of excitement as he walked beside Teresa Adams toward the Ruth's Chris Steakhouse on Freedom Way. When she had accepted his invitation for dinner, as a bonus she also agreed to view the baseball game together at the hotel's lobby bar after eating. On the way to the restaurant, the latent heat of their sidewalk conversation warmed the cool evening air around them.

For Teresa, the walk represented another brief opportunity to score some late-in-the-game points. She figured it likely her chances to interact with Tom Burns would disappear after the following day. Her flirtation with the pastor over the past months simultaneously confused her and thrilled her. She found the minister charming and exciting—something of a real, live, action-figure hero dressed as clergy, and he had aroused feelings that hadn't stirred in years.

She understood little about baseball, but when she saw the Pittsburgh Pirates sticker on Burns's briefcase, she mentioned her love for the Cincinnati Reds, not knowing the two teams were to play each other that evening. Disguising herself quickly as a true fan, Teresa effectively induced both the additional chatter and the all-important wager. When Burns later made the invitation for dinner, Teresa felt she was on a roll. Now she wondered if she should risk her advantage with one additional bold move. *Screw it!* she thought. *What have I got to lose?*

"Tom," asked Teresa, "does the church require you always to wear that clerical collar?"

"It isn't a strict obligation. I guess, for me, wearing it became sort of a habit. In my professional pursuits, the collar helps to establish me. Outside of the profession, the collar sends a message that might otherwise require a long conversation. Why?"

"No reason, really. I just find myself wondering what you would look like without it on."

The couple had arrived at the front door of the restaurant, and Burns stopped to face Teresa. During this split second, his mind spun. *Boom!*

he thought. *Right between the eyes!* Had Teresa just defeated him in the flirtation game, or did he just beat her?

His mind still in turmoil, he knew he needed to answer her. Teresa's eyes locked on his, showing a hint of anticipation. Failing to think of a snappier reply, Burns asked quietly, "How hungry are you?"

"Not very."

"Me neither." Burns took her hand, and the couple retraced their steps back toward the hotel.

———

The official-looking envelope from the University of Cincinnati School of Law surprised Jaden when it came to the city office where he worked instead of his home address. The document inside astonished him even more:

Mr. Jaden Stokes,

Congratulations on your selection to receive the Cincinnati Community Foundation Scholarship. The scholarship is new and funded by generous members of the Cincinnati business community. Funds will be awarded annually for the life of the financial trust established for the scholarship to this university's third-year law student with the highest grade-point average through the first two years of our School of Law. Funds from the scholarship will secure payment for all tuition costs and purchase books and other materials required during your final year of law school.
Thank you for your hard work and outstanding accomplishments at this University.

Dr. Alan E. Bernstein
President
University of Cincinnati School of Law

Jaden read the letter twice, then looked at the envelope it came in, shaking his head in mild shock. Jessica noticed the reaction as she headed to Jim Hargrove's office and stopped in front of her intern's desk.

"Everything okay, Jaden? You look like you've seen a ghost."

"Yes," he answered. "Read this."

Jessica read the letter and exclaimed, "Wow! Congratulations! Why aren't you jumping around with joy? This is terrific."

"I'm not sure where the letter came from. I didn't apply for any new scholarships, and this just fell out of the sky somehow."

"What don't you understand, Jaden? It's a new scholarship funded by some nice businesspeople in the community and goes to whoever has the highest grades—which is you. You didn't need to apply. Dr. Bernstein's signature doesn't appear forged. It's legit, Jaden!"

Jaden smiled. "Thanks, Mrs. Jones. I never expected something like this and feel . . . feel—"

"*Good* is what it's called. The feeling is good—and you should start getting used to it. I'm proud of you. Give me that letter. I want to show Mr. Hargrove."

———

An employee poked her head into Junior's cubicle. "Junior, there's a man out on the back truck bay who asked for you."

"Okay," said Junior. "Anybody we know? A customer?"

"No, but he has the same last name as you. Are you related to somebody named Jaelyn Bridges?"

Junior stared at the woman, wondering if she might be involved in a sick joke, but she didn't break under his scrutiny.

"What should I tell him, Junior?"

"I'll be right out, Sheira. Jaelyn Bridges is my father."

Junior found the man standing by himself near one of the trucks that had recently been cleaned. Jaelyn shuffled from one foot to the other as Junior approached, and when Junior came within a few feet, he said, "Hi, Junior. Sorry to surprise you like this."

"Is everything okay? Are you sick?"

"No. I mean, yes," Jaelyn stammered. "I mean, yes, everything's okay, and no, I'm not sick. Junior, let me reword that. No, everything's *not* okay, and yes, I *have* been sick. What I did to you three years ago was not okay, and I think I was sick in the head to do it. I made a mistake, and I'm sorry."

Junior, nearly speechless and fighting to avoid tears, said, "Dad, I made a big mistake, too. We all make mistakes. But what made you come here today?"

"Can you spare a few minutes? Can we talk someplace?"

"Sure, Dad. Nobody's in the break room. We can talk there."

When Jaelyn and Junior sat at a table in the sanitation-department lunch area, Jaelyn began the conversation. "I called your mom in Minnesota last night and apologized to her. Tunisa didn't do anything wrong, and I treated her badly."

"I bet that surprised her."

"Yep. The call did. We both had a long cry, but you know what, Junior? She forgave me. She's the one who convinced me to come to see you today."

"Well, I'm glad you did, Dad. What made you change your mind?"

"A strange story, Junior, but one I want you to hear. It doesn't present me particularly well. Do you know a man named Theodore Jackson?"

"Yes. He's a businessman who helps us down at the Catholic church with clothes drives and stuff. Have you met him?"

"Oh yeah. Thought it was by accident, but now I'm not so sure. Every day after work, I stopped off at the Moose for a beer with the other men. That visit used to include several beers, but Silvie—that's my wife's name—put a dent in that train. So now I drink a single beer and go home. Anyway, I started seeing this dude I didn't recognize sitting by himself, drinking a beer at the beginning of the summer. He didn't look like the rest of us scumbags, but he seemed friendly enough and never bothered anyone. One night, while I ordered at the bar, this guy happened to be retrieving a beer at the same time. When his change came back, he told the bartender to use it to pay for my beer instead of taking it. I thanked him, and he extended his hand, telling me his name."

"Jackson?" asked Junior.

"Yes. When I told him my name, he asked if I was, by chance, related to Junior Bridges. That stopped me for a few seconds, but I admitted I was.

He waited for me to elaborate, and when I didn't, he asked if I might be an uncle or something. I eventually told him our relationship and what happened years ago."

"What did he do?"

"He stared at me. He stared at me so long I felt uncomfortable. Then he shook his head and told me I had made a terrible mistake. He recounted how he knew you, what you did for the church, and about your job here. And then he told me something I'll never forget for the rest of my life."

Jaelyn paused for several moments, overcome by extreme emotion. Junior finally asked, "What did he tell you, Dad?"

Jaelyn composed himself and looked into his adopted son's eyes. "He told me that if he were ever lucky enough to conceive a son, he hoped that son would be exactly like you. I couldn't talk after he said that, and he left."

Junior couldn't speak now either, so the father and son sat at the table in the break room in silence. Then, finally, Jaelyn asked Junior, "Are you aware of the rumors about Theodore Jackson?"

"Yes. People have told me. The guy in the rumors isn't the man I see helping at the church."

"Well, the guy in the rumors isn't the one who helped me to understand my own terrible mistakes. Can you forgive me, Junior?"

Junior responded by hugging the older man. "Of course I can, Dad. Thanks for coming down here today."

CHAPTER 33

When Luci entered the video store's front door, she told the employee at the counter she needed to speak to Mr. Yi. The employee requested her name, then ducked through a door behind the counter. Within a minute, Yi came to the counter with the employee behind him.

"Ms. Adams," he said. "I hope you came to pay the debt you owe."

"Yes, Mr. Yi. I brought the money with me, and much of the cash is in small bills. You may want to count it. I also brought a release form for you to sign."

"A release? For what?"

"The form states the money I brought resolves all debt to you. I don't want to receive additional notices for more money later."

Yi rolled his eyes. "So, now that you found you aren't a model, you want to be a lawyer?"

"I'm neither. I'm a young woman who made a mistake, and I just want to be done with this."

"Follow me," instructed Yi.

Luci sat across from Yi at his desk and fumbled around in her large purse, finally producing a thick, plain envelope. Standing to hand the envelope across Yi's desk, she grasped the desk's leading edge with her other hand. Yi took the envelope, glancing inside it as Luci reseated herself. He made a show of dumping the bills on his desk to count them as Luci waited patiently across from him.

While Yi counted, Luci checked the security of the tiny device she had placed beneath the edge of the desk. The tape holding the button mic to the underside of the desk seemed tight, with the small device well hidden, so Luci risked no other hand movements in its vicinity. Yi scoffed at Luci's homemade release form but scratched an indecipherable signature on it before shoving the document back across to Luci.

"Thank you, Mr. Yi. I hope I never see you again," said Luci as she rose from her seat and left Yi's office.

Outside, in a construction van parked near the site that would soon house the new Victory Parkway Youth Center, two men wearing yellow hard hats and protective ear covering hovered over a small computer. When each heard through the earbuds inside the protective covering the words "Thank you, Mr. Yi. I hope I never see you again," they smiled and exchanged a quick fist bump. Fitzpatrick and Jones, sitting in the cab of a bulldozer nearby, heard two words in their headsets: "Surveillance established."

Fitzpatrick keyed his mic button twice to confirm the message's acquisition, then heard similar radio responses from others on the task-force team scattered around the area. "Here goes," he said to Denton.

———

Achieving a private meeting between Theo Jackson and Sun Yi inside Yi's office was critical to the mission. Without divulging the details for how he would accomplish such a meeting, Jackson assured the group he could do it. Since then, Jackson had recruited a valuable employee from inside Yi's organization, which bolstered his confidence. Jackson expected to deal with Yi, one criminal to another, leaving all others on the task force out of the most dangerous part of the operation's execution. After Jackson neutralized Yi, the Cincinnati police would finish the job and earn the public credit for the arrest. Pastor Burns never shared either the identity or branch of Mary's covert enforcement sources, but Jackson suspected members occupied strategic positions in the vicinity.

Before closing time, Theo Jackson appeared at the video store's counter and asked the lone employee if he could speak to the owner. The employee, who wore a cast on his right arm, asked Theo to wait and ducked through a door behind the counter.

When Yi appeared, Jackson suggested they meet in Yi's private office.

"I know who you are," said Yi. "What's this about?"

"We have spoken twice on the phone, and I would expect you to have researched my appearance. It's time for us to meet in person, but," Jackson said as he nodded toward the employee, "I think our business concerns something you would prefer to keep private."

Yi ordered, "Follow me."

Jackson stepped around the employee and followed Yi through the door behind the counter. A long hallway led to Yi's office in the back. Theo saw another hallway at the end of the building that he assumed connected to the other retail locations. When the two arrived at Yi's office, Yi stopped and faced Jackson. "Do you carry a weapon?"

"Yes. Do you?"

"Yes, but I own this store, not you. I make the rules. You must give me your gun until you leave the building."

"In that case, I'm leaving the building now," said Jackson. "You may wish one day that you did not make this choice."

As Jackson turned to leave, Yi stopped him. "Sit down at my desk. What's this about?"

"I'm here to recover the money that Lucretia Adams gave you earlier today. She's a friend of mine."

"Are you crazy? Ms. Adams owed me that money. But despite the fact it's a small amount, I will not give it to you. That isn't how things work."

"Well, then I'll assist her in a plan to expose GlaMore Photography. We know you traffic young females for prostitution to a ring fronted in Las Vegas by Foxee Modeling."

Yi reached under his desk and retrieved a small handgun. "Put your hands on the desk," he said as he rose and walked around the desk. "I don't know what you think you're doing, but you seem to have a death wish. I'm more than willing to accommodate it." While expertly holding the revolver close to Jackson's head, Yi retrieved Jackson's .38 snub-nosed pistol from its hiding place in Jackson's belt. He also took Jackson's cell phone.

"While you have my phone, touch the screen for messages. There's a prerecorded text message scheduled to go to the Cincinnati chief of police at five fifteen—about twelve minutes from now. Did you know an app exists to prerecord a text message on an iPhone?"

"No," said Yi. "Why should that interest me?"

"Well, I felt certain of what I would achieve in our meeting today. A copy of the text will also go to a senior official in Cincinnati's administration who does some work for you. The text details information you revealed to me in our interview."

"What the hell are you talking about? We didn't have any interview, and I haven't told you squat!"

"Not yet, but I decided not to take any chances about getting this information to the chief and the assistant city manager. Here's another news flash. Ten minutes after the text arrives on the desk of your contact in the city, Assistant City Manager Charles Roberson, an emergency alert text will leave his cell phone. That message will go to Gerald Story at Foxee Modeling, Sung Thi at Jet Sun Capital, and Marse Thibidou at International Fidelity First Bank in the Caymans. The message will warn those people of your cooperation with local law enforcement."

"You *are* crazy. When did you start working with law enforcement? Roberson knows nothing about Foxee Modeling, Jet Sun, or Fidelity. Even if he did, nobody at those places would believe him about your lies relating to me."

"Oh, I'm quite sure he knows about the investment firm and the bank, but it doesn't matter. Somebody in one of those businesses will check with contacts in your organization about what's going on. Your superiors may not believe you were disloyal, but they will be extremely disappointed you allowed local law enforcement to discover so much private information.

From what I know of the Santu, the punishment for incompetency is almost the same as the punishment for failure or disloyalty. Go ahead and read the text if you want, but you now only have about nine minutes before it's released."

While holding the gun with one hand, Yi tapped the screen with his other and read the message.

> *Hello, Chief. Mr. Sun Yi and I had a long conversation, and I discovered much about the Santu operations here in Cincinnati. He is considering your generous offer. I will provide more detail when we meet, but his contact at the passport office is Lucinda Shelby. Yi's contact inside the city is Charles Roberson, and the Foxee Modeling agency is one of the group's prostitution fronts in Las Vegas. Your suspicions about the communications gear on his roof are correct. I believe our city is now a regional administrative clearinghouse for Santu activities in the country. You already know his relationship with me. We'll talk soon.*

Yi screamed, "I didn't tell you any of that, and nobody will believe this garbage! I should shoot you now and throw your body in the river."

"Go ahead, Mr. Yi, or should I call you by your real name, Mr. Zheng? All the important people *will* believe the information because they know it to be true. Killing me won't stop the text message from going out in—let's see—seven minutes now. Throwing the phone in the toilet won't either. The message already resides in the cloud, and I'm the only one who can stop it with the right code."

"Then you better do it, now—or you die!"

"I sincerely hope you come to your senses because I don't want to die. But when your organization finds out about any part of the message, which they will, a quick death is the best of all possible outcomes for you. Looks like about five and a half minutes to decide, which isn't time to get Lin Song in here to start working on me. Oh yeah, I know about her, too. You could try to call all those who will get Mr. Roberson's text, but you won't reach them in time. Don't look so surprised. Put your gun on the table, return mine, and hand me the phone, *in that order*, and I'll reschedule the time for the message. You now have about four minutes to make up your mind. Remember, it will take me a few seconds to enter the code."

Yi perspired as he kept his gun pointed at Jackson's head, glancing back and forth between Theo and the clock on the wall. No doubt remembering the kinds of coercion he himself had performed with the Santu over the past decade, he also knew his organization would not bother to spend much time researching the integrity of the report on Jackson's phone. Human lives were not that valuable to the Santu leaders. With a minute left on Jackson's deadline, Yi decided to buy some time.

"Okay. I'm putting my gun in my pocket and giving yours back. Here's your phone."

"Those weren't my instructions, Yi. You have about forty-five seconds to put your gun on the desk."

"Okay, okay!" Yi placed his gun on the desk in front of him and returned Jackson's revolver and phone. Theo took Yi's gun, then executed a quick command on the cell phone.

Now holding his revolver on Yi, Jackson said, "I rescheduled the outgoing text message for ten minutes from now. I have much to do in that time, so don't do anything to delay me." Taking a long plastic zip tie from his trouser pocket, Jackson handed it to Yi. "Secure one of your hands to the plumbing pipe behind your desk, and we'll continue our conversation."

"Why should I do that? So you can hurt me? So you can leave me here for the police? I see no upside for me."

"Your upside, Mr. Yi, is that I'm in a position to offer you an alternative to the type of justice your organization will impose if they access, or become informed about, the message recorded on my phone. I don't plan to harm you, but I don't want to be concerned about you finding another weapon in a file cabinet somewhere while we talk."

"So, if I refuse, you'll just shoot me?"

"No. Worse. I'll leave you in this room while I depart the building. You'll have no time left to do anything about the message that will be released, and your organization will take care of you. Chief Fitzpatrick could still be interested in talking to you based on the information I provided, but my guess is that your organization will get to you before the police do. I don't care. There's nothing much in this for me."

Reluctantly, Yi wrapped the zip tie around his left wrist and attached it to the metal pipe. When he finished, Theo approached the plumbing line and gave the zip tie an additional tug to secure it. Then, he pushed Yi's office chair near the pipe. "You can sit now."

Theo executed a few commands on his cell phone and set it on the desk near Yi.

Yi grunted and stared at his knees. "You would never send a message to law enforcement implicating yourself. You lied about the text message. You're just another criminal and only here to avenge the death of your employee."

"I have more on the agenda than that, Yi, but you're right about the cell phone message. Do you play poker?"

"No."

"Too bad. The game teaches you about bluffing. In poker, a player with a weak hand can sometimes make a player with a better hand think the weak hand is stronger than it is. The weaker hand wins if the player with the stronger hand gets fooled by the bluff and folds. You folded the last hand. I won. Now we start a new hand."

"But you start this hand with a significant advantage because my wrist is tied, and you hold the gun."

"True. However, you started your hand against my friend, Reggie Lincoln, much the same way. You sought information about me, and I only want the same kind of information from you. I will start the recorder on my phone now, and you will answer my questions." Speaking toward the iPhone, Theo said, "I'm sitting with Sun Yi, also known as Lei Zheng, and he agreed to answer some questions for me. Mr. Yi, do you still have in your possession the cell phone you took from Reggie Lincoln?"

"Yes. It's in this desk."

"Please state the name of your immediate supervisor in the Santu organization."

Yi shouted to Jackson, "Turn that off. I'm not answering questions like that!"

Jackson switched the recording function of the phone off. "Is that also what Reggie Lincoln said when you asked him a similar question, Mr. Yi?"

"Your former employee and I are two different people, Jackson. He could sustain little pain and provided the information I required quickly. His cooperation earned a sudden and nearly painless death. Nothing you do to me in this room can equal what the Santu will do if I provide the information you request."

"I *can* speculate on what will happen to you for answering such questions—*unless* I provide a way to protect you," said Jackson. "The same thing that will happen if I leave you in this room without you answering. And I must tell you, Yi, I don't personally care how horribly you might die or how long the Santu process for that might take. You are scum and deserving of the worst fate possible. Strangely, however, I'm here to save your life. If you answer my questions honestly, you'll have a chance to live—behind bars, for certain, but you'll live."

"You're a common criminal no better than me. How can you make a promise like that?"

"Because I'm nothing like you and have managed to make important connections."

"That may be, but you're a fool if you believe safety exists from my organization behind bars."

"Knowing your potential value to the government, I could debate that. I won't, however, because I don't have the time. Democratic governments, burdened by so many silly rules for collecting evidence and extracting information, are disadvantaged compared to people like you and me. We don't have those sorts of rules, though, do we? Which allows us to get answers more expeditiously sometimes. Wouldn't you agree?"

"Yes, but I have already told you. I'm stronger than your friend Reggie Lincoln. You will not get answers easily or quickly from me, and neither will any government."

"Oh, I believe you, Yi. Also, I have no stomach for that sort of thing.

For this reason, I will leave the room and you in the custody of your former employee, Lin Song."

"What do you mean, former employee?"

"Ms. Song works for me now."

Theo touched a digit on his phone, and seconds later, Lin Song opened the office door. She carried a small-handled case big enough to hold a flute or a clarinet. "Good afternoon, Mr. Yi."

"In case you're wondering, Yi," said Theo, "I'm not bluffing. Goodbye, Mr. Yi."

Yi stared at the tiny Asian woman with terror in his eyes, and as Theo started to leave, he yelled, "Stop, you. Stop! You can't leave me alone with her!"

Jackson turned and stared back at Yi. "That wasn't my choice. It was yours. You warned that my efforts to obtain information from you would prove futile and a waste of my time. Did you change your mind?"

Yi's instinctual drive to survive now overcame his commitment to resist.

"Start your recorder, but get her out of the room."

"As you wish," said Jackson, and Lin Song left the room.

Inside a construction vehicle a block away from where Yi and Jackson sat, two technician agents breathed a sigh of relief and exchanged quiet high fives.

———

While Theo Jackson executed his part of the exercise with Sun Yi inside the building, two different task forces completed their assigned responsibilities outside. After Theo entered the building alone, team members outside watched from various hiding places in the vicinity. The plan mandated radio silence except for limited communications on a designated frequency. While plainclothes personnel working for an unnamed confidential federal agency provided backup perimeter support, Cincinnati police officers were tasked with securing the building once Theo went inside. Their job included quietly removing remaining employees in the building after Theo and Yi headed for Yi's office. Besides Yi and Theo, officers allowed only Lin Song to stay inside the building.

As planned, two uniformed officers entered the front door of the video store shortly after Theo. They found a single dark-skinned male employee near the front counter. The officers requested the employee's keys to the store, then escorted him from the building, explaining that the area was a crime scene requiring evacuation. After searching the two adjacent shops' front areas, the officers found only Lin Song in the photography store. The patrolmen locked the exterior doors of the video store as they left.

If all went as planned, when Theo completed his questioning of Yi, he would depart the building by the back door with Lin Song. Denton's group, masked to conceal their identities, would enter through the front door to arrest Yi. Once placed in an armored police vehicle, Yi would later transfer to a federal car for transport to an undisclosed maximum-security facility. Classified top secret, the plan's details redacted the names and identities of personnel participating in the effort. The Santu reputation for retribution caused the mayor to insist on the same extreme precautionary measures for her involved city employees as those for the federal agents.

———

Denton and Colonel Fitzpatrick stared toward the building with binoculars from inside the cab of the bulldozer. In the thirty minutes since police officers evacuated the building, no other activity had occurred. Over the secure frequency, the agent monitoring communications from the listening device Luci had installed reported, "We have passwords, some chain-of-command information, and eight locations. How much longer before initiating extraction?"

An unknown coordinator responded, "Ten minutes. Team Two, acknowledge."

The Cincinnati police, designated as Team Two, had responsibilities for entering the building on command to make the formal arrest of Yi. Fitzpatrick keyed his mic and said, "Team Two, copy."

At that moment, Denton alerted Fitzpatrick, "Car stopping at the front door."

"Got it," confirmed the chief. "Two males, Asian, exiting vehicle. Heading toward video store."

"Right. Most likely just customers. When they find the doors locked, they'll hopefully return to their car and leave."

"Probably," answered Fitzpatrick, "but I'm going to alert the others." Fitzpatrick made the radio report and received a series of audible double mic clicks on the network, acknowledging his transmission.

"No luck," reported Denton. "One has keys out, and they're going in. I need to get over there."

"Why you, Commander?" asked Fitzpatrick. "I'll send one of the patrolmen."

"No, Chief. I think I need to go. I can get there quicker than anyone else, and I'm also the only one Theo would recognize."

"Do you think Jackson would start shooting at our officers?"

"No, I don't, but he knows my size and voice, which eliminates two variables for potential confusion. He's not expecting company in this phase of the exercise."

"Okay," said Fitzpatrick. "Put your mask on. I'll alert the team you're going in. We don't have time to signal Jackson to leave before those two get inside."

———

In the building, Theo continued to ask Yi questions, recording the responses on his cell phone. He was certain task-force members also monitored the responses through the listening device Lucretia had placed beneath the desk. All had agreed on a limit of forty-five minutes for this phase of the operation, so Theo prioritized questions in order of importance.

Theo estimated the planned deadline for the interview had neared and felt for the other cell phone in his trouser pocket. Not able to risk bringing a radio into the meeting with Yi, Theo's signal that police were about to enter the building to arrest Yi would be the vibration of a text message arriving on the extra cell phone.

Hearing low voices outside the office door, Theo stood to ensure the door remained locked. He checked the spare cell phone and confirmed no text message had arrived.

"Are you expecting company, Yi?"

"No."

Presuming the voices in the hallway were not police officers, Jackson picked up both his revolver and Yi's from the desk and stood quietly to the side of the closed door. He motioned for Yi to also remain quiet. The light from beneath the door changed as feet moved on the other side. Then a voice asked, "Sun Yi, are you in your office? Is everything all right?"

Jackson shook his head toward Yi, warning him not to reply, and the same voice commanded, "Unlock the door, or we'll start shooting through it!"

———

Denton raced across Victory Parkway to the building's front door, grabbing his revolver from the shoulder holster on his way. He hoped to have no cause to use it and that the two who entered the building were merely employees returning for something they left earlier. Glancing through the open door, Denton saw that nobody occupied the front area. He stayed in a low crouch as he entered, positioning himself behind the front retail counter to listen. Voices came from the hallway that led to the office, and Denton darted to the side of the door connecting the hall and the retail area.

There he heard, "Unlock the door, or we'll start shooting through it!"

Denton took a quick peek and observed the two men with guns drawn on either side of the closed door. He heard no reply from inside Yi's office, but when one of the Asians raised his weapon to fire through the door, Denton yelled, "Drop the gun! Police!"

The two men turned and responded with a barrage of bullets in his direction. Pressing his body against the wall next to the door, Denton returned fire to the general area of the two men in the hallway. After his volley, another short burst of firearms occurred, and Denton glanced from behind the wall. Two men lay still and bleeding in the hall; Theo Jackson stood in the office doorway, holding two guns. When Denton shouted, Theo turned at once, pointing the two guns in Denton's direction.

"It's Denton, Theo. Are you all right?"

Lowering the guns, Theo said, "Yeah. I'm fine, but these two aren't. You aren't either, friend."

In the excitement of the past few seconds, Denton had not even felt the pain from the bullet hitting his right side slightly above the beltline. Blood now covered his shirt in that area, and he instinctively put his hand over the wound. Theo rushed toward him and grabbed a cloth from under the retail counter to hold against Denton's injury.

"You got a hole in the front of your shirt and the back," said Theo, "so no souvenirs in your body. We need to stop the bleeding, though. Let's get you outside."

"Is Yi still in here?" asked Denton.

"Oh, yeah. He's zip-tied to the plumbing in his office. We should remove him before more of his reinforcements come. I recorded what we need from him for now. The guys outside probably got the same thing through the bug."

"Whoops. Too late," said Denton as he watched another car roll to a stop at the front of the building. "Lock the front door. I'm sure they have a key, but having to unlock the door will slow them. Our side has plenty of reinforcements out there, which I'm sure are responding as we speak."

Theo slammed and locked the door.

"What about the two back there? They dead?" asked Denton.

"Yes, multiple times, I'm afraid."

"How did they know to get here so fast?"

"I would guess by the employee present when I arrived," said Theo. "You didn't arrest him, did you?"

"No. We just told him to get lost and took his keys. We didn't want to raise any alarms."

"Guys like him learn to be suspicious of everything. Let's move further back. I hear some screeching tires out there, and we don't need to take any stray bullets through the doors or windows."

Theo and Denton retreated to the office where Sun Yi sat in his office chair, tied to the pipe. They heard shouting outside and the sound of someone speaking through a bullhorn, but no more shots. Theo found several towels in the adjacent bathroom, which he secured around Denton's waist with a telephone cord he ripped from the wall.

In minutes, the front door opened, followed by a bullhorn command. "This is the police, and we have the building surrounded. Come out unarmed and with your hands in the air."

Denton yelled back, "Guys, this is Commander Jones! It's only me and—"

Theo put his hand over Denton's mouth. "Just tell them only you and Yi remain here. They don't need to know about me. I'll hide in one of the other offices and slip out the back door once everyone leaves."

When Denton started to argue, Theo said, "It's better for everyone this way. Trust me."

Denton yelled, "Sun Yi and I are the only live ones back here, and I'm a little shot up. I'll come to the front alone, and then you can enter to retrieve Yi. He's zip-tied in the back office to a pipe."

"Okay, sir," answered the bullhorn. "We will wait at the front door."

Denton made his way from the building, holding his side. When officers saw the blood, one motioned for medics to bring a stretcher from a waiting ambulance. As police officers helped him on the stretcher, several armed men in plainclothes rushed past into the building. Assuming these were members of the auxiliary forces provided by the secret element of the federal government's task force, he breathed a quick sigh of relief that the mission was complete. Then he heard the crackle of renewed gunfire inside the building.

Raising his upper body from the stretcher, he demanded, "What's going on? Where's that gunfire coming from?"

The medic replied, "Not sure, sir, but we're ordered to get you to Cincinnati General right away."

During the ambulance ride and his check-in at the emergency room, Denton couldn't take his mind off those last sounds of shooting on Victory Parkway. As he rolled down the hall on a gurney, drifting into unconsciousness, he wondered what happened after he left.

CHAPTER 34

"Hey, Commander. How do you feel?"

Nauseated and trying to focus through blurry vision, Denton attempted to locate the voice's source. Finally discovering it, he took a breath and said, "I'm fine, Colonel. Just a bit groggy."

"Understandable. You lost a lot of blood, but the wounds were clean, and the bullet only grazed the outside of a kidney. Doctors believe you'll be out of here in a couple of days."

"Great," said Denton, fighting to land his mind someplace solid. "I assume you have Yi in custody?"

"Yes. The tape Mr. Jackson recorded will prove useful. We did good work yesterday."

"Good, good," said Denton, his head clearing a little. "Chief, before the ambulance took off yesterday, I heard more gunfire coming from the building. What was that about?"

Fitzpatrick sat quietly; Denton glanced in his direction to confirm he was still there. At last, Fitzpatrick said, "We're not sure exactly what happened, Denton. When you came out, the undercover guys went in. They apparently encountered resistance and returned fire. After a minute or two, they yelled to our officers that we could safely enter. We went in, recovered Yi, and came back out. Our plainclothes friends were busy putting three casualties in body bags."

"Three?" exclaimed Denton. "There were only two dead bodies in the building when I left it. So where did a third come from?"

Pausing a moment, Fitzpatrick said, "It was Jackson. As I said, we aren't yet able to piece together what happened, but somehow Jackson died in the building. Our guys told the confidential units as they entered to expect to find only Yi back in the office, based on what you told them. Was Jackson still there when you left?"

"Yes. For some reason, he didn't want to come out with me. He said it would be better for everyone if he disappeared out the back once our guys picked up Yi and left."

"Strange," said Fitzpatrick. "It's possible he panicked at the sight of the plainclothes folks coming his way rather than uniformed officers."

"Makes no sense. Jackson had plenty of time to go to a different location while I exited the building."

"I can't explain it either, Denton, but I'm sorry."

"Jackson was part of our team. He's the one who created the whole setup. He had Yi cuffed to a pipe so that Yi couldn't reach a gun, and the two unknown Asians who entered the building were, without doubt, dead when I came out. So that can only mean someone on our side killed Jackson."

"It appears that way, and as I told you, I'm not sure how. It didn't happen intentionally. The undercover guys reported they encountered gunfire when they came to the hallway, and they returned it."

Denton struggled to absorb what his chief told him, his mind still fogged from the effects of anesthesia. "Did you see the bodies when the plainclothes personnel brought them out?"

"I saw the body bags come from the building, but I didn't examine them. As you can imagine, our group was in a hurry to clean and exit the area as soon and as quietly as possible. The feds took the three corpses to one of their facilities for identification."

"Have they communicated with you since?"

"Yes. A few minutes ago. One of the Asians showed up on an international database. Ngo Diem, a Santu member, wanted in two countries. No record yet in any of our databases. The other Asian hasn't been identified. The person with whom I spoke confirmed the third body was Theodore Jackson's."

"Through fingerprints?"

"I didn't ask. Probably fingerprints or dental records. Again, I'm sorry. I'm aware your friendship with Jackson goes way back. The incident was unfortunate."

"Colonel, Jackson and I had a friendship as children, not since. Jackson was an ally, not a friend, in the matter relating to the Santu presence in our city."

"I didn't mean to insinuate anything. I admit my respect for some aspects of Jackson's character grew over the past several weeks. A proverb originating before Christ suggests the enemy of our enemy is our friend. I don't apologize for my recent collaborative relationship with Mr. Jackson."

"Thank you," Denton sighed. "I'm having difficulty processing the whole thing, especially with a mind still impaired by medicine."

"I'll leave you alone now. I'm not supposed to be in here anyway. The doctor says you need several more hours of rest before the effects of the anesthesia completely wear off."

"Thank you, Chief."

When he closed his eyes again, Denton's mind struggled to work through a haze that prevented efficiency. Lying on the hospital bed, he thought—or maybe he dreamed—in semiconsciousness. *Theo—body bags—fingerprints—Pastor Burns—'Better for everyone this way'—Santu.* Then the random thoughts would repeat as if on a carousel. When he next opened his eyes, a welcome sight greeted him.

"Hey, you," said Jessica.

"Jessica, how long have you been here?"

"Almost since you got here last night. By the time I arrived, doctors had you in surgery. You've been out of it for most of the time since. Doctor Findley says you'll fully recover, though."

"Thanks for the report," said Denton. "Maybe I dreamed it, but I seem to remember Fitzpatrick here earlier."

"You *were* probably half-dreaming when he came to your room. He slipped in without the nursing staff knowing and got in quite a bit of trouble. You know Jack, though. He doesn't believe rules apply to him."

Denton smiled briefly. "I hoped his visit *was* a bad dream. He gave me news I didn't want to hear."

Jessica reached across the bed to hold her husband's hand. "I know. I'm sorry, T."

His mind now marginally clearer, Denton asked, "How much do you know about what happened yesterday?"

Jessica seemed confused by the question. "Not many of the details relative to the planning, but the chief told me how you got shot and how his men extracted Yi."

"Right. Did he tell you about Theo coming out of the building in a body bag?"

"Yes, and he felt terrible. He believes the plainclothes guys might have shot Theo by accident in the confusion."

"Right, Jessica, but think something out here with me. Did Fitzpatrick tell you how the feds identified Jackson?"

"Yes. He said they took Theo and the others to one of their facilities to establish identities. I understand they still haven't confirmed the identity of one of the Asians."

"Right. Fitzpatrick told me the same thing. He presumed the federal authorities identified Theo by fingerprints or dental records."

"Yes," agreed Jessica.

"You spent a good part of this summer researching Jackson's record in the city. You couldn't find a single violation. When you checked national databases for fingerprints, dental records, or anything else relating to Jackson, you found nothing, right?"

"Well, yes, but your fed friends might have more extensive databases than ours."

"That could be, but Theo Jackson isn't just a high-profile drug dealer in *our* city. Federal enforcement in our country and several others have an interest in Jackson. Our department here collaborates with a joint task force consisting of other state and federal agencies. If the federal government *does* own a better database than the ones we can access, don't you think they would allow us to access it to help catch Jackson?"

"What are you getting at, Denton?"

"I don't even want to say what I'm thinking out loud, Jessica. I don't believe records exist anywhere with Theo Jackson's fingerprints or dental records. Theo told me as much. I'm not buying Fitzpatrick's story, but I'm sure I don't want to expose the inconsistencies. Theo wouldn't come out of the building with me when our guys arrived, and I think he had a reason. Lying here in semiconsciousness thinking for the past . . . I don't even know how long I've been here—I keep remembering something Tom Burns said way back on page 217."

"Page 217? What are you talking about?"

"Oh, sorry. I'm still a bit delusional. A while back, as we put the finishing touches on the planning for yesterday's events, I expressed concerns to Pastor Burns. I worried that if we succeeded, Theo's role would likely be discovered by the Santu organization. Knowing the organization's reputation for retribution, Theo would have more than police or rival drug lords to worry about the rest of his life. Burns agreed and changed the subject, but he said something like, 'If everything works out, maybe we can take care of that too.' Perhaps he did take care of that."

"What? By having Theo killed?"

"No. By making everyone, including the Santu, *believe* Theo died."

"Whoa!" exclaimed Jessica. "How can we find out? You think Fitzpatrick is in on it?"

Denton didn't answer for several moments, then squeezed his wife's hand. "We don't do anything, Jessica, except go along with the charade—if that's what it is. Would you like to know why I think I'm right? You might find it a little spooky."

"You don't scare me, mister. Shoot!"

"For my entire life, as far back as I can remember, a sixth sense warned me when danger was near. While this sense sometimes alerts me for no good reason, it has never failed to alert me when a good reason *does* exist. So I have this extra sense I named the *bad feeling*."

"And," interrupted Jessica, "you have a bad feeling now about all this involving Theo?"

"No. The opposite. I had an unexplained bad feeling ever since I first drove by Mr. Yi's stores on Victory Avenue this summer. The closer we got to yesterday, the stronger that sensation got. When those two Asians went into the building, my system sounded full alarms. When I partially woke up to speak to Fitzpatrick, I looked all over my mind for that feeling, and I couldn't find it—even after Fitzpatrick gave me the bad news about Theo. The feeling wasn't there anymore. Not a trace! I thought the reason I couldn't find it might be the drugs."

"But you don't feel it now either?" asked Jessica.

"No. I don't. I have a good feeling."

Jessica didn't respond—only smiled.

CHAPTER 35

Jessica retrieved Denton from Cincinnati General Hospital two days after being admitted, with instructions to keep him convalescing at home for at least another week. A surgeon repaired the slight tear in his right kidney caused by the bullet, and the entry and exit wounds were healing well. Once the effects of anesthesia wore off, Denton became clear-headed with no significant pain.

He tried to discover the results from Sun Yi's arrest during that period, but details seemed sketchy. On the day following the sting, *The Enquirer* featured a small article on page two documenting an arrest made at a small business on Victory Parkway. However, the story listed no names and only stated police held a local businessman for questioning relating to a murder. The other deaths did not get mentioned, and the article included no photos.

From the car and over his wife's objection, Denton called Chief Fitzpatrick. After the briefest of conversations, Denton winked at his scowling wife and said, "The chief is meeting us at the house."

"Denton Jones! Forty-eight hours ago, you lay on a gurney heading for the emergency room with two bullet holes in your waist! Doctors only released you because you promised you'd take it easy at home, and you're back at work before we're even out of the hospital parking lot."

"Come on, J. Chief Fitzpatrick wants to brief me, not take me on a stakeout. Lying on the couch listening to him isn't going to take much energy. Aren't you a little curious about what's happened since we picked up Yi?"

"Yes," she admitted. "Don't you dare let him start talking until I'm in the room too."

"Deal!"

As advertised, Fitzpatrick's government vehicle sat parked in the Joneses' driveway when Jessica and Denton arrived. After helping Jessica set up the couch for Denton, Fitzpatrick pulled up a chair to the coffee table.

Before he could say a word, Denton held up his hand. "Wait for Jessica."

When the couple was ready, Fitzpatrick updated them on events since Yi's arrest. As Denton had surmised, the different agencies involved in the exercise successfully kept most of the details confidential. Jackson's "big bluff" strategy worked, gleaning more information from Yi in a short time than could have been accomplished through interrogation inside a government facility. Besides confirming the murder of Reggie Lincoln, Yi provided the names and locations of several Santu members in his chain of command, the passwords for three computers in his building, and a description of the responsibilities of the Cincinnati location for the Santu. When Yi confirmed Jackson's suspicions about GlaMore Photography and Foxee Modeling, the feds heard all they needed for probable cause. After the arrest, the federal tech agents had a field day with Yi's computers.

"Terrific!" exclaimed Jones. "Did Agent Warren get everything he wanted?"

"Of course not," replied Fitzpatrick, "but way more than he thought possible. For example, one of the IT guys found the account numbers for nine different offshore bank accounts, with detailed records of transactions, dates, and balances. It only took him about ten minutes to execute a federal order to freeze those accounts, but in that tiny bit of time, the Santu successfully shut down six, cleaning them out of funds."

"How could they react so quickly?" asked Jessica.

"Way over my level of banking expertise to understand," answered Fitzpatrick. "My guess, once agents froze the first account, an emergency transaction procedure automatically initiated. Our guys successfully sidelined over three hundred million dollars of assets in the three accounts we accessed, though."

"Wow, think what the total would have been with nine accounts," said Denton. "What happens to the money?"

"It will take a while to sort out," said Fitzpatrick. "It's doubtful the Santu would try to claim it, so eventually the federal government will distribute the funds. Rules for that kind of thing are in place. Some of it could filter back here to fund local efforts relating to trafficking initiatives."

"What about Yi? Where is he?"

"At an undisclosed maximum-security federal facility where authorities will never release him into the general prison population; neither will he ever be paroled. That probably doesn't bother him. He knows what the Santu will do if he ever gets out of prison. He'll have a relatively quiet and solitary life of reading and TV inside a place where he's safe and served three meals per day. More than the bastard deserves!"

"Did the federal guys impact any other Santu operations?"

"Oh, yeah." Fitzpatrick related what he knew about other federal initiatives occurring soon after Yi's arrest. Within hours of the Cincinnati incident, strike teams swept New York, Houston, Las Vegas, Atlanta, and Miami. A related international agency performed similar sweeps in three other countries. Agents made hundreds of arrests and closed dozens of businesses. The resulting interrogations and evidence review would require months to complete.

"How about victims? Any recovered?" asked Jessica.

"I don't know much about that," said Fitzpatrick. "The information is still coming to Agent Warren faster than he can digest it all. He said that like the phenomenon involving the banks, Santu members abandoned many of the raided businesses. Employees, mostly sex slaves, were just left behind."

"Well, thank you, Chief," said Denton. "If we didn't cripple the Santu, sounds like maybe we at least wounded them?"

"Yes, it seems. Interesting side note—remember that employee of Yi's, Lin Song?"

"Yes. I heard Jackson mention her name during the surveillance. The sight of Song terrified Yi."

"Right. Well, Jackson must have recruited her before going in to talk to Yi. Agent Warren says her nickname among the Santu is Tufu, which in Chinese means 'The Butcher.' Warren and Jackson had at least one meeting, maybe more, that I didn't know about. Doesn't matter, but I think Warren made an immunity deal for Song in one of those meetings. Anyway, that's working out for Warren pretty well."

"How?" asked Denton.

"The day after our exercise here, the feds rounded up a bunch of Santu folks in those cities I told you about earlier. Agent Warren put Song on a private FBI Cessna Citation jet to Miami, Atlanta, and Houston. When she walked into interrogation rooms, her presence produced the same results in several that it did with Yi. Santu suddenly started spilling their guts, metaphorically."

"With no other threats?"

"According to Agent Warren, none."

Denton laughed. "Sounds like Song might be a good investment. How will the feds keep her safe from the Santu?"

"They'll spend some money on her—they can afford to. She'll end up looking different and running a flower shop in North Dakota or someplace like that."

"Wonder if Warren had the same thing in mind for Theo?" asked Denton. "I don't think Jackson would give up information relating to a former employee, knowing the feds listened, unless he had a deal worked out with Warren in advance."

"I thought about that, too," admitted Fitzpatrick. "It's possible. Shame it didn't work out for him. Everything in the interview with Yi went just the way Jackson thought it would, except for the end."

Denton stared at Fitzpatrick, looking for a hint—of anything—but saw nothing. Fitzpatrick either possessed exceptional acting skills, or he honestly thought federal agents killed Jackson by accident.

Maybe that was precisely what happened.

EPILOGUE

Two Years Later

"Congratulations, Chief! How do you like your new office?" asked Jessica.

"I've only been in it about an hour so far. What brings you up to this floor so early?"

"I helped Jaden move some things to his new office, so I thought I'd stop by."

"Jessica," said Denton, "you aren't supposed to lift things. You know that!"

"Yes, dear, but relax. The *things* I moved consisted of two small pictures—one of you and one of me. I don't think the doctor would have a problem with that."

Jessica, now seven months pregnant, spoke to the new chief of police, Denton. Jaden Stokes was the newest city councilman, and they all reported to recently elected Mayor Jack Fitzpatrick. After deciding not to run for another term, former mayor Shirley Guzman asked Fitzpatrick to take her place in the election. He soundly defeated a local businessman for the position.

"Okay," said Denton. "I guess not. How's Jaden feeling about being the youngest person ever elected in the city to a council position?"

"Relieved, I think, but also a bit overwhelmed. You know Jaden, T. He tends to overthink everything, and he worries citizens will focus on his age versus his abilities."

"Well, they will until he starts showing them results—which will occur in a matter of weeks, if not days after he engages in the position. After that, it won't take Jaden long to prove he was the right choice."

"We know that, but you might give him a call later this morning with a pep talk. His close election gave him a stressful two weeks."

"I'll go see him a little later. The campaign contribution from the Independent Avondale Restaurant Association made the difference in his race, I guess, right?"

Jessica immediately understood what Denton *didn't* say. "Mmm, yes, probably so. Jaden doesn't know why the association gave him the money since he has no ties to the local hospitality industry. Now he's worried someone from that organization will expect a favor he can't provide."

Denton laughed. "I doubt anything like that's gonna happen. Tell him the association has a considerable vested interest in the success of the business community in our city, and they only want good, honest city management."

"I'll tell him. Not sure I'll convince him."

"He did the legal work for the transaction on the Children's Ministry building, didn't he? The Restaurant Association's contribution to the ministry should prove their strong sense of citizenship and financial commitment to community improvement."

Again, Jessica laughed. "Denton Jones, you're having too much fun with this, aren't you? You think either Junior or Jaden will ever make the connection?"

In addition to assisting Jaden with his campaign finances, the Independent Avondale Restaurant Association called Mayor Guzman six months earlier with another proposal. Someone informed the association of the International Children's Ministry Organization's pending expansion into Cincinnati, and the association found a building in their inventory they didn't need. The group offered to sell the building to the city at an extreme bargain if the city used it as the ministry's regional headquarters. Shocked at the association's offer, Mayor Guzman accepted the proposal with no negotiation. She instructed the city attorney to prepare the legal paperwork and asked the city treasurer to write the one-dollar payment check requested.

At the end of the current year, Cincinnati would lose their assistant sanitation supervisor, Junior Bridges, when Junior assumed full-time responsibilities as district chairman of the Midwest region, International Children's Ministry Organization. Junior didn't apply for the new position, but the organization's chief executive officer, Sven Nielsen, contacted him. According to Mr. Nielsen, a member of the ministry's board of directors recommended Junior, citing Junior's work over the past six years with Elements, Cincinnati's youth development program.

The promotion for Junior surprised neither Denton nor his wife, and both thought him an exceptional choice. The mystery of who on the board might have been aware of Junior's work required minimal research. When Denton downloaded the ministry's board of directors from its website, he saw Pastor Tom Burns's name. Denton suspected only he and his wife knew the connection between the association's gift and Junior Bridges.

"No, Jessica," answered Denton. "I doubt if either Jaden or Junior will ever connect those dots, and I think their secret benefactor is okay with that. In many ways, the man responsible no longer even exists."

"Right," mused Jessica. "Are you surprised you haven't heard from Theo?"

"No. Theo, or whatever name he goes by now, is too smart to do anything to expose himself. But if I needed him, I could probably get a message to him through the Restaurant Association. I bet Tom Burns also knows how to reach him."

"Did you ever tell Burns you figured out what really happened?"

"No, and I never will. Some things are better left unsaid and undisturbed."

"Probably right. Theo might be in a better position to help Burns behind the scenes."

"And both of us have jobs that allow us to help, when we can, *on* the scene. We can also do our part by adding a few more good men to the world," Denton said, grinning.

"Men?"

"Or women," said Denton. "Wouldn't you like to know now which now?"

"Nope, because I don't care. Do you?"

"No. I hope if it's a girl, she looks like you."

"And if it's a boy?"

"That he looks like you," said Denton.

Jessica laughed and punched her husband lightly on the shoulder. "Well, I don't care about that either. Dr. Crispin says we shouldn't plan to travel anywhere around New Year's."

"Except maybe to the hospital?" Denton came to the front of his new desk and hugged Jessica. "I can't wait. How much longer will you try to work at the office?"

"At least another month. I feel fine, and the work keeps me from obsessing about my mammoth size—which reminds me, I need to go. Gunnells's staff meeting starts in ten minutes."

"See you this evening, J."

———

The pink telephone slip with Teresa Adam's name lay among several others, but Denton pulled this one from the pile on his desk. He didn't feel like doing work today, and he suspected Teresa's call had nothing to do with police business. When Teresa answered the phone, Denton said, "Ms. Adams, it's a pleasure to hear your voice again. This is Denton Jones, returning your call from this morning."

"Thank you, Denton—or should I say Chief? Congratulations on the new job."

"Thank you, Teresa. I assume you also heard that Lucretia got the job with the mayor's office?"

"Yes. That's why I called. Thank you for your help and the reference. Luci is thrilled."

"You're welcome for what little I did. Lucretia won the job on her own merits. Mayor Fitzpatrick and I knew about her help two years ago, but she would have earned the position anyway. She was by far the most qualified candidate, in addition to being the most personable. I only worry that this job may interfere with her educational ambitions."

"It won't. Luci finished junior college this summer, and she's enrolled in evening classes at the university. It may take her a while, but she'll eventually earn a degree."

"I think Mayor Fitzpatrick mentioned to me that Luci also does some modeling now?"

"She sure does, but not with anyone like Foxee Modeling. She has a part-time gig with Nordstrom's and models for online and catalog sales."

"She's a busy lady. How did she get the Nordstrom's job?"

"You'll laugh when I tell you," said Teresa. "She sent her portfolio from GlaMore Photography to Nordstrom's New York City office."

"Good for her! And how about you? I know you moved Theodore Jackson Investments from Cincinnati, but I wasn't sure to where."

"Oh, I'm great. I can do most of my work for the company online, so I moved the headquarters to a place with a little better tax rate. Sorry, Denton. Nothin' against Cincinnati, and most of our holdings are still in your city."

"I understand," said Denton. "No apologies necessary. As I recall, Theo didn't like keeping much on paper, so your job must be a nightmare at times."

"Not really," Teresa answered. "We own property, leases, trusts, and parts of partnerships scattered all over the area, but Theo closed down the most difficult parts of our business during his last weeks in Cincinnati. I can monitor most things from up here with a few calls each day. The business also helps with several important charities down your way that I take care of."

"I'm aware of a couple of those," said Denton.

"No surprise."

"I'm impressed, Teresa. When I visited the office here, Theo told me you were much more than an administrative assistant. It appears he had an excellent succession plan in place."

"He did. For the most part, we operate as if Theo never left."

"Interesting. Well, thanks for calling, and I hope you'll stay in touch."

"Oh, I will. We have significant investments down your way, so I'll be visiting every once and again to check in."

When the call ended, Denton picked up the pink telephone slip to update his contact information for Teresa Adams: 681-459-2424. The area code seemed vaguely familiar to him, and on a whim, he tapped the contacts icon on his cell phone. Scrolling to the number for Tom Burns, he found 681-459-4848. Coincidence? He thought not.

———

When Jessica left after dropping off the pictures, Jaden stepped to his new office window and admired the view. From eighteen floors up, Cincinnati looked magical. The Ohio River formed a giant, lazy S to create the city's southeastern boundary, and Jaden could see the four bridges connecting Cincinnati to Newport and Covington, Kentucky. Like beautiful gemstones on a liquid finger, Riverfront and Paul Brown Stadiums hugged the riverbank on the Cincinnati side. Jaden had difficulty detaching from the mesmerizing sight. Most city council members maintained professional and employment positions in other companies, but Jaden planned to place his legal career on hold for at least the first year of his term. The sixty-five-thousand-dollar annual salary for council members would sufficiently cover his spartan lifestyle, and Jaden entertained broader political ambitions beyond city councilman.

A pretty woman standing at his doorway interrupted his reverie. She held a sheaf of papers in her arms and an angelic smile on her lips. "I'm sorry," she said. "I have documents for you to sign from Mayor Fitzpatrick's office. I can put them here on your desk and come back later to retrieve them if you'd like."

Jaden stared at the woman a split second too long before realizing it was his turn to speak. "Oh, sorry, certainly. On the desk is fine. I'm just starting to get settled and am a bit unorganized, I'm afraid. My name is Jaden Stokes."

The young woman blushed a little. "Yes, sir. I know that. Your name's on the door here. I also voted for you, Mr. Stokes. My name's Lucretia Adams, and I'm Mayor Fitzpatrick's new administrative assistant."

Feeling like an awkward schoolboy at his first high school dance, Jaden replied, "Right. I guess that is my name on the door. Of course. And thank you for your vote. Uh, you can call me Jaden if that's okay."

"Great," replied Lucretia. "Then I think it's okay if you call me Luci. That's the nickname my friends use."

"Good. Luci. I will," Jaden answered, struggling to think of a way to extend the conversation. Failing, he said, "I guess we'll be seeing a lot of each other around here."

"I hope so."

As he collapsed in his chair after she left, Jaden thought, *I think I'm going to like this job.*

———

Denton surveyed the city sprawling below him, his view including the new Avondale Youth Center. He reflected on that first meeting about the building with Theo Jackson two years ago and the whirlwind of events that created the path to his current office. When the joint task force raided the Santu enterprise on Victory Parkway and captured Sun Yi, the Cincinnati police and Denton specifically received much of the credit—and all the publicity. While Denton felt neither he nor his fellow city officers deserved much of the recognition, he also understood why those who did would, and could, never be known. To this day, he had little knowledge about many details behind the complete execution of the coordinated federal, state, and city initiatives.

Despite his efforts to deflect the attention relative to his role, Denton's stature as both a police officer and city leader rose due to his publicized involvement. When Chief Fitzpatrick recommended Denton as his chief of police to the city manager, nobody on the police force or in city administration objected. Just as he had been the youngest police officer in Cincinnati's history to become a district commander, he now served as the youngest chief of police. If Fitzpatrick's selection disappointed more senior officers on the force, none expressed it. The elections for mayor and council seats were competitive but not contentious, and Denton had an unexplained good feeling for a change.

City Manager Haley Doolittle had not yet named an assistant city manager to replace Charles Roberson, who quietly retired before the elections. Roberson escaped prison time and public humiliation in return for a promise to assist the city in understanding the means and methods for political corruption in the city. Roberson honored the commitment but ultimately offered little. He could provide no evidence corroborating his long-standing suspected relationship with Theo Jackson, and with Jackson's drug empire seeming to disappear entirely after the Yi arrest, none in enforcement exhibited much interest in reviewing the old history. With little fanfare, no retirement party, and scant pride, Roberson had left the employment of Cincinnati after over thirty-five years of service.

"Chief," came a voice from the telephone intercom, "you have a package out here. Would you like me to bring it into your office?"

"Sure, Susie, do you need any help?"

"No, sir, the box is light. I'll be right in."

Susie Helton came through the door with a medium-sized box in her arms and placed it on Denton's desk. "I don't know what's in this box, Chief, but it sure smells good."

"Thank you, Susie. If I find something in the package to eat, I'll bring it back to you."

When Susie left, Denton stared at the plain white box, searching for a label or advertisement. None existed, so Denton opened the box and found a single folded piece of paper lying on the tissue hiding the box's contents. When he opened the single fold, he read the two words: *Congratulations, Chief!*

Beneath the tissue lay several layers of brownies. Surveying the contents, Denton noted a mix of light-colored blondies and dark-colored brownies.

Leaving the box on his desk, he went to Susie's desk outside his office.

"Susie, who delivered this package?"

"A man came out of the elevator a few minutes ago and set the box on my desk. He said it was for you and then left. Is something wrong, sir?"

"No," said Denton. "The box contains brownies. Could you describe the man who delivered them?"

Susie appeared uncertain how to answer the question but said, "Well, he was darker than me and nicely dressed, maybe a few years older than you. He was short and very polite."

"Okay. Thank you. You didn't notice anything else?"

Susie squirmed in her seat nervously. "There was something else a bit unusual. When the man put the box on my desk, I noticed he was missing the little finger on each hand."

"Thanks, Susie. That explains a lot. The brownies look delicious. I'll keep one for myself, so you'll have twelve light ones with white chocolate and twelve dark ones with fudge to share with folks."

"Thank you, Chief. What color was the extra one?"

"Light."

ACKNOWLEDGMENTS

Thank you, Penni Askew, Word Summit Editing, for your meticulous editing, encouragement, and inspiration. Also, thank you to "beta readers" Elizabeth Cottrell, Cindy Rinker, and Alice Wilcox, who made this book better with their suggestions.

A NOTE FROM THE AUTHOR

Thank you for reading *The Other Side Of Good*. I wrote the book to be an entertaining work of fiction, but the specter of human trafficking in our world is *not* fictional. It is real, it is serious, and it is a much larger issue than most of us are aware. According to an International Labor Organization report, nearly twenty-five million people are trapped globally in modern-day slavery, and trafficking earns illegal profits in excess of one hundred and fifty billion dollars annually. That makes human trafficking one of the top three most profitable criminal enterprises on the planet.

I happen to agree with Theo Jackson that while the illegal drugs and arms trades represent vile crimes, these pale in comparison to the depravity of slavery. Many fine organizations exist to combat and stem worldwide human trafficking, including Unicef (www.unicef.org), Stop the Traffik (https://www.stopthetraffik.org/), the Freedom Network (https://freedomnetworkusa.org/), the Polaris Project (https://polarisproject.org/), and www.newcreationva.org.

I encourage you to contact any of these groups to learn more about how you can help to address this appalling world problem.

Thank you,

E. A. Coe